WHAT PRICE A
KINGDOM

WHAT PRICE A
KINGDOM

Dr Dmis

Contents

CHAPTER 1

The Welcome Gift

Andrew is brushing glaze on the last of the loaves to go in the oven. "Two hundred and twenty-two." He mutters to himself as he opens the oven door and loads the last tins onto the end shelve. "Five down on yesterday for the same amount of ingredients," he says under his breath as he shuts the door and turns over the last of the twelve twenty-minute sand timers lined up above the door of the oven. He leans back against the kneading and proving table while folding his arms, trying to work out in his head how he can be five loaves short when his weights were right on the scales he uses to size out each loaf. 'Water, yeast and salt quantities were the same as always, so how could it have happened?' he wonders to himself.

He checks his balance scales with various combinations of weights on each side before concluding that it must have been the sack of flour he used that was a little light. For it is the only thing he uses that is not weighed out by himself, as the mix he uses requires one whole sack that is fifty pounds in weight. A ping from a small bell rings out and resonates through the bakery as the first sand timer rotates after emptying and strikes the edge of a small brass bell. Indicating that the first loaves are ready to come out of the oven. Andrew swiftly moves to the left-side oven door, pulling it open and sliding in a huge paddle to collect the first batch of loaves. He rotates and spins them out onto the table before he returns for the rest of the tins on that oven shelf. As these hit the table he rests the paddle between the two ovens and closes the door. Then he returns to line up his tins in preparation for the next stage. Andrew turns each one over, tapping the base with a hooked wooden club that has a smooth, well-worn and amber colored surface from years of use against the hot tins. Once the bread drops out, the tins are stacked ten high, and the loaves placed on a cooling rack in a matter of seconds.

As the first batch of bread is placed on the wire cooling racks, an elderly lady comes through from the next room to start collecting the loaves. Her hands are not as hardened to the heat as Andrew's and she takes three at a time in a cloth and starts to fill the shelves in the shop window. 'Ping', another timer touches a bell and the process is repeated again and again until after half a hour, all the bread is out of the ovens and moved to the to the front of the shop.

Bread finished, Andrew clears away the tins ready for tomorrow and looks around at what he has left to make some sweet pastries. Due to the state of the country there is little in the way of luxuries and the choices are limited. He places what he has available on the table and looks it over. Some eggs, butter, a little cream, apples, dried fruit, honey and a little jam. Deciding the best way to stretch out the ingredients is an important part of his day as the more he can make, the more people he can feed. Today, he chooses to make a sponge with a jam and cream filling, apple and honey pastries and to finish off with some fruit cakes. Decision made, he starts to make the pastry first, then peels and boils the apples for the filling. Over the next hour he creates his works of edible art for his customers, utilizing every scrap of pastry and filling he has available.

In front of the bakery, widowed Penelope Johnson, Penny to her friends and all the customers she is well known to, opens the door to the shop and turns the sign to "Open while it lasts". They do not have much to sell, just four styles of bread and the few treats in the form of sweet pastries and cake, but it is good quality and very fairly priced in comparison with the state-owned shops in the area. It does not take long for the first customers from the ever-growing que to enter for one of the warm loaves of bread, as many have been waiting outside for some time. Almost everyone who buys from the shop is a regular and known by name. In an effort to spread the bread out as far as possible, they only sell one loaf per person and up to two pastries when available.

"Hello, Penny," says Sandra. "Usual, please."

Penny puts the scored bloomer on top of the counter and Sandra picks up her bread, pays and leaves the shop in a hurry to get home and feed her family. It's typical of the times; everybody is just about surviving, there are no easy lives for the common people round here. A few more customers enter the shop, but they do not buy anything yet, just stand there making conversation. It does not take long to work out why though, as when Andrew starts to bring out his pastries to the front of the shop, people immediately line up to buy what they are allowed; a treat for their children, wife or loved one. Whatever the reason, within an hour and a half of opening, the shop is sold out of produce and closes until the following day.

For Andrew, his day in the bakery comes to an end once the last of the pastries have been taken into the front of the shop to be sold. He will be up early and back in again tomorrow to light the ovens and start baking, as he is five or six days a week depending on the availability of flour and other ingredients required. As for Penny, her day is only half done, she will take the money earned from that morning and try to source the items needed to cook with and have them delivered ready for Andrew to start baking again at 4.30 the following morning. A difficult task in these desperate times, but with years of experience and many contacts and old friends across the town, Penny always seems to come through somehow, allowing Andrew to produce the food so greatly needed by the local people.

As he walks home, Andrew passes a group of children sitting around a small fire, some pushing more sticks into the flames to gain a little more heat, while others just huddle together for extra warmth. They are dirty, look half-starved and one of the girls only has one shoe on her feet. As always, Andrew takes pity on them. He stops, takes the loaf of bread from inside his jacket and starts to break off chunks, handing it out to the little one's piece at a time. The smile of appreciation from them all lifts his spirit a little, but he is sad that this is a sight he sees so often on his walk to and from the bakery. He keeps a third of the loaf back for himself and after wrapping it back up, he places it back under his coat for the journey home.

With a wave and many a thank-you from the children, he continues on his way. *How can the country have gone so badly downhill?* he wonders to himself. Young children homeless on the streets with no families to look after them. People in such poverty they are barely able to support themselves or their families. It was only ten years ago that the small country of Kelsey was the envy of all Europe. A long, narrow sliver of land between Hanover and Denmark and boasting a population of just under a million people. It is not the largest country around, but the volume and quality of all the products and trade goods coming out of this land through its three ports and land borders had been highly prized with other countries and kingdoms.

Once famed for its great variety of cheeses, fine cattle and smoked, spiced, and salted fish as well as fine quality jewelry and metal for use in the production of armour and weapons. It made Kelsey a desirable country to trade and have commerce with as it could supply much needed resources to neighboring countries. This abundance of trade goods also made Kelsey wealthy and important nation to have political ties with, ensuring prosperity to its people. The country's legendary white and gray Ambulette horses were prized across the known world for their stamina and strength in battle; the best of them worth a princely sum that only nobility could afford, or indeed, even allowed to own outside of their native country. Strong in the shoulders, with a powerful gallop and unflinching under fire, these gentle giants of the equine world have been at the head of many a battle involving heavy horse and lance across many European battles.

Now, however, the country is on its knees, torn apart by a corrupt government that holds its own people in a vice-like grip to line its pockets with all it can. Taxes cripple the poor with the middle classes not faring much better. As for the royal family, well, since the assassination of the king and queen near fifteen years ago, the child who was to inherit the throne when she came of age was now under state control. Even when she finally reached the age of eighteen and was due to take back control of the country and rule the kingdom by her own hand. It was not to be, for the government had been plotting and scheming for years. Putting in place new laws and legislations to contain her, restricting her powers and ability to rule. They kept control of the country for themselves under the guise of it being for the good of the state, citing that she was unprepared and ill-equipped to handle such a momentous undertaking. Moving back the age she was to take back control, year upon year as they plotted to seek her demise and remove her from office permanently.

The last five years had seen the worst of the decline in the country, families torn apart by those wanting to rebel and others wanting to make the best of what they have left. Barely anything the country now produces sees any return to its subjects as the now ruling government takes almost all the proceeds in taxes and other extortionate charges. In the past year alone, the government had sent in the National Guard to enforce law and order, pitting families against each other as politicians added more and more restrictions and taxes to ensure the people could not break free from the stranglehold they had over them.

Andrew, like so many, barely makes enough to get by. For many more with families, life has become an up-hill battle just to survive and get through each day. Alcohol is prohibited in most cities unless sold by the state for an extortionate price and gatherings of over fifty people are now illegal unless state-run. Trading on the black market is now the only way some people can survive; swapping or selling things they own for items they desperately needed to make it through these harsh times.

To the people of this country, life had become nothing more than a giant prison, the entire border contained within miles and miles of fencing and patrolled by armed soldiers. Nobody was allowed into the country unless sanctioned by the government, or it was a pre-planned state visit overseen by the ministry in person. All wishing to leave Kelsey must also have documentation supplied by the government and approved by ministry officials. Jobs that allowed access to the outside world had been restricted; for example, all merchant sailors' families were put under house arrest until their return, to ensure they did not abscond or complain to neighboring countries about living conditions and the true state of the country.

As for diplomatic guests and nobility on state visits from adjacent countries, they were always well entertained in the capital; the place where all Kelsey's government ministers and their families are housed, along with the privileged few who still had money to maintain their position. Visitors that are entertained by the state see this country as a place of absolute beauty with grand buildings, spacious parks and wonderful shops, restaurants and public buildings like opera houses and theaters.

They are even taken out to the country on organized visits to see cattle farming and horse training in a model village close to the capital. If only they had the chance to go just a little further, just another mile or so, for they would then see the truth and the true state of the people of this country under the control of The Three Heads.

The Three Heads was the name given to the three top politicians and government lawgivers, for they now run Kelsey and are considered by themselves to be above all others who reside in their domain. They have put each other in key positions to control the entire country and all within it, including the monarchy. The capital has now been split into three sections, with each of them running their third of the city from a palace, converted national library and a state Museum. Buildings that have been taken over by them as they grew in power and influence. All three establishments are fully equipped with all manner of amenities, sparing no expense to ensure absolute luxury.

William Bonner and Herbert Mallory are of about equal power of the three of them; cold, ruthless and, above all, dedicated to getting all they can for themselves and their bank balances. They both fear Alexander Stone as he has his own army in the National Guard and complete control on all mercenaries and bodyguards, with powers above all others in law enforcement. He has the final say on everything and all the jails and holding cells of the entire country are almost entirely filled with people he has had incarcerated for the good of "his" empire. There is nothing these three men would not do to maintain absolute power and complete control of Kelsey. Those that attempt to oppose them are branded traitors and revolutionaries and imprisoned without any formal hearing or court appearance.

Andrew finally reaches his little thatched cottage with its ornate wheat sheaf patterns in the thatch. Inside, he places the remainder of his bread on the table and throws his coat over the back of a chair, then goes out into his garden. Closing his eyes and taking a deep breath through his nose, he smiles as he smells the scents of the flowers. He tries to picture in his mind which one he smells first, but it's a tough call. Opening his eyes, he looks round at the beautiful array of blooms, for every area of his garden is full of flowers of different colors, shapes and sizes. Every wall and trellis is alive with plants and fruit bushes, all eager to worship the sun and put themselves on display.

He collects two wooden buckets from the side of a small potting shed and walks to the end of the garden and down four small steps to a narrow brook, where he fills the buckets with water from the fast-running stream. Then, makes his way round the garden, giving every plant a much-needed drink on this chilly late spring day, checking each one for pests or infection while deadheading any old and withered flowerheads, until he is satisfied his work is done.

His next stop is at his two beehives, positioned on each side of a compost heap, Andrew watches them for a while to ensure their behavior is normal. The one on the left is a larger hive and will soon need another shelf added to the stack to accommodate the growing population, but not just yet! For now, he is content that with both hives growing and functioning this well at the start of the season, the year should be a bumper one for honey come the autumn. With the garden in good order, he takes his favorite seat against the back wall of the cottage and runs his fingers through the mint that grows beside and under the seat. Sniffing the strong, sweet fragrance left on his hand he sits back to relax for a while, listening to his army of pollinators hard at work.

For an hour he sits, away from everyone and everything, just the sound of bees buzzing around him and the waft of different scents from his flowers, depending on the strength and direction of the breeze as it moves through the garden. For this brief moment in time, he is free from all the worries of the world and his eyes soon begin to close.

He is woken from his daydream by his stomach rumbling and demanding sustenance. Stretching out while yawning, he gets up and heads back into the kitchen, collecting a part-used stick of butter and a pot of honey from his pantry. At the table he spreads the butter and honey on the last of the loaf, comforted by the fact that it was his bees that made the honey with nectar harvested from his flowers the previous season.

Later that day Andrew is sitting in front of his fire in an old armchair passed down to him from his sister some years back. It is worn and lumpy, but still comfortable and reminds him of her. Soon, though, he will have to get up and get ready to go out, for today is the last Friday of the month and, as with every last Friday, there is a state-sanctioned event in the town hall; a competition all are eager to enter, for the prize is a large hamper of food that would supplement many a family. Andrew has always wanted to win, as the hamper is always full of different preserves and dried fruits unavailable to him to purchase due to their price, and he could make such fine cakes and pastries with them. Also, the various types of cured meat and fish would also provide a welcome change from his usual diet of bread and honey.

He gets changed into his best clothes and combs his hair, then makes his way into the center of the small town. It is a good twenty-minute walk away, but the cost of a carriage is not in his budget. For once, though, he is in no rush, for all get one chance to enter this particular event as it lasts several hours. On arrival he books himself in and waits to be put into a group of eight. Once the group is called, you head to a table, are given twenty tokens and begin to play cards. The winner is the person with all the tokens from the rest of the people around the table, or the most tokens if the game lasts over half an hour.

Whist, four-card stud poker and speculation are amongst the many games that could be played, but only at the start of the night would anybody know which game would be on the agenda for that month. Andrew and seven other people are taken into the main hall, and, as he takes his place at the table the adjudicator announces that the game this month is knockout whist. It is a tense and nervous moment as Andrew and his group are seated at a table and begin to look around at each other. There is no time to get acquainted as the cards are swiftly dealt and the event commences. Many do not understand the game, they are here purely because food is the prize on offer. Within ten minutes Andrew is through to the next round and over the next hour or so he is on fire with his best run at the game ever, moving from table to table as he wins with a great run of cards that does not seem possible: queens, kings, it seems whatever he needs to build a hand just drops for him.

Within four hours he is on the final table, facing seven others for the prize hamper that is on display next to them. He has never got this far before; his hands are sweaty, and it takes all his willpower to stop them shaking and maintain his expressionless gaze. Looking at the others around the table he can sense he is out of his league by the way they roll chips around their fingers and stack them ready to play. At this stage of the competition, the chips for each finalist are doubled and an audience of those that have already lost builds as they all wish to see who wins the event. The competitors all look at each other with shifty eyes; that is all but one, for at the end of the table sits a woman in her late twenties or early thirties. She's perfectly poised and has her hair up, revealing a pale, elegant neck. Her clothes are neat and tidy, but the dark green color and embroidered frills of her cloths are a little frumpy by today's modern standards. The brooch and few items of jewelry she wears look old fashioned and dated, more like family heirlooms than fashionable accessories.

Andrew watches her as the cards are dealt. She shows no

expression or emotion as the others around her banter with each other in an attempt to distract or glean advantage; she just picks up her cards, looks at them and places them face down to wait her turn. There is something about her that is captivating and intriguing to him. Andrew is sure that has never met this woman before, yet she seems somehow familiar to him, in a way he cannot explain.

He gets back to the game at hand. In the first couple of hands dealt, he and the lady opposite have a win apiece and gain a few chips each from the others round the table. The next round they both fold and it becomes a three-way tussle between the more aggressive players in the group; in the final stages one man goes all in and pushes his chips into the center of the table, quickly followed by the other two sliding all they have into the pot. There is a tense silence with all the crowd watching from afar as the men look at each other before the first man places jack, queen, king in mixed suits down on the table. He has a smile on his face as he does so, but it is short-lived as the next person places down a ten, jack and queen of spades. The balding man smiles, showing his blackened teeth and a deep hearty chuckle as he reaches forward with his hands to claim the pot thinking he has won. As his hands touch the chips, the final bearded man throws down three aces on top of the pile, pulling a huge gasp from the intensely watching crowd.

The second man is incensed at his loss as he clearly thought he had the winning hand. He swears and curses the gentleman who beat him as he storms away from the table, escorted by some of the government organizers to ensure no trouble ensues. In truth, all of them had good hands, but with three aces only one of them earns the right to stay at the table and he now has a huge advantage over the others still in the game with the number of chips he has amassed. Over the next couple of rounds, he tries to force out Andrew and the lady with some strong bidding, but they have both played what they have been dealt well and win a game each, reducing the man's stack by half and eliminating the other two competitors in the process.

With half the allotted time left and all three of them about even on chips, the contest becomes a bit cagey and caution enters the game for the first time. Andrew is next to take a couple of small wins before the other two competitors get into a high-bidding game. Andrew drops out with a poor hand and watches as the game between the lady and the other man heats up. Still showing no emotion and keeping her composure perfectly, she applies pressure by ramping up the bid slowly on the first two rounds and then pushing with a hundred-chip final bet, forcing the man to make a decision that could win or lose the game for him. If he calls her he will have just eighty chips left should he lose, if he folds he will have lost most of his chips to the pot, so he makes the bold decision to go all in and try and bluff his way out of the situation. The woman stares at him intently before pushing all her chips forward, forcing him to play his hand first. He looks solemnly at her as he turns over a run of four, five, six, and smiles at woman, thinking he has the winning hand. As the crowd applaud and mutter amongst themselves, she pauses for a moment before slowly turning over three tens while looking directly back at him.

The man realizes he has been outplayed and smiles while shaking his head. He stands up and leaves the table, only looking back and nodding to her from afar as he departs the room.

Now, only Andrew stands in her way. The next two hands are small wins for him, but with time now fast running out he needs to get in a good hand to have any chance of winning the Hamper. The clock continues to tick down as he looks at his newly dealt cards. It's not very good with just a pair of sevens and an ace, but with only two minutes left to play, he has no time to fold and wait for a better hand; as she has more chips than him, so will win if the timer runs out. Andrew takes a deep breath and closes his eyes as he pushes all his chips into the middle; he does not have enough to take all her chips, but, if she matches his bet. More than half the chips will be in play so the winner of this round will take the win.

The lady stares at him, pauses for a moment, then slides all her chips into the middle, making it truly an all-or-nothing hand. There are gasps, murmurs and comments from the people standing around watching the game as they are aware that if she had just folded, she would have won the game without having to play the hand.

The clock on the table chimes, signaling the end of the competition and the room falls silent. With all the chips in play, the game must now be finished to find a winner to the competition. The spectators start to move forward towards the table, eager to watch the final hands be turned over. As Andrew has been seen by the woman, so he must lay down his cards first. With trembling hands, he slowly turns his two sevens and an ace over and lays them down on the table while looking at the lady's face. A very slight smirk reveals her only emotion of the night as she leans forward towards her cards. Andrew knows instantly that she has beaten him and his heart sinks after coming so close. She puts her hand over the cards, pauses as she looks him in the eyes, then slides them toward the middle of the table without turning them over, conceding the hand to Andrew.

The crowd roars and cheers Andrew as they rush forward to shake his hand while Andrew stares at the woman in disbelief. She again shows no emotion as she picks up her belongings and overcoat and turns to walk away through the many people rushing past her to congratulate Andrew. He knows for certain she had him beat and is desperate to look at her hand, but the rules will not allow him to touch a conceded hand if the player chooses not to turn them over. He just has to watch as the dealer stacks all the cards together and shuffles them, destroying any chance of finding out what hand she had.

Andrew is escorted through the crowd, some cheer and praise him, while others are resentful and disappointed at not winning themselves. He moves towards the waiting officials to collect his prize. A family-size hamper filled with prime goods, ranging from food and drink to medicine and small gifts. It is a great prize indeed and he is unaware of the envy many of them show towards him as his mind is elsewhere, wondering why the lady did not claim the prize she surely won. He looks for her in the crowd, but she has long since disappeared into the masses and will not be seen unless she chooses to show herself. Andrew takes the applause from the people still around at the presentation and shakes the hands of the officials. One of them gives a small speech about the generosity of the state as the prize is wheeled in and shown to everyone, leaving many jealous at Andrews good fortune.

From that moment on, everything happens so fast that it becomes a bit of a blur to Andrew. Within minutes the officials leave the room and the people who were surrounding him led away to the exits and dispersed by the organizers. A man moves forward, closes the lid on the wicker hamper and ties up the straps, then stands up and turns to Andrew.

"Well done young man, please allow me to help you get this to the door as time is close to curfew and I must clear the building".

Andrew and the man lift the hamper off the table and between them they move to the nearest exit of the building, lowering the hamper to the ground on the other side of the door.

The man then shakes Andrew by the hand, gives him a small nod and steps back through the doorway, closing the door behind him. Andrew hears the clunk as the top and bottom bolts are locked, then fading footsteps as he walks away from the door. He looks around from the side street he is now standing on and sees nobody. Then, with an icy shudder down his spine, it dawns on him. He is in a city full of starving inhabitants, miles from home in an area where a curfew comes into effect in less than half an hour, carrying a basket full of food along the road. Adrenalin now kicks in, together with fear for his safety, he grabs the handles of his prize and begins to stagger towards the main road. His only hope is to flag down a horse-drawn cab, but with so many people leaving the building earlier there are precious few around and the ones he sees already have people in them hurrying to get home.

Pushing on towards his home, he gets the feeling he is being watched from every dark corner and entrance he passes. Looking around in the poorly lit street, he spots a face in the doorway here and someone smoking over there. It is very unnerving for him as he begins to feel more and more vulnerable with every step. His heart pounds faster and faster as he begins to hear footsteps and muffled whispers. Three men appear from an alleyway running between two houses, stepping out into his path with menace in their eyes, one tapping his leg with a long wooden club. Andrew begins to feel that it will not be long now before he is attacked and wonders how much it will hurt as he looks around for any chance of escape. He will not give up his prize without exploring every option first, but the situation does look desperate as he stops and places the hamper on the ground, ready to make a last stand.

Suddenly a carriage draws up beside him and stops, he hears a pistol or rifle click as it is cocked above him and he closes his eyes expecting the worst, but several seconds go by and nothing happens. He opens his eyes and watches as the three men in front of him start slowly walking backwards and into the shadows down the side of a building before disappearing from sight. He looks up and sees the driver of the cab pointing a rifle in the direction of the receding men.

"I suggest you put that basket on the back of the coach while I keep watch, my boy," says the elderly man. "Once on, you had better get inside so we can be off before they come back in greater numbers."

Andrew does not need to be asked twice. He staggers round to the back of the coach and pulls out the luggage hatch, placing the hamper into the opening. He then moves back around the side of the coach, opens the door and climbs inside as the driver calls out to him again. "Where to, my boy?" as he flicks the reins and pulls away.

Andrew leans out of the window and replies, "47 Brook Road, just off the main road, past the bishop's monument." As he sits back down, he looks up and notices a cloaked person sitting opposite him. He watches as the person slowly pulls back the hood to reveal her face. To his astonishment, sitting opposite him is the woman he was playing cards with at the final table. He cannot help but stare at her, unable to get the words he is thinking to come out of his mouth.

"I think you had better close your mouth as the expression does not seem to suit you," she says with a very slight smile on her face.

Andrew closes his mouth and thinks for a moment. "I presume it is you I have to thank for saving me back there? A moment longer and I fear that my life would have been in danger."

"It would seem that the streets are not as they once were, that is true, but I do not feel that you were in danger, just the food you were carrying. For a man who fought so hard to claim his prize it would not do for you to lose it while taking it home to your family," she says.

Andrew smiles at her. "You are mistaken, my lady, you had me beaten. I know that for a fact, yet you folded your hand and gave me the win and I know not why!"

She gives him a curious look. "What makes you think that I gave you the win, perhaps you had a better hand than me and I just wanted to hide my bluff."

"No, I am not buying that, I saw it in your face as I turned my cards and if you still want your prize you can have it. I would not feel bad about the rightful winner taking what they had won."

"What would your family think of you giving away such food when all around are so hungry?"

Andrew shakes his head. "I have no family at home. I entered the competition as I can use the food to make more things in my bakery. Times are hard for all around here and I struggle to get ingredients. I like to give food to the children I walk past on my way home, for they have no parents to look after them and, in some cases, not even shoes on their feet." The woman seems to be taken back by his words and looks to the side as if to hide her disappointment, then looks back at him.

"Is it really that bad that children are left to fend for themselves?"

Andrew nods. "Times are not good at the moment, but I can only hope they will get better."

The driver pulls up outside Andrew's house. "We be here, young sir, best you collect your hamper and get inside, for we do not have long to get back to the house before the curfew is in place."

Andrew steps down from the carriage, but, before he leaves, looks back at the lady. "Are you sure you do not want the basket, for it is rightfully yours?"

She looks at him. "Take it and do with it as you will, but I ask you give something to the children for it saddens me that they are the ones left on the streets of this once-fine town."

Andrew closes the carriage door and takes down the hamper from the back of the coach. No sooner has the basket hit the ground than the carriage takes off at a brisk pace down the road. Andrew lunges forward to close up the hatch and watches as the carriage rounds the memorial and heads back toward town. He follows it with his eyes until it's out of sight before picking up the wicker basket and struggling into his house with it. It is only as he closes the door that he realizes that he still does not know the name of the lady who came to his aid when he most needed it.

Dragging the hamper into the kitchen, he starts to unpack its contents onto the table and then around his kitchen. It fills his pantry with more things than it has ever seen before: pickled vegetables, preserves, cured meats, cheeses, bottles of wine, biscuits and sugared candies, to name but a few. He plans what he can take to work the next day to make some tasty treats to sell, then takes a small knife and carves himself a few slices of ham to eat before heading off to bed, for in a few hours he must be at the bakery again.

By ten o'clock the following day Andrew has been busy in the shop for several hours and has produced a few more pastry items than usual with the help of some ingredients from the hamper. They are selling out fast, but he has held back several cheese and ham pastries for himself. With his work done for another day, he places his apron on the side and collects the bag with the treats for the children. As he passes Penny at the front of the shop she stops him and gives him a hug and a kiss on the cheek.

"I do not know how we would survive without you, my dear, as you always seem to make enough to keep everybody fed around here. But know this, one day somebody will reward you for all your kindness, you mark my words, my boy." Andrew went to walk away but she pulled him back. "And please keep some of them pastries for yourself to eat, you are no use to anyone if you do not stay healthy and you are surely needed, more than you realize."

Andrew smiled and kissed her on the head. "I will, but someone has to help the children; they are our future."

As he walks along the path, his mind is still on the woman from the card game. Her calmness and presence made him feel good and he wonders who she was and what her name is. He would dearly like to see her again, but with no way of finding her, it will just have to remain a pleasant memory of a moment in time.

Soon, he arrives at the fire pit where the children can usually be found, but today nobody is present and the area constructed of rocks and tree stumps has been kicked around and everything is strewn across the floor. He looks inside the two derelict buildings nearby in the hope they are sheltering inside but finds no trace of the children. Andrew begins to worry for the safety of the little ones he has come to know, but is also aware that if they were in danger they would scatter to places only they know to hide and be safe in. So he starts to rebuild the rocks around the old fire pit, then collects wood and other burnable items and builds a fire. Once the fire is built, he lights it with a strike-a-light and gently blows on the embers to get a flame burning. He rolls back the large log and places the stools and other stumps that have been scattered about around the fire area and sits down to warm his hands.

It takes around ten minutes before he hears footsteps and the sound of people walking on loose rubble, but does not look round, just stares at the fire, poking it with a long stick. A few minutes later, a small boy takes the seat beside him, then another, closely followed by two more. Finally, the five girls, ranging in age from about ten to fifteen or so, arrive as a group and stand around the fire to warm themselves. The older one is bruised, her clothes ripped, and she has a small cut on her bottom lip. Andrew waits for them all to sit down before handing one of them the bag containing the pastries. She takes one and passes it on to the next child and so on until the bag returns with one pastry left. Andrew takes it from the bag and starts to eat, and, as he does, the others start to eat as well.

"What happened?"

For a while there is silence before one of the boys speaks. "Last night some men stinking of grog come looking for the girls. They nearly got Anna, but she wedged herself in a drain against the bars. We threw rocks at them as they pulled at her until they gave up and moved back to the fire. It was very scary." The boy takes a bite from his food, chews and swallows it before continuing. "They got very angry and smashed the place up. They get very nasty when they do not get what they want."

Andrew looks at Anna, who is nibbling on her food and watching him intently. As he stands up, she turns to run. He puts the palms of his hands out in an attempt to reassure her, but he can see fear in her eyes. He steps away from the children and starts to walk away; he does not want the children to see the tears running down his face.

"Thank you, mister!" Anna yells at him, but it only makes Andrew feel worse and the tears begin to flow more readily. He stops and wipes his eyes, looks back at the children, then heads off toward his house, angry that his country has become such a terrible place to live and that he can do nothing about it.

When he arrives home, he storms straight out into the garden, tears still flowing as he drops to his knees and shudders, trembling with rage and sadness at the same time. He falls forward onto his hands. "How can it get this bad? Those children deserve better than this." He mutters to himself.

"I called to you, but you did not answer," comes a voice from the kitchen.

Andrew freezes, then wipes the tears from his eyes as best he can before getting back to his feet and turning around. To his amazement, the lady from the card game is stood in the doorway, and behind her the driver of the carriage holding two full sacks in his hands. She sees the state Andrew is in and looks at the driver, who puts down the sacks and disappears.

"I did not mean to intrude, but you passed me with such haste that you did not hear me calling out to you."

Andrew wipes his eyes again and looks at her with a smile. "Please come through and take a seat." He gestures her to a wooden bench in the garden. The lady steps forward and is instantly taken back by the display of flowers and bushes that make up the garden. She can smell the lavender and honeysuckle in the air and the range of colors and plants in such a small place is quite captivating.

"I had some spare clothing and shoes at home, leftovers from the children that used to live there and I thought after yesterday's conversation that they might be of use to the little ones you spoke about." Walking over to the bench, she takes a seat and looks round the garden, spotting the two beehives nearby. "Does it not worry you, being so close to them?"

Andrew looks in the direction that she is facing and spots the honeybees flying around. "In the five years or so that I have been beekeeping, the only time I have been stung is when I accidentally sat on one of them." They both smile before Andrew continues. "I'm sorry to be so rude, I have not even introduced myself yet. My name is Andrew," he says quietly.

The lady looks at him. "It is a pleasure to meet you, Andrew," she says in a composed manner.

Andrew wipes his eyes again while waiting for her to tell him who she is, but with nothing coming back he bravely asks, "It would be nice to know with whom I am having a conversation?"

She pauses for a moment. "If I tell you my name, I would like to know what saddens you so in return."

Andrew thinks on her words for a moment while looking at the bees flying around, then nods his head. "I tell you my name, but it is for you and you alone, I do not wish for anyone else to know it, is that acceptable to you?"

He agrees with another nod.

"My name is Margaret Dessola, but to you I would sooner be known as Marge."

Andrew puts out his hand. "It is a pleasure to finally know the name of the finest card player I have ever seen," he says with a smile. Marge seems reluctant at first, but eventually puts her hand out and shakes Andrew's open hand.

"Now, Andrew, pray tell me why you are in such a state, for it saddens me to see you in such a way."

He looks at her, rubbing his hands nervously. "It is the homeless children down the road. They were attacked last night by drunken men trying to get at the young girls, in particular a girl called Anna. She is a bit bruised, scared and her clothes were ripped, but she did get away." He sighs heavily as he thinks on his words. "I don't know how this country has got so bad, but for young children to be abandoned by their parents and left out in the streets to fend for themselves puts us all to shame. The people who run this country have a lot to answer for."

Andrew can see in Marge's face that this disturbs her. "Perhaps we could go and see the children now, we could take the clothes I brought—"

"No, if they even see a carriage pull up, they will run and if they see a strange man like your driver, they will hide through fear of what might happen."

"I want to help."

Andrew thinks for a moment. "If I take you to see them, you will have to walk from here, just us two."

She stands up. "I will have a word with my driver, would you be so kind as to bring the sacks?" she asks as she leaves to speak with the man outside. Andrew follows her, picking up the two full sacks as he passes.

By the time he gets outside the front door, Marge is already across the road, speaking to the driver on the carriage. He does not hear much of the conversation but catches the last part as Marge gestures at him. "You will do as I say and wait here, that is my final word on it." She reaches into the coach and pulls out a coat and wraps it round her as she walks back across the road to join Andrew.

"Tell me, Andrew, you are a man who is not afraid to speak his mind, what do you think is wrong with the country to have put us in this terrible state of affairs?"

They set off toward the children and Andrew thinks for a while before cautiously answering, "We lost our sovereign monarchy. We never had this problem with a King and Queen on the throne, but when they died the politicians took over and changed everything. The country has suffered ever since and with these greedy people in charge no one can afford anything but the bare basics anymore. As to where all the money that is collected in taxes goes, I have no idea." Andrew stops talking to reposition one of the sacks on his shoulder. "I was young, but I do just about remember my mother and father going on the protest march in June '92 at the big house in the capital run by Alexander Stone, and they never returned. Since that day I have been on my own. I make what I can in the bakery in town and feed all that live locally until the supply is gone each day, but it is never enough. All I can say is the people and children deserve better than to just survive, but some will not even allow that as these children are witness to on a regular basis."

They are walking at a steady pace and Marge is listening intently to all Andrew says. "How far would you go to bring this country back to the old ways?"

There's a short silence before he answers. "I was nearly beaten for some food yesterday; children are starving on the streets. I lost my mother and father for protesting for their rights to live free. Me myself, I would give my all to protect that girl Anna and the other children left abandoned. So, in answer to your question, I would say that to bring this country back to what it was and could be, I would give all that is required of me."

Marge nods at the answer he gives her. "You are a brave and good man Andrew, one of the few I have met in recent times. Unfortunately, most people in power and high position put themselves before others, it's just how it is."

Andrew puts his hand out to slow Marge down to a stop, then places the two sacks down on the floor. "They be just around the corner here, please wait while I see them first to assure them you are a friend." He picks up the larger sack and walks towards the children. Margaret looks at him before picking up the smaller of the sacks and follows him round the corner, away from the road toward a partly collapsed pair of buildings.

Between the buildings and Andrew is the fire he rebuilt, with four children sitting around on old stools and a stump, the other children are already up and moving away while watching Margaret intently. Stepping back nearer the houses, ready to run if needed.

Marge calls to them to come toward her, but it has the opposite effect and they move further away, taking one step backward for every step she takes forward. She looks at each and every one of them in turn. They are filthy, one of the boys has a bad cough and the trousers and shirts of the boys and dresses of the girls are, as Andrew said, in a poor condition. It saddens her greatly to see such neglect.

Andrew takes Marge by the hand and leads her to a spare chair by the fire. "Take a seat and wait," he says to her before turning to the children furthest away. "Children, this lady is the one that helped me get the food you had earlier, she has come back with some things you might find useful." He opens the sack he is holding and lays out the coats over the spare chairs and logs, putting shoes and other items on the floor. Marge starts to do the same with the sack she was carrying and soon the girls move a bit closer.

Anna's eyes light up as she makes for a pale-blue dress, kneeling down beside it and sliding her hand over the top of it. "Can I have this one, miss?" she asks, looking directly at her. Marge's eyes are welling up as she nods. The girl picks up the dress and runs to one of the houses, disappearing inside behind a crumbled wall.

The others scramble to pick up items and start to put them on. It is only a short time since Anna has gone, but in that briefest of moments she has changed into the dress and as she steps out from the rubble of the derelict building. The smile and pride on her face lights up everyone looking at her. The dress might not fit as well as it should, but a new dress is a big thing and Anna is very happy. "Thank you for the dress, miss, it is very nice, I will look after it as best as I can," she says while approaching the fire. She then spots a pair of shoes Andrew has just put on the floor. They are of a color that nearly matches her dress. She picks them up and measures them against her bare, dirty feet; they look just about right and she nods to herself as she sits down and puts them on, doing up the two buckles on each side.

Margaret is heartbroken to see the children so dirty and left abandoned, she cannot believe it is acceptable for the state to leave them to fend for themselves when others are so greedy and have so much. While she is thinking these things, Anna stands up and walks around the fire smiling and near-dancing in her new shoes and dress. After two or three laps of the fire she sits down beside Marge. "Miss, why do you help us when you have never seen any of us before?"

Marge looks at her with a sad look on her face. "It is because I can, my dear. Nobody deserves to go through what you have been through in the past couple of years, and I aim to make it stop just as soon as I can."

Anna looks at her. "Nobody can change what's been done, and you cannot change the future on your own, we just have to make the best of it while we are here."

Marge leans forward and pats the back of the girl's hand. "You would be amazed at what can be done with a strong will," she says. "That dress looks lovely on you, Anna, and the shoes set it off wonderfully."

"Thank you, miss," Anna says with a smile. "I feel better to be wearing something so pretty; it makes me feel a little bit special again, like I used to when I was a child."

Marge looks at her with a surprised expression. "Well, to be fair, you still are only a young girl."

"Ha! I am old when it comes to living on the streets Marm, not many girls make it past my age before something happens to them. Take a look at young Billy here, eleven years old he is, can speak right proper, hold a conversation better than I. But he would have been dead in a week without me to watch over him. He's just not sharp or quick-witted enough to survive on his own."

Marge is shocked to hear Anna speak this way but does not push her with any more questions as she does not want her to feel that she is being cross-examined.

The pair of them spend an hour talking and laughing with the children before they get up to leave. Marge has been taken aback by how nice the children were to her despite all they had been through. She has become particularly fond of Anna, who has been living longest on the streets. Despite the dangers she faces on a daily basis, she looks after the others as best she can. Marge puts her hand in her pocket and pulls out a beautiful metal-finished hairbrush and passes it to Anna.

"This is a gift from me to you, Anna. It was my mother's, and I am greatly fond of it, but I want you to have it and remember me by it when you use it." Anna takes the brush, looks at it and back at Marge, then steps forward and gives her a big hug.

"Thank you, miss," she says while holding onto her tightly.

Marge is shocked and a bit stiff; she is not used to this kind of contact and does not know how to react.

"Well, I must go now, it has been wonderful to see you all and I will visit again soon, I promise you."

Marge turns and walks away, taking several steps before waiting for Andrew to finish speaking to the children.

"I was not expecting them to be so nice," she comments as they start walking.

"They are children, not wild animals, Marge. They respond to human kindness as all children do, they just happen to be a little more appreciative due to not having had much in their lives."

"This used to be a village away from the town, but, as it grew and expanded, it sort of swallowed up the village and continued building around the old cottages. Some have fallen to ruin as they are incredibly old. My house is nearly a hundred years old and it is one of the newer ones." He comments to Margaret as all too soon they reach Andrew's house where they stop, and he turns to face Marge. "Thank you for buying the children some clothes, for I could not help but notice the price still on one or two of the coats. It was a kind thing you did."

"You were not to have known that they were purchased, it was a mistake for the price to be still attached," she snaps, disappointed that Andrew has noticed what she has done.

"Maybe so, but I did, and the children are very grateful, as am I, for your kind gesture." He pauses.

"I have enjoyed showing you my garden and talking to you as well, it has been a long time since another person has shown interest in the lost children of this country or in myself. I am just sorry that you have seen the way the people have been left by what is going on in this country, as it never used to be like this around here."

Marge takes one more look at him and gives a small nod and a grimace before turning to walk back to her waiting carriage. As she moves off she has a look in her eye as if she is about to do something that may be pushing the boundaries a little too far. She speaks no more, just steps into the waiting coach and takes her seat. Marge does not even look out of the window at Andrew as the carriage is driven away.

Andrew, however, looks on and watches as the driver flicks his reins at the horses and the coach moves off, slowly disappearing into the distance. Once gone from sight he turns and enters his house, closing the door behind him. He takes a seat in his living room and stares blankly at the unlit fireplace, thinking about how eventful the day has been. He now knows her name but thinks that there is far more to her than she lets on. Will he ever see her again or was what she had just seen too much for her to take in? For that also would not surprise him in the least. He wonders if he will ever know anything about this elusive woman and where she is from. So many questions run through his head as his eyes begin to close and he slowly falls asleep in his chair.

CHAPTER 2

New hope

Over the next two weeks Andrew thinks about Margaret a lot, he is still using the last of the preserves and other items from the hamper in the bakery. These additional pastries and tartlets bring in a little more money, allowing Penny to purchase more ingredients. Allowing Andrew to expand the amount and range of breads and cakes he can produce, filling the shelves a little more and feeding a few more people from the local area than usual.

The children also benefit as Andrew has a little surplus stock to feed them more regularly. He also supplies them with soap and blankets, along with a few simple toys for the younger children. He has even had Anna in the bakery helping out with the fetch and carry of bread and helping Penny serve in the shop on a couple of days during the second week.

Whereas Andrew and his little bakery have been making things a little better for the local people, conditions in the town itself have been getting worse. There has been more civil unrest, with people retaliating against ever-greater rent increases and taxes on owning livestock and the cost of food. Riots have led to the army taking on additional roles guarding state buildings, food stores and escorting politicians. Constables continue to patrol the streets, in ever greater numbers, to help maintain law and order. It's often difficult for them as families are divided themselves as to how the country is being run and the conditions they are living in. But, with The Three Heads threatening to bring the National Guard on the streets if they don't assist, it is better for the people if they try and reduce the hostilities as most of the National Guard are mercenaries and violent, corrupt soldiers from other countries who do not care about the citizens of Kelsey. Not that their own government seems to show much in the way of caring for the people under their control either.

It is Saturday morning and Andrew is running a little later than usual. He was expecting Anna to turn up and help as he is becoming accustomed to assistance in the bakery, but she did not arrive this morning. He tries not to worry about her absence, just puts his head down and gets on with his work. Knowing he will be taking food to the children food later and check on her then to ensure all is well. For the moment though, he has many more people relying on him to supply bread for their families and he does not want to let them down.

A carriage passes swiftly through the Town and into the old village area, then slows down to a walking pace for the remainder of its journey. It makes its way along the road while the people inside look out the window, alert to everybody walking past. Within a few minutes it nears the area where the children are to be found and a voice inside the coach calls out to the driver to pull up.

As soon as the carriage stops, Margaret steps down and looks around, accompanied by a man in a top hat with a leather bag in his hand. She looks up at the driver. "Wait here, for I do not wish to scare them. I will return shortly and, for God's sake do not worry, you can see me from where you sit." Margaret and the man walk toward where she had seen the children with Andrew. "All I ask you to do is to check them over and ensure they are in good health; one of the boys has a nasty cough and another had been very ill when I was last here."

The man looks at her. "As you wish," he responds, "but I must say that this is a little irregular to say the least, your——"

Margaret stops suddenly, putting her hand out to stop the man in his tracks. "No, no, no!" she says as she swiftly crosses to the empty firepit with the older man struggling to keep pace with her speed.

The stones and stumps surrounding the remains of the fire have been kicked around. Margaret looks for any sign of the children but can see nothing, then, on the floor outside one of the derelict houses, she spots something she recognizes. A pale-blue shoe. She rushes over to it and picks it up. Looking around, she calls out, "Anna, where are you. Anna?"

She walks thorough the derelict buildings looking for the young girl, heart pounding with fear and dread. As she moves around the rooms she spots one of the young boys she had seen before, sitting in the rubble with blood smeared over his face.

"I tried to stop them, but they just hit me and carried on," he says as she rushes to him.

She parts his hair that matted with blood to examine the cut, as the boy points to the far corner of the room. Margaret has a terrible feeling come over her, it's all she can do to look round, and, as her eyes focus into the darkness, she can see something blue in the corner of the room. She turns, leaving the boy in the hands of the man who arrived with her and slowly approaches, knowing what she will see but hoping against hope to be proved wrong. Her heart sinks as she gets close enough to see Anna, wedged so tightly into the crumbled corner of the building that only half her back can be seen. The blue dress that she was so proud of has been torn and she has bruises and even a muddy boot print on her back.

She crouches and reaches forward to touch Anna's back, but it's cold. As she eases her out, Anna falls, lifeless, into her arms. "Anna, oh, Anna, what have they done?" Margaret lifts the child from the corner of the room into the light and lies her down, head resting in her lap. Anna's legs and arms are covered in cuts and bruises and the front of her dress has been ripped open; dried blood streaked down her legs. Margaret turns to her companion, who is attending the small boy. "Please take a look at this girl," she says in a quiet voice.

The man comes over, taking the girl's wrist to feel for a pulse. He looks up at Margaret. "I cannot find a pulse."

"Check her again!"

The man opens his bag and takes out a small mirror, placing

it just above the girl's mouth and nose. He holds it there for a moment, then looks at it. "She is alive, but barely."

"Look to her."

Margaret puts Anna to the floor, then stands and walks out of the building. She spots the driver of her carriage and waves him over. He pulls the coach right up to the side of the building.

"Wellesley, come here and help the physician. Load her carefully into the coach and take her home."

Wellesley jumps down and disappears inside. "My god, who would do such a thing?" he murmurs, picking her up with the most tender care. He carries her to the coach, easing her through the door and onto the seat. The physician climbs in, taking the place beside her. The driver looks back at Margaret. "To your home?"

"Yes, home, and have Beth stay with her until I return. Now, go quickly. Collect me when you are done. Bring George and that old seadog of a friend of his, Westerfield, for I have a use for them both. Tell them to come prepared."

Wellesley looks at her, shocked. "Leave you here alone?"

Margaret looks at him, steely-eyed. "Go, the sooner you go the sooner you will be back." The man rushes to mount the coach, cracks the whip and, within moments, he has turned the horses and they are away up the road.

As the carriage disappears from view, Margaret starts to weep. The boy approaches, dragging a large stool with him. He offers the seat to Margaret.

"Has Anna gone to Heaven, miss?"

Margaret smiles at the boy and puts her arm round him. "Heaven is where she will go eventually, my dear, but, for now, let's hope we can keep her with us a little longer," she replies, wiping her eyes with a handkerchief.

"They came late last night as the fire was going down, as they have most nights this week, drunk with grog as they always are, staggering in from all directions and calling out for the girls. Anna got away from them at first, all five of them. She also got everyone else away too, that is all but me, they got hold of my leg as I climbed up on the roof and dragged me back down. They kept hitting me, said they would keep on until I was no more unless she took my place. I tried to be brave and not cry, as boys should not, but I am not as strong as Anna."

The tears flow anew, down Margaret's cheeks. There was an anger and a shame inside her that she could not control. The more she hears what happened, the more she knows she must do something to protect these children.

"She came back, just stood there. She said run, so I did. The last I saw was her being pulled to the ground. I threw rocks at them to try and stop them but had to run when one came after me with a knife. Big, it was, and I was too scared to stay any longer. I'm so ashamed to have left her, but I was so scared. I am only little, miss, if I were bigger, I would have stopped them, I swear I would have."

Margaret wipes her eyes, again, and looks up to see a man heading toward them, whistling and swinging a big cloth bag in his hand.

As the man notices somebody in the children's camp he hesitates a moment, then, recognizing Margaret, smiles and walks on. Only when he is ten or twelve yards from her does he notice that she is crying. His pace quickens and as he reaches her, she stands up. He instinctively takes her in his arms, her arms coming tight around him as she trembles.

"Those men, they got Anna," she sobs, clinging to Andrew. "They got her, and we did nothing to prevent it."

Andrew holds onto her until she is ready to be released. Eventually, he sits her back down.

Turning to the boy, he says, "Billy, what happened to you? Where is Anna?"

The boy points to Margaret. "Miss had her taken away in a big carriage with horses."

Andrew looks at Margaret.

"I had my driver take her to my home with a physician I was going to have the children looked over with. I only hope they will be able to keep her alive until she can go to where I had planned."

Andrew looks at the ground, then back at Margaret. "Then I

will come and see her with you."

Margaret shakes her head. "The place she is going would not allow you to enter, but, trust me, she could be in no better hands. If she survives the journey."

Before Andrew can say another word, Billy asks him, "Is that food in the bag, sir?"

"Yes, I baked some special pies for you and the others," Andrew says, still thinking about Anna.

"They won't come out now, not after what happened. They'll all be hiding, afraid to be seen for a while," Billy says.

Margaret thinks for a moment before standing up. "Andrew, why don't you give the pies to Billy so he can find the others and share out the food while we take a walk?"

Andrew nods, passing the bag to Billy, who looks inside. "Wow, look at them pies, they look delicious. Thank you!" Then a shadow passes over his face. He looks up at Margaret. "I'll take these to the others, but what will I say about Anna, miss?"

"Just say she will return when she can, but for now she needs time to get better," Margaret answers. Billy nods once and runs.

Margaret takes Andrew's arm and walks with him toward his house. "Anna is being taken to a dear friend of mine. After what those men did to her it is touch and go if she will survive. Her body was cold and so ravaged we could not even feel a pulse to start with. She might still live. If she does, it will be down to the skill of my friend Beth." She sighs deeply.

"I know so little about you, Marge, yet here you are, helping the children so many have left for dead or treat no better than animals. I get so angry that the people who run this country allow this kind of thing to happen anyone, let alone to children."

"Better circumstances would have been nicer for us to meet again, please take me away from this place, Andrew, we can do no more at the moment as nobody is here but us."

Andrew looks around at the empty derelict buildings and rubble strewn floor. It is an awful place and not one that should be acquainted by a lady like Margaret.

"Come, Marge," he says as he leads her away. "Let us make

our way to my garden, it will at least be a better place to sit and talk compared to here. If only to take your mind off what you have seen here and to tell me a little more about where you have taken Anna."

When they reach Andrew's house he opens the door for Margaret, leading her through the house and out the kitchen door into the garden, where he sits her down on the bench.

"If you would excuse me, I will light the fire and make us something to drink." Andrew leaves her and busies himself in the kitchen while Margaret makes her way round the garden, looking at and smelling all the flowers that are in bloom. For a small garden it is crammed with ornate and unusual blooms and she is fascinated by the two beehives. She sits back down and watches as the bees busy themselves around the garden, flying this way and that to various flowers, over her head and right past the tip of her nose in some cases, paying no attention to her presence whatsoever, just going backward and forward from the flowers to the hive.

Andrew steps into the garden with a tray, on which are homemade biscuits he made yesterday and a pot of tea. He has also made her a cup of his usual lemon and honey tea that he passes across for her to try.

"This is very nice and unusual, it has a fragrance I know but am unable to remember what it is, still it is very refreshing."

Andrew smiles as it is a herb from his own garden called lemon balm, but he does not tell her the name of the ingredient that she knows is present but cannot put her finger on.

"How was it you happened to be here today, visiting the children, more so with a physician accompanying you?"

Marge takes another sip of her tea before answering, ensuring she is careful in the way she answers the question.

"My appointments were canceled, and, with an empty schedule, my associates had no need of me for the rest of the day. The physician is an old family friend and I asked him to accompany me and meet the children. To advise on what ailed one of the boys and how to aid his recovery…"

The two of them continue to talk for several hours about the children, the bakery and what Andrew produces for the people. How the country has fallen into such a terrible state and what could be done to improve the lives of those who live in it. Much of the conversation was also about Anna, Andrew explained to her about the little he knew of her past and just as he asks about where she has been taken and who will look after her. There is a knock at the door.

Andrew pauses and listens as the door is rapped on two more times, he gets up to see who it is; Margaret knows exactly who it will be. When the door is opened, he is confronted with the coach driver.

"Would you kindly let Margaret know I am outside when she is ready?" he says to Andrew before turning and walking back to the carriage.

Andrew closes the door and turns around to go back outside, but Margaret has followed him into the house.

"It was my driver, wasn't it?"

Andrew nods. "Yes." He is saddened that she must go, for it has been a long time since he spent so much time in the presence of a woman he feels so comfortable with. "Will I see you again?"

Margaret thinks for a minute. "I am not sure yet, but I must ask you not to go back to the children tonight, for I have organized for those men that attacked Anna to meet with a surprise should they return, and it will not be pretty."

Andrew nods in acknowledgement and as she reaches the door he goes to open it, then suddenly pauses. Turning around, he steps forward and wraps his arms around her. She responds. After a few seconds they both step back and look at each other. Andrew looks into her eyes as something seems to take the air away from his lungs and he is unable to draw breath. His heart is pounding as if it will burst out of his chest at any moment. He steps forward again and gently kisses her on the lips. Margaret surprises herself by responding to his kiss, staying in his embrace for a few moments before stepping back.

As she steps out of the doorway, she turns to him. "My driver will pick you up at ten tomorrow." Margaret walks over to the coach and steps up into the open carriage, disappearing inside as another hand reaches out to close the door behind her and the carriage moves off. Within a minute it has turned the corner and is out of sight.

Andrew can hear the sound of its wheels rumbling on the stone surface and the rhythmic tapping of the horse's hooves for a while, but soon, even that fades into silence.

He bolts the door behind him before moving to his favorite chair and sits by the grey stone fireplace, pushing at the logs with a brass-handled poker to add more heat to the room. He has a warm feeling inside him as he thinks about seeing her tomorrow.

A thousand thoughts are now rushing through his head. After a while he manages to get them in some kind of order and perspective as he thinks firstly about young Anna and where she might be right now, how she is doing in a place full of strangers, and whether she will survive what happened to her. A feeling of anger and rage builds up inside him; he wants so badly to take revenge on the people who attacked her and violated the girl in such a terrible way. But he also realizes that the attack on Anna affected Marge as well and for some reason he feels that she has something planned that will be far more reaching and damaging than anything he could do in the short term.

Why did he instinctively kiss her? He wonders to himself, for it is not like him to do anything like that on the spur of the moment.

Andrew's eyes slowly begin to close. He fights to keep them open, but the warm fire and comfort of the chair sap his resolve and within a few minutes he falls asleep in the chair.

Margaret is looking at the men opposite her. "How is the girl doing, George?"

"It is too soon to tell; everything possible is being done for her, but she was so close to death that I fear her strength may not be enough pull her through," replies one of the men.

"That child showed more courage to step forward and knowingly take what was coming to save a little boy than we have all shown in years." Margaret takes a deep breath and then continues. "It is *our* fault that the country is like this, we have allowed poverty and despair to become part of everyday life. Some of our people have turned into animals, and it is time we take back control and rebuild our nation. Those men did a terrible thing, but what I have seen over the past weeks shows that there is still good in many people around here. The punishment for these men must be severe."

George nods. "That is why I have brought along this gentleman. His name is Jacobs, Horacio Jacobs, and he has an idea to present to you."

"Tell me what you have on your mind," Margaret prompts when he doesn't speak.

The man tilts his cap and starts to explain his plan to Margaret in great detail. Margaret listens, then nods in agreement.

The coach pulls up some two hundred yards from where the children have been living. Three children are sitting round a relit, smaller fire. The men slip out and move into the shadows, one of them carrying a small, heavy brown sack. Quietly, they move closer as the coach drives on and away off into the distance. George points out a good spot to the others where they can observe the children sitting and still have enough cover to settle in for a long wait.

Darkness has fully fallen and, as the town clock chimes 10.00 p.m., the three men are starting to feel like they have wasted their time waiting for the men. George is scraping out the tar in his pipe with a small pocket knife, while Horacio is rubbing his hands together to generate a little friction to warm them.

Westerfield stands up to straighten his back out. "Surely I am too old for sleeping outside, I've got used to my bed and the comfort of my wife in old age," he comments, making the other two chuckle.

A glass bottle is smashed somewhere in the distance. The other two men get up and start to listen intently. Soon, laughter and slurred singing can be heard coming from the town side of the buildings the children use. Minutes later, five men come into view, two walking in front and three locked in each other's embrace as they stagger ever forward toward their goal.

"D'you think she's still around?" one of them says to the others.

"Course she'll be there, she has nowhere else to go. 'Sides, she'll be wantin' to see us again, I'm sure of it," another slurs as he takes a swig from his bottle of homebrewed vodka.

"Ease up on that grog, Finley, it be strong stuff! Let's leave them alone tonight. It wasn't right what we did last night."

Finley looks back at Daniel. "Shut up, you wimp, you've always been less of a man than the rest of us. Now, if you don't like it, you can keep a lookout like before, you coward."

As they approach the camp the children have already heard them coming and have disappeared back into the darkness and the safety of the building and its drainage system below ground. One of the men relieves himself on the fire while the others stagger around the buildings looking for Anna.

"Here, girlie, girlie, I have something for you," one of the men calls out, then trips and falls in the rubble. The others laugh as he struggles to get to his feet. "Where the hell can that girl be?" he bellows.

The man by the fire hears or sees nothing, as a priest swings through the air and lands with a thud as Westerfield whacks him round the side of the head. The man is caught by George before he hits the ground and laid away from the fire. Horacio has another man in a chokehold until he drops to the ground, with another swift strike of a priest he is laid to rest and dragged next to the already downed man. George staggers and laughs as he catches up to another man, who thinks it is one of his friends until a punch to the jaw puts him on the floor. By now the other two are looking round, they can sense something is not right but it is too late; they are set upon and dragged back to the others by Horacio and Westerfield. All are clamped in irons and linked together with a long chain taken from the sack they brought with them. The two men who are still conscious are panicking and scared.

"Who are you and what do you want? We have no money and

if you want the drink just take it, it's yours with our compliments," one of them yells whilst trembling and shaking.

George leans over him. "Scared, are you? If I had my way you would be feeding on your own bollocks by now, for I saw what you did to that little girl and I am disgusted."

The man looks up at him. "It was just a bit of fun with some tart of a girl who lives on the streets, who cares about her?"

Before George can answer, Horacio has rushed him and punched him hard in the face, knocking him backward and into the embers of the fire. He screams as the glowing fragments burn the side of his face and neck. As he rolls away, embers fall off his face leaving two large burn marks behind.

George has no pity for him. He pulls the man back to where the others are positioned and stares at him. "Now you will always have something to remember this night, just like that young girl will. If she survives, that is, and by god you better hope she does, for the things I will do to you if she does not would scare the Devil himself."

"Is the girl that badly hurt?" asks Daniel.

"What do you care, you got what you wanted from her yesterday, didn't you?" Horacio says.

Daniel shakes his head. "No, it was wrong. I had no part in it, just the shame of doing nothing. I should've done more to stop it happening. Please tell me she'll be alright, that's all I ask."

Horacio stares back at him for a while before speaking. "It does not look good at the moment, filth."

George walks over to the sack and pulls out a thunder mug. Sitting it on one of the stumps around the fire, he primes it, finally adding a bit of fuse wire about ten inches long. He lights it, then walks away.

As he stands there waiting for it to go off, Westerfield comes to stand by him.

George turns to him swiftly. "I saw what those animals did to her. And, do you know, as I helped lay her on the bed she held onto my wrist and asked, 'Is the boy OK?' With all that she had been through and suffered, that little girl was more worried about the boy she gave herself up for."

"I have two daughters around her age, I doubt they could get through the day without help but this girl, abandoned by all who knew her, looks after a dozen other children in these ruins when all the adults around do nothing." He pauses for a moment. "Yes, I feel angry and ashamed. Like *she* said, we should never have let it get to this state. But I fear more for these men now, for I saw the look in Wellesley's eyes, a look I have not seen in many a year. Not since we came across the massacre in the lowland village of Helmsburg by those raiders. That night, when we caught up with them, I saw Wellesley take on and kill a dozen, the last two with his bare hands. If anything happens to that girl it will take a small army to hold him back. I think when we have finished here we should let Lord Ashby know what has happened, or there may be another massacre before sentencing is passed."

With that there is a thunderous explosion that lights up the sky with a trail of red as the flare shoots upwards several hundred feet. Within minutes lights start to appear in the houses all over the edge of town, windows start to open, people even go into the streets to see what is happening.

"Well, that's woken a few people," George says. "I hope the wagon master has seen it, I don't want to set another one off as people will see that we are here and question what we are doing with these men."

Sure enough, half an hour later, as the last of the people have gone back inside their homes, an iron-bar-lined prison wagon arrives. As it draws close, Horacio waves it over to the group of men. When it pulls up, a man jumps off the front and goes to open up the door of the wagon. They bundle the five men into the wagon cell, close and lock the door, then George climbs onto the top of the cage while the other two sit down on the passenger bench beside the driver. The wagon turns and heads to the magistrate's office. It takes nearly an hour to get to its destination on the most bone-shaking ride George has ever experienced. As they pull up outside the courthouse, the three of them cannot wait to get off and seek a better place to rest and sleep while the five men get processed inside the building.

Westerfield beckons the other two to follow him down the road. "I have a place for us to stay; they will have food and beds ready for us." George and Horatio have no objection to the offer and soon the three men can be seen entering a nearby building.

It is some seven hours later before the three men return to deal with the prisoners. In the courthouse the five men are sobering up and the realization of where they are is sinking in. One is yelling out that he is the son of a politician and demands contact with his father, another from a wealthy family offers bribes and payment for his release. The man with burns to his neck and face is whining about the loss of his good looks, while the last two just sit in silence. They have nothing to offer and can only wait to see what is in store.

The five men are individually collected and taken from the cells to an enquiry room. As each one enters, they see the three men who apprehended them sitting at the table with an empty chair opposite them. Each one of the five men in turn is sat at the table and the questioning starts off in the same way.

"You know if the girl dies you will be hung for murder," comments George.

"For now, we have repeated assaults on minors, rape, actual bodily harm of a minor and we caught you going back as a group to find and assault and rape that girl again. That does not look good for you, does it, Finley?" continues Horacio as he lays on the pressure.

"What are all the people of this fine town going to think about having a rapist of children like you around?" adds Westerfield. "I think they will want to hound him out of town, especially if they have children."

George continues, "You think so? If I had children around here, I would be tempted to make it a more permanent arrangement and end the risk of them ever returning."

Finley is shaking and trembling, trying to put on a brave front, but they can see they are getting to him. "You're just trying to scare me, you can prove nothing. I want out of here so you either charge me or let me go."

George looks at him. "So, you just want to go, that's no problem to me. If you want to go and take the risk of a mob hanging that's fine, just sign that you want to be released out of magistrate custody to your country, Kelsey, and you can go."

"What do you mean sign out of custody to my country?" Finley asks.

"Well, you can give me your address where you can be contacted should I need to speak to you again, or just sign that you will be in your country of Kelsey for the next ten years and go now."

Finley thinks for a few seconds. "Where do I sign?"

Horacio pushes forward a double-folded document for him to sign. "Can you write?"

"Of course, I can write, you fool, I'm not ignorant."

"He was only asking as it helps if you write the following, 'I sign at my own free will into the country of Kelsey,' then sign it and date it, and we will countersign and date and you will be gone from here," George says.

Finley takes quill and ink and writes what has been requested, then signs and dates the document, passing it back to George and watching as he and the other two also sign and date the parchment. George then opens up the sheet of paper and places it on top of the other four signed and dated sheets of paper to his right.

"Well, that's all five of them signed and dated. Out of all of them, only that lad Daniel seems to feel any sense of shame for what has been done to that girl," George says.

"Aye, you're right, but as the lad says, he should have done something to prevent it. In his own words, he's as guilty as the others. It is a real shame for him though, for he is the only one that shows any kind of potential," Horacio says as he stands up and leads the three of them out the room.

Finley follows, but as he leaves the room a guard grabs his arm. "This way with you, sir, you need to wait in your cell until the wagon is ready to take you from here," he says as he leads Finley back to his cell.

Sometime later, all five men are escorted from the cells, through the building and out the back to the courtyard. There, the prison wagon they arrived in is waiting with the back open, and, beside it, George, Horacio, and Westerfield watch as the five men approach, each one with a guard by his side. More men appear from around the side of the wagon brandishing leg irons and the guards grab the five prisoners and throw them to the ground. The guards pin them down as they try and kick out while screaming and yelling, as the officers apply the leg irons and then stand them back up on their feet.

"What the hell is going on here? My father will hear of this," one of the men shouts as Horatio steps forward and stands in front of him.

"Oh yes, your father will hear of this, but he will not see you or any of your friends for the next seven to ten years, for now you belong to me, filth!" Horacio yells at him.

"You have waived your rights to the magistrates and their courts, so now the ears of politicians and their bribing ways cannot help you. You are now in the hands of the country and we do not take kindly to people who assault, rape and beat children who are sovereign citizens of this land. Sentence is ten years at sea on one of our ships of the line and, by God, you will be the better for it," George says with a smile.

"You cannot do this, I know my rights!" yells the politician's son, Limington Smyth.

Horatio walks up to him and head butts his nose, splitting it and knocking him to the ground. The young man struggles to his feet with one hand on his nose, holding back the flow of blood. Finley steps forward and is instantly punched in the stomach by one of the guards; he buckles over but manages to stay on his feet.

"Get back in line, you scum!" the guard yells at him.

Westerfield is next to speak. He steps forward and looks at the five of them one at a time. "Seven to ten years walking the decks learning how to sail a ship, and, more importantly, discipline and how to be a gentleman of society, that is what you have to look forward to. Oh, the fun we are going to have with each other is going to be so entertaining." He pauses to think for a minute before continuing to speak. "You might not want to go to sea, but you're going anyway. You might decide that you are better off jumping overboard. If you do, you will die, and I will not care at all. You might not want discipline in your life, but you're going to get it. I will teach you how to become sailors at sea and gentlemen in society. You might not want that either, but, by God, you going to learn to be both. You see, you had a choice with what you did in life and you wasted it. That girl Anna laid down her life to save another child from you animals and she paid a terrible price. Make no bones about it, you are only alive because she is. If she dies, the chances are that you will find that fate better than what I would put you through, for I would cut off your manhood before I start work on the rest of you piece by piece: fingers, toes, ears and nose. But for now, be assured that if she lives, in ten years' time, should you survive the sea and its many dangers, you will return to these shores a far different person from the sniveling shits you are today."

He flicks his head at the guards who respond instantly and push the dejected men toward the waiting wagon. None of them say a word as they are loaded aboard for the journey to the coast and the gunship *The Vigilant*. The ship is being stocked with provisions ready for its voyage to protect the country's ports and trading ships from the pirates and buccaneers that frequent the seas around the coast. Horacio and Westerfield take to the front of the wagon, with Westerfield holding the reins and flicking them at the horses to get them moving. George watches them leave before going into the building to finish off filing the paperwork on the five men that have now been sentenced. The five men in chains inside the wagon fall silent; there is nothing they can do now except take the punishment they have been dealt for the actions they took on poor Anna and the other children.

CHAPTER 3

The Date

Andrew has tossed and turned all night, thinking about the day to come with Margaret. The loud explosions that woke him up around midnight did not help as he could not get back to sleep. He finally gets up at 7.00 a.m. after an extended lie-in from his more usual time of 4.00 a.m., but it is Sunday and his only day off for the week. Unfortunately, due to the lack of sleep, he feels more tired than when he went to bed. Being excited yet nervous at what might happen today, Andrew decides to wear all his best finery for the occasion.

As he looks at himself in the mirror he realizes a shave is definitely in order and decides on a trip to the barbers for a haircut as well. Besides, getting a close shave from someone else will remove the risk of him cutting himself through nerves. It is barely past eight when he leaves his house for the local barbers, and he arrives just as the doors have opened for business. He has a huge smile on his face and the brothers who run the shop, Reggie and Tony, can tell he is excited about something.

Andrew jumps straight into the middle chair and waits for one of the brothers to walk over. "The usual, please, and also a close shave."

Reggie and Tony look at each other, then back at Andrew. They both move closer and inspect the stubble on his face, then look at each other again.

"Let me get my spectacles," Tony says to his brother as he walks over to the side and puts on a wire-framed pair of glasses with small round lenses in the middle. He approaches Andrew and leans in to have a close look at his chin. "Hm, ah," he comments as he carries out his inspection. "Ah ha," he says, pointing to the edge of his chin.

Reggie moves in with a pair of scissors and snips at the air above Andy's chin. "Got it!" The brothers roar with laughter.

"Really, I come to my friends for a cut and a shave, and this is how I am treated?"

The brothers look at each other again, then back at Andrew. "No, there are many places you can get a cut and a shave, but this is the only one you can come to and have our special treatment and conversation." Reggie chuckles again. "Now I presume that this must be for a special occasion as it is so early in the morning?"

"A woman, perhaps?" adds Tony. The brothers look at the slight smile on Andrew's face as they start to prepare him for a shave, then back at each other. "Ah, I presume she is still alive and not blind?"

"Not that it is any of our business, dead or blind makes no difference to us if that's what you like," adds Reggie. Andrew sighs deeply as the brothers laugh and joke at his expense.

Soon the lather is on his face and Tony gets to work with a cut-throat razor. "Keep still and this will not take long, and I mean not long, for I think wiping the lather with my little finger would remove what little fluff there is."

The brothers are as fast and efficient at what they do as they are with the banter and within ten minutes Andrew is shaved, cut, pampered, and on his way out, dropping his payment in the pot on the counter.

Reggie takes the coins out of the pot and puts them back in Andrew's pocket. "No, my friend, there is never a charge here for a man who fed us for nothing for so long, for we would never have made it without your help. Now go and see this woman, perhaps she is the one, yes?"

"If she is, we want to be the first to see the one who has got a good man," adds Tony.

Andrew laughs. "Thank you, my friends, we will see how it goes today." He leaves the shop and returns to his house with Tony and Reggie watching him through the window while talking to each other.

Andrew's mind is still full of what-ifs, he can barely hold a thought long enough to make sense of it. That being said, the journey to his house is done and over before he realizes.

He goes straight out into the garden and starts to inspect his plants, watering with buckets of water taken from the stream and deadheading a few of the flowers that have finished blooming. Back inside, he fills a bowl with water and has a final wash before getting into his best clothes: trousers, waistcoat and jacket, all with a dark-blue pattern, a white shirt and black shoes. Dressed, he takes a seat and waits for the carriage to arrive. There is nearly half an hour to go, but he can think of nothing more to prepare, so he sits there listening for the sound of horseshoes clipping on the road outside.

On the dot of ten he hears a coach and horses pull up outside. He is nervous and starting to sweat as he opens the door; the driver has not even put on the brake before Andrew is slamming the door shut behind him.

The driver looks down at him. "Come sit by me for a while, I wish to talk to you."

Andrew thinks it a little odd, but as the driver puts out a hand he takes it and climbs up onto the front of the carriage, positioning himself next to the driver. As he does so, the driver flicks the reins to get the horses moving, they pull off and head toward the town. Strangely, the driver says nothing for a while, just navigates the cobbled roads, turning this way and that before taking a left and heading away from the town and into the country.

Andrew looks at the driver two or three times, observing his chiseled and granite-like features as he waits for the man to speak, but he makes not a murmur. Andrew starts to build up his confidence and is just about to speak when the driver pulls the horses to a stop. Andrew's nerves return as the driver finally turns to face him.

"What do you know about the woman you are about to meet?" he asks, staring directly into Andrew's eyes.

Andrew is a bit taken aback by the question and looks down

at the ground between the horses, but soon comes up with a response. "Well, her name is Margaret, she is good at cards, folds when she has won and beaten all, looks stern and emotionless but there is something about her, something quite special," he pauses for a moment.

"There is a kindness and honesty about her that is beyond words. She feels responsible for everyone, even the children near where I live." Andrew looks back at the driver. "I do not know what it is about her, but she has a way of making me feel needed and I enjoy her company."

The driver nods, then flicks the reins to get the horses moving again. "She has a lot on her mind, bless her," he says, glancing back at Andrew.

"I do not know what she sees in you, but if you let her down in any way I will tear out your heart and leave you to rot in some field somewhere. By the way, my name's Wellesley."

Andrew does not know if Wellesley is being serious or just being protective of his employer, but it does make him think about what he is doing, traveling to see a woman far above his station in society, being driven to God knows where with nobody at home aware that he's gone. If this man were to do what he has threatened, nobody would even know Andrew was missing until the bakery opened tomorrow and there was no bread. He begins to wonder if that is all he would be remembered for; a baker baking bread and pastries for the masses whenever he could get the ingredients.

He sits for a while, wondering what to say that would put him in a better light. "Have you known Margaret long?"

Wellesley slowly turns and looks at him. "I were outside the door when she be born, watched over her as a child, seen her grown to a fine woman, stood with her through tragedy and despair and I stand with her now in a time she is most needed. Yes, I know her as well as any man alive and would give my life willingly for hers."

"Well, could you tell me the things that she likes or is good at so I can have an idea of what to say or do, for I do not want to disappoint her, or upset you for that matter?"

Wellesley thinks for a while. "She be good with a blade, well good for a woman anyway, a crack shot with a pistol and rifle, especially with her rifled barrel marksman's iron. Take the nose right off your face at a hundred yards, she could. Knows a bit about healing and how to comfort them that are in need of it. Smart and sharp she be, has a good understanding of the law of the land and how it be applied. As for her dislikes, people who are dishonest, lie, manipulate, or put on others that what they would not like done to themselves. I pity them that play her for a fool, for she will bide her time and when ready, bring the wrath of God when she strikes back with the vengeance and the fury of a great storm."

Andrew is wondering if he has bitten off more than he can chew as the driver continues steering his team of horses along the road, then turns onto a country lane through fields and large woods. Within the hour they are driving along the side of a great estate set on the right-hand side of a huge forest that spreads back as far as the eye can see. Andrew can only look and admire the sheer beauty of the gardens full of topiary, bushes, plants, and statues, with a huge water feature that forms the centerpiece of the garden. Behind the gardens sits an imposing stately house of granite and stone, with ornate marble pillars and high chimneys.

Around the outside of the building are various gargoyles and grotesques that are joined into the corners of the guttering and cylindrical towers to give a spout for water to flow off the buildings' rooves when it rains. Flying from the very highest tower is the national flag and below it another showing the coat of arms of the royal family of Kelsey, an image of a gold griffin with talons forward on a black background, with three angled rows of gold lines and the words in Latin for "courage comes from within." Andrew cannot read the words, but knows they are there as many of his elderly customers talk about them, especially in the current climate.

On the second to largest tower is a huge red weathervane in the shape of a dragon with a long curly tail and its wings swept back. It is pointing southeast, meaning that the wind is coming off the sea and across the land and bringing cooler weather for the time of year.

The coach continues on until it reaches the main entrance to the estate. Grooved white marble pillars stand either side of a wide stone archway depicting gods and heroes from days of old, riding and battling mythical beasts and monsters. Its beauty and exquisite workmanship catch Andrew's eye as they pass. This entrance leads onto a long gravel driveway and as the coach slows down and turns into the entrance, Andrew recognizes the building from pictures he has seen in books. Brendlelake Palace is the residence of the Queen of Kelsey during the spring and summer months. Behind the palace should be a huge lake with a river feeding into it via a manmade waterfall and at the other end another, smaller drop off as the water flows through a maze of boulders and rocks to continue on its way to the sea. The coach is inspected and waved on by several armed guards who seemingly know the driver and carriage well and have been expecting it back for a while.

No sooner are they entering under the archway than Wellesley takes a sharp turn left and follows a sidetrack for around two hundred yards to a gatehouse cottage built in traditional hard blue stone and topped with a stunningly patterned golden thatch roof. There are corn heads cut into the weave of the straw and a pair of wooden pheasants built into the roof fabric along the ridge. It's as beautiful as a picture postcard, the cottage surrounded by its own small garden full of all kinds of flowers, shrubs and small fruit trees with a stone slab seating area backing onto the cottage wall.

Wellesley pulls up outside the house. "Time you were getting off, Andrew, Margaret will be inside or back any moment."

As Andrew climbs down, Wellesley tilts his hat, then flicks the reins and moves the carriage away down the gravel drive toward the palace. Andrew heads toward the back door of the cottage. It is open, but he still raps the knocker and waits for a response. He does not wait long as Margaret appears in front of him carrying a tray with a teapot, cups, and saucers, along with some fine cakes and pastries. Andrew takes the tray from her and carries it outside to the seating area and places it on the table, then turns back to greet Margaret with a smile. He can see that she is glad to see him by the very slight smile on her face, a quirk he has noticed before.

"Well, I guess I have a little explaining to do," she says as she pours the tea. "I have not been totally honest with you, Andrew, but that is because I have rules I must follow. Being a lady-in-waiting and an advisor to the queen, I must be incredibly careful whom I associate with or talk to. I had to be sure who you are and where you are from before I could bring you to my little cottage as I reside in the grounds of the palace. Also, should I be needed by the queen I must attend immediately, but for now I am not required and have some time to see you."

Andrew is somewhat stunned at Margaret's words as they start to drink their tea while he thinks what to say in responce. "It is a beautiful cottage and the garden is quite exquisite, and you look absolutely stunning in that dress, Margaret," Andrew comments as he adds a stick full of honey to his tea.

Margaret smiles and does the same, also adding a piece of lemon to hers. "It would seem that I have picked up some bad habits from you in the short time I have known you."

"I must ask," Andrew says after a short pause "How is Anna, will she recover?"

Margaret puts down her tea and looks back at him. "She is gravely ill and it is too soon to tell if she will pull through, but I was allowed to take her to the palace and she is under the care of the queen's own physician, so she cannot be in better hands. My only regret is that I cannot take you to her, as you may not enter the palace."

Andrew nods in understanding. "I hope she will recover soon as I miss her greatly, as do the other children. I cannot always be there for them and without her they are in danger of those men returning and causing problems, as it was always Anna who kept the girls safe."

Margaret shakes her head. "No, that is one worry you will never have again, for those men have chosen to go on a journey for a while. You can tell the children they are safe and will not be bothered again, I also have friends in the area that will check on them from time to time from a safe distance so they will not know they are being watched."

"Journey?"

"Yes, they decided to travel a while with some associates of mine, but don't worry, they will return," she replies. "In good time they will return as better people, I am sure of that, so rest assured, Andrew."

The two of them spend the whole afternoon first walking round the cottage small garden, then round the fabulous grounds of the estate and its stunning lake. Arm in arm, they amble along, admiring the beautiful flowers and shrubs. Margaret talks about the history of Brendlelake Palace and by mid afternoon they return to the cottage, where they step inside and close the door to the outside world. Andrew sets and lights the fire in the front room, noticing that the fireplace has not seen any form of fire before as there is no soot nor ashes present, but thinks to himself that she must spend most of her time in the palace. With the fire going and catching hold of the logs, they close the red velvet curtains and take their places on a large floral-patterned suite facing the hearth for its warmth and light. Andrew takes Margaret's hand, then leans forward to gently kiss her and Margaret responds. Slowly the kisses become more passionate. Just as things are starting to get even more heated, there is a knock at the door. The first knock does not stop them, but the second, louder, knock cannot be ignored.

Margaret gets up to answer the door and Andrew watches as two ladies whisper to her. She nods as they speak before she closes the door and returns to him. Andrew stands up to receive her, and, as she comes closer, she takes his hands in hers and kisses him gently.

"It would seem that the queen has been requested in the capital for a few days on state affairs. I am sorry, but I must go with her. Wellesley will be here shortly to take you back home. I do so dearly want to see you again, perhaps after your work next Saturday? I could have Wellesley pick you up around midday and you could join me here again to continue our conversation?"

Andrew nods and kisses her several times before she turns and walks toward the door. As she leaves the cottage, he can see there is sadness in her eyes.

"Until I see you again I will think of you, Andrew," Margaret says, taking one last look at him before the door closes.

Andrew sits back down, thinking of the wonderful time he was having up until this moment. He does not have to ponder long before he hears the sound of the carriage being driven over the gravel to the cottage. "*Everything is so efficient and precise with her.*" He thinks to himself as he stands up and sighs heavily. He looks around the immaculate room one last time before heading for the door, where Wellesley is just pulling up outside. Reluctantly, he walks over to the carriage and climbs inside, sitting back in the seat as Wellesley moves the team of horses forward. All Andrew can think about during the long drive home is the wonderful time he was having with Margaret before she had to leave.

It seems like no time at all has passed, but it has been well over an hour and as Andrew looks blankly out of the coach window, he realizes he is nearly home. Moments later, the carriage pulls up outside his door. Andrew steps out and looks up at Wellesley to thank him, but he has vanished. As Andrew looks round he hears a thud from behind the carriage and turns to see a large trunk that Wellesley has just dropped down from the back of the coach.

"She wished for you to have this and said you might find its contents of use to you. Now grab the end and I will help you into the house with it."

Andrew rushes over, picks up the end nearest him and walks backward to the doorway, fumbling with the catch with one hand while struggling to hold onto the trunk with the other. When he finally manages to open the door, the men bundle the large traveling chest into his house, placing it on the floor by the fireplace.

"Thank you for driving me today, sir. I'm sorry I did not sit and talk on the way back, but I had a lot on my mind," Andrew says.

Wellesley does not answer, just nods in acknowledgement before leaving the house and climbing back up onto the coach. Once the horse and carriage are out of sight, Andrew closes the door and goes to light a fire to start warming the house, as it is a little nippy.

As the fire takes hold he goes into his garden and checks on his plants and bees. It takes him until dusk to finish watering his plants, along with deadheading all the flowers, which he adds to his compost heap, giving it a good turn as he does so.

With a final check on his bees, he returns to the house to wash up and see what he has left in his pantry in the way of food. Within the hour he has heated water on the fire and made tea, finding some leftover bread and cheese in the pantry. He sits by the fire to eat and only now starts to wonder what is in the chest, testing his resolve by finishing his meal before going over to see what is in it. Andrew undoes the two big straps and lifts up the top of the chest, letting it fall over the back. There are several wrapped packages and a selection of fine clothes neatly folded in the bottom, but what catches his eye is an envelope on the top with his name Andrew and an x by it. He picks up the letter and looks at it as he sits back down in his chair. Opening the envelope, he unfolds the letter inside and begins to read it to himself.

Dear Andrew,

I have written this letter in advance of your arrival in case I do not have long to be with you, for my duties may call me away at any time and I have no choice but to go when requested. I am deeply sorry that I could not tell you who I was before as it may attract the wrong type of attention from the worst type of people. But feel safe in the knowledge that I do wish to spent time with you when circumstances allow.

Please find in the chest a few items that I thought you might like. I chose them myself, but with little experience of getting gifts for a man I might have got it wrong. In the bottom is a bag of money; this is to ensure you always have enough to buy the ingredients to make food for the children and perhaps some clothes or a few toys should you feel they need them.

My thoughts are with you always.

Margaret xx

Andrew reads the letter a couple of times before folding it, putting it back into the envelope and placing it on the mantelpiece above the fireplace. Then he turns his attention back to the trunk and starts to open the packages. One box contains a dozen containers of fruit preserves, another a small sack of sugar, a real treat for Andrew as just the smallest amount ground into cream or pastry makes a real difference to the taste, and dried dates and a selection of assorted nuts in another small paper-wrapped package. He takes out the clothes and shoes and tries them all on and is amazed that all the items fit him perfectly.

"How did she manage to get it all right?" he mutters to himself as he works his way through the chest. Next a few garden tools and a selection of bulbs and tubers with the names of the flowers and how best to grow them written on pieces of paper wrapped round each one. Most of them he has never heard of, but it will not stop him from doing his best to grow them.

Finally, at the bottom of the chest is a hand-sized pouch. When he opens it and pours its contents into his hand it soon becomes clear that there is more value in these coins than he has ever see before. He looks round the room as if people might be inside the room watching him, then splits the money into four piles. He puts one behind a brick in the fireplace beside him, then stands up and collects the sugar and preserves and heads to the pantry. Placing all the preserves, the fruit, nut bags, and sugar on the empty shelves, then moves a small beam to one side and puts another quarter of the money behind it and replaces the wood to hide his prize. He gathers up the clothes he has been given, goes upstairs, and puts them all in the wardrobe and wooden chest of drawers in his bedroom before hiding another quarter of the money under a section of floorboard he uses for his own personal poke, not that there was ever very much there in the first place.

The last quarter of the money he puts around him in small amounts: a little on the mantle above the fireplace beside the letter, some in his work trouser pocket to use on more ingredients, a little more in his jacket pocket, and finally some outside in a small box that slots in the side of one of his beehives. The selection of tools and bulbs he places by his little shed, covered with an old sack ready to sort out when the light of day returns. With everything tidied neatly away, he moves the much-lighter chest upstairs into the spare room and places it against the far wall. He can use it for storing blankets and other items for the children as he collects them from the shops or has donations given to him in the bakery. Standing back and looking at the chest, he cannot believe that Margaret has given him such a fine array of gifts, so many things and all of use to him. He shakes his head and smiles to himself. "What a woman," he murmurs, "what a woman indeed".

Andrew then heads to bed, for he is back at work tomorrow and will have a lot to do at the start of the week. As he climbs into bed, he takes one of the two recipe notebooks that sit next to the bed and flicks through the pages for inspiration, they were once his mothers who used to write down items she had made or seen on her travels. It has been a long day, and within half an hour he has fallen asleep with the book open on his chest.

The following week seems to fly by, time and days rush past in a blur for Andrew. With a little more money for ingredients, he makes more bread and pies in his shop; this in turn allows him to sell more as nothing wasted and for the first time he starts to make a small profit. He has more people than ever coming to his shop to buy bread and in the hope of a few pastries and cakes and he is not letting them down. The days in the kitchen are longer as he has no Anna to help him and there is always a lot of preparation to do. On his way home he drops off food and supplies to the children, usually sitting and talking to them for a while and ensuring they are as well as can be. One of the lads, Kris, has shown an interest in baking and Andrew has been considering using him in the bakery until Anna is able to return. He decides to give the young man a start the following Monday morning and see how he gets on.

It is odd, though, for twice this week he is sure he has felt that someone is watching him as he talks with the group of youngsters, but when he looks round he cannot see anyone who stands out from the crowd. On one occasion he took a walk round the area, but all he saw was a man walking a large black dog on a thick rope. Still, Andrew cannot afford to let his guard down as the lives of these children may depend on it one day, so he always stays alert and vigilant to his surroundings when he is with them.

The week finishes as it started at a fast pace in the bakery. Once the baking is done, the kitchen cleaned, and the shelves full of bread and cakes, he says goodbye to Penny and his patrons. So many of them want to shake his hand and thank him personally for keeping the prices low and helping them when they are short of money for payment.

As he steps out the door he hears a young woman comment, "No, Rosie, not today, perhaps next week we can get you a cake." Andrew stops in his tracks, turns and takes two cakes from the rack and puts them in a bag along with a few coins from his pocket, passing them to the little girl as they leave the bakery. "Take these, Rosie, they are a special treat for a special girl."

"Thank you," she says with her eyes wide open and a huge grin on her face.

All her mother can do is smile at Andrew. "You are too kind, Andrew, God bless you".

For Andrew, Margaret's coins were given to him to help as he sees fit to do so. It is not just children who are hungry in these difficult times, whole families are struggling to stay together. On his way home he calls in on the children and gives them a bag containing the food he has prepared for them. Today it is chicken and mushroom pies and a couple of loaves of bread, and for the younger ones he has made a few fruit tarts.

On his arrival home, he rushes round to get all his chores in order, watering the plants and ensuring his bees are in good health. He has a quick wash and gets into some of his new clothes and waits impatiently for the arrival of Margaret's driver. It would be a lie to say he is not excited; he has thought of her every day since last week. The only thing that he is worried about is if she is still at the capital with the queen and is unable to return home. On that fear, he soon has his answer, for he can hear the sound of hooves clicking on the road as a coach approaches at pace. He hopes and prays that it stops outside his house and when he hears Wellesley's voice calling his horses to a halt he is up and out of his chair like a scalded cat. He tries to calm himself as best he can and puts on his coat for something to occupy him while he waits for the knock at the door.

He goes to the kitchen and takes the large bunch of flowers from the bucket he has been standing them in, dries the stems and wraps them in the paper he has ready on the side. Tying them neatly with a bow made from a piece of red ribbon, he stands by the door to wait for a knock. After five minutes, impatience gets the better of him and he opens it to see if the coach is still there. Sure enough, there it is, just yards from his door. Looking up at Wellesley, he sees him sitting there staring right back at him.

"You know I be waiting for you, so hurry up and climb up here with me," Wellesley comments as he reaches down with his free hand.

Andrew hesitates. "I have these for Margaret, I will just put them inside the coach for safekeeping."

"They can go inside the coach, but I'm afraid you will need to be up here with me." He bangs the top of the carriage with his fist and a hand covered with a dark leather glove reaches out from below the cloth covering the window. It clicks its fingers at Andrew, who looks at the hand before passing it the flowers. The hand retracts inside the coach with the flowers with Andrew watching out of the corner of his eye as he mounts the carriage.

"Things are not always as they appear, my young friend, and I would ask you to wait a while before asking me any questions as they might be answered in the fullness of time." Wellesley says as he flicks the reins and clicks at the horses to get them moving, maneuvering them expertly round in a circle and heading back up the street. They take the same route that they had done the previous week, heading first toward the town center, and then moving round the outskirts of the city. Andrew does not speak, just watches the road. He has little understanding of what is going on and is afraid to ask the wrong question.

They are twenty minutes into the journey when they round a corner and are confronted with a man slowly pushing a wooden hand cart. As they bear down on him he looks behind and panics, twisting around on the cart and falling to the ground, pulling the cart over with him and spilling its load of thick wooden logs across the road.

"Woah, centurion!" yells Wellesley, pulling back on the reins to stop the horses before they trample the man. Two men come running from either side of the road and thrust pistols through the coach windows, yelling for the people inside to get out, while the man on the ground begins to get up from the floor. On the side that Andrew is sitting, a hand comes through the curtain over the window, grabs the villain by his necktie, and pulls his face violently into the side of the coach, smashing it into the doorpost and dropping him to the floor. The man on the other side fares no better as something inside the coach grabs his hand. He screams in agony as an animal begins growling and ripping at his fingers and wrist. A pistol sticks out of the carriage door and points at the man who is still screaming.

"Release!" orders a man inside the coach, and with that the man retracts his ripped and mangled hand and falls to the floor still screaming and yelling in pain.

The coach doors on both sides open and two men get out, one with a large black wolf-like dog on a thick rope lead. They forcefully pin the two men to the ground to clamp them in irons as the man on the floor with the hand cart stands watching all that is going on while reaching inside his jacket pocket. Andrew hears two clicks and looks over to see Wellesley has cocked two pistols, pointing them at the man in front of them.

"I would think again before pulling out that pistol as I will shoot you dead," Wellesley says as he readies himself to fire. The man looks up at him, pauses for a minute, then slowly takes his hand from his waist coat pocket, holding a pistol between his thumb and forefinger. He stretches it out in front of him and drops it to the floor. The two men from the inside of the coach watch the gun fall and only Wellesley notices the man raise his other hand with a smaller pistol. He fires both barrels at the man, hitting him in the shoulder and the right kneecap. The impact throws the assailant's aim off target and the bullet clips Andrew's arm.

Everything happened so fast that initially Andrew does not feel anything. His adrenalin kicked in at the sight of the first gun, his heart pounding, the shock of what has just happened stunning him into silence. The man on the floor is moaning in agony and pain.

"Still alive after two shots, you must be losing your touch, Wellesley old boy!" comments one of the men from the coach as he rolls the man over and puts metal handcuffs on his wrists.

"Of course he's alive, but only because I want him that way for questioning. A shoulder shot would have been enough, but this way he will never walk properly again, and his masters will have to find an excuse as to why their men were here attacking a royal carriage. Now, you know where to take them while I deliver this man to Margaret," says Wellesley.

"Better you than me, for she will be none too happy with you when she notices what has happened to him," replies the man with the dog.

"Oh, and why would that be so?"

"The lad has been clipped on the arm, and, if I remember rightly, you said to her he would not be in any danger."

Wellesley looks round at Andrew and sees the blood that is starting to seep through his shirt just below the shoulder. "Oh damn," he mutters as he turns to inspect the wound. "There will be hell to pay for this," he says, taking a red handkerchief from his pocket and tying it round Andrew's arm. He looks at Andrew. "Are you well, lad?" He taps the side of Andrew's head. "Can you hear me, boy?"

Andrew turns to look at him, dazed. "Who… Who were those men?"

"They work for the Government, or should I say for Alexander Stone and his two associates, William Bonner and Herbert Mallory," Wellesley explains. "We got wind that they are now after the queen's advisors in hope of finding out about her plans for the future, as they are unable to get close to her and believe she is planning to take back control."

Andrew thinks for a moment. "So, why would they want to question me?" He pauses. "Oh, it was not me they were after, it was Margaret."

Wellesley nods. "These men will stop at nothing to keep the queen from her rightful place."

Anger starts to take over the better side of Andrew. "Can you not just shoot them now and be done with it?"

Wellesley smiles slightly. "I like your spirit, but they are cunning and ensure they are safely engaged elsewhere. They use men like these to do their dirty work, and there are always plenty more mercenaries out there to take their place when they fail, it is just a matter of price and opportunity. For now though, we will question them and find out what they know before sending them away to a place where they can do no harm. As for you, young Andrew, I need to get you patched up and over to Margaret so you can keep an eye on her for me while I have words with these men. It seems she might have a soft spot for you, not that she would tell me mind, it is just a feeling that's all."

Andrew flexes his arm out. "I have cut myself worse in the garden at home…" He pauses to think on Wellesley's words. "Does Margaret really think on me?"

"It is a possibility." Wellesley takes up the reins and gets the horses moving. As they pass the men being marched off, Andrew cannot help himself and kicks out at one of the men, knocking him to the ground in a heap.

"That's for thinking you have the right to touch Margaret, you traitor."

Wellesley looks at him as he straightens back up. "By God, boy, you have some fight and passion in you when riled. I'm beginning to like having you around."

They pull up outside the small cottage. Andrew hardly waits for the carriage to stop before he climbs down; his arm is a little stiff and he uses the other to take most of the weight of his body, letting out a small grimace as he opens the carriage door and to retrieve his flowers. Lifting them from the seat, his heart sinks; they have been crushed and flattened. He takes a deep breath and throws them back in the carriage.

This has not gone unnoticed by Margaret, who is standing in the doorway watching. He hears footsteps approaching and looks around, smiling as he realizes it is Margaret. He turns to greet her, but she walks straight past him to look at what he threw into the carriage. Looking at the crushed flowers on the floor she steps back to look up at Wellesley, giving him one of her severe, stern looks before turning back to Andrew. Only now does she see his blood-stained arm and the red handkerchief wrapped round it.

"We shall talk about this later, Wellesley," she says in an angry tone, without even looking around.

Wellesley sighs heavily. "It was an ambush. A lot went on in a very short time; the lad is fine, just a little nick, that's all."

Margaret glares at him for a few more moments. "Well, be gone and leave us alone, before I forget my manners."

Wellesley does not even comment, just grits his teeth and mutters to himself as he moves the horses on, for he knows better than to argue with her when she is in that kind of mood.

Margaret, on the other hand, takes Andrew by his good arm and walks him toward the cottage. "Come, my dear, let's see to that arm of yours." As the door closes behind them it starts to rain. In Kelsey, when it rains it really hammers down, and this downpour looks set to last for the rest of the day. Inside, she sits Andrew down at the table in the kitchen, places a small knife on the side, and heads to the kitchen stove with a small bowl to collect some hot water from the pot she was heating to make lemon and honey tea. She takes a clean muslin cloth from the sideboard drawer, honey from the pantry shelf, and a large metal spoon that was hanging over the stove. Sitting the spoon on the flat iron top, she pours a small amount of honey into the bowl of the spoon and allows it to heat up on the stove.

Back at the table she undoes the handkerchief around Andrew's arm and cuts away at the sleeve so she can look at the wound. Taking a piece of the muslin and dipping it into the hot water, she starts to wipe away the blood and shirt fibers. Andrew does not move or flinch, just looks at Margaret. He is conscious that not a word has been spoken between the two of them yet.

With the wound thoroughly cleaned, Margaret cuts the muslin into two strips an inch wide and about three foot long. Then she brings over the bubbling honey on the spoon and sits it across the small bowl for the honey to cool a little. While it does, she takes the sleeve and handkerchief and throws them on the fire in the lounge. Returning to the table, she takes one of the strips of muslin and dips the middle three inches into the honey and leaves it to soak.

"This may be a little hot, but it will stop the wound getting infected, so be brave, my darling," she says as she places the honey-soaked strip over the wound. Andrew grits his teeth ready for the pain, but finds it is just about bearable. Margaret wraps the rest of the strip round his arm and ties it off in a small knot, wrapping the second strip over the top for added protection and trimming the ends with a small knife.

"There, all done." She kisses him gently on the shoulder, then on the lips and goes to move away, but Andrew has other ideas. He stands up and turns her around, holding her in his arms and kissing her again.

"I have dreamt of doing that to you all week," Andrew says, looking deeply into her eyes when they finally separate. As always with Margaret, she is impeccably dressed; today she is wearing a dark-green outfit with black floral patterning and her hazel-brown hair is held high with a small green hat to one side, finished with three small feathers in a tight curve. "How is that you always look so good?"

"Well, I hope it was worth the week long wait," replies Margaret with a smile on her face. She starts to clear up the mess that has been made while Andrew wipes the honey from the spoon with his finger and tastes it.

"That's a good drop of honey."

"I had some plans for us today, but this weather is unexpected and now I do not want the wound on your arm, which should never have happened, to get wet," she comments while making tea for the pair of them.

"Well, we shall just have to adapt, then. For now, though, I think I should cook something for you in return for the attention you have shown my arm."

Margaret looks at Andrew. "I have no idea what we have, for I have been away all week. One of the girls left a box of something in the pantry, but I have not yet looked at what is in it. Even then I am not much of a cook."

Andrew laughs. "How would you survive on your own, I wonder?" he asks as he walks into the pantry, bringing out a large box and arranging its contents on the table.

It soon becomes apparent to Andrew that there is food enough for a meal for two people twice over in the box. He adds more wood to the burner beneath the stove top and starts to prepare a meal. Within twenty minutes a stew is simmering on the top of the stove, its rich aroma filling the room.

"We have an hour or so before it will be ready to eat," Andrew says as he looks out of the window. "It's looking no better out there."

He pokes the fire and adds another two logs to the embers before sitting down with Margaret, putting his uninjured arm around her shoulders. "How is young Anna doing, is she making a good recovery?"

Margaret looks at him with a smile. "I was wondering when you were going to ask. She is healing well. She got up yesterday and has been slowly walking round the palace a little. I was with her a few hours ago and she was talking about you and the other children. I think it will be a long while yet before she is fully recovered and ready to return to her friends as her injuries were quite extensive. Three cracked ribs, a tremendous amount of deep bruising across her back and arms, and she needed stitches to areas that were torn when she was violated. The physician has said that, physically, she should make a complete recovery. But, Anna's mind and trust of people will take a long time to heal, if she ever fully gets over it."

Margaret asks about Andrew's encounter with the men who attacked the coach and they trade stories and adventures, asking questions of each other on what they have done in the past. Andrew cannot hope to match the meeting of royalty and famous people Margaret does on a daily basis. But it seems that Margaret is just as eager to learn what it is like for the people who live around Andrew and his bakery and how they cope with the day to day, living in such poverty.

Andrew gets up and checks the simmering stew. With a few stirs of the pot he calls out to Margaret, "The food is ready. If you come through, I will serve."

As Margaret takes her seat, Andrew spoons out the stew into a bowl and places it in front of her. He has already cut up some bread and put it on a plate, placing the butter in a small dish in the middle of the table.

Dishing out himself a bowl too, he takes his place at the table opposite her, smiling as he sits himself down. After a few mouthfuls, Margaret smiles at Andrew and nods with approval. "You are a talented cook, Andrew."

Andrew smiles at her. "I have made far worse things taste edible in the past, for I have not always had such fine ingredients to use." They continue to talk over dinner. Margaret describes some of the dishes she has been served at state affairs in the past. Andrew pauses and shakes his head, "I think even I would draw the line at a boiled sheep's head, even if it was considered a delicacy."

Darkness has long since set in and Andrew has closed the shutters and pulled the drapes across the windows. They move to the fire, gazing into each other's eyes.

"You have not yet told me when your driver will be picking me up."

"Do you wish to go, then?" she asks, quietly.

Andrew is already shaking his head before she has even finished speaking. "No, not at all, I was just thinking that it was getting late, that's all."

Margaret puts her arms around him, kissing him gently. In an even softer voice, she says, "I was hoping you would stay the night."

Andrew looks at her. "Here?"

Margaret nods slowly.

"With you?"

She nods again.

"Yes, with me, unless you would rather it be with someone else?"

"God, no! I mean yes."

Margaret looks confused and Andrew looks up at the ceiling, trying to think of the right words to say. He looks back at Margaret, then wraps his arms around her waist and kisses her. "Of course I want to be here with you tonight, there is nobody else that I would rather be with."

Margaret lets out a sigh of relief. "I was beginning to think that you—"

Andrew interrupts. "There is nobody in this whole country that I want to spend time with more than you, Margaret, for you mean a great deal to me." They hold each other tightly for several minutes, not needing to say a word to each other. Andrew can feel her heart pounding where she is pressed against him. He holds her tight to his body, giving her a gentle kiss.

Margaret is so nervous she begins to tremble, It has been so long since she trusted anybody with her feelings, but she has finally found a man she dearly cares for and is convinced that he feels the same about her. And yet, if she goes through with tonight, there will be no going back. She would have gone against all protocol and stipulations associated with working for and serving the royal household.

After a while Andrew gets up to put a couple of logs on, but Margaret interrupts him.

"Don't bother with them, Andrew, for I wish to retire anyway." She kisses him gently on the neck and whispers in his ear, "Give me five minutes, then join me." Andrew watches as she lights a lantern by the fireplace and ascends the stairs. She does not look back, just disappears into the room above the stairs.

Margaret begins to undress, undoing the clasps on the front and side of her dress before unbuckling the waist belt and sliding the dress down, stepping out of it and placing it neatly over a nearby chair, then adding a chemise and undergarments to the collection. She takes out her hair pins and lets down her hair showing it to be far longer as she shakes her head and flicks it all over her shoulders and down her back. Finally, she folds back several layers of bedclothes and climbs into bed, shivering at the cold for a moment before her body heat starts to warm the blankets as she waits for Andrew.

Meanwhile, downstairs, Andrew has been pacing the floor. It has been a while since he has been with a woman and he is very nervous. *What if I am no good or cannot do it?* He takes a deep breath and goes upstairs. As he enters the room he can see her looking at him with those beautiful eyes, her hair all let down. He takes off his waistcoat and shirt, then his shoes and socks.

"Please turn out the lamp, for I am a little shy," Margaret interrupts as he starts to undo his trousers, looking at him with pleading eyes and a nervous expression. Andrew does as Margaret asks and turns down the wick until it goes out. With nothing more than a sliver of moonlight through the window to see by, he finishes undressing and makes his way toward her and the bed.

It is mid-afternoon when they finally wake, still wrapped around each other.

"Morning, my dear, I hope you slept well," Margaret says with a tender smile on her face.

Andrew stares at her for a moment before he too smiles and kisses her on the nose. "Not really, I seem to have had a strange dream of being kept awake by a demanding woman, wanting more and more from my body."

"Oh, and what did you do about this?"

"Well I did what any good man would do with the woman of his dreams and gave her my all."

She touches the side of his face with her fingertips. "Do you think you were good enough?"

He smiles and kisses her again. "Well, I gave it my all, so I hope she was satisfied with the performance."

"I think she was," Margaret replies, kissing him once more and holding him tightly.

It is almost another hour before they get up. Andrew is up first, dressing himself and going downstairs to clean and light the fires to warm the house, scattering the ashes from the day before over the flowerbeds to enrich the soil. When he goes back inside Margaret has appeared in the kitchen and is filling a pot with water to boil and make tea. She is dressed, but still has her hair loose and the sight of her takes Andrew's breath away.

They kiss. Again.

"You do know that not every time we stay together will be like last night, don't you, for I may be called away at any time."

Andrew thinks for a moment. "Then, as in my dreams last night, I will have to spend every bit of the coin I have when the time comes."

She slides her hand inside his trousers and cups him, giving him a gentle squeeze. "I think the cup is truly empty this morning, my dear, perhaps some time to recharge is required."

He gives her a gentle hug. "And now, breakfast? I saw some eggs in the pantry and some bacon and cheese are still left in the box, so, with your permission, I recommend a bacon and cheese omelet à la Andrew."

Margaret smiles and takes her place at the table. "Permission granted. I shall sit here and watch as this mysterious omelet of yours takes form, mon cheri."

Andrew beams as he starts to prepare food for his woman, heart full of pride and feeling as big as a house. He has never felt so happy and content in his life. A chance meeting with Margaret at a game of cards several weeks ago has changed his life forever.

After breakfast they spend the afternoon walking round the grounds of the palace, looking at the fine architecture. "The queen's great-grandfather commissioned the building of this house, had all the marble used around the windows and arches on the doorway's imported from quarries in Italy. The steps and stairways leading into the building are all hard-wearing Bluestone from Ireland," Margaret comments as they continue moving along arm in arm.

"It is a pity I do not have more time, Andrew, but I will soon need to get ready to join the queen and support her as she takes on the politicians in another round of cat and mouse negotiations on policies. Let's just hope that it does not take too long, for it has been nice to just be myself for a day and enjoy your company without others around.

Before long, Andrew is saying goodbye from the front of the coach where he is sitting with Wellesley, a spot he now prefers and feels safer after the incident inside the coach with the would-be assassins a few days ago.

Andrew waves to Margaret and looks back for as long as he can see her, then, after she is gone from sight, he turns and sits back down beside Wellesley.

"Andrew, are you sure you are up to the task?" Wellesley asks after a short silence.

Andrew thinks before answering. "I get the feeling that the queen puts on her a lot of responsibility and duties, but if she can handle the pressure, it would be a poor show if I could not stand by the woman I care for so much."

"Ha!" laughs Wellesley. "I feel there may be hope for you yet, young man."

CHAPTER 4

Life-Changing Times

Over the next six weeks, Andrew's life remains the same. He works, checks on and feeds his growing number of orphan children on his way home each day, and all but one weekend he spends time with Margaret. He now has two or three of the older children working in the bakery as the workload continues to increase. Penny is somehow managing to find greater supplies of flour and other baking ingredients more regularly and at a better price and Andrew is able to hold more than enough stock in his stores to cover each day in advance, making it easier to plan what he will produce the next day. The bakery output has greatly increased, along with the number of people coming to the shop. For the first time in years, he has filled the whole shop window with all sorts of cakes, breads and pies, not that there is anything left by the end of the day. However, they are able to feed more people at an affordable price and the shelves are holding their own for a good part of the day. Penny has even had to use one of the older girls to help her serve behind the counter all day as the queue now always spills out into the street.

Andrew's bakery and commitment to helping the community with affordable prices and support of the homeless and orphaned children over the years has made him quite a celebrity. Many people want to help him and assist in whatever ways they can, with that in mind he has made several trips to the local mayor and councilors for the area, and, after several meetings, he has been able to purchase the derelict houses the children use as a home for virtually nothing, providing he rebuilds them for the re-homing of orphaned youngsters from the local area.

With the money from Margaret, he has been able to employ two builders to start taking down the old buildings, recycling and stacking all the bricks and tiles along with anything else that can be reused to save costs. After a week or so of watching and distrust of the two strangers, several of children are now helping to fetch and carry and assist where they can. Putting the two men well ahead of schedule and allowing them to start working on what will be the footings for the great build.

Many locals have also been donating what they can at the bakery or assisting in the build with time, labor, and, in some cases, even finances or materials. It is becoming more and more of a community effort than Andrew had ever anticipated. His plans are to make the two buildings into one, having a line of bedrooms upstairs, each one housing two bunk beds on each side of the room, and downstairs a large open room with space for the children to play and learn, supervisor quarters, a kitchen and bathroom with three or four baths in it and two large open fireplaces to heat the house in winter. It will not be elegant by any stretch of the imagination, but it will be functional and have room enough for thirty or so children to live in a safe environment.

Last week Margaret had stayed with Andrew at his house, the first time that she had ever visited and remained the night. He was able to show her what the money she gave him was going towards and how the project on the housing was moving forward firsthand. Margaret met all the children and visited the bakery, where, as a special treat, the children had baked her a small sponge cake filled with jam and cream with a frosted top. It was not quite the standard Andrew worked to, but it was a good first effort and tasted great.

Margaret had explained to the children that the queen had taken an interest in Anna and offered her a position on her staff, and that Anna, with typical stubbornness, had said that she would only take the position if the queen would help with the problem of homeless children. With what Margaret had seen today, she was going to report back and recommend financial assistance not just for Andrew's project on the house, but for several of these projects around the country.

As she was about to leave, the children gave her a bag filled with cards and little gifts for her to take back to Anna; even the few that did not know her wished her well. No doubt Andrew had helped them all with the spelling and wrapping, but all had done their best, leaving Margaret with the task of delivering the gifts to their friend.

It was now the seventh week of the relationship and the bonds between the two of them were growing stronger with each encounter. It is around midday, and Andrew was desperate for the coach to arrive and take him to see his beloved Margaret. He paces up and down the room in anticipation of its arrival and is on constant alert for the sound of horses coming down the cobbled street. After an agonizing wait and near to giving up for this week, he finally hears the sound he has been waiting for; faint to start with, but soon getting louder. As the coach pulls up, he is already at the door with a small case in hand. He places the case in the coach with his coat on top and is about to climb up to sit by the driver when he notices it is not Wellesley.

"You are not the usual driver," Andrew comments as he stands there looking at the man.

"No, sir, that be why I am a little late, for I got lost getting here," he says. "I am sorry for being late, but if you would be so kind as to get in the carriage there be a note for you inside."

Andrew is now cautious and a little hesitant, the experience of the attempted assassination on the coach and knowing the risks Margaret lives with, make him now more alert to danger. But does recognize the carriage and the horses look familiar as he has seen them many times. He peers inside the door and, sure enough, there is a letter for him to read on the seat. He takes the letter and looks at the front of it; it is written in the most elaborate calligraphy, all it has on the front is his name.

Climbing inside, he takes a seat and unfolds the letter to read its contents.

My dear Andrew,

I have often told you that it is sometimes complicated for me, and this is one of those times. To ease your mind that it is me who wrote this letter, I will admit that the first time we met I had a full house with an ace on top.

The driver has been instructed not to move off until you bang the roof three times. He will not be taking you to my cottage, but to a place in the little village of Glennsford, just over halfway between your house and my cottage. I may not be there when you arrive as I will be assisting the queen in her duties and tied to her requirements and schedule. But help will be at hand to assist with what needs to be done. Do not lose faith in me now, my darling, as I need your strength and your shoulder to lean on more than ever in these difficult times.

My love always,

Margaret
xxxxx

Andrew bangs on the roof and then, as the carriage moves off, reads the letter over and over again until he has virtually memorized every word. Once finished, he folds it and places it in his pocket. He sits back in his seat and folds his arms; there are a lot of thoughts going through his head, but the one that is most on his mind is how Margaret is doing and why the change in location for them to meet. He also wonders where Wellesley is, as he has slowly become more of a friend than a driver and he enjoys the banter with him during the journeys to and from meeting Margaret.

The time passes slowly in the back of the coach for Andrew, with nothing to do but look out of the window or sit back in his own thoughts and ponder the world. On the half-hour mark the coach driver slows his horses to a stop. Andrew looks out of the window to see what is going on, but quickly retracts his head as another carriage moves past in the opposite direction within a foot or so of where his head was. *God all mighty*, he thinks, letting out a relieved breath, *that was close.* As the carriage pulls forward again, he looks out of the window, this time keeping his head inside the coach, and sees that they are crossing a large stone bridge over a river that spans around forty yards of water across its width. On the other side of the river the coach moves at a slow walk, then turns right and follows a small path along the side of the river for several minutes before turning left onto gravel track, judging by the sound under the wheels, before finally stopping.

"We are here, sir," the driver calls, but Andrew has already opened the door and stepped down from the carriage. Landing on the gravel with a crunch, he takes a few steps forward and looks around. A short distance away are two enormous oak trees, just beyond them is a river running along the side of the garden and lined with large willows. The garden spreads out on either side of the gravel driveway at the front and stretches around the back of the building, with several flowerbeds and established fruit trees scattered around the well-maintained lawn.

The house itself is about four times the size of the cottage where they usually meet, with the same blue stone walls and twelve windows across the front. It stands three stories high and has tall chimney stacks at each end of the building, both showing thin plumes of smoke. The roof is made up of square-cut gray slate tiles and sets the house as a typical country-style manor. Andrew reaches into the coach and takes out his case and coat and heads toward the arched front door, stopping briefly to admire the flowerbeds on his way past.

As he reaches the front of the building, the door opens and a beautiful young girl in a fine summer dress steps out smiling at him. Andrew recognizes Anna instantly, though she looks far, far cleaner and better dressed than he has ever seen her. She looks well, and Andrew cannot help but smile as he moves towards her. Anna rushes up to him and gives him a huge hug and a kiss on the cheek.

"They thought it was better for you to be greeted by a friend rather than a stranger," she says as she grabs his arm and leads him into the house. "Come this way and I will show you around.

I hear you and Margaret are a little more than friends now," she adds, smiling at him.

Andrew is lost for words, not that he could get any out anyway as Anna does not stop talking about what she has been doing and who she has seen, along with asking many questions about how the children are doing and how the bakery is going. They head into a reception area where Anna takes his case and places it on a side table and hangs his coat on the wooden coat rack.

"It would seem the queen saw fit to allow Margaret to use this family house when she was off duty as it was more reflective of her position and role serving the royal household. She has also decided to give the small cottage to the head gardener and his wife so they can be permanently on the grounds they attend. As for me, I now have my position helping the queen as one of her handmaidens, allowing Margaret more time to step up as her chief advisor and personal confidante and do more planning and organizing of her duties, roles and requirements for the good of the country," Anna finishes.

Andrew looks at her with a huge smile on his face. "You seem to have come a long way in a couple of months, Anna. I had been worried about you for so long with only Margaret's assurances you were doing well. Now, seeing you here, it warms my heart to finally see you with my own eyes again, especially when you seem so happy."

Anna cannot stop smiling as she answers. "More so than I have ever been, although there was a time at the beginning that I just wanted it to end, but the people who helped me were the best, and I mean all of them. I owe my life to them for what they did to get me back on my feet. As for the queen, she spent so much time visiting me and building up my confidence. She is an amazing woman, Andrew, I feel so proud of her and what she has done and is doing for me and all the others around her. I want to serve her as best I can as she is a remarkable woman under so much pressure." Anna's tone of voice changes. "So many politicians want her out of the way or hidden from sight; they want to remove all her powers and prevent her from taking her rightful place ruling this country. They don't want her helping the people get back on their feet and putting the politicians back down where they belong. So, she needs all the help we can give her, for the lady will never give up the fight for her subjects. This is why Margaret is so special, she holds everyone together, and with you by her side, she seems that much more determined that nothing will stop her helping get this country back in its feet."

Anna sighs heavily and takes a few breaths. "That's why I want to help all I can to get her into this house. She supports the queen and holds back those that want her out of the way. Now I am well again, the first duty the queen tasked me with was to get this place ready for dear Margaret to move in and get comfortable in the months ahead. Do you know, I have been here five days with a group of people getting this dirty place reopened and ready to be used as a home again? There was years of dust and debris everywhere inside and all the furniture was covered in sheets and blankets. We've had to have both fireplaces lit round the clock to dry the building out and make it warm and cozy again. The only thing that seemed to be maintained in this whole place was the gardens. As they were always on view to people looking in, a local gardener was commissioned to maintain the grounds, but, inside, well *that* was a different matter."

Andrew laughs at Anna's constant chatter. "Well, I must admit the first thing I looked at when I arrived was the garden and its borders. Then, when you stepped through the doorway and smiled. Well, I knew it was you, but your presence still took my breath away. What a fine young lady you have become young Anna."

Her smile lessens slightly. "Here, less of the lady, I am still Anna, the same Anna from the streets you helped save me from. I also understand from Margaret that you have purchased those old houses. She says you are re-building them for the children to live in and get off the streets for good, and that you have some of the children helping in the bakery like I did, that is so good of you."

"I only chose where to spend what I had been given by her, well that and the little profit from the bakery and local donations have helped to keep it all ticking along." Andrew pauses and smiles a little. "To be fair, I think Margaret is helping a little more than I know, because things seem to be a little easier lately, not that she will admit it to me you understand."

Anna takes hold of Andrew's arm again. "Come, let me take you around the place before Margaret arrives, for there is so much to show you and so little time left for me to be here," she says, leading him round the building.

Andrew looks at her. "You mean to say you are not staying here with us?"

Anna shakes her head. "I would love to, but I am instructed to leave in the coach that Margaret arrives in and return to continue the queen's duties in Margaret's absence. Besides, I should think that you and Margaret will have a lot to talk about with all these changes."

The pair of them move from room to room with Anna explaining all that was done to each area, along with any of the building's history she has been told about during the past five days by some of the longer-serving staff that had been working with. They end the tour back downstairs in the main lounge, taking seats by the large open fire. On the walls around the room are paintings of previous kings and queens, including the last couple with their young daughter. As Andrew looks round the room, following all the pictures in turn, he notices above the fireplace there is a lighter square area in the wall above two crossed swords.

"What happened to the picture up there?" he asks curiously.

"Oh, well, I was hoping you would not notice that until I repaired it," Anna says, flustered. "When we pulled down the sheet covering the picture, it caught on the edge of the sword and ripped the picture off the wall and broke the side of the frame. It went back to the palace earlier today and should be repaired and back by next week."

The pair of them continue talking about Anna's training and the duties she has been carrying out for the queen. How she struggled for weeks after her attack to come to terms with what had happened and how badly it had affected her until the queen had encouraged Anna to work for her and given her a purpose. Anna may not have the airs and graces of those born in society or be able to represent nobility, but she was able to get a job done, read people, smell a rat, observe without being seen, and adapt to changing situations. She was a useful addition to the queen's arsenal.

For the queen these traits were far more important at this moment in time than ever before, providing Anna wanted to help, she would have her taught in the arts of defense and attack, along with the skills needed to look the part in society. For a smart, pretty woman with sharp skills would be an asset to have around in the coming years as the queen slowly puts her long-term plan into motion.

Close to an hour had gone by before they hear a coach coming up the gravel driveway. Anna jumps up and goes straight to the nearest window to see whose coach it is, then turning excitedly to Andrew. "She's here. Oh, damn, what I mean to say is Margaret is arriving. I'll go into the kitchen and get her lemon and honey tea on the go and see to some food before I leave."

Anna has already disappeared before Andrew has even got out of his seat, he heads to the entrance to welcome in his beloved Margaret. As he opens the front door he can see Wellesley struggling to pull up the reins of the carriage while holding his shoulder. Finally he manages to stop the horses, just a few yards past where Andrew is standing. Before he has a chance to step down, Andrew is at the door to the coach and opening it for Margaret, arm stretched out ready to assist her down the step.

The last thing he is expecting is the pistol that comes through the doorway and points into his face, but as Margaret comes into view she lets out a sigh of relief and lowers the pistol. Andrew is shocked by how exhausted she looks, more so than having a pistol pointed at his face, as she steps down from the coach she wobbles on her feet. Andrew steadies her as he helps walk her to the door of the house, taking her through to a seat by the fireplace.

"Thank you, my dear. Now please go and help Wellesley, for I fear he may be injured."

Andrew pauses to reassure himself that Margaret is well, then rushes back outside to see to his friend. As he approaches the carriage, Wellesley is just sitting there, the reins still in his hands. Andrew can see lines of blood running from his shoulder down his arm and onto his leg.

"Come Wellesley, let's get you inside," he says as he steps up and begins to help his friend down from the buckboard, tucking his head under his good arm and slowly helping him to the ground. As they turn and head toward the house, a group of riders arrive at the gallop, pulling up sharply a few yards from them. Andrew looks up to see soldiers in green uniforms, blooded sabers and lances drawn as they bear down on their position. Acting on instinct, he pulls the pistol from Wellesley's side and goes to point and cock the weapon, but, as he raises it at the first soldier, Wellesley knocks it back down.

"They are with us, Andrew, and, besides, it is not loaded. The thought was good, just not the right one this time my lad."

All five riders swiftly dismount, one taking the reins of all the horses and three of them reloading their pistols while the officer rushes over to help Andrew get Wellesley into the house.

"With your permission, sir," he says as he takes Wellesley's other side, and together they stagger into the house and through to the kitchen. They sit him down on a chair just as Margaret arrives via the other door.

"Captain, get your men inside by the windows, tie the horses to the wagon for now, and have one man go upstairs and look to see if we have been followed." Margaret orders

"I want you all in the house for now." She turns her to look at Anna, "Anna! get some more water on the boil and collect my small brown case from under the seat in the coach. Andrew my dear, get that shirt and jacket off Wellesley's back so we can take a look at the damage and see what we need to do."

No one hesitates to follow Margaret's orders. Andrew undoes the buttons on Wellesley's jacket while noting how efficiently everybody works during the emergency. Even Anna shows no fear as she drags another pot of water to the top of the stove and then heads outside to retrieve Margaret's case.

As Wellesley's jacket and shirt come off, the five soldiers file in through the back door and take up their positions, the fifth one catching his lance on one of the drapes by the window as Margaret looks up.

"John Bull, you know better than to bring in an eight-foot lance into a house to fight with. Pistols and blades at close range will be the order of the day, should they come. If you must have that with you, break it in half so it can be used better." She shakes her head as the other men smile and chuckle.

"Here, load this for me," Margaret says as she throws a pistol in the direction of one of the other soldiers. John leans his lance up against the wall and kicks down on it to break it in half. Picking up the half with the spear tip on it, he holds it in two hands and does a couple of practice jabs with it, nodding with approval before looking back out of the window again.

Anna comes through the door and places the medical case on the kitchen table. "Now get some white cotton sheets and start ripping them into strips for bandages," Margaret says to her. "Andrew, see if there is any honey in the pantry. If there is, you know what to do." She turns to the officer. "Captain Hawkswell, put your buckle knife in the fire below the oven to heat up and pass me your hip flask for I will need it to clean items before we use them."

"Hip flask, ma'am!" he protests.

"Captain Hawkswell, do you think I don't know about your famous brandy hip flask you took from a general in battle many years ago? We all see the bulge in your breast pocket when you ride, so hand it over or shall I be forced to take it from you." The men looking out the windows cannot help but smile and try to hold back their laughter as Margaret cuts their captain down to size. Hawkswell throws her the flask and Margaret catches it, giving it a shake. "It's still full, as I expected. I knew you would never drink on duty, you are too good an officer," she says as she puts the flask on the table. Anna arrives back in the kitchen tearing small strips from one of the large sheets she has collected from upstairs, making a pile of the pieces on the table.

Margaret grabs two of the strips and goes over to the small pot on the stove that Anna was going to make the tea from, dunking the strips in the hot water before returning to Wellesley. Gently, she starts to wipe the blood and sweat away from the two wounds, one in his shoulder and another in his side that runs front to back along his ribs.

"Wet two more strips for me, Anna," she calls out and Anna arrives swiftly with two more hot, wet strips. Margaret takes them and continues wiping around the wounds, getting closer and closer to the actual cut in one area and the hole in the other with each stroke.

"Wellesley, we need to take the bullet out before it gets worse. You have a choice, we c—"

"No, I don't, Marge. I can feel it pressing inside my chest. Do it now before it ruptures. If it is to be fatal, I would have it done by you rather than that butcher back at the palace."

Margaret gives one sharp nod and looks around the room to assess what she has available to assist her. "Clear the table and let's get him on it. Anna, get a cushion for his head, you two men help lift him carefully onto the table," she orders, pointing at two of the soldiers stationed nearby.

Margaret opens the case to reveal a complete medical field kit. Pulling out a probe and a pair of long tongs, she pours brandy over them and wipes them with another strip of bandage material before pouring more brandy over them and flicking them at the ground to shake off the excess liquid.

"Riders heading for the bridge," the soldier upstairs shouts down. "I count twelve, thirteen, no, fourteen of them."

"Just watch them," the captain yells back. "Keep us up to date with their direction, but do not shoot or give your position away."

Ignoring the shouting, Margaret prepares to push in the probe. Slowly, she moves it into the hole in Wellesley's shoulder and down into his chest area. Wellesley is fighting back the pain to remain motionless while Andrew and Anna watch, waiting for instructions.

"They are heading over the bridge," calls the lookout. Moments later he calls again, "They are over the bridge and continuing at a canter." A minute goes by. "They are heading toward the woods about two miles away."

Margaret has not looked away from her patient and finally feels a dull thud on the end of the probe. "Damn, I've hit cloth. Andrew, lay his jacket and shirt out on the floor." Andrew does as requested while Margaret picks up the long tongs and starts to follow the probe down the wound. Tears are running down Wellesley's face, but he does not move.

"You were leaning forward when you were shot and the ball is down at an angle," Margaret comments as she pulls the probe out and continues with the tongs alone. As she makes contact with the pistol ball, Wellesley winces. "Easy, my old friend, I will do this as quick as I can."

Margaret grips with the end of the tongs and starts to retract, this pulls on the hole and creates a vacuum trying to keep the bullet inside. Slowly, as the pressure is released, the tongs are retracted until they are finally out and Margaret releases the lead ball onto the table, then picks it up. Peeling off the pieces of material wrapped around the bullet, she passes them to Andrew. "Do these fragments fit the holes in his jacket and shirt?"

Andrew sizes up and rotates the pieces of cloth. "Yes, they fit, but there is still a piece of ribbon-like thread that is missing from the jacket."

Margaret goes to the medical case, coming back with some tiny, thin pincers with a curve on the end. She pours brandy over the pliers, wipes them, then pours more brandy on the pliers as she did with the other instruments she used. Not deep, but along one side of the hole she lowers the nose of the tool and begins to tug at a piece of thread until it comes loose. As she lifts it out of the hole she takes it in her fingers and pulls a piece of crinkled ribbon two inches long from the hole.

Margaret passes the bloodstained piece to Andrew. "Does that fit the missing area, my dear?"

Andrew takes the piece and sizes it up to the area missing a strip; it takes him a while to pull it all into shape and fit the area that it was once attached to. "Yes, that is all of it, down to the ends of the thread," he replies.

"Thank God for that," Margaret mutters, letting out a sigh of relief. She takes another piece of bandage, wets it in the hot water, and wipes over the two wounds again. Looking about the room she spots the item she needs next. "Captain, your leather riding glove, if you would be so kind." He passes her the glove as Margaret turns to Anna. "Anna, get the knife from the oven fire and wipe the glowing blade with a wet cloth." Anna does as asked, making the blade hisses and spit at the contact with the water. As Anna is doing that, Margaret returns to Wellesley. "I need you to bite down on this and brace yourself, my friend, for this be the worst part." He opens his mouth and takes the leather glove roll in his teeth, holding onto the lip on each side of the table with his hands while Andrew and the Captain brace him in position.

Anna then steps forward, passing the blade carefully to Margaret, who runs brandy down both sides that instantly lights into flames. With a couple of flicks of the wrist the flames are out and Margaret turns back to Wellesley.

"On the count of three, ready?" Wellesley nods, preparing for the inevitable. "One…" She places the blade down over the wound for a few seconds. It hisses and spits, the heat of the blade cauterizing the wound as Wellesley tenses and lets out a muffled scream before passing out.

The glove falls from his mouth as the air fills with the smell of burning flesh. Margaret inspects it to ensure it is sealed. Margaret throws the knife into the sink and returns with a small pan of hot honey and puts it on the table beside Wellesley. She looks at Andrew and the captain. "You two lift him up and support him while I wrap this round his body." She dips the middle of a bandage strip in the honey to cover about a three-inch section and lifts it out of the pot to cool a little, then places it over the wound on his ribs and ties it on the other side of his body. Then she wraps two more strips over the top of the first piece and knots them in place. The next strip of material she wraps around her hand to make a puffed-up square and dips that in the honey, again she waits for it to cool a little before placing over the pistol hole. She wraps the rest of the bandages over and around his shoulder to hold the padding in place, securing it with a tight knot. "Anna, throw all the used bandages in the fire to get them out of the way." Margaret says as she inspects the work she has performed on Wellesley. With a nod of approval she relaxes, letting out a huge sigh of relief and sitting down.

Margaret picks up the flask and raises it to the captain. "To you and your men, Captain, for you showed all the courage and bravery one could ever ask, without a thought for yourselves." She takes a sip from the container before passing it to the captain; he takes a sip and passes it to Andrew. Andrew does the same then offers it to each of the soldiers in turn, including the man upstairs, and on his return passes it to Anna, who shakes her head at the offer.

For the next hour all in the house is quiet as they watch and observe from several vantage points to see if the pursuing riders return. Anna makes all the men a cup of tea while they clean up their swords and equipment. Margaret remains close by Wellesley with Andrew standing at her shoulder. Finally, he stirs, first moving his hands then opening his eyes. He takes a few moments to get his bearings before looking at Margaret.

"What happened to two and three?" he asks as he tries to sit up.

"It was taking too long to get there." She comments as she smiles at him. "Now be still, we have been waiting for you to wake up before the coaches head back to the palace."

"What about you?"

Margaret looks at him with a stern gaze. "With no coaches or horses this place will be of no interest to anyone and myself and Andrew will be fine for a day or so. Now rest yourself, as I am putting the captain in charge of the coaches and Anna in charge of looking after you, and that is an order."

As dusk falls, the coach is loaded with Wellesley and Anna and the soldiers mount their horses. The second coach, that Andrew arrived in, also joins the group. With Wellesley unable to drive, one of the soldiers has to take on that role, but before he climbs up the carriage he walks over to Margaret.

"Ma'am, I know it is not my place to speak to you, but I need to say this. All of us here would go to Hell and back to serve our country, but for you I would do it twice over, God bless you." He salutes her before turning and mounting the buckboard, collecting the reins in his hands and prepares to leave.

"Private." Margaret calls, the soldier turns to look at her. "Any man who stands by me like you have done today has the right to approach and speak to me whenever they want. I look forward to the next time we meet, for I will remember what you gallant five have done today."

With Anna looking out of the carriage window, the group leave, moving off up the road at a steady pace. Andrew and Margaret watch, arm in arm, as they disappear into the gloom and mist that has started to roll in from the river, then return to the house and close the door behind them.

In the end room they take a seat by the fire on a large bench style suite, Andrew sitting upright and Margaret sliding down and lying along the suite, using Andrew's lap and chest as a pillow. He strokes Margaret's arm and kisses her on the head as she snuggles into him.

"I would ask what happened today, Margaret, but I am sure you will say that I am better off not knowing."

She looks up at him with her beautiful eyes. "That's why I love you so much, for you know that I do what must be done and you always support me." It is the first time she has used the word love and he feels a pride like never before. Andrew smiles at his beloved, still stroking her arm, and leans forward to kiss her tenderly. Margaret responds and the kiss becomes more passionate.

"I was going to ask you to make something to eat, but it has been a testing day and I would much rather an early night and eat in the morning. How would you feel about helping me upstairs?" She comments as she sits upright on the seat.

"Your wish is my command, my dear." Andrew comments as he stands up and lights one of the oil lamps sitting by the fireplace, then places the fire guard in front of the fire. Picking up the lamp, he returns to Margaret and offers her his hand, helping her up. They hug tightly, then head toward the stairs and slowly make their way to the bedroom above. Andrew puts the lamp on the side and dims it, then goes over to the bed and pulls back the sheets, leaving Margaret to get changed in the shadows, as she prefers.

Andrew, on the other hand, just strips everything off and piles his clothes on a chair before climbing into bed. To start with the sheets are cold to the touch, but after a few minutes the bed starts to warm up. By the time Margaret arrives in her nightgown, Andrew is warm and comfortable wrapped in the blankets and as she tugs on the sheets to climb in, he tries to resist, holding onto the sheets as best he can. To start with he is winning the battle of the bed, but Margaret changes tactic from brute strength to a few kisses and the lure of passion causes Andrew, like most men, to relent and release the sheets. Margaret slips into the warm area of the bed, turns her back on him and reverses her cold body into his, putting the finishing touch on her victory by placing her cold feet on his legs to warm them.

"Really," he comments as Margaret starts to chuckle, "I feel that all I am becoming to you is a bed warmer." He allows her to wriggle into him and get comfortable, then slips his hand over her waist and cups her breast, kissing her neck gently.

"Well, you do not want us getting cold now, do you?" she replies.

He kisses her again. "*We* were not cold, my dear, for I was quite warm. Only you were cold."

Margaret puts her hand over his and slides it down to her stomach. "No, my dear, I meant us." Andrew gently caresses her stomach while kissing the back of her neck for a while before he suddenly stops.

There is total silence for a minute as Andrew absorbs Margaret's words, then more silence as he dissects them and tries to find the right words to say in reply.

His hand starts to gently rub her stomach again. "Am I hearing you right?" he asks quietly.

Margaret turns her body to face him and, as she does, she moves her leg over his hips and straddles Andrew, climbing on top of him and lying on his chest. She starts to roll and curl his hair with her fingertips as she speaks. "It would seem that we might be three, my dear. What would you think of that?"

Andrew's mind fills with a million thoughts; fear, pride, excitement, wonder, too many emotions to grasp at the same time. He looks into her seductive eyes as she lies on him like a cat that has just got the cream.

As with all men, when it comes to saying the right thing at the right time, he cannot help but get it wrong. "How?"

She lifts her head up and looks at him. "Well, if you want me to tell you how to make a baby I will explain," she replies.

"No, what I meant to say was, really, we have a child coming?" Andrew starts to grin, the grin grows into a beaming smile. He puts his arms round her and kisses her. "When?" he asks.

"Well, it is only a strong possibility, but I would say sometime in the spring. We will have a few things to plan and do before then if it is so, as it is going to get complicated." She pauses for a moment. "I was hoping to go through them with you in the morning as we will have the day together to discuss things."

Andrew answers swiftly: "We could talk about it now."

Margaret shakes her head at him before kissing him on the lips, again and again. "Tomorrow, my dear, for now this lady requires a more personal attention and you better be up to the task for in a few months it will be off limits." She grinds her hips against him. Andrew smiles at her as he rolls her onto her back, positioning himself on top of her. He kisses her neck and slowly nibbles his way down to her firm breasts. With a lust for life and each other, they pass the next couple of hours in a frenzy of passion and desire before curling up in each other's arms and falling asleep, exhausted from their efforts.

It is early, the rays of light are barely breaking through the gaps in the curtains, Andrew, as always, is the first to wake, laying on his back and looking up at the celling. There is smirk on his face that has not left him all night as he thinks on Margaret's words. Sitting up, he looks at the curled-up woman asleep beside him, kissing her gently on the forehead he stretches and yawns before getting up and dressed. There is a cold chill in the morning air as he heads downstairs to clean out and get the fires lit to warm the house through before Margaret gets up. He has a huge, permanent grin on his face and a spring in his step that only the news of being an expectant father could have caused. Within the hour both fires are set, lit and well on their way to a perfect glow with the rooms warming up by the minute. The hot water is almost boiling on the stove and he has a pan sizzling away with thick-cut bacon and sausages he found in the larder, he is about to crack the eggs into the pan when Margaret arrives in the kitchen.

"That smells good, my dear." She makes her way behind him and kisses his neck, holding his waist as she peers round to see what he's cooking.

"Take a seat at the table and I will be with you in a minute," Andrew says, giving her a quick kiss before cracking the eggs into the pan. He places a large pot of tea on the table, then opens the oven door and takes out some warmed plates, cups and an empty roasting tray. Putting them all on the table, he collects bread, butter and cutlery and sets them with all the other items on the table.

Margaret pours the tea through a strainer before adding honey and lemon pieces, while Andrew plates up the food. As he slides the plate toward her, she looks at what is on the plate; two sausages, two pieces of bacon, one fried egg, and a few mushrooms. On the plate in front of Andrew are three sausages, four pieces of bacon, two fried eggs, and a whole heap of mushrooms. Margaret looks past Andrew out of the window, causing Andrew to turn to see what she is looking at. As soon as he does, Margaret switches the two plates and picks up her cutlery and begins to eat. Andrew turns back and spots the deception, reaching forward to swap the plates back and is instantly jabbed with a two-pronged fork.

"Ouch!" He shakes out his savaged hand, then rubs it.

"Don't even think of coming between a pregnant woman and her food," Margaret snaps at him with a savage growl, stabbing a whole sausage and biting half of it off in one go. Andrew concedes to Margaret and her wicked grin, shaking his head and smiling at the same time.

They eat well and clear up before heading into the other room to sit in front of the fire, Margaret stretches out, using Andrew as a cushion while Andrew slides his hand over her stomach and begins stroking her belly.

"The queen is the only one who knows I am with child other than us. I am hoping you will agree to keep it this way for a while until it becomes noticeable," Margaret says quietly.

"It will be difficult, and I know of two people in particular who it will be hard to hide it from, but I understand it would be best for now until we are sure."

She looks lovingly up at Andrew. "The queen wants to help and thought that this estate was close enough to both of our places of work that we could see each other more regularly while also continuing our duties and obligations. The problem is, Andrew, if I leave her side the politicians will tear her apart, so I need your support and help more than ever."

Andrew looks down into her eyes. "What is it you need me to do, my love?"

"I need you to have finished the house for the children and have trained someone to be able to at least cover running the bakery in six months' time, ready for you to look after our family here, in this house. I will be here as much as I can, but I must continue helping the queen defend the people or this country will fall apart. But I fear that without your bakery supplying food to the desperate, and a place for the children to live safely, they will suffer terribly as well."

Andrew thinks on her words. "Is that all you need from me?"

"No. I know you will get round to asking eventually, but I need you to do something for us next week, so will you ask me to marry you today so I can say yes and we can marry next weekend quietly, without fuss or pomp. A proper wedding can and will follow, but I need to be protected from those that would like to disgrace me and separate me from my duties and also from you."

"Oh, is that all?" he answers lightly, not even shocked at her request.

Margaret looks at him with her usual stern but hopeful

expression. "I seem to bring you nothing but requests and demands. If you want to say no or leave me, I will understand and not question your decision as I know I put pressure on you and ask things of you without a valid explanation. In time this will not be always the case, my dear, I promise. But I do really need you more than ever; you give me the strength and will to do the right thing and I would struggle with what needs to be done without your support and belief in me."

As Andrew looks down at Margaret, he can see that tears are beginning to roll down her cheeks as she gazes unseeing at dancing flames of the fire. The only other time he has seen her in tears was over Anna and what those men had done to her. He knows she organized for the men to be punished for their crimes against the children, using friends and the contacts she has from her role as advisor to the queen. He thinks for a while on what she has said and what he has been through in the past few months before replying, stroking her arm as he speaks.

"You, my dear Margaret, have surely turned my world upside down. More has happened in the past few months than in many a year gone by. Through it all though, one constant has remained. I fell in love with you from the moment I set eyes on you at a game of cards. You took my breath away then and I still have yet to breathe properly in your presence. I feel no less about you now with all that has gone on around us than that moment you entered my world. In fact, I feel more for you now, knowing what you risk being by my side and allowing me in your life." He holds her tightly and leans forward to kiss her softly on the cheek, then moves across and kisses her on the ear before whispering into it, "Margaret Dessola, lady of mystery and thief of my heart, would you do me the greatest honor I could ask of you and become my lawful wedded wife? I have only these hands to hold you and this heart to love you with, but I swear to God I will stand by your side and protect you until my dying breath and even then, should you still be alive, I will watch over you until we meet again in the hereafter."

Margaret wipes the tears from her eyes, bottom lip trembling as it always does when she is sad or upset, but this time it is because of the words spoken by Andrew are so passionate and meaningful. She wraps her arms around him, putting one arm round his back and sliding the other up to the hair at the back of his neck.

"God yes, my darling, with all my heart I say yes!" She looks into his eyes and kisses him again and again. "I have never asked so much of anyone in my life before, but I promise you that between us we will prevail and I will love you to no lesser degree than you have shown me thus far."

Margaret holds him tightly and does not let go for several minutes, not that Andrew is in any rush to be released, for he also has his arms around her waist and kisses her passionately. "My dear Marge, as this is to be our home, shall we go for a walk round the grounds and see what it has to offer?"

"In a minute, my love," she whispers in his ear. "For now, just hold me and comfort me, for this is one of the times that I need your strength and shoulders to hold on to."

Later, the pair of them are walking the grounds of the country manor, slowly ambling along the border beside the crystal-clear river lined with trees and reeds and the flower beds of the garden. They can see brown trout and grayling darting in and out of the silt weed and cabbages beneath the water line, while moorhens and coot's squabble in the water's edge for the best feeding grounds. They pass the edge of the small wood at the end of the garden and along the dry rock wall on the border and head back to the house. Talking about what will have to be done to make their partnership work and how to fit in all that will need to be achieved before the baby is due. The deep and intense conversation continues on until late in the afternoon when the two carriages return to take the pair of them in opposite directions. Even then they continue talking and holding onto each other until the very last moment.

With a final farewell hug, they kiss passionately and say their goodbyes before leaving the new house and each other's company to go to their different destinations. For the weekend has passed and it will be another long week apart until they are due to meet up again, that is unless something happens in the meantime.

CHAPTER 5

Promises, Promises

From the moment Andrew arrives home he is unable to hold a thought in his head, so many things to think about and plan and so little time to action it all. He is nervous about getting married to Margaret, worried about getting everything prepared and in order before becoming a father. Disappointed about needing to move away from his beloved cottage, the children and bakery. The risks his beloved Margaret always seems to take for the queen, and his limited knowledge in the use of pistols and swords when danger is present plays heavily on his mind. As he worries he would be unable to help or defend her with any real skill or ability should the need arise.

He spends the morning working as usual in the bakery, getting his young team of apprentices up to speed with working in the kitchen. It is now a higher priority to plan for his life going forward with Margaret, something he has already been putting it into action, showing the young men how to time and organize all the items they bake each morning. After finishing at the bakery, he goes to oversee the building work for the children's home, which seems to be on schedule according to the timings he has in his head. He is quick to pay any bills or material costs needed to ensure everything keeps moving forward at pace.

As usual, he feeds the children and takes care of their needs and any problems before returning to his garden to plan preparations for his own life. Not just for the weekend but now for the long term with his bees, garden, flowers and house. Sitting in his favorite chair by the fire, he starts to plan out what he requires to do and achieve for himself and Margaret. Planning comes easy to Andrew as he always takes the most practical approach and adapts easily if something unforeseen comes to light. His ability not to panic or fold under pressure, but just reassess and move forward is a key aspect of his nature.

Andrew concludes that his best option for the garden is to pot up the plants he wishes to move to his new house over the coming months, but not move them until the last moment so his bees can still feed on and pollinate them. He can dig some borders and planting areas at the new house, ready to move all his favorite plants later in the year, and then relocate his beehives in January when they are in a near-comatose state and not feeding as much. He decides he will sell the house when he has moved out to give him and Margaret a buffer in finances and ensure they have some cash available for any changes they might need to make once the baby arrives.

As for protecting Margaret, he decides to speak to Wellesley for assistance in learning how to use a sword and fire a pistol as he knows what to do or at least knows people who may be able to help Andrew learn. It is of particular importance to him that he learns these skills well as the events that happened the previous weekend showed up how little use he was when a life-threatening situation was at hand, and he is determined that that will change.

This only leaves the terrifying task of getting married at the weekend. Terrifying because he knows nothing of the plan, how it is going to happen or where, as Margaret said that she would organize everything, he just had to trust her to finalize all the requirements.

Andrew understands why it is so important to her to have the wedding as soon as possible, given the position she holds serving, advising and supporting the queen in these difficult times. As the weekend has just shown, a lot of people seem to want Margaret out of the way. In Andrew's mind this must be the work of the Three Heads, wanting to contain the monarchy so they can remain in full control of the country. For he has seen the passion and drive Margaret has for the queen, the country and the people that reside in it. He only has to look at Anna and the other children to see the lengths she will go in order to help the needy and see justice done on those that take advantage of others.

From the way she organized the defense of the house when they were in imminent danger, he can see why the queen puts so much trust in Margaret and her counsel. Her organizational and command skills were formidable and the knowledge she demonstrated on weaponry, tactics and healing show why Margaret is respected by all around her. Including the officer in command, who was not averse to taking advice. Yet humble enough to have a private soldier approach and speak to her before they left. There is no doubt in Andrew's mind that he has been blessed in being lucky enough to find the most perfect woman in the world for him. He feels so proud of her and all she does for everyone and soon, in a matter of days, this wonderful woman will be his wife.

Andrew decides that he must get the wedding ring. It might not be to the standard others could provide, but it will be from him, and in his mind, that is all that matters. He heads upstairs to his private stash under the floorboards to see what he has squirreled away; seventy-six crones, a small bag with his mother's jewelry and what is left of what Margaret had given him a few weeks ago. Andrew puts it all in his pocket and heads into town. It is a long walk to where he wants to go, but he is on his way and even the rain that is hammering down will not stop him from getting to the jeweler's.

As he arrives at the shop, he peers through the window at the display. Everything he views is either poor quality, too modern in the way it is made and presented or is out of his budget by some margin. After nearly an hour of looking, Andrew decides to head further into town to the pawnbrokers at the end of the street to see what he can get for his mother's old jewelry so that he knows how much he has to spend. It is a dingy old shop full of all kinds of oddities and curiosities, old wooden display cases show off items that can be purchased and there is a faint smell of old tobacco in the air.

After inspecting what he had to sell, the offer they gave him for all the items was decent and more than he expected, but if he accepts the offer he would still be way off what was needed to purchase any of the rings that had caught his eye in the jeweler's. Andrew is heartbroken and near to giving up on his quest when something catches his attention. A ring on top of the cabinet, mixed in with several other items. It is dull and dirty and has not been cleaned in a long time, but it has potential and is the style he is looking for. He picks up the item and looks at it; a chunky, wide gold wedding band with carved leaves and vines running round the sides. Set into the middle of the band are four dirty sapphires and three dull diamonds; the middle one has seen better days and is chipped, but it is in that old-fashioned style that Margaret loves.

The ring is a bit dated for modern tastes but would have been very expensive to make many years ago, and it shows very little if any wear to the inner side of the band. It is exactly what he has been looking for.

The owners of the shop tell him it was going to be stripped for its few good stones and the gold melted back down with the other items on the cabinet, to be reused in something else. It is not a cheap ring and the price is more than Andrew has, but after nearly twenty minutes of haggling, pleading and damn near begging, Andrew gets them to agree to sell it to him for all he has on him. With so little in the way of profit for the shop, Andrew must take it as is, without being cleaned or polished. It is a deal he can live with as it is the only ring he has found that he thinks Margaret would like and he can afford. He places it in the small bag that he had his mother's jewelry in and tucks it into his pocket. With the shopping part done he now needs to find a way of cleaning the ring; for that he only knows one person and he heads back to the bakery.

Andrew arrives as the last of the bread is being carried out of the door by a couple of triumphant elderly ladies. One of the children is sweeping the floor as Penny is counting the takings. He takes her to one side and shows her the ring.

"Do you know anyone who can clean this up?" he asks her.

"Andrew, this is so beautiful," she exclaims as she rolls it round in her hand. "It will need all the stones removed and reset, and the middle one is unfortunately chipped." She thinks for a moment.

"I do know somebody who might be able to help, but it may take some time to be done."

Andrew sighs deeply and shakes his head. "I only have two days."

"Two days, that's barely enough time to even ask around." Penny puts the ring back in the bag and places it in her pocket. "Leave it with me and I'll see what I can do after I lock up. Now go and rest up, for I have things to do, young man."

Andrew leaves the bakery and heads home, stopping to speak to the children and help the builders with some work on the house. He lugs stones, bricks and timber around according to their instructions and helps with other simple laboring tasks. As he stands back and looks at the structure, he can see that it is coming together faster than expected, with one of the builders erecting the end chimney while the other is working on the wall surrounding the fireplace. Several of the older children are supplying cleaned, recycled bricks while the younger ones are just playing in the local area and making a nuisance of themselves. With a couple of hours work put in, Andrew heads home for a wash and some sleep before the start of his shift early the next morning.

Thursday goes by in the blink of an eye, and Friday morning is not much different. Andrew has been flying round the kitchen like a man possessed, baking bread, cakes, pastries, and even two small birthday sponges that were special requests. The last items to enter the ovens for cooking are the meat pies and pasties and some bacon and cheese turnovers which go in as the ovens begin to cool and lose their heat as they cook at a lower temperature than the bread. He mainly makes these items for the children as a whole meal in one, but they have also become very popular with customers in the shop, often selling out faster than the cakes. There has yet to be a time when the bakery has had something left on the shelves for the following day, but it is a challenge Andrew tries to achieve every day he works.

Andrew has seen and spoken to Penny many times in the last two days, but he has refrained from asking her about the ring and whether she was able to get it cleaned and polished. Now that there are only a couple of hours before he will be finished in the bakery and just a few hours before being picked up. He is desperate to ask her if she was able to help repair and clean the precious ring.

An hour later, as the last of the items he has prepared are displayed in the shop front, he can wait no more. He tries to catch Penny's eye to ask her about it, but she is constantly serving people and the queue, as always, never seems to get shorter.

"Andrew, would you be a dear and bring out the two birthday cakes?" Penny calls out. *Finally, a chance to speak to her,* he thinks, but no, no sooner does he walk in with the cakes than Penny and her helper Sophie take one each and pass them over the counter to the waiting families. Half hour later and the front of the bakery shows no sign of slowing down. Andrew has finished clearing up out the back and his two apprentices have bagged up the bread and pies for the children and are heading out the door with them.

Andrew waves them goodbye and turns back to look for Penny, but she has disappeared. After looking round the front of the shop he spots her through the window speaking to another elderly lady. Moments later she comes back inside, walking through to where Andrew is standing out the back and passing him a small blue box.

"It was close, but they came through for us, Andrew," she says.

Andrew's heart skips a beat. It's all he can do to reach out and take the box from her and he just stares at it for a moment before opening his prize. The gold ring has been polished to a fine yellow glow, the four sapphires are aqua blue like the deepest ocean and stand out amongst the three sparkling diamonds. He can see that the middle stone has been replaced as it is no longer chipped, but the set of three match each other perfectly, sparkling and reflecting light from all angles. The engraving looks as if it has only just been cut, such is the sharpness of the vine and leaf pattern and scrollwork. Andrew looks at Penny. He has no words to say as he is in awe of the finished product.

"It was a good job it is in the old style, my dear, for we are all old now and so is our jewelry, and between us all we managed to find another diamond that matched perfectly."

Andrew still cannot speak and instead he hugs Penny, kissing her on the top of her head. "God bless you, Penny, it is absolutely beautiful," he says eventually while still staring at the ring.

She closes the lid on his prize. "It is about time you left, my dear. I hope she likes what you have done for her because, if not, I would not mind it myself." Penny smiles and laughs at Andrew who is still beaming with excitement at what has been done to the ring.

Placing the box in his pocket he kisses Penny on both cheeks. "You are the best," he says before picking up his coat from the rack and turning to leave the bakery.

He does not remember much of the journey home and for the first time in many a week he walks past the children, giving them only a wave as they sit eating their food. He is still in a daydream as he enters his house and walks through to sit in his favorite chair in front of the fire. His small traveling case is already packed beside him, with his best jacket lying over the top of it. Over the next hour he taps his pocket many times just to ensure the box is still there, wanders round his living room countless times, clean's and sets the fire for when he returns and checks his bees at least a dozen times.

Finally, after what seems an age, he hears a carriage coming down the street. He waits to see if it stops near his house but, when the sound of the hooves clipping on the stone road surface disappears into the distance, he knows it is not the one for him. It is another half hour before he can make out the sound of another coach driving down the road. Again, with bated breath, he waits to know if it will stop. As Andrew hears the coach pull up and the horses stop clipping on the surface of the road he gets up, grabs his coat and case and heads for the door. It is difficult for him not to show his disappointment when he sees the new driver and not Wellesley, but he does his best. Smiling and raising his hand to the coachman before opening the door and entering the carriage. He places his case on the floor and throws his coat across to the other seat as he sits down.

"Really, without even looking you throw your clothes at me," says a voice from under the coat Andrew had just thrown.

Andrew jumps back. "I am so sorry, sir," he says as he lifts the coat off the man. To his great relief it is Wellesley, bold as he always is, wearing a fine dark-green military uniform with all the medals and sashes of a hero. The white and green plumes on the side of his regimental officer's hat sets the look off a treat, and even the sling strapping his wounded arm up is of matching green and fitted to perfection.

Andrew has a huge smile on his face. "I am so glad to see you, Wellesley, and what a sight you are. I knew you were no ordinary man, but I did not imagine that you would be so decorated."

Wellesley swipes at the air with his good hand. "Ha, most of it is pomp and fluff, my boy, my real soldiering was many years ago. But now and then it is nice to know I still fit into my old uniforms, seems like Margaret keeps me running round enough so I do not get too fat in my old age." They both chuckle, "It would seem that you will be in need of a man to represent you and that person just so happens to be me. This is a request of the queen, so before you think this is voluntary be aware it is an order from my commander-in-chief."

Andrew looks at him. "I would have been asking you myself even if the queen had not, for I know of no better man to represent me," he replies.

"That may be so, my boy, but I do not think you really know the danger you will be in. You are not yet remotely prepared for the challenges to come, but then again you have heart and have come this far, so perhaps you will yet find a way to succeed. No man has ever captured Margaret's heart like you have, and that must say something about you."

Andrew thinks on his words for a while, then passes him the small box from his pocket. "If you are to be my second, I think that I should be leaving this with you until it is needed."

"May I?" Wellesley asks.

Andrew nods nervously. "I did not want to go into this empty-handed and after looking everywhere this was the only thing I found that I thought Margaret might like."

Wellesley looks at the ring, then reaches into his pocket and takes out a small pair of spectacles to have a better look. "Well, I will say this for you,' he says, returning the spectacles to his pocket, "you know what she likes. I think that you have chosen wisely, my friend, she will love this and it is far better that the plain backup one I had in reserve." He takes the ring from the box, places it inside a white glove, which he tucks into his tunic, and chucks the box out of the window.

They travel on for some time before Wellesley speaks again. "You will be residing with me tonight, for it is tradition that you do not see the bride until the day of the wedding, even when the circumstances are as strange as this. However, the night may not go how Margaret would have wanted for you, as the queen, well, she has different ideas and believes that you should be seen by the people who would be protecting you should the circumstance arise. If you are to enter into a life with her advisor, you need to know the people to rely on. So, what goes on tonight stays with us, Margaret need not know all the details."

To say that Andrew is apprehensive at what he has just been told would be an understatement, but Wellesley is his friend and, whatever else he may think, he trusts him completely.

A little over an hour has passed and, looking out of the window, Andrew does not recognize any of his surroundings. They enter a large, wooded area and continue deep into the forest for another ten minutes or so before the horses stop. The creaking sound of large doors can be heard opening before the carriage moves through the entrance in a thick wall of stone. Andrew can see battlements, ramparts and soldiers in green uniforms everywhere.

"Welcome to my home, Andrew," Wellesley says as they approach a large building with two armed guards standing before it. "This is Stoneheart Manor, home of the queen's own 1st Royal Grenadiers, or their more commonly used name Green Devils, and the queen's own 1st Royal Sea Marines, often referred to as the Sea Devils. They are the finest military soldiers and sailors the country has to offer, handpicked from all the forces and best people in the land. They have one duty and one master, to protect the queen and serve the queen. She and her entourage are looked after only by these men and in some cases women. At any time 500 sailors and 500 soldiers of all ranks make up these two units. You can join them by invitation only, position in society means nothing here; you are accepted on merit and merit alone.

"You met some of them last week Andrew. They were part of the cavalry battalion protecting Margaret, only ten of them charged five times that number. Three were injured and two killed, and just over a dozen of the enemy mercenaries survived, as you saw for yourself that day. I know not of any braver men that serve in this country or any other, for that matter."

Andrew looks at Wellesley. "I knew they were no ordinary soldiers as they were riding Ambulette horses. I've read about them in books and recognized their markings, all gray and white with black fetlocks."

Wellesley nod his head. "Very good, young Andrew. These are the queen's own stock and lines, eighty-four active and working for the crown, twenty-two breeding mares, eleven foals or colts, six stallions and fourteen retired and used for training purposes, last I recall. All have a history or bloodline that goes back at least 200 years if not more, and all are here within this one and a half thousand-acre site. Only Lord Ashby has better, and these and his are all closely related. They are war horses and will stand by their rider to the end, and their riders, well, they will stand by their mounts to the bitter end as well. None finer, my boy, none finer."

Wellesley steps out from the coach and turns to Andrew. "If you would be so kind as to follow me to your quarters, you can get changed."

"Changed?" asks Andrew.

"Yes, changed, all who visit Stoneheart Manor wear the same uniform, either dark green as a soldier or dark blue for the navy. Nobody wears civilian clothes here, including the queen and her advisors. It is for your own protection and to show respect for the people defending you."

After a salute from the guards to Wellesley and vice versa, they enter the great stone building and make their way down the corridor to the guest quarters. All the walls are covered in historical portraits of military figures and battle scenes, weapons, flags, rolls of honor and other military items.

Everything that Andrew sees looks like it belongs in a stately home; tables, chairs, even the crockery he glimpses in a dining room. It seems that all the military personnel are treated as ladies and gentlemen, and they respect all the items in the building as if they were their own property, as a lot of the items are clearly old but in immaculate condition.

Andrew is shown to his room and left to get changed. As he walks around the small area, he is amazed by all the antiques and fineries he would not expect in military accommodation. On the bed are two sets of uniform, one blue and one green. After considering the options, Andrew decides to put on the green uniform. As he dresses himself in the new attire, he is amazed that it is a perfect fit and not uncomfortable to wear. Around the seams and shoulders the uniform has surprising stretch and flexibility and is extremely comfortable; whoever designed and selected the material for the army uniform made it a well-crafted and practical piece of clothing.

Once the transformation from civilian to soldier is done, Andrew stands in front of the full-length mirror to observe what he looks like. He adjusts the small cap to match the way the others he had seen walking around the barracks wear it and sucks in his stomach to make the fit better. Satisfied, he ventures out of his room and along the corridor, viewing a lot of the pictures of battle scenes as he goes.

"Excuse me, sir," calls out a voice in the distance. "Would you follow me, please?"

Andrew looks up to see a man in uniform similar to the one he is wearing beckoning him toward a doorway. As Andrew approaches the room he can see Wellesley speaking to several army and naval officers inside, including one or two he recognizes. The captain from the incident at the house the previous week, the man who had a large black dog in the carriage, and the other man who also assisted in foiling the assassination attack that day.

As Andrew enters, the group of men look up and beckon

him over to them. They greet him with smiles, handshakes and reintroductions to the men he has seen previously and first-time introductions to the ones he has not met before. Andrew is shocked that they all know so much about him and what he does. They are fully aware of the bakery and the rebuilding of the two houses for the children, but it is not an uncomfortable conversation for Andrew. Far from it, the men are all most polite and accommodating. Once they have had their time to talk to Andrew, he is introduced to the rest of the men and women present and spends the next couple of hours talking to more people than he has ever spoken to before in his life.

For Andrew, the biggest thing that stands out about everyone is how normal they all are, not one ignorant or selfish person amongst them. Their passion for their country and belief in the queen and her advisors to get it back on track and back to what it used to be is refreshing. There is genuine interest in what has been going on with the homeless children and what Andrew is doing for them, and he is surprised to hear that some of the soldiers are adopting a similar approach in at least two areas of the capital as well. They have been organizing the rebuilding of an old school and a church to home and accommodate vulnerable children and young mothers to keep them safe and away from those that would prey on the weak and homeless.

Andrew is invited to join them all for supper, and again is surprised to discover that the entire barracks eat together in the main hall, be it soldiers, sailors, civilian personnel, officers, or even on occasion the queen and her many advisors. Spirits are high as they head down the corridor to the canteen, and Andrew is shocked, if not slightly intimidated, when he is put next to Wellesley on the long top table. The food is the same for all ranks, and Andrew is impressed to be told that the camp is mainly self-sufficient. They cultivate crops and rear their own livestock, the first-year training cadets catch seafood on fishing boats used for learning sea skills, and some local game is hunted by marksmen if the opportunity arises or they need to cull an overpopulation deer, wild boar or smaller game.

Andrew learns that it has become very obvious to the people training here that the ruling politicians of the state, the Three Heads, want this barracks closed and their own government forces to protect the queen and act as her security on a daily basis. No doubt there would then be a terrible accident involving the queen and they would be able to claim total control over Kelsey. By being almost entirely self-sufficient, however, and the queen and her associates funding any additional requirements. They manage to stretch their meager budget and keep the army and navy forces intact and out of reach of the influence by the Politicians.

After the meal the officers retire to the lounge for cigars and rum for the navy, port for the army, a tradition for the sailors and army the world over. Many of them raise a toast to the queen, then settle down in small groups for conversation. Soldiers from the ranks that have distinguished themselves in the service of the queen are also invited to the lounge in appreciation of their deeds done and Andrew is delighted to see Captain Hawkswell lead in his men, two still in wheelchairs and one hobbling on crutches. They are all immensely proud at being formally invited and making it into the room under their own steam. Andrew is first to walk up to them and shake their hands, followed by Wellesley, other officers applauding and congratulating them on their endeavors.

These brave men take their rightful positions at the top table and are served drinks and cigars by their commanding officers. For these few it is a life-changing moment and the loyalty and sense of worth they feel will go through the whole regiment by tomorrow. Each of the men also receives a handwritten letter from the queen and a small gift in a box, which they each tuck away to look at later.

As the evening moves on, the celebrations and conversation get more rousing by the hour, so many toasts to the heroes and the queen have been said that most in the room are merry. Andrew has been offered drink after drink and has been polite in accepting all of them, but not being a great drinker, he has been discreetly disposing of them where he can. For one poor palm tree in particular this has been a bad night and Andrew isn't hopeful of its chances of survival. He also notices that the amount of drink he has been pouring on this plant does not equate to the level of liquid rising in the bottom of the pot. Somebody else must have been adding to the collection, and at some rate as well.

It is the early hours of the morning when Andrew returns to his guest quarters. He has had a great time, meeting and speaking to many people who all have interesting opinions and ideas. Each one of them wanted to speak to Andrew and the one thing that stood out to him was the control they all showed without realizing. Not one person, male or female, talked about their military duties or boasted about killing or taking a person's life, nor did anyone get too drunk and act like a fool. It was probably the best night he has ever had with a group of people, not that he is one for going out a lot, but as a night of entertainment, this one would be tough to beat.

He is soon asleep and only awakes to the sound of a trumpet being played for the second time at 8.00 a.m. sharp, signaling the start of breakfast to the barracks. He had slept right through the 6.00 a.m. trooping of the flag, but now he gets up and looks at the blue naval uniform. Once shaved and washed he puts this uniform on to ensure that he has worn both during his visit to Stoneheart Manor as a sign of respect to the military personnel present. As he steps out of the room, the first thing he notices is eight cadets carrying four palm trees in their containers out into the grounds. He watches from a distance as they empty the liquid out of the bottom of each pot, dunk the matted roots in a stream, replant them in the pots and bring them back to the officers' quarters. He chuckles to himself as the cadets curse the stink of stale alcohol as they pass.

"Cost of replacing the damned things is expensive, it is better to try and keep them alive if we can," a voice comments from behind Andrew. He turns around and is confronted by Captain Hawkswell. "You are not the only one who uses the pots, most of us do not like to lose control, but we also do not like to refuse a toast or cheer as we never know if it will be our last."

"Do you lose many people?" Andrew asks.

The captain nods slowly. "Far more than we would like, for

it takes years for these men and women to reach the standards we require, unlike the politicians who can just pay for assassins or mercenaries from all over the world with taxes taken from our own people. We here are all homegrown and loyal to the rightful ruler, the queen. They try to get at us through our friends, families and even ambush us when returning home, so many of us live here, cutting ourselves off from our families to protect them."

Andrew nods in acknowledgement. "It must be difficult to take yourself away from your families when life here in this country is so difficult for the people at the moment."

The captain grimaces. "If we do not do this now and plan for the future, we will not have a country to call home, so all here support the queen and her plans for taking us forward. You have seen firsthand with Margaret the risks we are forced to take in support of the monarchy. Now I have spoken long enough, it's time we got you to breakfast, for you no doubt have a long day ahead of you and I have my duties to attend to, so a good meal now will not go amiss to set us up for the day."

The two men enter the canteen and join Wellesley at one of the tables. As they take their seats, plates of bacon, eggs and sausages are placed before them, along with mugs of tea by the serving cadets.

"By God, that is fast service," remarks Andrew, making the captain and Wellesley laugh.

"That's because you are expected to be out of here within fifteen minutes of you sitting down, my boy, so best you tuck in," Wellesley says, almost finished with his own breakfast.

Exactly twelve minutes later, the three men leave the canteen and head toward Wellesley's office, in a part of the building with several rooms leading off into different departments. As well as the army and navy, there is a room dedicated to finances and accounts, commerce, transport, politics and negotiation, farming and livestock, and finally law. Captain Hawkswell continues with his duties while Wellesley takes Andrew into a small office and sits him down, closing the door to ensure that nobody is listening to them.

"We are being picked up in an hour's time," Wellesley tells Andrew, "So you need to decide if you will be in blue or green. Whichever one you choose, that will be the color you will be married in and will represent at formal events and meetings going forward, so will it be army or navy? The choice is yours, Andrew."

Andrew thinks for a while. "This all seems so impersonal when marriage is spoken about like this. I only know people from the army side, so I guess it will be green."

Wellesley stands up and shakes his hand. "Good man," he says, then steps to the door, opens it and calls out to somebody, "Green." He closes the door and sits back down again. "I do not understand the reasoning for this myself, boy, but Margaret wants you to be her husband immediately on paper, so I will abide by her wishes, but are you ready for what is required of you in these trying times?"

Andrew thinks for a moment before answering, "I love Margaret with a passion, I know her reasons for it being now and I will support her unreservedly. We will be married today and that will be an end to it. As for me, I also have a lot to do in the next few months. I do not know how I will complete it all yet, but it will be done and finished in time. However, what I do need from you is help with another matter, I need to be able to defend her in the case of an emergency and no one else being around. I must know how to shoot a pistol accurately and handle a sword with confidence."

"That will not be easy," Wellesley replies after a short silence. "We can only do it when Margaret is not around, for she will not approve of this. I do agree with you though, as I see it as a good last line of defense for her should the worst befall those that are defending her." Wellesley takes a deep breath and slowly lets it out as he thinks. "Leave that to me boy, I will have the best men I know come up with a plan for how this can be done discreetly and without her knowing."

The two men talk for nearly an hour before there is a tap at the door. "That be the signal that the coach has arrived," says Wellesley, standing up and leading Andrew out of the door. They head straight out of the building to the waiting carriage, where Captain Hawkswell is sitting up top holding a rifle. Beside him is the private that had spoken to Margaret so kindly before leaving last weekend, he smiles and nods his head at Andrew before collecting the reins ready to move off.

As the two men enter the coach, Andrew notices two full uniforms on the seats, along with two ornate ceremonial swords, and between them a large ledger book.

"Well, lad, there be no going back now. These be the full-dress uniforms and we will need to be in them when the coach arrives."

Andrew's nerves are finally taking their toll and he lets out a big sigh and takes in a gulp of air as he studies the uniform on the seat next to him.

"You're lucky, boy, every time I put this particular uniform on it seems to get heavier. There are fewer of my comrades left alive each time I wear it so the memories of what it represents saddens me more and more," Wellesley says with a heavy heart.

Nearly an hour later the carriage stops at the house where Margaret and Andrew met up the weekend before. The two of them slip into the house to get changed into the dress uniforms before returning to the coach and setting off again. This time they make their way to the small village of Brambly by the Larch, just around the corner from the house. The coach pulls up at side of the small village green and Wellesley is quick to step out first, in his full-dress uniform with matching arm sling complete with a dozen medals for bravery and suchlike pinned on it.

Andrew follows in his uniform carrying the ledger book, adjusting the sword hanging by his side once out of the coach. The captain steps down from the front of the carriage and collects the large ledger book from Andrew. The coach then moves off round the corner while the three men take the short walk across the green and enter a very small, quaint village church. Andrew and Wellesley walk to the front of the altar and stop on one side of the vicar, while the captain continues past and into the small adjoining room, placing the large book on the table inside. He leaves the church and closes the door behind him, standing guard to one side and awaiting the arrival of Margaret in her carriage. They only have to wait a few minutes before the sound of horses can be heard approaching the building.

Andrew is more nervous than he has ever been in his life. As the door to the church opens, he looks up to see Anna dressed smartly in a blue naval uniform entering the church followed by Margaret dressed in her titled uniform of admiral commander-in-Chief. Despite the medals, ribbons and gold thread everywhere, her beautiful, hour-glass figure shows through in the right places, looking absolutely stunning to Andrew. As for the vicar, he has to double-take as Anna, with a huge smile on her face, leads Margaret down the aisle to stand beside Andrew and Wellesley. Both are very nervous and excited at the same time, but the village vicar appears shocked to see two such well-decorated soldiers as Margaret and Wellesley, and especially with Margaret being a woman.

With a little coaxing from Wellesley to get him going, the vicar starts the ceremony. "Dearly beloved, we are gathered here today..." The vicar continues through the same speech he has done thousands of times before, finally getting to the names of the bride and groom. For Andrew it is straight forward, just Andrew Johannsen, but for Margaret it is a little more complicated as her full name is Margaret Maria Babette Katerina Tatiana Dessola.

When Wellesley passes the ring to Andrew to put on Margaret's finger and she sees it for the first time, putting a smile on her face as she looks lovingly at Andrew.

"It's beautiful, my dear." At that moment she knew that she had chosen the right man for her, as the old-fashioned style ring and beautiful arrangement of her favorite stones could only have been chosen by a man who really knew what she liked and it was perfect. As the vicar is asking her to repeat the words, her eyes never leave Andrew's. They seal the wedding vows with a kiss, holding each other tightly.

Wellesley is a lot more reserved, showing very little emotion at the event, partly because he knows the risk and danger Margaret has taken to do this. Nevertheless, he is pleased to see the little girl he has looked over for so many years happy and content. As the group walk into the side room to sign the village church register and the ledger that they had brought with them, the reality of what Margaret and Andrew have done starts to sink in as they look at each other and realize they are now married and bound together. The newly married couple fill in and sign both the books first, followed by Anna and Wellesley to witness the marriage, then, finally, the vicar also signs and dates both books. He shakes the couple by the hand and congratulates them, wishing them a long life and a glorious future together before he turns, closes the books and takes the church register to the large oak cabinet and locks it away for safe storage.

Anna picks up the other ledger and follows Andrew and Margaret as the four of them leave the room and make their way out of the church. The captain is holding the door open with a huge smile on his face, and the private soldier is standing by the open carriage door ready for them to enter.

It takes less than ten minutes to reach the house, and the driver slows to a stop on the driveway, allowing Andrew and Margaret to get out of the carriage before driving on. Following the path back up to the road. Anna cannot help but lean out of the window and wave with both hands while cheering and yelling, while Wellesley just watches until they are out of sight.

Andrew turns to Margaret and kisses her passionately before picking her up and carrying her through the front door of the house. As they enter they can see that Anna has been busy, for the house is filled with flowers, decorations, and paper bows, to a very exacting standard. The fires have been lit at both ends of the house and are at a perfect orange glow, making the house warm and cozy. On the table is a selection of fine roasted meats and fish, and on the far side a small cake with a male and female soldier on the top looking exactly like Andrew and Margaret, made of spun sugar work. A small card is wedged under the side of the cake, which Andrew picks up, opens, and reads out to Margaret.

"Please accept this token gesture of our well-wishing until we can celebrate in style, from all at Stoneheart Manor and the palace."

Margaret crosses the room to her husband and kisses him several times before speaking. "There will be a time when we will celebrate our wedding again, publicly, with all our friends and family present, I promise you, but I am afraid now is not the time, my dear."

Andrew shakes his head. "I do not care, for you are now my wife and that is good enough for me."

Andrew holds her tight as Margaret looks at the ring on her finger closely. "This is so very beautiful. It will never leave my finger when we are together and never leave my body during official business," she says, holding it up in the air to get a better reflection off the stones and see how the wide band of gold looks on her finger. "I will have a pendant made and this will fit in the center as the focal point. As I love it so much, that way I will be able to wear it as a brooch when on official duties." Andrew chuckles to himself. "Why do you laugh, my dear?" she asks curiously.

He looks at her lovingly. "It is just that it is all so fast and fairytale-like, with more twists than a book. In a little over three months, we have been through more in our lives than most people in a lifetime. In just the last half hour we have been married in a church by a vicar who nearly swallowed his own teeth when he saw you walk down the aisle wearing more decorations than a veteran soldier."

Margaret laughs to hear Andrew put it like that. "I hate to tell you, my love, but this is dressed down from what I should have worn. You see, I have done a few things in my time for the service of my country, but none more important than marrying you." She kisses him passionately, again. "Now, would you please help me out of this uniform for we can barely breath inside here."

"Oh." He pauses, then *oh* as he cottons on to what she means. He takes off her sashes and undoes the buttons on the front of her uniform, freeing Margaret's breasts inside the thinnest of cotton vests in an invitation that Andrew finds hard to resist. He gently kisses and nibbles at her nipple while undoing the buttons along the back of her high-waisted trousers, and, as the last button comes undone, she wraps her arms around him and kisses his ear.

"There be time enough for that later, my love," she whispers, "but for now, after two days of rushing around organizing and not getting much to eat, I'm hungry and I want to put a dent into that food."

With her trousers and tunic thrown on the floor, Andrew cannot help but laugh as Margaret walks over and sets to a joint of beef with a knife and fork.

"Mmmm, God, this is so nice," she comments, chewing on a piece of the succulent meat. Soon both have piles of food on their plates and are heading to their favorite chair by the fire. Andrew sits upright in the corner while Margaret leans against him, bare toes pushing against the opposite arm rest. "It is so good just to be here alone with you, Andrew," she says between mouthfuls of food. "All day from dawn till dusk I am pulled pillar to post, with people needing things done or opinions on problems that are so insignificant or just too daunting to comprehend. Moments like now are all I have to relax and let my mind rest and have time for me and us."

Andrew slides his hand over Margaret's stomach and rubs her tummy gently. "In a few months you will need to be taking it easy anyway, with a baby on the way. Have you thought about when you are going to let people know of your condition?"

She looks up at Andrew. "Yes, and our decision is to say nothing and wait to see who will notice first. I have many tricks up my sleeve to hide this baby from prying eyes. Who knows, I may be able to hide it all the way to the last month and then, with some good fortune, leave others to support the queen while we retreat to this place and I enjoy being a mother and a wife for a while."

"Anna will be the first to notice," Andrew says.

"Oh no, it will be Wellesley, for he spots everything not just visually, but he tends to notice changes in people and their behavior," Margaret replies. They place their empty plates on a side table and continue talking for an hour or more, while wrapped in each other's arms as couples do in moments of peace and quiet.

"I think that I am good at understanding you and your moods and needs, my dear wife," says Andrew with a smile.

Margaret pinches his leg. "You think so, do you? So what am I thinking about, right now?" she asks.

Andrew laughs. "That's easy, it's been over an hour now, you will be wanting some more food, especially the beef as it is your favorite."

Margaret nods. "I will not say that the thought has not crossed my mind, but, no, the food will still be there later." She stands up and pulls Andrew up with her, holding him in her arms and kissing him passionately. "This lady is a newlywed and desires satisfaction, and, if you are not able to, I will find a man who can."

Andrew smiles and chuckles as he twirls her in his arms. "My dear, as alluring and captivating as you are, most men could not handle a woman so demanding and authoritarian as you. In fact, I would go so far as to say that there is but one man in all these lands who would be brave enough to take you on and have a chance of surviving your wrath, and that man now stands before you as your newly appointed husband."

He spins her around again and holds her tightly as he kisses first her neck, then an ear, her nose, and finally her lips before looking into her eyes. Margaret looks radiant and absolutely breathtaking to Andrew; he holds his wife in his arms as he slowly rotates the pair of them round as though they're dancing. "I never imagined that a man could love a woman so much, yet now with you in my arms I can barely breathe or hold a thought in my head. I would walk to the ends of the world for you, my dear, should you wish it."

Margaret smiles and kisses the tip of his nose. "The end of the world might be needed later, but for now how about getting me to the top of the stairs, for I still need to see if I got a good deal in this marriage or not."

The two of them move as one. Toe to toe, they continue rotating and shuffle their way to the stairs while kissing and fondling each other. Attempting to undo Andrew's tunic without looking where the buttons are becomes a major challenge for Margaret while Andrew is intimately working his way around her body. Finally, with great relief, Margaret throws his jacket to the floor and they are overcome by passion.

When they finally emerge from the bedroom on the following afternoon, Andrew's theory on Margaret is proven right for the first thing she does is to attack the beef that she is so partial to. He watches, chuckling, as she cuts slice after slice before turning around and seeing him laughing. It is only then that she remembers what he predicted the day before.

"The baby is hungry, what can I do?" she says while placing another piece of beef in her mouth before smiling at her husband.

CHAPTER 6

Plan in Place

Despite how complicated Andrew and Margaret's life is, it always somehow manages to work out for them and over the next four months they still tend to spend part of each weekend together. It may be only a day or, when chance allows, two nights and a day, but their bond is strong and they are working toward a better future for many people, not just themselves. Andrew spends the time when Margaret is absent learning to use a sword with the help of the recovering Wellesley and Captain Hawkswell, along with pistol and rifle shooting using targets floating on the river beside the manor house.

Progress on the children's home has been swift, the outside and roof of the house have been completed and the interiors are well on their way to being finished. All the flooring is down, the kitchen and bathroom are complete and only the living accommodation and supervisor's area need finishing. The children have been working with Andrew on the garden, where they have created a vegetable patch, planted some fruit trees and bushes, and even made a small herb garden and some flower beds.

In the bakery, the bread and other fineries are now being regularly produced by the young men Andrew has been training. Although they still need some guidance and help with the timings and types of bread and cakes produced, they are slowly getting to grips with perfecting everything they make and also starting to add a few new creations on their own. Not quite to Andrew's exacting standards, but edible enough for the orphaned children, who they use as tasters on any new recipes.

Out the front of the shop, Penny has done a grand job of

teaching two of the girls the art of serving the customers and controlling how much each customer can buy or take in any one day, as word has spread about the affordability of these staple foods, more and more people have come to rely on the shop to provide for their families.

One of the recent arrivals to the group of abandoned children is Rose. She is more educated than the others and was left alone when her parents were killed defending their herd of horses and cattle from being taken by the state. An only child with no family to help her in her time of need, she has been living hand to mouth, doing whatever was needed to survive. Only Penny knows the truth of what she had to endure to get by and it has made a strong bond between herself and Rose. Being a little older and wiser, Penny has been taking her to help source the stock needed for the bakery in the afternoons, freeing up more time for her to help at the orphanage. Penny has also taken an interest in helping with the interior design of the children's house and has asked Andrew if she could be the one to supervise and run the building once it is complete and ready for the children to move in. Explaining to Andrew that she has a good few years left in her and she wanted to teach the children about life and all it could be for them. "I want to show them how to get the most out of what they have, guide them in how to make a difference to the world around them and support others who may be in need of help." Were her exact words to him.

This had been Andrew's plan all along, for Penny is loved by all, from the children who will do absolutely anything for her, to the locals and customers she has known most of their lives. As for Penny, she will always have people around her to ensure she will never be lonely or without help as she gets older and her life's worth of knowledge will be invaluable in teaching the children who end up staying at the house while they grow and mature in a safe environment.

* * *

Another three weeks goes by, the house for the children is now complete and with additional funds donated from Margaret's ever-deepening pockets. The beds, bedding and provisions required to start bringing the children into their new home are all in place. Penny has moved into her new position and has been organizing the final touches while Rose has been running the front of the bakery with the help of Andrew and two of the younger girls. So far all is working well and Penny has not been needed in the bakery, although she does pop in most days to check and make sure that all is the way she likes it to run.

Donations and gifts from people and families in the community in the way of clothes, blankets and other items for the growing number of children have been overwhelming, enough not just for the children here at this house, but a surplus that can be used to supply other areas of the town where children struggle to survive on the streets.

As each bedroom in the house is completed, Penny moves the younger, more vulnerable children in so that she can work with them and asses their needs. For many, they are traumatized by their ordeals and need encouragement and help to cope with being abandoned or orphaned by their families. Over the past few months, the number of homeless children has grown until all but three of the beds have already been allocated, the children ranging in age from around eight or nine to Rose who is pushing eighteen. She also helps run the house and assists with the younger children daily. It is not just a place for the children to sleep, it must also be as self-sufficient as possible as costs will always be a problem. Rota's are drawn up and all must pull their weight to make the project work, from helping in the kitchen to prepare food, clothing and cleaning the younger children, setting the fires and filling the coal scuttle and wood piles.

Washing and wiping up the assortment of dishes and plates is down to the younger children, and with the help of some of the local people who have volunteered time, some schooling and education each day for all the children living there.

It is a Friday afternoon and Margaret has just arrived at the children's home with Wellesley and Anna. As they walk up to the house, they find Andrew outside putting up a wooden sign on the front of the building by the side of the doorway. It is a long, angled piece of oak, heavily stained and carved with the words "Dessola House". Andrew looks round as Margaret speaks.

"Well, I do not know if I deserve that, but it does look nice and makes me proud."

Andrew kisses his wife on the lips. "Without your care and financial support, we would never have got the children off the streets, my dear, you deserve far more than just a name on the front of the house. Anyway, this is just the first of many that I hope will be built to home the children this country has lost along its way," Andrew says with a smile.

Wellesley and Anna have not taken their eyes off Andrew since they have arrived, and as he steps back to check the sign is level, he starts to feel uncomfortable with the looks he is getting. "Do you not approve of the name of the house, Wellesley?" Andrew asks, as if it is the sign that has offended the two of them in some way.

"It's not the sign that disturbs us," Wellesley huffs out. Only when Margaret walks a few feet away to speak to the children do they turn on him like a pack of wolves.

"When were you going to tell us, then?" snaps Anna.

"Did you think we would not notice the change?" adds Wellesley.

Andrew looks at them, bemused. "What are you talking about?" Anna looks at Margaret to ensure she is looking away from them before turning to Andrew and rolling her hand over her tummy to signal a bump. "Something wrong with your hand, Anna?" Andrew asks.

"No!" she snaps. "Is she…" And she repeats the gesture.

"Is she what?" Andrew asks with a blank expression.

Wellesley clenches his fist and shakes it in Andrew's direction. "Tell me, boy, before I knock it out of you!"

With Anna and Wellesley focused on Andrew, no one notices Margaret turn and look at the three of them, a huge grin on her face, for she knows what the two of them will be asking him as they have clearly been wondering for a while now.

"Is she?" asks Wellesley through gritted teeth.

"Is she what?" asks Andrew with a puzzled expression on his face.

Anna finally comes out with it. "Is she with child?"

Andrew looks seriously at them. "Have you asked her?" Both Wellesley and Anna frown at him and his hesitation to answer the question.

"No, of course not, you cannot ask a woman like her that kind of question! She would rip your head off for asking, especially if she has just put on a little roundness," Wellesley rants.

"Is everything all right, my dear?" Margaret asks Andrew as she arrives back with the group.

Andrew takes her hand and kisses it gently. "Oh yes, my love, Anna and Wellesley were just asking about you, that's all."

"What would they be asking you about me for? Surely the two of you would be speaking to me if there was anything you wanted to know?" Wellesley and Anna look at each other with their heads hung low, then back at Margaret.

"Enough, I cannot take it anymore!" Anna says, braving herself to ask the big question. "Wellesley and I have noticed some changes with you and we were wondering if there was anything that we should know about."

Margaret has that stern *you're going to have to work a lot harder than that for an answer* look on her face. It is an expression Andrew has experienced many times and he has become a master at seeing through it. He looks away to hide the grin on his face as Margaret responds.

"Pray, what kind of changes are we talking about? You will have to be more specific if you want me to understand and answer the question correctly."

"Good God, woman, you don't make it easy for us who know you best and want to support you! Despite your best efforts to try to hide it from us, we have come to notice that you have gained in size considerably and eat more than the rest of my regiment put together in one sitting. This and the fact you are often under the weather in the mornings, head in a bowl much of the time and downright vicious with it, leads us to conclude that perhaps there may be something afoot here," snaps Wellesley. After a brief pause to regain his composure and think his words through, he continues. "All we want to know is, are you with child or not? I cannot take the suspense anymore."

Margaret looks at him with a shocked look on her face. "'Head in a bowl'! 'Downright vicious! You are speaking to me with those kinds of words, are you? A married woman no less, and, asking me in front of my dear husband if I am with child because I have gained a little weight! You, my good man, presume too much. This is not the kind of questioning I would expect from a so-called officer and a gentleman, let alone my protector and commander of the queen's own forces."

By now Andrew is struggling not to laugh and give the game away as Margaret's performance is excellent and he is enjoying watching her make the two of them work for her replies. "I would have you know that I have just been a little more peckish than usual, that's all. The fact that I have been under the weather once or twice is due to the poor preparation of the food, which reminds me that I must address that with the cook and get to the bottom of the problem as I think it is a little too spicy for my stomach."

"Stubborn, impossible woman," mutters Wellesley as he tries hard to control what he really wants to say. "The food is not the problem here, madam, as we all eat the same meals, it is just some require a little more than others and one individual has a lot more."

As Margaret goes to speak she starts to feel faint and wobble, but before Andrew can react Wellesley is at her side, holding her up. Anna moves to support her other arm as Andrew looks round for a place for her to sit down.

"The bench behind you," he says as he points to a garden seat across from Anna. They all help Margaret over to the wooden seat and gently lower her down. It takes a minute or so for the moment to pass before Margaret comes round and takes Wellesley's hand in hers.

"My dearest friends, we wanted to hide it as long as possible before telling you both, to protect us and you from people who may take advantage of my situation. Andrew and I were wondering who would notice first; we did not anticipate you both knowing at the same time."

Wellesley looks at her with solemn eyes. "I have to confess we have known for some time now. You can hide nothing from young Anna; she has been on to you for many a month now," Wellesley comments as he smiles at her. "As for being in danger, look over my shoulder to the old-looking man on the crutches by the wall, and across the road at the three men working on resetting the wall of that old house."

Margaret looks over at the man, then the builders working in the garden. "What about them?" she asks.

"That be Lord Ashby with the crutches, and his son and two officers working on the wall. There are a half-dozen others dotted around the area and nearly four hundred more men and women waiting their turn to watch over you, Andrew and that young 'un you have been hiding. You must understand, to us you are a national treasure, and we dare not let anything happen to any of you, for you mean that much to so many, including the royal household and monarchy."

Margaret gets to her feet. "I will speak to Lord Ashby, for old Dicky should not be standing out in this heat for so long, he should have retired long ago."

"Ah, leave be Margaret, he is already retired from most active duties and is doing this for love of you and what you are doing. They would all be terribly disappointed if they knew you were aware of their presence. Every one of them knows you and wants to do their part, they adore you. Let them help and rest assured they will watch over you."

She thinks on Wellesley's words for a while before answering. "Then I think the four of us need to leave here and head for the house to plan the next couple of months. It will be difficult to hide this from those that would take advantage of our situation."

Margaret says goodbye to everyone at the orphanage and then leads the four of them back to the carriage. As she does so, she turns to a man standing by a nearby coach and gives him a deep nod, the man tilts his cap in response and moves off round the carriage, swiftly returning with two others carrying a huge chest. As Margaret and the others step inside, the chest is loaded on the back, masked by their movement as they sit down.

Andrew cannot help but look back out through the window at what has been achieved in so little time. He is proud that they have a safe place for the children, but at the same time he is realizing that changes are happening and soon he will have to step back from running the bakery and overseeing the children on a regular basis to look after Margaret and his child. Not that he will give up his achievements, just let others take a more leading role in their day to day running while he enters a new phase of his life with Margaret. He is surprised to notice two men appear from the back of the carriage as he pulls his head back in, one of the men turns and tilts his cap at him before swiftly moving on with his companion. He is about to call out to them but is distracted by Margaret touching his arm.

"Are you well, Andrew?" she asks, worriedly.

Andrew nods. "Yes, my dear, just a little tired, that's all," he replies.

As Wellesley bangs the roof of the coach to signal the driver to get moving, Andrew sits back in his seat and sighs heavily. He lowers his eyes to the floor, looking at nothing in particular as he contemplates all that is going on in his life. *Am I strong enough to do all this?* he wonders to himself, for so much has passed so quickly and a large amount of what has happened has been out of his control and in the trust of others. Margaret is watching him and knows it is going to be difficult for Andrew to let go of it all. She clasps his hand in hers and smiles at him as he looks at her.

"My dear, life moves in the strangest of ways. I too feel like the weight of the world is sometimes on my shoulders. In such moments, when I find it is too much for me to take, I gain strength in the knowledge that you are by my side and my friends are around me to ease the pressure. I would not say our life together so far has been in any way normal or easy but believe me when I say that I would not have it any other way now you are here with me.

There is a strength in you, my dear, a strength far stronger than you realize. I see it in your eyes and feel it when I am around you. In time we will all come through this and it will all be worth the pressure we find ourselves under at this moment in time. My father used to tell me that 'courage is not given to a person, it is found when most needed'. For the longest of times, I never understood its meaning. Now, all these years later, I think I am finally beginning to understand what he meant."

Margaret pauses for a while, thinking, before she continues. "Our country and its lands have been brought to their knees by corrupt politicians and scheming diplomats for far too long. Out for their own gains and profit, they have no feelings for the people of this country or concerns for their lives or those of the children who struggle every day. They want it all: money, status and power to do what they want. They believe that if they have total control over the people, they will not be able to break free of their tyranny. They do this by ensuring the people have barely enough money and food to survive and keep them fighting and bickering with each other rather than uniting against the politicians. For years they have been ensuring there is no way of removing them from office and high status by making up laws, decrees and government red tape that prevent any kind of diplomatic recourse. In their eyes, all the people of this land are here for one purpose only, and that is to support their way of life, nothing more."

Margaret lets out a long, deep sigh, as if the whole world was on her shoulders. "You yourself have seen it with the abandoned and orphaned children, the way so many people live in poverty, deprived of many of the basic needs of humanity. In your bakery, you do what you can to help those most affected with cheap prices and good food to keep their families going. For many this is not living, this is existing at its lowest level, holding on to the scraps of life when they should be enjoying what life really has to offer them.

"I, on the other hand, when assisting the queen on her state duties, see what the culprits are doing firsthand to the nation. The poison they sow into the lives of good people just to twist them and make them turn on each other, turning good people into bad and bad people into monsters. It breaks my heart to see the suffering and depravity that has hit those that live in this country, so terrible they would abandon their children or be lost while trying to protect them from this regime.

"If only the queen could have seen this betrayal years ago, the undermining and scheming going on behind her back, she could have fought back then, when she had the support and the will of all people behind her. It would have been far easier than it is now for her to right the awful wrongs that have been done over the years. But it was so cleverly hidden from her, masked in plain sight; cunning in design and so buried in paperwork and bureaucracy, that she did not see them for what they really were or what they had planned until it was too late."

Margaret shakes her head as the words continue to come out. "To try and right such a terrible wrong, we are forever looking over our shoulders for the next person to take a shot or try to bring us down in the political arena. It needs to stop now, and the country needs to be restored to its rightful ways. The people deserve a better standard of life than the one that presents itself at the moment."

Andrew watches Margaret. She is sitting very still and upright, looking straight forward at the space between Anna and Wellesley on the carriage wall. Tears are rolling down her face, but she does not move or break down, just keeps her position and composure while holding Andrew's hand.

"Do you think that the queen can really fix the problems that this country has, my dear?" Andrew asks quietly as he reaches for a handkerchief and passes it to Margaret to wipe her eyes. She turns to give him a reassuring look.

"I know she is doing all she can, but the cost will be great and she may have to risk more lives of the ones she loves to see it through to the end." She sighs and rubs the back of Andrew's hand before continuing. "It would seem that it is the price a mother pays for the love of her children these days. We have lost so many of her children already and the battle is far from over."

Anna also has tears rolling down her face, she knows only too well the price paid by people as her parents and brothers could be counted amongst the number lost to the country's corruption. She goes to move to comfort Margaret, but Wellesley holds her back with his arm and a stern shake of the head.

"Not now, lass," he says quietly, leaning toward her. "Let her get this out, she will be the better for it, I promise you." He comforts Anna with an arm around her shoulders.

Andrew has seen and heard none of the action between Anna and Wellesley, for his eyes have not yet left Margaret's face. "There is a lot these politicians need to answer for," he says, thinking of his mother and father who never returned from the protest all those years ago, when he was but fifteen years of age.

"How far would you be prepared to go to take down these evil men, my dear?" Margaret asks him.

Andrew thinks on his answer for a while before replying. "As far as you need to go, my love, for it seems that you have the greater role and the bigger part to play. But know this well, should anything befall you, queen's decree or not, I will snatch the life from those men at cost to my own if need be. So spend my life wisely my dear, for I only have the one to give."

Margaret dabs at her eyes with the handkerchief before she tucks her arm under Andrew's and holds on, leaning her head on his shoulder. "It seems we will have a lot to talk about and plan this weekend." Then she looks up at her two friends opposite. "So, now you know for certain that I am with child, this is not to be spoken about with anybody. Apart from the four of us, the queen, and my physician, nobody can know for now as the risk is too high."

Opposite, Anna nods as she wipes the tears from her eyes with the red handkerchief she has lifted from Wellesley's pocket. As she discreetly blows her nose he looks round and notices his initials on the corner of the cloth. He reaches up with his right hand to feel inside his empty waistcoat pocket.

"Why, you little sneak, you are learning far too well for my liking!"

Anna turns to him. "Who better to practice on than the man who says it could not happen to him?" she asks with a cute smile, fluttering her eyelashes at him. She folds up the red handkerchief and tucks it back in his pocket. "Thank you for the loan of your military, by the book, crisply folded, corner to corner creased and measured—"

"Yes, yes, I get the message," Wellesley butts in. It is a lighthearted moment that puts a smile on Andrew and Margaret's faces and as they start to chuckle it lightens the mood with all four of them as they continue on their journey.

When they arrive at the house Wellesley is first up and out of the carriage, holding the door open for Margaret and Andrew to disembark. Once they are out, he goes to climb back into the coach.

"Where, may I ask, are you going, Wellesley?" He looks round and is met with Margaret's glare.

"I thought you would want to be alone with Andrew, as usual," he responds.

Margaret stares at him for a moment. "The time for me and Andrew to be alone has long since passed, as you have already noticed. Andrew's work for now is all but done for the foreseeable future." A shriek of laughter is heard coming from Anna, still inside the carriage. "Don't be thinking you are out of here either, young lady, you can make your way into the house and get the fires going and water on the stove for tea." Anna's shocked face appears in the doorway. "I will be needing you as well this weekend for we have many things to discuss and plan, so move like you have a purpose."

Anna steps down from the carriage and speeds off into the house to do as requested, while Wellesley closes the coach door behind her. Margaret then turns her attentions to the driver.

"All the luggage can be put in the hallway James. Wellesley and Andrew will assist you to carry in the larger trunk on the back, for that must go up the stairs and into the large room on the left-hand side. It weighs some, so take it easy and mind you do not scratch the wooden rails or walls as you take it up there."

They look round and notice the enormous dark leather and wooden trunk on the back of the coach. Wellesley scratches his head. "I did not see that on the back when we left this morning."

"That's because it was put on by two men when we were leaving the children's house earlier, now be a good man and help take it in for we will need what is inside to formulate and prepare coming events."

Wellesley thinks for a moment. "You must have had this all planned out for some time now, to prepare the trunk without my knowing. Come to think of it, you were not even that surprised when Anna and I asked about you being with child."

"Of course not, you two are as subtle as a thunderstorm when you are talking around me. I have heard you two bickering with each other for weeks now, it was only a matter of time before one of you finally plucked up the courage to ask the question. Now I have to consider how to keep this information away from the eyes and ears of others who would take advantage before we are ready with our own plans."

Andrew smiles and shakes his head, amazed at how Margaret is always ahead of the rest of them and planning for things that they have not even considered. He moves towards the trunk with Wellesley following and begins to unhook the item from the back of the carriage. Between them and the driver they manage to carry the trunk to the front door where Margaret is holding it open for the staggering men. She watches with a wicked smirk on her face as they pass and continue to drag the heavy chest up the spiral staircase to the room above. Moments later she enters the room and passes the men, pointing to an area on the far side.

"Over there against the back wall please, gentlemen," she instructs with that stern look on her face. It is a look Andrew has started to read quite well, and he has a feeling that this time it is the look of knowing a daunting task is ahead that she is apprehensive to start.

With the chest in position, the driver and Wellesley head back down the stairs to deal with the rest of the luggage while Margaret just stares at it. Andrew walks up to her from behind and rests his hands on her hips. She does not move or turn around, just puts her hands over his.

"This was my grandfather's war chest. He took it into battle on three campaigns over his lifetime to secure the positions of our borders, with the help of allied kingdoms supporting us. It passed to my father when he died and was used in his battles when he secured our ports and trade routes with the rest of the known world. It held charts, maps, and instruments to navigate the seas as well as his personal belongings aboard the ship he served on. Now it has been passed down to me, and in my hands it may very well hold the key to saving the country from itself, if you believe what the queen says. I just do not know if I am strong enough to start, let alone stay the course it will take us on."

Andrew gently kisses her neck. "I do not know what you have planned, my dear, but if the queen chooses to put her faith in you, and if the people I have met since we have been together have anything to do with the outcome, she has made a wise choice. You are loved and cherished by so many, I know you will do all that is needed to get the task done. Let's face it, from the very first day I met you, danger and adventure have come hand in hand with what you do and how you live. It is what makes you the person that you are."

He pauses for a moment. "You will always have me by your side, so when you are ready to face this next task she has set for you, I will be ready to assist when and if needed."

Margaret turns to face Andrew, looking him in his eyes before stepping forward and holding him in a tight embrace, head tucked into his shoulder. "I would not be able to do what must be done without you by my side, my dear, but I also need my private time with you, away from all the madness I must endure. So, for that reason I must ask you never to enter this room after today. Not because I do not want you here, but because I will need your opinion on things as they arise and the answers must come from an outside perspective and not from someone who is immersed in the scheming and planning that will go on in this room. You have put up with so much secrecy and mystery when it comes to my duties and myself, few would ever have considered me worthy of such devotion and I love you all the more for the tolerance you show. I am asked to do a great deal in the service of our country and the time I must give to the queen and her requests leaves so little for us, but please be patient. You mean so much to me and your support and understanding is the foundation I need to keep me going. This political war will not last forever and once it is over we will have the rest of our lives to be together."

Andrew holds Margaret in his arms, stroking her back and thinking on her words as he always does before answering. "If this is what you wish of me, then of course I will support you, but I feel before this room gets up and running we will have a larger issue to address. It will not be long before we will be bringing a new life into the world and you will not be able to hide that from those who want to separate you from the queen."

As always, Margaret has a swift and concise response. "If I can get through the next three weeks at court, the queen will have got to her summer break and will have no need of me for a while as she will be leaving for her six-week retreat, as is tradition. This is time usually spent entertaining kings and queens and other such royalty from other countries at Montebello Castle, on our northern coastline. But the staff in the castle has been infiltrated by pro-government spies and possibly assassins and the queen has decided to spend it instead at the only safe place left to her, Stoneheart Manor. She will be safe there from the prying eyes of the politicians as she will be amongst her own soldiers and officers as she works on her plans to restore the country to better times. With the queen safe and with good people around her, I will be free to come here and spend my summer with you and, God willing, our child."

The pair have still not yet released each other from their embrace. "Anna should have made the tea by now, shall we head down and partake in the refreshments before she starts to yell up the stairs?" says Andrew.

Margaret looks up at him and nods. "It would be a shame to let good tea go to waste, and we must talk with Anna and Wellesley to plan a safe environment for our child and how we are going to cope with the changes."

They make their way down the stairs and into the kitchen, where Wellesley and Anna are waiting for them. As they enter the room, Wellesley pulls a chair out from the back wall for Margaret to sit on as Anna waits for the nod to pour the tea. Margaret willingly accepts the seat as standing on her feet for long periods of time is now rather uncomfortable, letting out a sigh of relief as she sits down.

"I was thinking, Andrew, you will be moving into this house soon to prepare for the arrival of me and our child. I know you had intended to sell your home to raise money for our needs going forward, but, to be fair, there are no needs that we are anticipating in the short term and I have a better suggestion for the use of such a fine cottage. We have two injured men from the last skirmish, one missing a leg and the other an arm, and we need to give them purpose under the service of the crown to keep them gainfully employed and paid a wage fitting of such brave men. I would like to propose that you delay selling the house and have the crown rent your cottage as a place for them to live for the time being. These two men could discreetly watch over the children's house and the bakery while you are here, as well as take a few trips to the city to discreetly monitor certain politicians over the coming months. As I think it is about time we start to build up a picture of their habits and what they get up to as I am tired of them hounding us and using mercenaries paid by our own people's taxes to hurt those that serve the queen and their country."

"It would be nice to keep the cottage and to have someone watching over the children and the bakery as I have noticed that with more people coming to the shop now, we have attracted interest from one of the local gangs. They offer protection for a price or wreck and damage such places until they are forced into paying to be left alone."

Margaret looks at Andrew in shock. "You have said nothing to me about this new development, how long has it been going on?"

He grimaces. "Well, it is only recently that I have noticed people watching the shop. Some of my regular customers pointed it out to me and told me who they work for." Andrew sighs deeply.

"You have been very busy of late and I was going to look into the matter after the weekend and find a way to resolve the problem."

The conversation soon moves on to what is needed before Andrew can move into the new house and the preparations for Margaret and the arrival of the baby. They consider all aspects of the move, from the linen needed, a cook along with food and supplies, and a doctor to be on call, to security in the form of some of the queen's guards, who will reside in the local village as they will also be required to work in the room where the chest was placed.

Nothing seems to be left to chance. With Anna and Wellesley taking notes and offering solutions and ideas to all the questions Margaret and Andrew raise, they soon put a plan together that will cover all eventualities and problems that might arise. Andrew suspects that Margaret had already thought of everything beforehand and that this exercise was only a courtesy, allowing her friends to offer their ideas and conclusions to the questions raised.

For him, the biggest change would be the arrival of a friend of Margaret's, Beth, who would be in charge of the housekeeping. Once the baby was born, she would then take on the role of nanny when required as Margaret would still be supporting the queen in her official duties and would be away from home.

Andrew would also need to travel now and then to check on the children's home and the bakery to ensure the standards were maintained to his exacting requirements and the children remained safe from any harm.

Anna had smiled when Beth's name was mentioned, as she was the woman who had tended to her many months back when she had been attacked. Beth had also been the one to encourage Anna to take up the position she now has as a lady-in-waiting, as well as using her streetwise abilities when asked to do so by Margaret and Wellesley.

Later in the evening Andrew heads to the log pile with Anna for more fuel as the nights can still be a little chilly and, with a clear sky, the temperature will drop drastically overnight. No sooner had the pair of them left, than Margaret turns to Wellesley.

"These people watching the bakery, I want them out of the way, we have come too far to let something like this happen now."

Wellesley nods. "I have already sent the driver away with instructions, we will have no problems in a day or so. The admiralty can always do with fresh, willing recruits for the ships, so I took the liberty of telling the navy to supply the muscle needed."

The weekend ends up being entirely spent in planning and preparation. Security is uppermost in Wellesley's mind as he insists on being in charge of all the arrangements and personnel. Margaret, as usual, has something to say about her needs, forcing Wellesley to threaten her with speaking to her majesty the queen when she tries to reduce the extent of the arrangements he suggests.

This does not go down well with Margaret, who gives him the stern and disapproving look in front of the others, but eventually they reach a compromise and peace is restored. One of the rooms is set aside for the baby and another for Beth to stay in during the week as she will not be able to travel backward and forward from her home on a daily basis.

All aspects of the move have been covered and rechecked at least a dozen times over the weekend, with the only moments Andrew and Margaret able to spend alone together being at night and the few times after a meal that they walked around the garden arm in arm. There is no doubt that the bond between them is strong, but in these testing times even these few moments alone have helped them strengthen the feelings they have for one another.

As the weekend comes to an end, two carriages return to the estate house to take everyone back to their current duties, the group of friends says their goodbyes to each other. Margaret and Andrew are able to have a last brief moment together before they separate for another week. The next time Andrew sees Margaret he will have moved into the house permanently, and his own place will be used for the good of two soldiers in need of a home and a job to suit their abilities.

Andrew can see that Margaret is tired and in need of a rest. She is heavily laden with child and still planning and scheming for her queen. Although Andrew is concerned and would dearly like to insist she steps back and relaxes a little more. He knows the strength in this woman and her sheer stubbornness to continue would only cause them to have heated words. Instead, he bides his time, for it is only a matter of weeks before she will have the opportunity to rest, and with the baby due soon, she will not be able to do much at all. With a final kiss and embrace, the couple prepare to depart company for the time being and head away from each other for another week. As the coaches leave the driveway and turn in different directions, Andrew and Margaret take one last look at each other out of the windows before sitting back and thinking about what will happen next. The two of them are both great thinkers and planners, though Margaret rather more so as she has had to live on her wits for many a years to survive the attentions of the Three Heads and their attempts to remove her from society.

CHAPTER 7

The Ball Starts Rolling

Andrew has been up for not much more than an hour, packing the last of his personal belongings when he hears a knock at the door. He looks at his pocket watch to check the time. *Seven o'clock on the dot*, he thinks to himself as he hears the church bells in the distance start to chime the hour. He responds to the knock and is confronted by two men he has never seen before and behind them a large, open-backed wagon.

"We be here to move the last of your belongings that you require transporting to the estate house, sir," one of them says in a heavy country accent.

It is the moment that Andrew knew was going to come, but that still does not make it any easier for him as he has lived here for so long. After a short pause he nods at them with a raw smile and waves his arm in a way as to invite the two men into his humble house.

"There is not much left to move, just some clothing, several boxes, a couple of dressers, some plants in pots and the two beehives out the back."

The men look at him with strange expressions on their faces before turning and looking at each other. "I thought they were messing with us when they said about moving bees from the house," one of them says uneasily.

"Oh no, there is no messing with you. That's why you're here so early in the morning as the hives are still cold from the night. I have just sealed them up for the journey to the house, so we will be loading them last of all. Now we must move fast as they do not like to be kept contained for long."

The men tilt their caps and begin to load all the items and boxes that Andrew has put to one side. It does not take the three of them long to finish collecting all the things in the house and start on the plants and pots in the garden, leaving the bees until the very last minute. As the two men gingerly carry the first hive to the back of the wagon, they can hear the hum and grumble of the insects in their enclosed space looking for a way to get out of their imprisonment. To the unknowing men, the bees sound angry, like they are looking to attack and take revenge on their captors by stinging them, but, for those that know, the bees just want to get out and start to work on collecting nectar for the hive. The humming is caused by the beating of the bees' wings, which pushes air around the hive. There are small vent slits along the wooden layers allowing for the bees to breathe, regulate the temperature of the hive and cool the nest to the optimum conditions to keep the queen content.

They gently slide the first hive into position, then turn to collect the second one as another wagon pulls up behind them. Andrew recognizes the driver and his companion as the two injured soldiers he had met when visiting the barracks before his wedding day some weeks back. The two men are swift to dismount the vehicle and approach Andrew. They have smiles on their faces and an arm out each to shake Andrew's hand.

"I'm Ned, sir, and we were hoping to see you," one of them says with a huge smile on his face. "It is ever so kind of you to offer us your house to live in and a chance to still serve in the queen's forces, we will forever be in your debt." Andrew looks at them; one has lost an arm and the other a leg. *How can they be so grateful to me when they have suffered such debilitating injuries?* he wonders to himself. "You can rest assured, sir, we will look after this place, the children and the bakery as if they were our own, so help us God," Ned says, still shaking Andrew's hand.

Andrew is taken back by the willingness of these men to thank him when they have lost so much in the line of duty. In this case it is more poignant to him as they were protecting his beloved Margaret and Wellesley, as well as others. All Andrew has done is agree to them living in his cottage while he will be with Margaret in a huge house in the country.

"It is good to see you both again," he says with a smile. "I know you will look after the children well and watch over the bakery and its staff, I just hope this cottage serves you as well as it has done me over the years. Come, let me show you around the place while these men load the last beehive on the wagon, for there are a few little secret spaces the house has to offer."

As the three men enter the house, Andrew points to the lintel above the fireplace. "There are front and back door keys if you need them, I have always left them up there as I rarely have had need of using them." Andrew takes them around the house upstairs and down, showing them all the rooms, little hidden cubby holes and secret spaces he has found in the time that he has been living there. Finally, they move through the kitchen and into the garden which, despite having a few key plants missing, is still full of flowers and looks a picture.

"It will be a grand place to live and I mean that with a full heart," says one of the men. "I have known of no home to call my own before, just the workhouse where I was left as a babe, then the streets of the city when we ran away, then the service of the Crown where I started as a drummer boy at eleven. For that be when Wellesley found the two of us, half starving and near drowned in a broken coal hut on the side of a derelict house. I still remember it now as clear as day, sitting on a white horse all upright and proud in his green uniform, a fine young officer he was then. He dismounted, put both of us up on his mount in his place and led us back to his barracks. The dirt and coal stains that ran from us changed the color of his horse and saddle such was the rain came down that night and the filth on our bodies. He had us cleaned, gave us fresh cloths and fed us from his own table, for the first time in I know not how long I felt like a real person again. I swear if it was not for him, we would not have lasted out the next couple of days in that place. Now, with near thirty-five years of service behind us, we get the chance to live in a house we can call our own and still serve the queen in these later years, despite our injuries.

I feel the good lord has rewarded us far more than we deserve."

Andrew looks at the pair of them. "But you have lost an arm, and he is missing a leg. Surely you must feel anger at such a loss?"

Ned puts his hand on Andrew's shoulder and shakes his head. "Boy, I have seen many a comrade and friend fall at my side, have loved them all as if they were my own brothers and sisters. Put the spade to their very graves with my own hands too many times to count and shed more tears than many a river has carried water. To get this far after so long with just an arm missing, or a leg in the case of young Dick here, is more than a little fortunate. We have been lucky to dodge the full swing of the reaper's hand many a time in the past. For him upstairs has taken so many from our number, more so now the Three Heads have taken to running the country and robbing the people blind. They have bounties on all our heads, you know, hunt us down like rabbits when there is a lot of 'em. Some have made a good living out of it, lining their pockets on the blood of our comrades, but three or four to one, we usually give them a licking most times, make them earn their ill-gotten gains. The Three Heads are using our own people's taxes to fund an army of foreign mercenaries and spies to do their bidding and make the people suffer more." He spits on the floor in an exaggerated manner, then pauses before continuing. "Our only hope of getting our country back from them evil men is to help our queen take back the control from the stranglehold they have on this land and its people. Rid the land once and for all of these parasites and bring harmony and peace to those that still live in it. If we can still serve her in any way at all, we will do it, even if it costs another arm and leg, so help me God, for she has put all on the line for her people."

Tears start to well up in Ned's eyes as he stares blankly at Andrew and thinks of all the people he has seen lost to those men. It is several seconds before he snaps out of it and comes back to his senses. He grabs hold of Andrew tightly with his one good hand and looks into his eyes, tears still flowing as his emotions run wild. "You, you should know this better than the rest of us, for you are in this up to your neck with Margaret. You and she are the reason we have got this far, you must see that, you are our only hope."

Dick steps in and pulls Ned away from Andrew. "Now, now, Ned, let's not be getting all upset and emotional on Andrew, he has to go and see Margaret and we have things to be getting on with settling in here." He turns the distressed and trembling man away from Andrew, then looks back at him as he holds Ned tight. "I'm sorry about that, sir, he has been through so much in the past few months. He is a good man, please do not think less of him."

Andrew shakes his head and steps forward to support Ned as they move him to a bench to sit down and calm himself. "You have no worries about that, my friend, for you two are some of the bravest men I have ever met." Andrew goes to the kitchen and fetches a cup of water for Ned. "Here, drink this, it will steady you." Ned starts to sip the water while staring at the floor.

Dick turns back to Andrew, keeping one hand on his friend's shoulder. "He gets like this every now and then. Struggles with still being alive when we lost so many of our friends in the service of our country." He sighs heavily. "We lost a few close comrades when we took our injuries, including a young lad who looked up to him as a father figure, Bernhard was his name, he'd only just turned twenty-two days before he died. Ned had taken quite a shine to him, helping him to read and write in the time we had spare. Now he thinks that he should have been the one to die, not Bernhard, for he had his whole life ahead of him still." Dick turns and reassures Ned before continuing to speak.

"Truth is, if it was not for Ned, I don't think any of us would have survived." Dick pauses for a moment to pat him on the shoulder before continuing. "You know, he dropped three men on the first charge through the enemy, then turned and chased down two more before he was shot in the arm. Even when they put a sword through his shoulder, all the way down to the hilt, he fought on. His last charge at them was with his reins gripped in his teeth, sword poking out of his back and him leaning forward in the saddle, pointing his saber at his next victim. Another was taken by that sword before they shot his horse from under him. I still see him now, waving that sword while standing straddled across his dying horse 'Bella', yelling and cursing at the enemy for the loss of his mount. He rallied us into one last charge that turned the tide of the battle, but it was really him that put the fear of God into them. They outnumbered us many times over, but they were already terrified by Ned's actions and his refusal to go down in the fight, some were already fleeing when we had at them that final time. We just kept the pressure on and rode after them, cutting at the ones that fell behind." Dick smiles as he pushes Ned with his hand. "Now that very sword we pulled from his shoulder is up on the wall in the mess hall, along with all the other trophies and items of note that have honored the regiment over the years."

Ned looks up at his friend. "That hurt more pulling it out than it did going in, but some of me feels that was because it was you doing the pulling."

The three men start to chuckle before Dick stops and looks past Andrew to the two men who have just walked into the garden from the kitchen doorway.

"We be ready to leave when you are, sir," one of them says while staring at Ned. "I could not help but overhear you talking," the man comments, gingerly approaching them as he takes off his cap. "Is that there man really Ned, Corporal Ned Pepper of the queen's own?"

Dick turns to the man. "Yes, that be him."

The man shuffles forward a few more paces. "My boy spoke often of you, claims that you saved his life on more than one occasion when he rode in your company. Showed him the way to be a cavalryman, he said. Not that I would expect you would recall him, but he was right proud to be with you a few years back and I just want to thank you for looking after my boy."

Ned slowly looks up at him. "What's your boy's name?" he asks quietly.

"Parsons, sir, Robert Parsons."

"Shiner Parsons?"

"That be him, sir, though I never did know how he got the name Shiner!"

Ned beams at the man. "We gave him the name as he always

seemed to have a black eye, always challenging larger men in the navy to a fist fight. He thought that it would toughen him up for when he would have to fight in combat for real. Not that he needed toughening up, he was a brave lad in his own right and always gave a good account of himself." Ned pauses. "Where may I ask, is the young man now, for I do not recall when I last saw him?"

"He was asked to take a commission in the city by his commanding officer. That was near a year ago and I have had but two letters since he left, so I cannot tell you where he be now, nor if he is well or not."

Ned and Dick look at each other; there is a deathly silence between them before Ned speaks again. "I am sure he will be home soon, then we will all meet up and talk some more over a meal. I'll tell you of your son's escapades from the years past when he was with me, for I am sure he would not have told you some of the adventures we got up to in our time together."

The man nods his head and replaces his cap. "That be a day that I would surely look forward to, sir," he says as he turns and heads back through the house. He stops at the doorway and looks back at Andrew. "We'll be on the wagon waiting for you, sir."

Andrew nods in acknowledgement. "I will be there shortly," he replies as the man moves off through the house. Andrew looks toward Ned and Dick. "Be safe, gentlemen, and look after yourselves as well as the children and bakery. Many people do not realize that the bakery is where many of the most vulnerable and poor around here get the only food they can for their families. As for the children, don't just watch over them, speak to them, tell them stories of your bravery and valor. For most have lived on the streets their whole lives and they have suffered so badly. Perhaps a few real heroes who also started off on the streets could bring them a sense of hope and I know they will love to hear of your adventures."

The two old war horses smile and chuckle. "Maybe a few stories, but some we will keep to ourselves, as all the ladies love a man in uniform and those stories would not be appropriate for the children."

Andrew smiles and lets out a small chuckle. "Look after the house, it has served me well and I know it will be make a good home for you just as it has me." He shakes both the men by the hand.

"We thank you for allowing us to stay here and the children will see us daily, that is a promise," Dick says. "But you must do something for us. Look after Margaret and keep her safe, for she is the heart and soul of us all and sometimes she takes a risk too many. I would not dare say anything out of turn, but she is not as tough as she makes out, and, knowing she loves you dearly, you have her ear more than most of us. We all need her now more than ever, but Ned and I are no longer able to be by her side for protection, so you must ensure she stays safe. That woman, as stubborn and headstrong as she is, be loved by us all and may well be the key to unlocking this country and making it a better place."

Andrew cannot help thinking there is more that Ned and Dick want to say about Margaret. He knows they have been by her side for many years and probably know more about her past than he ever will, but now is not the time to pry and ask questions. He has to leave and get the bees to the new house before they get really agitated and start to swarm. Andrew wishes the men well for a final time before leaving their company. Passing through the house, Andrew has one last look around the place before stepping out into the street to mount the wagon and leave with the two laborers.

As he steps up to join them, his mind switches thoughts to where he is going. In an hour or so he will be with his wife, living with her for more than just a few days at a time, and soon his first child will be born. With the bakery now doing well in the hands of others he has trained and the children safely in their new home, Andrew can finally focus on being a good husband and an expectant father.

With a flick of a whip, the wagon lunges forward as it moves off along the road, bringing Andrew back out of his thoughts. Each turn of the wheels takes him closer to his destination, as they pass the house he built for the children, he can see some of them playing in the front garden while others can be seen through the window exploring the house.

"We can stop the wagon here if you want to take a look around the house, sir," the driver says, as he notices Andrew looking at the building and children.

Andrew smiles and shakes his head. "I have seen it many times, I am just glad that we got it finished before I left. From now on it is for others to look after, my part is finished," he says with a proud smile.

The wagon continues down the road, rumbling on the cobble stones as it goes, within minutes the bakery comes into view along with a que outside the door of around thirty or so people. A strong smell of fresh bread and savory pies fills the air with a tempting aroma long before the wagon reaches the front of the shop. As they pass the waiting people Andrew recognizes many of them as regulars he has known for years. Some turn and wave to him while others start to clap in appreciation of all he has done for them and soon all of them are clapping and wishing him well. It takes Andrew by surprise as he was not expecting anyone to bother, but as he smiles and waves back the driver pulls up his horses beside the applauding people.

The door to the bakery opens with a ping of the bell and two of the young men that he has been training for the past few months step through holding a large cloth-covered wicker basket between them. They shuffle through the people and up to the wagon, then load the basket onto the rear of the cart before walking round to Andrew.

"You didn't think you would get away without us making something for you to go with, sir?" says one of the young men. "Mind you, it is not to be viewed until you are with Margaret as is for the both of you. It is a thank-you from all of us, and we hope to see you here again soon."

Andrew is lost for words and near tears, but before he can say anything one of the horse's spooks at something in the crowd of people. Rears up and lunges forward at a brisk trot, taking the other horse and the wagon with it. Andrew is left laughing and waving back at his customers and friends as his transport hurtles down the road with the driver pulling back on the reins and calling out to the horses as he tries to regain control. The line of people continues to clap, wave and laugh at the wagon as it disappears around the corner and out of view. It takes a good five minutes for the driver to get the horses back under control and down to a walking pace before finally getting them to a standstill. By then the men can hear the bees humming in anger in the back of the wagon, unnerving the two men beside Andrew.

"I'm sorry about this, these dammed horses have a mind of their own when they want to, we can go back to the bakery if you would like sir." The driver offers while keeping one eye on the two wayward horses and his hands tight on the reins.

Andrew turns and pats the man on the shoulder. "No, that was as good as it could get, the horses made it easier for me to leave without getting too upset, and to be fair, what more could I say to them?" Andrew turns back to look forward down the road. "Come, let's be on our way. I cannot wait to see what they have made for us, from the smells coming from the basket I think we will be in for a real treat."

The wagon sets off again, slowly making its way down the narrow streets and along the outskirts of the town. Andrew settles back, stretches out and takes a deep breath, for all is about to change in his life, a new beginning with Margaret. He has achieved all he had set out to do with the bakery and the home for the children, now it is time for him to spend time with his own wife and soon-to-be child. He will, of course, still visit and help out when he can, for both the bakery and children mean a lot to him and Margaret.

It is not long before the houses start to thin out and the countryside begins to take over. The rumbling of the metal wheel hoops chattering on the stone roads gives way to the quieter earth tracks, and all seems more relaxed and tranquil as the wagon ambles through the country paths toward its destination.

* * *

Back at the bakery it is like every day, the line of people never seems to shorten. The two girls in the shop are serving as fast as they can and the bakers keep the bread and pastries coming through, topping up the shelves and display cabinets almost as fast as they are emptied. There is no doubt that this little shop is turning out more than any other bakery in the area. They may be serving more people and baking more items, but the rules remain the same on the limits of how much each person can buy.

Just up the road from the bakery, two men from the local gang are watching the shop. 'The Penny Rips', as they like to call themselves, have had the run the East side area of the town including the old village area for some time now. Some say that the name came about from their first gang mugging when only a penny was found on the victim, but whatever they started as, they are now very much a force to be reckoned with. Due to them always being armed and up for a fight to enhance their reputation and fear factor in the community, the constables of the law enforcement would sooner turn a blind eye than confront these gang members as they fear injury or death from the encounter.

Everything bought and sold in the area has them involved in some way or another, that is everything except this bakery and even the supplies the bakery uses to make its goods have not been tapped by the group. Anyone affiliated with the gang is easy to recognize as they all wear silk neck scarfs in different colors and flat caps. Due to the poverty and oppression in the city, the gang has grown from strength to strength, with only the most hardened people making the grade and able to join. With a collective gang membership now pushing forty-five people, they are larger than most in the area and have more numbers to throw in at any rival gang should they have to.

"I don't know why the boss has been waiting for so long, usually he just takes what he wants and the Devil to pay with anyone in our way," says one of the men to the other.

"Would be right in most cases, but it would seem that others are involved here and the boss has been unable to trace the suppliers they use for the ingredients. It may even be an outside firm undercutting us and setting us up for a takeover attempt. Anyway, until he gives the nod we watch, report what we see, and wait for instructions," the second man replies.

There is silence for a while as the two men continue to watch the people entering and leaving the bakery in a constant flow. Finally, for one of the men, it gets to be too much.

"This is killing me. If we want to find out about this place, we need direct action." He steps out from the side street as his friend makes a grab for him.

"Murphy, where do you think you are going? Get back here!"

Murphy flicks his arm away and stares back at him as he walks away.

"Grow a pair, Rabbit. I'm going to check out that old boy over the road with the crutch, I've seen him around a few times now and I just want to ask him a few questions, that's all."

With that, Murphy crosses the road and struts along the path to an old man leaning up against the wall of a house with his crutch under his left arm. He wipes his brow with a handkerchief, taking a break from shuffling along the road. As Murphy approaches the old man, he looks around to see who is watching, and with nobody paying him any attention he confronts the old man.

"Seen you around here a few times too many, old man, now let's me and you have a talk." With one last look around to ensure nobody is watching, Murphy grabs the shoulder of the old man and pushes him down the side of a house along a narrow alleyway. "Now let's have a few words about why I keep seeing you here, you don't seem to ever be entering the bakery or any other shops and you sure as hell don't live round here as I would've seen you before, so who are you?"

"No, no, please, sir, leave me be," yells the old man as he turns to cower against the wall.

"Don't turn your back on me, old man, I want some answers from you now or things are going to get a little rough on you."

Murphy grabs the old man, turning him round and raising his other hand to strike his face. As the old man is turned around, he hooks his crutch over Murphy's arm, twists it round to push it up his back, and clamps him up against the wall. He leans on the crutch, pinning the bemused Murphy with no way of getting free.

"Crafty bastard," Murphy says as he reaches down into his pocket with his free hand and pulls out a stiletto knife, flicking out the blade as he raises it up to strike. The old man grabs the hand holding the knife and positions the point of it on the thigh of his opponent before raising his knee and smashing it into his hand, ramming the blade into Murphy's leg. "Aaahhhhhhhh." Murphy screams out while grimacing with pain.

"Thought I was an easy target, did you, laddie?" says the old man as he twists the knife to inflict more pain.

"Jesus Christ!" Murphy yells out in response to the knife being rotated.

"No, lad, he will not help you here, for you are way past saving by words alone. Now, let's us have that conversation, shall we?"

"Do you not know who we are, old man? Look at the scarf and cap, we are The Penny Rips and you have just sealed your own death," Murphy yells.

"Really? I thought it was going to be harder than this, boy," says the old man, "but I guess you are not used to people who know how to fight back."

There is a shuffling sound from the entrance to the alleyway and both men look round to see Rabbit standing there, staring straight at them.

"Now you're for it, old man, let's see what you do with two of us to deal with."

Both of them watch as Rabbit staggers slowly toward them with a large knife in his hand. He takes three or four steps before dropping to his knees, then forward onto his face where he remains motionless on the floor.

Murphy lowers his head as he sees four more men enter the ally and approach them. Two of them stop to pick up the fallen Rabbit by the arms and drag him along, while the other two take hold of Murphy and pin him up against the wall, allowing the old man to get back up on his crutches and step back from his captive.

"He took a good clout to the head, but he will eventually come round, Lord Ashby," one of the men says as they pass him and move deeper down the alleyway with the unconscious Rabbit in tow.

Lord Ashby turns to the man who tried to knife him. "Well, it would seem it is not your day after all, young man. Now, I have a few questions of my own for you."

"You'll get nothing from me but my fist in your face, old man," replies Murphy, and he spits in Lord Ashby's face and then chuckles to himself.

Lord Ashby wipes the saliva from his face with a cloth from his pocket and stares back at the nasty little creature in front of him. "I used to be against this kind of treatment in the wars and service of my country. However, soldiers were always honorable on both sides of a conflict. They may not have understood what they were fighting for, but they would always make the best of a terrible affair and give aid and compassion to the enemy's fallen and wounded after the battle. As for you and your kind, you prey on the weak and the old, inflict pain and suffering on your own countrymen for profit and gain. You have no kind of honor or respect for others, just an insatiable appetite for greed, money and power."

Lord Ashby does not take his eyes off the man in front of him as he speaks. He is old school, born from tradition and loyalty, a man who would give all for his country and monarchy, stand by a friend in need even if it put him in mortal peril. He grabs the knife that is still embedded in Murphy's leg with his right hand and continues to speak as Murphy winces with the pain that this action inflicts. "Now, I would like to know where your group of thugs and bullies are hiding out, so if you would be so kind I will not have to inflict any more pain on you."

Murphy stares back at him. "You haven't got the balls, old man. When I get out of here I'm going to carve my name in your skin." He spits in Lord Ashby's face again and laughs at him.

As Lord Ashby wipes his face, then twists the knife in the man's leg.

"Argh, you bastard!" Murphy yells. "I'll fucking have you!" The knife is withdrawn and plunged into the front of the other thigh and Murphy screams again.

"I have no time to waste on you, you either tell me what I need to know or I will bleed you out here and start on your friend." Lord Ashby turns to look at Rabbit, who is now on his knees and being forced to watch as his friend is being worked on. "You're next, my lad, so get ready and brace yourself as only one of you will leave here alive."

Rabbit is trembling with fear as he looks into the solemn, cold stare of Lord Ashby's eyes.

"I have friends that have come to grief at the hands of your gang. You break into homes, rape, murder and abduct young girls to work the streets. In the case of you, my boy, I will start by removing your Jacobs, before you get the chance to produce any more like you, that would surely be a good place to start."

Rabbit is absolutely terrified. "Tell him, Murphy, for God's sake tell him!"

"Shut your hole, you little shit, they won't touch us. We're protected by people high up in the capital, so you have nothing to fear," Murphy yells back at him.

Lord Ashby knows he has Rabbit where he wants him and the information will come from him if he pushes, but he is determined more than ever to break this man Murphy, for he is a nasty piece of work. Now Murphy has mentioned being protected by people in the capital, he needs to find out who he meant. "Now tell me, who do you think protects people like you?"

With no reply, Lord Ashby looks round at what is available to him and, after a moment's thought, calls out, "Olson, give me your splitting axe, I have a use for it." He undoes the trouser belt around Murphy's waist. "Drag the worthless carcass over to this thick tree branch."

The two men holding Murphy do as requested and drag the man toward the branch. He fights, twists, and pushes back in a fruitless attempt to prevent getting to the branch, but soon his arm is being placed over the limb and his wrist bound firm by the belt. As the axe is passed to Lord Ashby, Murphy begins to panic, pulling and yanking at the belt to try and free his hand. For the first time he has real fear in his eyes as the thought of losing his hand becomes a real possibility. He looks at Lord Ashby, trying to think of something that would intimidate him and put a stop to what is about to happen.

"You would not dare, they would see you dead for touching me."

Lord Ashby just smiles at him, then turns to look at Olson. "How many limbs do you think this axe has cleaved off on the battlefield? Eight, ten?"

Olson looks down at the floor for a moment before looking back at Lord Ashby. "There be a dozen that I can think of that I have had a part to play in, maybe a few more, me Lord."

"I will ask you one more time, then I will remove this hand. Let's just hope this old man has the strength to make the cut in one go, one would hate to have to go back in with a knife and cut through all the little bits of sinew and veins that might be holding the severed limb in place. The thought of doing that makes me shudder. Still, if you have nothing more to say, let's get on with it."

Lord Ashby raises the long, narrow axe and places the curved blade on Murphy's wrist, then raises it up high into the air.

"You would not dare, Mallory would have your head for harming us!"

Lord Ashby pauses for a moment. "That was not the answer I'm looking for boy I want to know where your boss Vandenburg and the rest of the little shits in The Penny Rips are hiding themselves, and I want to know in the next few seconds."

Lord Ashby braces himself to strike the blow. Just as his shoulder twists to strike down Murphy screams out, "The market! They are at the marketplace in Old Square!"

Lord Ashby shakes his head slowly. "No, no, lad, that is where you were before you moved some time back. I will waste no more time on you." He raises the axe high in the air as Murphy starts to mumble and dribble.

"Oh God, this isn't happening," he mutters out as he first squints at the raised axe, then closes his eyes as Lord Ashby prepares to strike down again. "The disused brewery on the river at Oxbow!"

The axe slams into the branch, burying the blade deep into the wood above the man's hand. Murphy's eyes open to see the head of the axe within an inch of his wrist and he lets out a huge sigh of relief. Olson undoes the belt and slowly lowers Murphy to the ground while Lord Ashby turns to one of the other men.

"Petrov, you know what to do, check it out, we will be there in about two hours." He then turns to Rabbit and Murphy. "Have I got something special lined up for you two young men?" he says as he takes the silk scarves off both men and gets to work on Murphy's injuries. First he wraps one of the scarfs around the wound on the first leg, then he pulls the knife out of the second leg and wraps the second scarf, tying them tight round the bleeding wounds on Murphy's legs. "I don't want you to bleed out before you have a chance to repay this country with the service you are about to provide for the next few years."

Murphy grits his teeth at the pain in his legs, staring at Lord Ashby like a wild animal trapped in a cage. "What service? You will get nothing from me, old man."

Lord Ashby smiles at him. "By the time we have finished with you, laddie, you will either be a better man or dead. That choice is yours. I just hope you will be a better man."

Rabbit looks up at Lord Ashby and sees three more men coming down the path behind him. He can hear the sound of chinking in the air and, as the men get closer, can see they are carrying leg irons and chains.

"Oh God no, surely not." He breaks down and weeps as the men approach him and attach the irons to his legs and cuff his hands.

"Just on his wrists," Lord Ashby says as he pulls Murphy to his feet. "He will not go far with these wounds, and you will need to help him to the wagon for I do not want him to bleed to death before he starts to repay his debt to society."

Murphy mutters and mumbles under his breath as he and Rabbit are helped away by the guardsmen. Lord Ashby watches them as they disappear around the corner, staring blankly for a while as he thinks on the name Murphy mentioned.

Mallory! It is the first time they have managed to get something on him, perhaps now they can make inroads into finding out what he has to do with The Penny Rips. Slowly, he starts to move off on his crutches, his friend and first officer Olson by his side as always, ready if needed to help his mentor if asked.

"Come, my boy, we have a lot to do and not a lot of time to do it in." The pair of them make their way up the alleyway to the road at the top of the path, with the other two disguised soldiers following them close behind. "It has been a challenging start to the operation, but it is not over. We may have the name of a place they could possibly be using as a base, only time will tell if the information is good. The sooner the rest of the gang are apprehended, the better it will be for everyone in the area. They may even get lucky and catch Mallory at this place as well," Lord Ashby says as the men make their way to where their horses have been kept while they have been interrogating Rabbit and Murphy.

CHAPTER 8

Raising the Stakes

On instructions from Lord Ashby, Petrov and two of his unit are on a scouting mission and are creeping up on the disused brewery at Oxbow, approaching from the reed-lined riverbank on the north side. At this time of year, the river is crystal clear, running over a gravel bottom with clumps of streamer weed forming green sways in the winding flow of the water. The depth varies from three to seven feet, with deeper holes and cutbacks on the bends and behind the large boulders and slabs of rock that are scattered along its way. The water is cold as its source is high in the mountains and runs at pace making it not only very pure, but strong in flow to push the largest of waterwheels if positioned correctly. In the spring floods it is common for boulders to be pushed downstream with the force of the water and to settle where the flow slackens, making new features and changing the flow pattern on the river year on year.

At only sixty to seventy feet wide, it is not the largest river by any means, but the quality of its water has made it perfect for the production of beer and other ales for more than a hundred years. With a ban on private production now in place, the sale and consumption of alcohol outside government authorization makes it illegal for this plant to continue to produce. But with the underground market thriving, the production of alcohol has become a lucrative business for a lot of gangs to get involved in, particularly those with friends in high places who can help shield them and give advanced warnings of any raids. That is for a hefty cut of the profits of course, nobody does anything for nothing in these hard times. With homemade alcohol commanding a premium price amongst the people desperate to drown the misery of daily life, it is little wonder this brewery has the potential to be occupied and used by an opportunistic gang like the Penny Rips.

For now though, the river is just another obstacle that needs to be overcome, as Petrov and his two companions have no choice but to make their way across to other side. They leave their packs on the far bank and quietly slip into the water which soon reaches up to their waists as they move between the weeds and rocks where the water is shallowest. They keep their sharpshooter rifles, pistols and powder above the water line, the rest of what they carry must take its chances and hope their packs keep them dry.

As the men reach the far bank they slowly creep into the bull rushes and reeds and move up into position to look over the old brewery and see who is around. From their position the outside of the plant seems deserted, there is no movement from anyone or anything to be seen around the main building.

"There's nothing here, Sergeant, this was just another waste of time," comments one of the men.

"Be patient, Dunbar, we'll wait a bit. It's still quite early for a group like that to be up and about," replies Sergeant Petrov. The men remain motionless for several minutes before Private Dunbar speaks again.

"This is stupid, there's nothing there, it's just like it always is. I'm freezing sitting here, let's go inside the building and make up a fire and get warm again."

As the private goes to move, Petrov puts his hand on his shoulder and holds him down. "Be still, boy, for all is not as it seems."

The private settles into position again. "What do you mean, Sergeant? I see nothing out there."

Petrov looks at the man and smiles. "That's why you are still a private. We aren't looking for the enemy marching at us like on a battlefield. These are thieves and cutthroats, everything they do is sneaky, underhanded, behind closed doors or down an alleyway. Take a closer look by the double doors at the front; there are slits cut in the walls on the sides, perfect to shoot at anyone standing outside the doors. Above the gates the windows have had the top half of each boarded up with thick timber, the water wheel is still turning and collecting water and by the size of that gearing, it is driving something big on the inside." He then points down the road to the right, "The wooden bridge for the one road leading in and out over the river has small barrels on the posts, possibly wired to powder, and the large barrel beside it looks to have a thunder mug on top of it. That goes off and the whole world knows you're here before even you do, young private."

The sound of horse hooves trotting stops Petrov from speaking and they crouch down lower, watching as a horse-drawn wagon reaches the bridge. Two men step out of the small building to its right, the driver waves his arm in an arc three times and the men return to the building, allowing the milk cart to continue its approach to the main brewery doors. Upon arrival the horse is pulled to a stop and the brewery doors slide open, exposing an Aladdin's cave of sacks, boxes and distillery equipment being tended inside the entrance. Dozens of milk urns are lined up by the doorway and at least twenty people can be seen busying themselves in different areas. As they watch, four men, each rolling a milk urn in a rotating manor, move them out of the building. They roll them to the back of the dairy cart and switch them with the empty ones the driver has pushed off his wagon. Within a minute the milk cart is turning and heading away to deliver the next load, while the men roll the empty urns back inside, the doors close and it is like nothing is there again.

"Let's go, we've seen all we need to. We'll report back to Lord Ashby for our next set of instructions, not that I have any doubts what he will decide to do next," Petrov says to his men.

The three of them reverse back into the reeds, cross the river, collect their equipment from the far bank and leave the area, ensuring with several looks back over their shoulders that they have not been seen or worse, followed. They make their way into the woods, and at the designated meeting point they find Lord Ashby and seventy men from the queen's own Grenadiers. There are twenty mounted cavalrymen, twenty sharp shooters with their rifle-bored muskets, and thirty light foot infantry. Lord

Ashby always insisted on taking a group from several detachments to ensure all units were used in action and all could share in the achievements of such encounters.

As Petrov explains what they are up against and the senior officers form a plan. Once they have gone over it several times to ensure that all know what they have to do, Lord Ashby calls in all his men.

"Now, lads, I cannot afford to lose good men to this rabble, and I believe they will put up a stiff resistance because they know the consequences of being caught. We have a navy that will willingly take any if not all on a nice long trip to sea, but not at the expense of any of you here. So, take no chances, shoot first and be alert to any underhanded moves. Now get going lads, stay safe and remember your training, for you are better prepared than your enemy."

All the men nod and say yes or yes, sir, for Lord Ashby is much loved by his troop and even now in his late sixties, not that he would ever admit it to anyone. He still will not sit back and send his soldiers out without him being around to take the same risks. Most of the men are moving off to get in position for the raid, but a few he needs for special assignment are kept back for further instructions.

"Petrov, I need you to capture the next milk cart intact and take the man's place. Meet us just on the far side of the sharp bend before you get to the bridge and when you get there, we will go through the rest of the instructions then. Just remember we need the milk cart undamaged as it will be needed for the next stage of the attack."

Petrov nods and turns away, collecting his two chosen volunteers as he goes to carry out his instructions. Within minutes they are on horseback and cantering down the road.

Lord Ashby turns to the cavalry officer. "Lieutenant Cavendish, you know the mayor of this city?"

Cavendish nods. "Yes, sir, I know the man well enough to know he is a snake and has evicted good people from their homes to line his own pockets. Some of my men have friends and family members that he's treated poorly for his own gains. He's an extremely unpopular man with many of the locals and has to be protected by several armed men at all times."

Lord Ashby listens to the lieutenant's words. "How would you like to fetch him for me and bring him here? I would like to see if we could eliminate two snakes at the same time."

The officer looks at Lord Ashby with a wry smile. "It would be my pleasure, sir."

"Meet us about quarter of a mile before the bridge and I will explain what to do next, once you and our guest have arrived," Lord Ashby says. Cavendish turns and takes the first four ranks of his cavalry with him as he heads to town.

With most of a plan in place, Lord Ashby is helped back up on his horse. Olson is by his side as always, with his elite guard following as they move off across the field and head for the agreed point before the bridge. It has been Olson's main duty to protect Lord Ashby for several years now, with his instructions coming straight from the queen herself. In her eyes, Lord Ashby is considered a priceless treasure to the country and must be protected and kept safe at all times. A job Olson has had many a sleepless night over, due to the man always being in the thick of things for his beloved queen and country.

Olson is another person who, many years ago, led a different life as an assassin and mercenary to the highest bidder, sent to murder the queen when she was but a child. He was one of the few that actually made it past Wellesley and Lord Ashby and his men one night in the palace, but as he stood over her sleeping in her bed with a small doll in her arms, he could not bring himself to finish the task. He has never said why or what caused his change of heart to anyone, but come the morning, he was found sitting in the chair beside her with tears in his eyes. He had been wounded several times and his four accomplices were found dead at his feet, each one covered with a sheet to hide them from the young queen.

Lord Ashby was convinced he was ashamed of what he had become, while Wellesley believed that he must at some time have had a family of his own that he had lost. Whatever Olson's change of heart, there was no reason he could not have fled the scene and never been seen again, it would seem that he had just reached his lowest ebb and wanted his life over. After a long recovery, he ended up serving as one of Lord Ashby's elites. Over the years Olson became a good friend of Wellesley's and often spotted walking and talking privately with the queen. He does not say much to anyone, nor has he ever shown any emotions since that day, but his trust and devotion to his three friends is beyond any measure.

Within the hour, the sharp shooters have crossed the river and are set up in the reeds, the light foot infantry have made their way around the back of the building and are spread out in the scrubland, with a couple near the hut by the bridge.

Lord Ashby is around half a mile from the bridge with the cavalry, waiting for all the others to arrive. As always he is calm and collected and has absolute trust in his men to carry out their tasks without his interference. He is talking amongst them as if it were a day out riding in the woods, at ease with all that is going on around him as they wait for the others to arrive. It does not take long for the first party to be seen coming down the road; Lieutenant Cavendish leading the mayor of the city by his horse's reins.

The lieutenant salutes as they pull up beside Lord Ashby. "My compliments, sir, here is the man requested."

"Sir, I must protest most strongly," the mayor begins. "This man has dragged me away from a very important meeting with people from my community." He continues to rant and rave while the lieutenant gives his report.

"Found him in the Stiletto house, sir. Apparently he was explaining to two of his workers what rights they have. Just seemed odd that it was while he was in bed with them both and they were all naked."

The mayor looks at Cavendish, wide-eyed. "I explained that it was a misunderstanding. I was inspecting the room and sheets on the bed to ensure they were clean and to the standard of a guest house in that area."

Lord Ashby looks at him and sighs. "Mayor, I am really not

interested, but, if you want to continue, perhaps we should have this conversation at your house with your wife and children present."

The mayor goes quiet and thinks for a moment. "Er, um, I don't think that would be a good idea, for I do not think she would understand what I have to do in the role of mayor to maintain the town's standards."

Lord Ashby smiles at him. "Quite so. Now that is out of the way, shall we get down to business and talk about The Penny Rips and the fact they are running contraband out of the building down the road?"

The mayor looks uncomfortable and starts to sweat. "That is absurd, that place has been shut down for years. Nobody uses it anymore. I can categorically say that it has been closed since the making of alcohol by private enterprises was banned. And The Penny Rips do not exist; it is a rumor spread by a few disgruntled people who wanted an excuse not to pay their taxes like the rest of us. Anyway, you have been on several raids in the town with my enforcers and found nothing at any of the places."

Lord Ashby stares at the man. "The places you sent us to in the past had been long since vacated by the gang because they were tipped off. This time we have the upper hand and I want you here by my side to witness the event as it happens."

The mayor is looking more and more nervous, sweating profusely and becoming very agitated the more Lord Ashby speaks. Before he gets the chance to say another word, they hear the sound of horses coming down the road. They all look up and watch as a milk cart trundles down the road toward them. As it gets closer, Lord Ashby recognizes Petrov steering the horse. He has a silk scarf round his neck and a flat cap on his head and is supported by two riders behind him. As the cart stops, he kicks off the man who had been driving the vehicle; he is tied up, gagged, and a little bloody round the face, but in reasonable health.

Petrov steps down and walks over to Lord Ashby, staring in disdain at the mayor as he passes before stopping to salute Lord Ashby. "Seem to have caught up with him before the bend, sir.

This chap was on the side of the road having a drink of his own supply, so he was a little closer to the brewery than we expected." He pauses to catch his breath before continuing. "I have an idea, sir. I would like to make the exchange before we attack, if I can get away with it."

Lord Ashby looks at the back of the cart and notices something, then turns back to Petrov. "Yes, I think you are right. That would be a good idea, how long would you need?"

Petrov looks at the floor before looking back at his commander. "About ten minutes or so, to be safe."

Lord Ashby thinks for a moment. "Yes, by God, do it. Leave now and we will follow in five minutes."

Petrov salutes, turns, and runs to the back of the cart. His men assist as they move the milk urn's around and adjust the lids to prepare the containers before Petrov climbs aboard and takes up the reins.

The mayor, who has been watching all this time, decides to make his move. "I would like join this young man and ride with him," he says as he lights a cigar. "I want to see with my own eyes if anybody is around."

Lord Ashby considers him. "Yes, but only as far as the bridge, and take your own horse as I cannot afford for anything to happen to you." The mayor smiles at him, for he has got what he wants and is now feeling more comfortable with his position and what he must do.

Petrov flicks the reins and gets the horse moving. He is up to a trot instantly and heading toward the bridge, the mayor following beside him. As he approaches the near side of the bridge, two men come out armed with rifles. Petrov takes off his cap and waves his arm three times over his head. One of the men waves back and they stand and watch the cart travel over the bridge. The mayor pulls up his horse beside the two men and is about to dismount when two soldiers come out from behind the hut. They take down both gang members quietly with a knife to the back, while holding them around the neck and then dragging them backward into the undergrowth to finish them off.

The mayor is taken back by what he has witnessed. He looks up to see the cart arriving at the building and the doors opening, and soon men are rolling out more full urns of bootleg alcohol, collecting the ones off the back of the cart, swapping each one over in turn. He hears horses and turns to see Lord Ashby and Olson leading the charge of cavalry toward the bridge. Seizing the moment, he looks at the large barrel with the thunder mug on the top and throws his cigar into the scattering of black powder. It ignites instantly, with a flash of light and a puff of white smoke, but the thunder mug does not go off.

"Charge!" yells Lord Ashby as the cavalry cross the bridge.

Petrov points out the oncoming soldiers to the men rolling back the empty urns. They hasten to roll the empty containers into the building as the cavalry ride past, shooting at anybody inside the doorway. The doors slam shut as the cavalry ride on into the distance. Petrov has collected the reins and is charging back toward the bridge, where he pulls the horse up and dismounts from the milk cart. He walks toward the mayor while pulling a pistol form his side and raising it to point at him. Stopping at the barrel with the thunder mug on it, he picks up the heavy brass object and pours out the wet, porridge-like powder onto the top of the barrel.

"We had to be sure that you were the traitorous dog that we thought you were," he says, while cocking the hammer back on his pistol.

Back at the building the men inside are now shooting out of the gun slits and windows above at the soldiers as they begin surrounding the brewery. The sharp shooters are firing at the slits and hitting the odd person. Lord Ashby has dismounted his horse and hobbles over to the conflict area, yelling at his men to move back from the building. Soon, all the men start to fall back and take cover. The men inside the brewery keep shooting, thinking they have the army on the run. They are yelling and screaming profanities at the retreating soldiers, laughing and cheering.

Suddenly there is an explosion inside the building, followed almost instantly by an even larger explosion that blows out the barn doors and the men behind them. This in turn is swiftly followed by another more devastating explosion that rips open the building from the inside. Men are blasted out of the windows above where they were standing and shooting from, the roof is torn apart and hangs over one side of the structure, while fires from the burning alcohol and the storage of flammable and explosive goods rip through what is left of the building.

After a couple of minutes of hugging the ground and hearing the debris land all around them, the soldiers come to their senses and slowly stand up and walk toward the building. There is no need for weapons now, for there is barely a person left alive. As the men move forward they can see bodies strewn everywhere. Some have even been thrown fifty or sixty feet from the building and lay amongst the scattered wreckage. They start checking for survivors, one, two, three, they pull out the bodies and line them up. After nearly half an hour the tally is reached, thirty-one dead, seven wounded—mainly concussion, shock, and burns—and one found able to walk and speak. As for 'The Penny Rips' this is the end of the road, the leader of the gang and his two known seconds are now dead along with most of its members. What few remain alive are about to be incarcerated for the foreseeable future, ending the reign of terror they once had over the people of this area.

As for the soldiers that took part in this operation, two men have minor shrapnel injuries, while another is dead from a bullet to the head.

As Lord Ashby and his officers head toward the bridge and the mayor, Petrov turns to face them. "Must have had a lot of powder or alcohol stored in that building, sir, for only the first two explosions were from the powder charges in the urns."

The mayor sees that Petrov is distracted and takes his chance to escape. He kicks out at Petrov, knocking him to the ground as he turns his horse and kicks it with his heels to make a bid for freedom. Petrov quickly stands back up, composes himself and faces the fleeing man as he aims his pistol, letting loose the shot with a bang and a puff of smoke. The lead shot hits the mayor in the back of the knee, knocking his foot out of the stirrup. Three strides of the horse later, his unbalanced body falls to the ground, hollowing out in agony while holding his leg.

"Good shot, my boy, splendid aim!" Lord Ashby calls as he limps over to the stricken man. "We have known for a while you were a bad apple, but that attempt of yours with the thunder mug, well, that just sealed it for you, you traitorous cad."

"My leg, you shot me!" he yells up at them.

Petrov looks down at the man's leg. "In and out, sir. Kneecap is blown so I doubt he will walk properly again."

Lord Ashby steps on the mayor's leg and pushes down, causing the man to yell out with the pain. "Cavendish, you have a day to find out about what this man knows about Mallory's involvement with this gang and its operation. I want to know everything he is up to, along with anything that connects his criminal activities to Stone, Bonner and the other gangs. Then take him and the other prisoners to the war ship Vigilant, it is being repaired in the docks after a bloody battle with pirate ships. They have lost a lot of men and these few will help to swell the ranks again. They can all start to pay back this country by protecting our seas for the next few years."

The mayor looks up at Lord Ashby and is about to speak when Lord Ashby continues. "If this traitorous filth does not speak, apply the lash. If he dies, so be it, he will not be missed by many, I am sure of it. As for the others, though, they are only doing what they need to survive despite what we think of their methods. Make sure they make it aboard the ship alive. Their victims deserve satisfaction for what these men have been doing to them, and a lengthy service for the crown will be a good start. The two I got earlier, I intend to have in the army; there is something about them, especially Murphy. I think they have the potential to become something useful after some guidance and discipline has been applied."

Lord Ashby continues his rounds, moving over to the cart and the four urns on the steps at the back. He flips off one of the lids and cups his hand into the dark liquid, taking a sip. "That's not bad, not bad at all, Petrov, take it back to the barracks for the men to celebrate what we have done today. For the monarchy did not ban beer, *they* banned it to control the black-market production and distribution." He pauses for a moment. "Oh, better do that when I am not around and don't let the boys know I am aware of it, for it might not look too good for me if someone in authority were to find out what!"

His officers are chuckling as he makes his way back to his horse. "Better bury the bodies over in the scrubland behind the building, or the stink will travel to the town in a day or so. I will see the queen and let her know what has gone on here and the outcome of the day's folly."

Lieutenant Cavendish helps him up on his horse as he says this, his trusted companion Olson mounting up beside him as well as his unit of elite men. As Lord Ashby turns his horse and heads away, he shouts to his soldiers, "Well done, men, that's one in the eye against the Three Heads, what!" The men cheer back as he rides across the bridge and into the distance, for they are as proud to serve him as he is to lead his troops into battle.

* * *

Around the same time in the capital city of Ravenberg, the last diplomatic meeting between the monarchy and the politicians is coming to its conclusion. After five hours of debating inside the government chambers at the Grand Hall of Angels, the doors burst open and Alexander Stone storms out. William Bonner and Herbert Mallory are scurrying behind him trying to catch him up as he hurries halfway down the corridor before stopping and leaning with one hand on the shoulder of a statue of the angel Gabriel. His other hand is on his hip as he looks out of the window while shaking his head.

"That bloody queen has done it again. Every time I think I have a way to get rid of the woman, she finds a way to slip her head out of the noose at the last minute. Now again, she has got to the summer break without relinquishing her claim to rule and govern the laws and policies of this country. How does she do it! She always manages to belittle me with fancy words in front of all the politicians and diplomats without stepping out of line." He growls and mumbles to himself before turning to look back at his two followers. "Why is it between the two of you, you cannot get rid of just one person? Years ago she was only a child, now, many years later, she is still a thorn in my side, just like her parents were."

He turns and storms on, muttering and cursing to himself, then stops and turns to his associates again. "I presume we have people at her summer retreat by now."

Bonner and Mallory look at each other, then back at Stone. "Yes, yes we do, nearly half the staff from the kitchen and garden and several maids and servants in the main building, but…"

Stone stares at Bonner. "But what?" he says in a deep, stern voice.

Bonner lowers his voice as he replies. "It would seem that she has decided to reside somewhere else this year and not at the usual palace."

Stone takes in a deep breath and exhales fully. He shrugs his shoulders and looks down as he holds the top of his nose with his thumb and forefinger. "Don't tell me, that dammed Stoneheart Manor. You would presume that with a name like that I would be the one living there." He thinks for a moment. "Well, who do we have inside there we can use?"

The men look at each other before looking back at Stone. "We are still unable to get people inside, they just seem to disappear after a week or so," Bonner mumbles.

"Well send more people, I need to know what that woman is up to. If not then find a new angle, that girl I've seen with her the last few times," Stone snaps his fingers as he thinks, "er, er, Anna, that's her name. Find out about her, see if she can be bought or encouraged to work for us. Perhaps she will get us closer to the queen or at least tell us what she is planning. I have to know what she is up to, for she always manages to be just one step ahead of my plans to be rid of her."

Bonner and Mallory nod in agreement. "We will have people look into this opportunity at once, sir."

Bonner and Mallory move off together, plotting how to find

out about Anna, while Stone heads toward his private chambers. He walks into the room and pours himself a large glass of brandy, taking a deep drink before moving down a hall and opening a door into another area. There is a young lady present, and as he enters the room she stands up from the chair she has been sitting in and looks down at the floor. The large four-poster bed beside her is made up and the room is immaculately tidy. The young lady is in her late teens and does not look pleased to see him.

Stone stares at her for a while, taking another sip from his glass. "Who told you to get dressed?"

The girl does not look up as she speaks. "You told me if I did what you asked last night, my parents would be released today."

Stone thinks for a moment. "You misheard me, my dear. I said your parents would not be harmed, it will take longer to get them out of prison, for the charges against them are severe."

She finally looks up at him. "The charges against them are a lie, their only crime is that their daughter is pretty and has caught the eye of a monster like you." She spits the words at him as the tears start to flow from her eyes.

"Now, now, my dear, sticks and stones and all that. I think if all things go well we will have your parents out in a couple of days or so, providing there are no more situations to overcome. You see, if I have another problem they may never see the light of day again, do you understand?"

She looks at him with eyes full of hate but has the good sense not to respond. He takes another sip from his glass before placing it on the side table and walking over to her. He approaches her, putting his hands on her hips and kissing and nibbling at her pale-white neck.

"Now, I would suggest you resume where you left off and we can continue our time together undisturbed, for I have time to kill." She visibly shudders. As he starts to pick at the buttons on her dress, she closes her eyes and prays that she is somewhere else, anywhere, anywhere but here with this evil man. He lifts the dress off her shoulders and slides it to the floor, then brings his hands up to cup both her breasts and starts to squeeze them.

She trembles and bites her bottom lip as his hands move over her naked body, touching every part of her, making her tremble at the thought of what she is about to go through again. Within a few minutes, he is shunting her toward the bed.

The young lady thinks of her parents and younger sisters, convincing herself if she can get through this, they will be free and she will see them again. *Just got to get through this*, she tells herself.

"Don't think I am going to do all the work, my dear, for I would not take kindly to that." She takes two deep breaths, opens her eyes and turns to smile at him, then starts to kiss him as he lowers her onto the bed. "That's more like it, my dear, show a little passion and desire. You are with a man who runs a country, and, as such, I wield a great deal of power. You should feel honored that I choose to spend some of my time with you."

✳ ✳ ✳

Elsewhere, Bonner and Mallory are making their way out of the building. "Thank god we are done for a month or two, that man is beginning to let power go to his head," says Bonner.

"I feel the same way. Putting the chief magistrate in jail with his wife on trumped-up charges just to have his way with his damned daughter, it's madness, especially when you think of all the women he has at his beck and call," Mallory replies. "Wanting the queen removed from office; that man is playing with fire. She has been quite quiet up until now, why wake a sleeping giant? Should she want to fight back, she has very powerful friends and supporters. Not least Lord Ashby and Wellesley and their estates, or should I say professional army; their influence amongst the people is very real indeed.

Mallory thinks for a moment, "All the contractors and assassins that I have send to Stoneheart Manor end up missing or coming back to me years later demanding payment for time at sea. I spend more dealing with the failures than I do the successes, whether it be paying them off or having them removed. I am beginning to wonder if what we did all those years ago was worth what we are going through now. The people have been drained of everything, he cannot keep taking what they do not have or there will be a riot on a scale too big to control. I mean, what more does he want? We have houses everywhere, more money than we could ever spend, fingers in every enterprise, beautiful women whenever we want. We live like king's and he always demand's more. I just don't get it, we have got all that any person could possibly desire, why bite the hand that feeds you?" Mallory shakes his head in dismay.

"He wants to break her; she is the only person he has not been able to dominate or control. In all these years he has not been able to bend that woman to his will, and I fear if he ever does he will still want more, perhaps even extend our borders and invade a neighboring country," answers Bonner.

"What! You think he would be capable of starting a war just to satisfy his lust for power?"

"Who knows? But for now Mallory, I will look into this girl Anna, as he requested. You go to the meeting with the heads of the gangs and ensure they are playing by the rules and still giving us a fair cut in return for our ignorance of what they are peddling." The men tilt their tall hats at each other as they turn to get in their separate carriages.

"I will see you Monday at Stone's Estate," Mallory says. "We will review all our findings and make a plan of action going forward. Let's pray by then that his blood has cooled down and he sees sense again."

"Good luck with that one, I feel that he is beyond listening to us anymore."

As soon as both men climb their carriages, the drivers set off in different directions, with both politicians relieved that the government and political assembly are now closed down for a couple of months. No new laws can now be requested or debated and they have time to relax and enjoy their villainous lifestyles.

* * *

Margaret is already in her carriage and on her way to meet her husband. With all the affairs of state now done and all royal requirements and duties to the crown over with for a while, she can finally breathe a little easier. She has hidden her pregnancy from those that would most use it against her and for now at least, she can concentrate on herself, time with Andrew and prepare for her child. There is so much she needs to explain to Andrew, so many secrets and problems to overcome and resole, for he is her constant, forever standing by and supporting her. As she sits in the carriage, accompanied by her friends Beth, Wellesley and the ever-watchful Anna, she looks forward to a time when she can put all this behind her and live her life without the risks she takes at the moment.

"Wellesley, have you dispatched men to the retreat and closed it down as the queen will not be there this season?" she asks.

Wellesley gives her a reassuring nod. "Men and women from the troop arrived this morning. All the local and known staff will be paid off and sent home, the others we know about will be dealt with in the usual way. In the case of five of them, they are wanted across the border and Prince Frederik himself will be arriving later today at Stoneheart Manor to collect them. It would seem they might have had something to do with the abduction of his cousin, the Countess Della Dewinter. And as you know, he was more than a little fond of her."

Margaret looks back at Wellesley, a rare smirk on her face. "He is very fond of her, some would say too fond. If they had something to do with her disappearance, he will get it out of them. But whether they did or did not, they will never be the same again once he has finished with them. His methods are a little crude but very effective, I doubt they will ever be a problem to us again on our side of the border."

* * *

While waiting for the arrival of Margaret, Andrew and his assistant laborers have finished digging in the plants he had taken to the estate. The bee hives are placed in their new positions amongst the flowers at the end of the garden right next to the river. It's a prime spot as there are many flowering fruit trees and shrubs nearby to keep them occupied. After an hour of letting them settle, Andrew slowly takes the covers off the exit holes and steps back to watch what they do. It does not take long for the bees to start streaming out and within minutes, the air is filled with the humming and buzzing of angry bees circling and flying around the area. Andrew takes a seat and watches as the colony expands their aerial reconnaissance; wider and wider they fly, checking out everything in their new environment. They interact with the second hive and begin to set their boundaries with a few minor aerial fights, but no mass attack. He watches for some time and at one stage is sure one of the queens exited the hive and walked on the outside as there was a carpet of bees moving around the wooden structure for a while before heading back inside the nest.

Slowly, normality begins to creep back into the colony, the bees become less angry and fewer are circling around the air. Over the years Andrew has acquired an expert eye when it comes to how the bees think and work. He watches as scouts start checking out the flowers in the surrounding area and soon they are back at the hive. They dance and vibrate on the hive ledge to let the others know what they have found and where to find the better flowers for collecting nectar. The bees are beginning to start exploring the flowers and collecting nectar, although a little erratic to start with, it soon gains momentum with the bee's. It will take a few days for the hives to fully settle down, but it looks like for now, the queens in each colony are content with where they are, which means they will not swarm and leave the hives.

Andrew can do no more for now, he must leave them to get on with their lives the same as he must get on with his, and he returns to the house. On arrival he is offered tea and light snacks on a tray by the new cook, a woman in her early forties by the name of Bunty. He was aware she would be working here, but until that day he had never met her. A polite, thickset woman with large, dark eyebrows, wearing a cook's outfit and cotton hat, she has a comforting manner about her as she wanders around the kitchen, moving things about and continually bringing in more stock from a wagon parked outside and placing items onto the shelves and filling the many cupboards with ingredients and spices she has bought with her.

Andrew is at a loss to know what to do with himself, the fires are both lit at each end of the house, the wood stacks are full to bursting, all his belongings have been sorted and placed in suitable locations around the house and bedroom. The two men and the cart that came with the last of his items have left the premises, their duties now complete. He can hear the footsteps from the people pacing around in the 'war room' as he calls it, upstairs and to the right of where he stands. With nothing more to do he takes a seat at the kitchen table and drinks his tea as the cook re-enters the room with yet more items of cookware and pots and pans. She sees Andrew looking all forlorn and lost at the table and stops to speak to him.

"If you do not mind me saying, sir, this must be a great change to what you are used to." She smiles as Andrew looks up at her and nods his head.

"I have married a wonderful woman, of that I have no doubt, but I have also at the same time inherited the biggest collection of people in the deal that I could ever have imagined," he replies.

"I have known Margaret many years and I have never seen her happier than when she talks about you, or you're mentioned in conversation by people with her. You have given her a new perspective and happiness I thought she would never find. But, as with all people of such a prominent position, she does come with a lot of baggage. There is a whole country resting on her abilities to help the monarchy do what is right for the people. That kind of pressure can only be carried by the strongest of people, and even then they need the support of great people. From the sound of it, and the opinions of others around, there's none better than you, young man."

Andrew nods to himself. "Tell me, how long have you known Margaret?"

Bunty smiles at him. "I first saw her a week after her birth. I was the daughter of a maid when her parents were alive, it was my mother who got me a position in the kitchens peeling vegetables, cleaning, and helping the cooks with whatever they needed doing."

He is about to ask about her parents when he hears the sound of a coach and several horses coming up the driveway. He is instantly up on his feet and on the way to the front door, leaving the cook chucking to herself. "Oh, to be young and so in love," she says, shaking her head.

As Andrew opens the door, he can see a dozen cavalrymen in green escorting a coach to the front of the house. He recognizes some of the men as they approach, they smile and nod at him as they move past.

"She be well and inside, Andrew," says one of the officers with a grin on his face. Andrew has become a firm favorite of many of the officers and men he has met, not just because of who he is married to, but because he always has time for everybody and speaks to all with respect and decency. Not only that, but he has been in conflict with some of them and is well known for what he has done for the children on the streets. He is considered one of their own by so many of the men who serve Margaret.

The coach pulls up, but before the coachman or his companion have had a chance to step down from the carriage, Andrew is at the door, opening it and helping all down without so much as a word to any of them, he is so anxious to see his wife. As she moves into view, he freezes. The expressions of joy from the pair of them at seeing each other seems to stop time for a moment, they see nothing else but each other as he helps her down the steps to the ground. They hold each other in their arms and kiss as Wellesley waves off the coach and escort and Anna and Beth enter the house, leaving the couple behind. Wellesley keeps his distance and looks around to give the couple some privacy, but he is always alert to his surroundings and will never let the couple completely out of his sight while on duty.

"It is good to see you, my dear," says Andrew, and he then kisses her again.

"Oh, Andrew, what a couple of weeks it has been! I am so

glad we now have some time together. I think another day in the company of such horrid men like those politicians and I would have just shot them all and been done with it."

Andrew smiles at her. "I'm sure that would be the best solution, but, for now, come warm yourself by the fire, your cook has just made tea." Andrew helps her into the house, but as they reach the stairs she stops.

"I think I will get changed first, for this dress is beyond uncomfortable." She takes a step up the stairs, then turns to Andrew. "Would you help me out of this attire, my dear, for it is most uncomfortable around the middle?" Andrew is instantly by her side as they ascend the stairs together. When they enter their bedroom on the next floor, Andrew looks back quickly to check nobody is behind them, then shuts the door.

While the others downstairs make their way to the kitchen and help themselves to tea and cakes, Andrew helps his wife out of her dress. As the garment falls to the floor, Andrew is amazed at the size of her tummy, for she is now heavily pregnant and in her undergarments it shows just how far gone she truly is.

"Help me to the bed, my dear. I just need to rest a while," she says. It is becoming more apparent to him by the moment that Margaret has been struggling more than she has let on. He lays Margaret down and takes off her shoes. Her legs and feet are greatly swollen, and once he has positioned her comfortably with additional pillows to support her, he starts to gently massage her feet. He can tell by the expression on her face that he is helping to take some of the aches and pains away.

"Come lay with me," she says several minutes later, passing her hand down to him and encouraging him to slide up behind her. She places his hand over her stomach and he feels the movement of the baby inside her. He cannot help but be excited and keep his hand on her to feel it move again and again. He gently kisses her neck several times before she turns her head to look at him. "Forgive me, my dear, but for once I seem to be in no condition to take advantage of your presence." The pair of them chuckle together for a moment before Margaret's eyes slowly start to close and she falls asleep tucked into Andrew's body. He kisses her once more on the shoulder while still cupping her tummy and rolls a strand of her hair between the thumb and finger of his other hand.

"By God I love you, my dear, but I fear you take on too much for any one woman to handle." He chuckles to himself. "I know if you were to hear me talk like this, you would tell me you have a whole army around you, but to me there is only you, my beloved. For I see nobody who could fill your role if you were not here," he whispers as he watches her sleep. It is hard for him to see his wife put herself through all that she does, but it is just that which makes her so special to him. The way she can be so passionate about people and those in need fills him with admiration. He continues to watch her as she breathes and moves for a while, but his thoughts slowly drift away and before long his eyes also begin to close and he falls asleep, still holding Margaret in his arms.

Nearly four hours has passed before Margaret starts to stir. As she begins to move Andrew's eyes open, she puts her hand behind her back and feels Andrew's body tucked up beside her own. "I'm here, my dear," he quietly whispers behind her ear.

Margaret rubs the side of his body with her hand. "It's nice to have you with me, my love, I always seem to sleep better when you are around." Grabbing his hand, she tucks it under hers and holds it tight to her chest. "How was it for you to leave your house for the last time?" she asks while stroking his hand.

"Oh, it was odd to start with, but when I met the two old boys that were going to use the house, I felt rather proud. They were so humble and appreciative and thought more of you than anything else in their lives. They said that still being able to serve the crown and you after the injuries they had sustained in service meant so much to them. You seem to have such an effect and presence on everyone around you, so many love and adore you. I still do not understand how I was so fortunate you chose me with so many men to choose from, a lot of them had much more to offer you in wealth and position in society than I."

Margaret turns around to face Andrew. She holds his hand and kisses it gently. "I never chose you, you happened, your ways and mannerisms stood out from the crowd and how you think of others first before yourself sparked something in me. You have a strength and a way about you that is so special. You are not afraid to say your mind when needed, but so loving and understanding when it comes to my needs and me. You have the patience of a saint, allowing me to serve and do my duty to the monarchy, especially after you have seen the risks and dangers that we face on a daily basis. You have the strength of a rock by my side when I need it most, always there supporting me in my hours of need without question or an explanation." Margaret turns and looks into his eyes. "I think you have it wrong, my darling, I was lucky to find you when I most needed somebody by my side, for I do not think I would have had the strength and wit to get this far had you not come along when you did."

Andrew holds Margaret in his arms and kisses her passionately. "You came into my life and my world got turned upside down." He smiles. "I would not change it for all the wealth the world has to offer, my dear, for I love you so." He pauses for a moment, trying to find the right words to express himself. "It would not matter what you put me through, for I am in love with you, so if the Devil himself should come here and rattle this door looking for you, I would give him a run for his money, by God I would."

At that very moment there is a knock at the door. Margaret and Andrew look at each other with wide eyes and smiles on their faces. "He didn't waste his time in getting here, did he?" Andrew says, while Margaret smiles and lets out a little laugh. Again, there is a knock at the door.

"Well go get him, dear, you threw down the challenge, let's see you defend my honor with some vigor," Margaret says. Andrew gets up and heads to the door, grabbing the handle and swiftly swinging open the door. He is confronted with a shocked-looking Anna, who quickly composes herself.

"Lunch is ready if you are hungry," she says.

Andrew turns back to Margaret. "I reckon I have the edge on this one, shall I just shoot her with a pistol or go for the sword and use the point?" Margaret is trying not to laugh as Anna gives him a horrified look, then turns and runs back down the hall and stairs.

"He's gone mad, I only offered them food and he wants to kill me!" she yells as she makes her way quickly back into the kitchen and the safety of others.

Margaret slowly and carefully gets to her feet, grabbing a robe from the large ornate oak wardrobe and wrapping it round her as she heads out the door past Andrew while patting her stomach. "Baby needs feeding, my dear, guard my rear should the Devil follow, for I am certain he is not stupid enough to get between a pregnant woman and her food." Andrew is laughing as he watches his beloved stride down the hallway to the stairs.

Away from prying eyes, in the bosom of her mis-matched family of close friends, Margaret is now proud to show off her large bump to all who would dare to look. Up until now she has had to hide it from all but herself under layers of clothes and loose-fitting dresses. As she walks into the kitchen area, she has the eyes of all in the room.

"By God, how many do you have in there?" asks Anna with her jaw wide open and a bemused smile on her face.

Wellesley flicks her round the head while also staring at Margaret's belly himself. "That will be enough of that, young lady, now fetch the leather armchair with the extra cushions from the lounge and let's make our Margaret comfortable."

While Anna shoots out the door, collecting the arriving Andrew to help with the moving of the furniture, Bunty and Beth look at each other with huge grins on their faces, like a pair of old aunts. "I do not think we will have long to go, any larger and it will be popping out near full grown," says Beth as she walks over and hugs Margaret. "Congratulations, my lady, you do not know how long I have waited to say that, but now we are free from state duties I can contain myself no longer," she says as she helps Margaret into the armchair that has just been carried into the room by Anna and Andrew.

It is hard to imagine, for over eight months of barely talking or whispering about being pregnant through fear of the wrong people finding out, Margaret has kept almost all her pride and excitement to herself. But here, right now, surrounded by those that matter most to her, she can finally be herself and share her excitement with everybody.

"I will not miss the long walks down the corridors to the chambers, each time I would nearly get to the end I would be desperate for the privy," she says with a smile. Margaret then turns to Anna. "Well, you got me here on the pretense of food, my girl, there be at least two here waiting to be fed and if you're not fast I will start on you first." The close-knit group of friends starts laughing and chuckling at Margaret's words and before long all sorts of food is placed on the table before her and she starts to fill up a plate with items to eat.

"You had better keep some room at the end, my dear, for the boys and girls at the bakery have been busy and made a basket of treats for you and I" whispers Andrew into Margaret's ear.

Margaret puts her fork back down on her plate and swallows, then clears her throat. "Well bring it out, dear husband, let's see if all your training has paid off." Andrew smiles and disappears into the pantry, collecting Anna on his way through.

At the same time there is a rap at the front door. The room goes quiet as both Beth and Wellesley look at Margaret with concerned expressions on their faces. "I think it would be wise to close the kitchen door," says Wellesley as Beth makes her way over to see who it is. Margaret stands up and steps back from the table. "Beth, let them in, I am expecting some of our men. Wellesley, open the table and add the extension to the middle and Bunty, bring some more chairs from the far side of the room. I feel our guests will be hungry and be in need of a good meal."

Beth opens the door and before her stands Lord Ashby, with Captains Olson and Cavendish and the soldier Petrov behind him. Her concerned look changes to a smile as she knows Lord Ashby well and has seen the others many a time before. The hats come off all four men as she opens the door wider to allow Lord Ashby to hobble through, as he passes she puts her hands out to block the others. "Guns and swords on the table, please, gentlemen, then through to the kitchen if you would be so kind."

The three men disarm and place all their weapons on the reception table before following Beth into the next room. Ahead, Lord Ashby has already made his way through and is greeted by Margaret personally.

"So, this is where you have chosen to hide yourself this summer, then," he says. Then, as he sees the size of Margaret standing before him, a smile lights up in his face. "By God, you're, you're…"

"Yes, my dear Ashby, and a long way gone as well. I am so sorry I could not tell you before, but the risks were too great."

Lord Ashby steps forward and hugs her as if he was her father, kissing her on both cheeks. It is all he can do to not shed a tear as the words are not coming to him.

"Come, take a seat beside me and we will talk about everything that has gone on, for now I need you and your men more than ever."

The others arrive and are taken back when they see Margaret standing before them, then, when they see her condition, they are stunned and stop in their tracks. Lord Ashby turns to his men with a stern look. "You've all seen Margaret before, she is just a little bigger now. Besides, as I have said to you many times, in private we do not stand on ceremony round here, come through and sit at the table, you are all considered friends as well as soldiers."

Andrew is used to seeing stunned people around his wife by now and pays no attention to them as he continues undoing the straps on the wicker basket while others set up the table with more plates and cutlery. Wellesley has helped his old friend Lord Ashby be seated beside Margaret before shaking the hands of the other three men and showing them to the table. The soldiers are still stunned at what they have just seen and it takes them a while to get comfortable with the situation. But, as Andrew starts unloading various pies, cakes, and puddings of all types and varieties, and Bunty and Beth place them around the table, they soon become more relaxed and start to eat the food with the others. The conversation is light-humored and well-mannered, and the praise for the quality of the items from the bakery makes Andrew immensely proud of the people he trained.

They spend nearly an hour at the table eating, drinking, and talking before all of them have had their fill. As the plates are cleared, Lord Ashby asks Margaret if it is possible to take a few items away with him for a wounded man he knows. Margaret answers with a nod and a smile before she stands up and suggests that they retire to the lounge and leave the girls to clear up the table while they get down to business. The men follow Margaret and Andrew while Wellesley brings up the rear, he has a bit of trouble keeping Anna back as he tries to close the door, keeping her out of the room.

"I will tell you what happens later, Anna," he says as he pushes her back away from the doorway. Anna does not take kindly to being left out. "Later," he says again. She points at Wellesley with her finger and shows her teeth at him in defiance before storming back to the kitchen to help the others and he is finally able to close the door.

As Lord Ashby takes his seat, Wellesley pokes at the fire with a fire iron rod and adds another log to the glowing embers. Margaret starts to speak as he takes his own seat. "Well, gentlemen, as you have all now seen by my condition, Andrew and myself have a child due soon. There is no going back from this, not that we would want to anyway," she says, looking lovingly at her husband.

"First on the agenda, did you manage to deal with the problem with the gangs and what they are up to, as I do not think the people can take much more of their blackmail and bullying?"

Lord Ashby leans forward. "We have started on several of the main groups, but we had great success with the one closer to home. 'The Penny Rips' have been utterly wiped out, only a handful survived our incursion as they put up a strong fight. I have two with me for the army and the rest will sail in a few days, for they all have a debt to society to pay."

Andrew knows of the gang Lord Ashby is talking about, he says nothing but is relieved they are out of the way as he was aware they were watching his bakery as a potential target for extortion and racketeering.

"Oh well done, well done indeed." Margaret looks at Petrov

and Cavendish. "No doubt you two were in the thick of it again."

The men look at her with the pride only a soldier can have when recognized for their actions by a superior. "We did our part, that is for certain, my lady, but all had a hand in the elimination of this troublesome problem," says Cavendish.

Margaret turns to look at Lord Ashby. "These men may well show themselves to be as heroic as you one day, Lord Ashby."

He smiles at her with great pride. "I hope they all surpass me and go on to even better things, for they are good lads." He pauses for a moment. "We did get some information from one of them, though it would seem that they felt they are protected in their actions by the state."

Margaret looks at him. "Oh, and how does that work then?" she asks curiously.

"It was made clear that all the main gangs work under the guidance of a certain gentleman named Mallory."

"Mallory! That spineless little weasel, so he is the one dishing out all the orders on behalf of Stone, I should have known. That way Stone keeps his hands clean while others suffer the cost of his exploits." Margaret goes quiet, thinking about this new information and how it could be used to their advantage.

The conversation and planning go on well into the evening, and by the time business is concluded there is only an hour or so of daylight left. Wellesley shows the men to the front door while Andrew remains behind with Margaret, who is by now exhausted and very tired. The three men collect their pistols and swords while Wellesley and Lord Ashby talk alone outside.

"You do not seem to have many men around the place considering what is going on here and the importance of the people inside, my boy," says Lord Ashby.

"No, you're right, she is insisting that I am enough. I have the odd person around doing jobs by the river and woods, but it is not easy as she is on my case constantly. I have rented a farmhouse in the village with room for six men at arms, and have a cook and cleaner in place already, but have yet to get good men from the barracks to move down there."

Lord Ashby thinks for a while before answering. "Why don't I have my bodyguards, the six elites, move down there once we have left here? You know them well as you trained them at your barracks. Olsen and the other two are more than enough for me to have around until I reach the rest of my unit tonight. Keep them on hand for the next week or so, it will give you time to organize six more to replace them in a timely manner."

Wellesley smiles at him. "I was hoping you would say that old friend. Here is the address of the farm building, the woman is expecting them and the barn outside is clean and ready for their horses, with plenty of fresh bedding, feed and hay." Wellesley passes his friend a piece of paper and they shake hands, then he helps him onto his horse.

Anna arrives with a parcel of food for Lord Ashby. "That is grand, my dear, if you would pass it to young Olson, he will carry it for me. I am sure the men will be grateful for the items inside, for I have damaged one quite severely. Unfortunate, but necessary at the time, I am afraid." Anna passes the bundle to the mounted Olson who smiles at here, he takes the package as they turn and make their way down the driveway. The six security escort join the back of the group of four men as they continue trotting up the driveway and onto the track.

While watching them leave, Anna prods Wellesley in the ribs. "I am not happy with you old man, I should have been at that meeting. Do you know it took me nearly half an hour to find a place to hear what you lot were all talking about?"

Wellesley looks at her, shaking his head. "My dear Anna, if you were not on our side I would have you shot. No! I would have you shot then cut up into pieces to ensure that you were definitely dead and disposed of in the river."

Anna smiles at him with her typical innocent look. "Then who would you get to take messages to the six men you now have stationed in the village, for you know she will not have you leave the house while she is here."

Wellesley looks at her. "How in God's name did you hear me talk about that?" He sighs deeply and thinks for a moment. "One of them did not catch your eye, did they?"

Anna stops in her tracks and stares at Wellesley. "No man will ever touch me again against my will, not and live anyway," she says, pulling a stiletto-style knife from somewhere on her dress and rolling it across the back of her hand. She then turns and walks back toward the house, placing the knife back where it came from. As Wellesley catches her up, she puts her arm through his and holds on tight.

"I thought no man could touch you," he comments curiously.

"Ah, no man, but you are my Wellesley, and, besides, you're old enough to be my father." She stops suddenly, pulling Wellesley back with her. "You're not my father, are you?"

He looks at her in shock. "Oh God, I hope not, I could not take the stress of it all!"

She moves off again, pulling Wellesley with her. "So do you want to make love with me then?" she asks, batting her eyelashes at a now-terrified Wellesley.

"Oh God, she gets worse," he groans, as he tries to pull away from her grip.

"Because if you do, I am up for that. We can take the spare room upstairs and go at it all night and the next day if you want."

Wellesley slips from her grasp and gets in the house first, followed by the laughing Anna. As she steps through the doorway, she turns and closes the door then turns around still laughing. Suddenly stopping in her tracks as she is confronted by Margaret standing in front of her with her arms folded.

"Don't you think that was a little mean to him? You know he loves you like a daughter and would lay down his life for you," she says with a slight smirk on her face.

Anna thinks for a moment. "Maybe, but it is fun to see him squirm just a little. Besides, if it came to it, I am certain that it would be me protecting him as I could not imagine life without him watching over me." She lowers her voice to a whisper. "Not that I would let him know that." She lowers her head and moves around Margaret and into the kitchen under the cover of giggles.

Margaret cannot help but smile and chuckle to herself, for

Anna reminds her so much of herself when she was younger.

CHAPTER 9

The Family Grows

The first week of everybody living in the new country house has been a particularly difficult time for Andrew as he has been used to living alone and doing everything in an orderly and precise way for a long time. Now he has people who cook his food and serve it at exact times of the day and others who work in the garden and tend to everything that needs doing, most of the time before he has even asked for it to be done. His clothes are washed, pressed and back in his wardrobes as soon as he puts them down each day and his shoes are the cleanest, shiniest shoes he has ever had in his life.

There are so many people in and out of the house daily: military personnel, diplomats, people of influence and staff to maintain the running of this busy establishment, to name but a few. They are all kept away from private areas of the house and almost all of them do not see Margaret at all, while those that do see her do so only when she is sitting at a table to hide her pregnancy. Though Andrew does not often see all the people coming and going, he always knows they are around as he can hear them walking around the rooms and along the corridors throughout the day and evening. It often makes him worry that his wife could be compromised at any time and her life put in danger.

It is a lot for Andrew to get used to in a short period of time, but the benefits are that he is with his beloved Margaret a lot more of the time and that is priceless to him. Besides, he always has Anna and Wellesley watching over her when he is not by her side. Andrew has not lived with a woman before and it takes some time to adapt and learn to share, especially as Margaret's pregnancy makes her rather demanding. In some cases, he ends up doing or agreeing to things he does not really want to, just to keep the peace. When around others, he will agree to their way of thinking to fit in, however, when he is alone with Margaret he will only speak the truth, whether she likes the answers or not, and will offer his real opinion on the subjects that he has had issues with during the day. This is the way Andrew is and because it is advice from her husband Margaret often listens, she is beginning to appreciate Andrew more and more as she knows he is a methodical thinker and would only offer advice after thinking carefully about it.

Margaret is also learning to change her ways in this relationship, for now she shares her life with Andrew on a much closer level. Day in and day out she has a man she trusts beside her, supporting her whenever she needs a shoulder to lean on. She is also beginning to follow his lead, take inspiration from his opinions, and asks his thoughts on all manner of subject matter. This in itself is a big move away from what she has always done in the past, with only her own wits to keep the wolves from her doors. Margaret spends the early part of every day in the 'war room', as it has become known by all, This is one of the only times of the day that Andrew can get on with the things he would like to do without Margaret being around.

Once she enters the room and the door closes, he is free to engage in his passions of gardening and beekeeping, or, if Wellesley is around, a bit of sword play and pistol shooting to hone his skills. That being said, the core of Margaret's team, Wellesley, Anna, Beth, Lord Ashby, and Bunty the cook are now becoming an integral part of his life as well, as they are always with them in the evening, sitting around the fire and reflecting on the day's events and planning the next day's requirements.

It is on one such evening that Wellesley and Anna are playing cards and debating who is the better at cheating and not being caught. This soon becomes a testing point as both of them throw down hands containing the ace of hearts. Andrew and Margaret are curled up on a large suite laughing as Wellesley leans forward and holds Anna's arm on the table, pulling a couple more cards from the frills of her cuff with his other hand and throwing them down on the table.

"You are so bad at cheating, my girl, a blind man could see what you were doing!"

Anna reaches into Wellesley's waistcoat pocket and throws down two queens on the pile. "You're no better yourself," she says with a smug look.

"Anna, they are more of your own cards, that pocket is too far away from the table for me to use without being spotted," he replies, pulling a card from under his bare wrist and dropping it onto the table. "That is how you cheat, my dear."

Anna looks at him in awe, her eyes lit up as she turns over Wellesley's wrist to see where the card came from. "Wow, show me how you do that!" she says while feeling and pinching his skin as if trying to find a secret pocket.

"The student still has much to learn from the master, it would seem." He chuckles as he watches Anna try and work out how he had done such a move.

Margaret whispers in Andrew's ear, "This is why I never play cards with them, for I never know which one to keep an eye on." As she leans back, she twitches and sits back up, her expression changes as she feels different. "Darling, I think the time has come."

Andrew looks at her as she tries to get up, it does not sink in at first. "Oh" he says as it hits him, and he assists his wife to her feet.

"Help me to the bed chamber." Andrew gives Margaret a shoulder to hold onto while Wellesley moves to her other side for additional support, and as a group they slowly move to the door left open by Anna as she disappears down the corridor and out of sight.

They move along the corridor and up the curved stairs into another room that has been set up specifically for the birth. The men help Margaret to the bed, and, as they sit her down Anna reappears, followed moments later by Beth in her nightgown. They strip Margaret of most of her outer clothes before Beth speaks up.

"Gentlemen, would you kindly leave the room? I will call you if you are needed, until then please wait outside. Anna, get Bunty to put some water on the stove, we will need a lot of hot water, then get her physician, he is in the spare room on the top floor at the end of the corridor." Anna is out the door in a flash.

"We have a physician in the house?" asks Andrew.

"Yes, and a very good one at that. His name is Herbert, he delivered Margaret when she was born and was responsible for saving Anna's life as well. He arrived yesterday and I had him moved to a room away from all prying eyes until he was needed, and it would seem as if that time has now come. Now, would you two please leave, for I have work to do and Margaret needs to concentrate on the job at hand."

Wellesley leaves the room as Andrew is still standing by his wife, holding her hand. "It is time you went, my dear, for this is something you cannot help me with."

Andrew pauses for a moment, then kisses her on the forehead. "I will be just the other side of the door." With a heavy heart, Andrew leaves the room, closes the door, and waits in the hallway with Wellesley.

After a few minutes Anna walks past them, closely followed by the physician with small black bag in hand and spectacles perched on the top of his head. As she knocks and opens the door, he courteously tilts his hat at Andrew as he passes and enters the room, closing the door behind him.

From now on, it is a waiting game. Andrew paces up and down the corridor, listening to Margaret's moans. Hearing nothing for more than a few minutes is worse than hearing Margaret scream. Not for the first time, after a quiet period of around five or six minutes, his nerves are on edge and he reaches for the door handle.

"You cannot help Andrew, let those that know what they are doing tend to Margaret, Son," says Wellesley, trying to reassure and advise Andrew. Andrew stands motionless at the doorway, still holding on to the handle, then slowly releases his grip and turns to Wellesley. "I'm not sure who is the more distressed at this moment in time, Margaret in there giving birth or you out here turning yourself inside out. Calm down and let nature take its course. Women have been giving birth since the beginning of time, they know what they are doing. Your job starts when they are born, as you are to look after, protect and support them both. Margaret will need you at your very best, for the path she has chosen to walk is not one many would willingly take."

Andrew looks at Wellesley, sweat building up on his forehead as he continues to pace around and react to the slightest sound from inside the room. Never in his life has he felt so helpless as he stands here before Wellesley, unable to help his wife in her time of need, the thought of being a father looming over his head. His beloved Margaret is next door screaming out trying to give birth to their child, and all he can do is stand outside and wait. *What parent would ever want to go through this more than once?* he wonders to himself as he takes the hip flask Wellesley offers and takes a nip before handing it back with a nod.

More time passes, then there is another loud scream from Margaret followed by a deafening silence that seems to last forever for Andrew, but in reality, it has barely been a couple of minutes. Suddenly, the air is filled with the sound of a baby screaming its lungs out for the very first time. Andrew looks at Wellesley for what must be the hundredth time in the last hour, his eyes widen, then a smile appears on his face and he waits for the door to open and his first chance to see his child.

Minutes pass before the door handle slowly turns and Anna appears, beaming with a smile to match the one on Andrew's face.

"Margaret invites you to come in and see your child," she says as she holds the door open for Andrew and Wellesley to enter the room. It's at this very moment that Andrew freezes to the spot; he is so numb with excitement and fear that he can barely move his legs. Slowly he starts moving, turns the corner and looks into the room. Margaret is sitting up in the bed covered in sweat, her hair more disheveled than Andrew has ever seen it, while she is looking near exhausted. Yet she glows with a radiance of pride and satisfaction, holding a baby wrapped in a tartan blanket in her arms and looking up at her husband.

"Come, Andrew, come and meet your son."

He staggers toward the bed. "It's a boy, you say?" He moves the covers on his face to take a look at him.

"Say hello to our Henry."

Andrew is trembling as he takes the baby in his arms and looks closely at him. "We have a son, Margaret," he says.

"Yes, I know that, I've just given birth to him, Andrew."

Anna and Beth both burst into laughter, Wellesley is smiling and shaking his head while Andrew is concentrating so hard on his son, he does not realize that what he has said is so funny.

The physician is cleaning his tools and preparing some items on a table. "Margaret, we need to check you and the baby over. Apart from Beth, the others should leave while we see to your needs."

Andrew looks up. "Is anything wrong?"

The physician shakes his head. "Not that I am aware of, my boy, but she has just given birth and we need to do some checks. You will have the rest of your life to watch over them. But for now, I need to do my work, young man, so pass back the baby to Margaret and let us have a little time to assess them both."

Andrew passes the baby back to his wife and kisses her on the forehead. "He is the most beautiful thing I have ever seen Margaret, as for you, no words can ever be enough. I will be just a call away if you need me." Andrew steps back, still staring at his wife and baby. At this moment there could not be a prouder person, his eyes are so full of amazement and admiration for Margaret and his son Henry.

Wellesley, in his typical way, just nods at Margaret and smiles slightly as he passes and helps shuffle Andrew out the door. Anna follows them, she is beaming from ear to ear as she exits the room and closes the door behind her.

"Aww, he is so cute Wellesley," she calls out, and as he turns to look at her, she flickers her eyes at him, "I want one too, will you help me?"

Wellesley turns, shaking his head, and storms past Andrew. "That dammed girl is impossible," he mutters as he goes.

Anna is still laughing loudly when Margaret suddenly bellows, "Anna! Leave the poor man alone, your chance will come in the fullness of time!"

She stops laughing and follows Andrew down the stairs to the lounge. "I will get us some tea," she says and heads toward the kitchen.

Andrew takes an armchair by the fire next to Wellesley. "That be a fine boy you have there, young Andrew, he does both of you proud."

Andrew nods at him. "I am still in shock, it is hard to imagine being a father as I have not done anything yet, all the work has been done by Margaret so far."

"Don't you worry, your work is just about to begin, and I don't envy you, for Margaret and Henry will need a lot of watching over and protecting in the times to come."

"I had a feeling you would say that Wellesley. I just hope I am as good at it as you are, as I feel I still have a lot to learn."

Wellesley sits up and stares at Andrew. "I have no children; Constance and I were never blessed with little ones God rest her soul. We wanted them very much, right up until the day I lost her."

"Margaret often tells me how you and your wife were always around, helping her become the woman she is today."

Wellesley nods his head. "Those were difficult times for Margaret. Lord Ashby, Constance and I swore an oath that day: that we would not let her out of our sights, such was the peril she was born into."

Andrew does not push any harder on Margaret's childhood, as he is just beginning to understand that she has a complex past. "Margaret also explained that from the day you carried Anna from the carriage to her bed in a state of near death, you had been near constant by her side, watched over and protected her as if she was your own. As for Anna, she now watches over you in the same manner, just like a hawk watching its prey. Even I can see that she speaks and teases no other man like she does you, such is the bond and friendship between you both. That girl may not be from your loins and came a little older than most do, but seldom have I seen a closeness between father and daughter as strong as the one you two have."

Wellesley lets out a small "Hunh" and smiles as he thinks back. "I carried her in alright, cold as ice and barely a pulse, cut from the inside out she was, lost a lot of blood and not expected to make the night. But she had grit and fire inside her by God, more than any person I have ever known. That girl just would not let the Reaper take her without a fight. When she finally opened her eyes, I was beside her bed. Pale-green eyes she has, just like Constance. Her first words were to ask about a boy that they had been beaten. Not about herself, but the little boy Billy she had tried to protect at her own peril."

Wellesley is not an emotional man by nature, but Andrew can see by the light of the flickering fire that his eyes are welling up. "The first time I left her side I had vengeance in my heart. If it was not for Lord Ashby, those five men would have not made it past the first night in the holding cells at the docks, for it was him and Olson and near a dozen of the guards that held me and my blade back, pinned in a room until they had been moved out by others and boarded onto a naval ship destined for service at sea." He takes his hip flask from his pocket and pops the lid, takes a small sip, then offers it to Andrew, who politely refuses. Wellesley takes another sip then replaces the lid and puts it back in his hip pocket. "I will let no man harm her again, not while I live and breathe anyway. But do not let that little whippersnapper know how I feel about her, it will do no good her knowing that I have a soft spot for her. She is a handful as it is, without adding fuel to the fire."

Outside the half-opened door to the room is Anna; she has been listening to the conversation while holding a tray with a pot of tea, cups, an assortment of biscuits and a few other items. It was ready so fast as the cook Bunty, was already up and preparing tea while keeping plenty of hot water on the go for Margaret. Tears are running down her face as she hears the words spoken by Wellesley. It comes as no surprise to hear that he feels that way about her as she feels the same about him, for he is the closest person she has to a father now and has done more for her than any man alive.

With the tray getting heavier by the minute and in typical Anna fashion, she pushes the door open and strides in. "I bring tea and a few biscuits and other things courtesy of cook."

Both men stand up as she places the tray between them on a

small side table, then she walks straight up to Wellesley and throws her arms around him and holds him tight with her head on his shoulder. Wellesley is a bit shocked, but slowly puts his arms round her. After a minute or so she leans back and looks into his face. He can see that she has been crying by the shiny tracks down her face reflecting the light. Anna then kisses him on the cheek and tucks her head back into his shoulder.

"That is so you do not feel left out." After a minute she releases him and marches for the door, as she reaches it she turns and speaks again. "Oh, I really do want a baby of my own now, and with no man around I don't suppose you would consider helping me in that department, Well—"

"You little…" Wellesley throws one of the cushions from his chair at her, but she skips out the door, avoiding all contact as she laughs and giggles her way back up the stairs toward Margaret's room.

Andrew looks at Wellesley. "You don't suppose she heard us talking, do you?"

Wellesley sighs heavily. "Yes, I think so, it is what she is good at." He pauses, then takes his seat again. "There will be no living with her now, that's for sure."

Several hours later, the fire has burnt out and Andrew and Wellesley are asleep in their armchairs as Anna returns to the room. She enters quietly and approaches Andrew, shaking his arm gently. As his eyes open, she puts her finger on his lips.

"Shhh, Margaret wishes to see you."

Andrew looks to Wellesley, but he is still asleep. Andrew quietly gets up and leaves the room, while Anna slips into his warm chair, snuggles down and stares at Wellesley for a while. She reaches forward and waves her hand in front of his closed eyes, and when she gets no reaction gently moves the hair from his fringe away from his eyes and pushes up the corner of his mustache.

"What do you want, Anna?" he asks quietly, without opening his eyes or stirring.

Anna jumps and retreats back into her seat. "How did you know I was here?"

"For one, I heard you enter the room. Also, the scent you wear gives you away my dear. After years of living on your wits, you stay alive only by using all your senses, not just your eyes."

Anna is angry at being caught out by Wellesley. "I could have got you if I wanted."

"No, not this time, I had you made from the moment you entered the room young lady," he says calmly while still not moving and keeping his eyes tightly closed.

Anna is still searching for an edge over her rival. "If I was a wrong'un, I would've stabbed you before you were even aware I was in the room with you."

Wellesley sighs heavily. "No, you would not have had the chance. Besides, to do that you would have needed this." He raises his left hand, showing Anna the long, thin blade, she keeps down the side of her dress hem. He flicks it up in the air and catches the blade in his hand before passing it back to her, all the while keeping his eyes closed and his head tucked into a small cushion.

Anna feels down the side of her dress, realizes to her annoyance that she has been disarmed, and huffs in anger, then takes the knife back from Wellesley. "That won't happen again, I'll have another on the other side next time, you see if I don't!"

Wellesley opens his eyes and looks at Anna. "It is not the number of knives you carry Anna, and you are a good and resourceful lady, just not better than me."

Anna thinks for a moment. Of course Wellesley is right, but for a street girl like Anna it is a bitter pill to swallow. She sits in the chair beside him, tucking her legs under her body, and after a moment of looking at the floor and the fireplace she turns and looks at Wellesley. "Why do you put up with me? You don't need me around and you have always had *her* covered when any problem arises." She looks solemnly at the floor as Wellesley sits up in his chair and turns his whole body toward her.

"My dear, I need you now more than ever. We have three people that the whole of this country will depend on to get them out of this terrible state, whether they know it yet or not. The enemy bangs on the door near every day and there is a paid assassin on almost every corner. I have already lost too many people to these men over the years, our last chance is with us right now. I know you heard Andrew and me talking, you would not be Anna if you had not, and I should have known better than to talk about personal things with a partly open door nearby, that was my mistake. But the words spoken are true, you are very much like my Constance. She was completely unstoppable in her dedication to the queen and I know she would have enjoyed meeting you, for you have the same drive and fierce spirit that guides your actions as she had."

Anna looks at Wellesley. "What happened to your wife, if you do not mind me asking?"

Wellesley thinks back to the day it all happened as he shakes his head in regret. "We should have seen it coming. The signs were all there; a last-minute diplomatic meeting with an envoy from a nearby kingdom to discuss trade between our countries. They had the correct paperwork and credentials to represent a noble family we knew well. But the whole group was hiding a secret, a terrible secret that was to change the lives of all of us forever." Wellesley's mind goes back to the events that happened that day.

"The formal dinner had just finished and we were all leaving the dining table for the smoking room to enjoy some brandy and cigars. The conversation with the main negotiator over dinner had been a little vague, but not too out of the ordinary to be suspicious. But enough that I should have dug a little deeper as it was my duty to do so. The queen had said her goodbyes and was taking their very tired daughter to her bedchambers. She was closely followed by my Constance, who was always at her side."

He pauses and stares at the floor for a while as he thinks on what happened that day. "There was no warning and they had to have had inside help because when we entered the room the diplomats split up and moved to different areas and collected swords and knives that had been stashed by someone on the inside. They knew exactly where to find the weapons despite apparently never stepping foot inside the palace before. They were also smart enough not to use pistols, knowing the sound would have carried in the air and attracted more attention and that the bulk of the

King's bodyguards were in the nearby guard room. Besides, the assassins would not want to make much noise if they intended to escape the Palace alive.

"The two guards in the hallway were taken out first, hit from behind with no chance to defend themselves as the assassins blocked the door to prevent help arriving in time. King James and I defended ourselves with just the decorative ceremonial swords we were wearing for show, not combat weapons. Having said that, with the skill we had, we took out two or three of them before the men blocking the door joined the attack. I saw three others breaking off and heading after the queen, but there was no way I could go after them, it was my duty to stay and protect the king."

Wellesley lowers his head in shame as he continues. "They managed to force us apart by just sheer numbers. I watched as a man behind the curtains plunged a sword into the back of the king from the shadows. I managed to slice at the assailant's wrist, cutting him deeply, but I could not get back close enough to finish him off. I fought on and saw the king sustain two more injuries, one to the top of his arm and the other across his hip as he was turning away. But it was when the man behind the curtains fired a pistol shot into him that he finally fell to the ground, mortally wounded.

"I could tell instantly that the man who fired the shot was not part of the group of assassins as they stopped to look round and see who had given them away. Fortunately for me, it was all the distraction I needed, plunging my sword into the man in front of me, right through his heart and out his back. I took the sword from his hand and sliced the throat of the man beside him, then buried it in the neck of the third man, right down to its hilt. Wading through their bodies, I pushed into the man standing over the king who was about to finish him off. I grabbed a fallen sword and sliced across this belly, instantly dropping him to the floor holding his innards in his hands, then thrust the sword through the side of the another, pinning him to a piece of furniture behind him. It was at that moment that the door burst open and the royal guards rushed in, taking on and finished off anyone with the will to fight on. That is all except for the man I had pinned to the furniture with a sword."

Tears start to flow from Wellesley's eyes as he remembers his great friend the king, while Anna has moved to sit on the arm of his chair, listening intently to every word he speaks. "I dropped to my knees beside the King as the life ebbed from his stricken body. His last words to me were, 'Protect my wife and daughter my friend, for alas I can no longer be there for them.' He died as the last word left his lips and another shot rang out. The assassin pinned to the furniture had been shot in the head by the elusive man who had been behind the curtain. He had slipped through the glass door leading into the rose garden in the confusion and had taken the shot using a marble statue for an armrest. While the guards gave chase, I took some of the men to find the queen and Constance. To their credit, they had made it all the way to the princess's bedroom before the fighting had taken place. I presume they were attempting to get to a hidden passageway in the wall, but they didn't quite make it.

"In the doorway to the room was the body of the first man. No doubt Constance had been hiding round the corner of the door and taken him out with a small blade to the throat as he entered the room. There was no sword by him so she must have used it to fight the other two." Wellesley pauses as his lip trembles. He stares blankly through Anna as if she is not even there, to the wall behind her as he continues to recall what he saw that day. "The queen was next, lying over the second man with a dagger in her stomach and a wound to her shoulder. I would think that she took a sword point to the shoulder while running and turned and rushed her attacker with nothing but her bare hands in order to protect her child. The man she was on top of had scratches to his face and a wound to his side through his ribs that would have pierced his heart. Only an expert with a blade could have done that. So, I would presume that he followed the first man into the room, stabbed the queen in the shoulder from behind,. She turned and grabbed for his face taking his dagger to the stomach as she fought with him. Constance would have been at their side and must have been the one to strike the fatal blow with the thrust to his ribs. From there, the fight with the last man must have been a brutal one around the bedposts, as there were several cuts into the woodwork of the posts. The sheets and hanging curtains also had slashes through them and the last assassin was slumped over the bed with a sword still embedded in his chest.

"I found Constance propped up by the side of the bed dying. She had several cuts to her body and left arm, and her right arm was tucked under the bed holding onto a terrified little girl. She never spoke a word, just looked at me as I came to her aid. I had no time to say anything to her, it was like she had held on just long enough for me to get to her and the little princess. I could do nothing but watch and hold her in my arms as the light faded from her eyes and her head fell to one side as she passed away."

As Wellesley sits there motionless he begins to weep, for in the space of a few minutes all those years ago he had lost almost all that were dear to him. As he has done so many times before, he wonders what he could have done differently to save his friends and wife that terrible day.

Anna moves to kneel on the floor in front of him and takes his hands in hers. Tears are rolling down her face, as if a tap had been turned on. She was feeling the loss as much as Wellesley himself just from the words he has spoken. She comforts the man who has become so important to her as he mourns the loss of his beloved wife and the reigning monarchy. He had sworn an oath to protect them all, but on this occasion he had been undone. Even now it is a painful memory for him, to know that he failed in his duty as a soldier and worse, to have lived on when all around him had lost their lives. It does not matter to him that the odds were overwhelmingly against him, and that he had fought like a man possessed, defeating many of the assassins. Inside help, betrayal and pre-planted weapons had given the assailants a distinct advantage. But Wellesley is too proud to use that as an excuse. In his eyes he had failed in his duty and the cost of his failure had been the death of the King and Queen along with his wife Constance.

Anna is wise beyond her years, having survived as a girl on the streets for most of her life and lived through a terrible ordeal herself. She does not speak a word, just waits and allows Wellesley to come to terms with what he has told her. For a while, time seems to have no meaning to the pair of them, they both just remain in the positions they are in waiting for the silence to be broken.

"Did you ever find the man who betrayed the king and queen and shot the prisoner?" Anna finally asks.

It takes a while for Wellesley to answer as he continues to stare blankly through Anna. "No, but I am sure I know who it is, and, when the day comes, I have a special gift for him. One that will allow him to remember and reflect on what he did for a while before death takes him."

Anna leans forward and holds onto his arm and shoulder to comfort him. "Oh, my dear Wellesley, if ever you need my help in any way, you only need to ask and I will be ready."

Finally, Wellesley moves. He looks at Anna and raises his hand onto the back of her head. "My dear child, you already have. That day I brought you into the palace I asked God to let you live, it is the first time I have ever asked for anything from anyone since my wife died." Anna looks up into his gaze as he continues. "I do not know if it was God answering or your fight and sheer will to survive and I do not care, all I know is that you pulled through and are here today. You and that little princess from all those years ago give me a purpose to keep going. I have managed to stay the course and fight on despite often wishing to the contrary. In time there will be a day when this country takes back its soul from those that have sought to take it for themselves. Until then, you and I must protect those that will put most on the line, defend them from harm, and keep them safe while they prepare for that day. For mark my words, it will come, and, when it does, we will all have our revenge."

* * *

While Anna and Wellesley have been talking about the past

downstairs, Andrew has entered the room with Margaret and his son. She is now sitting upright, her hair returned to perfect order, and her face is glowing with pride and even a small smile as she sees her husband approach her. Their son is tucked in a pale-blue blanket and resting on the bed beside her with her arm around him. Quietness fills the air as they are alone for the first time in a while.

"Come my dear, sit by my side and say hello to your son again, for we have missed you these past few hours." Andrew approaches them, chest bursting with pride. He leans over his wife to tenderly kiss her on the lips before taking her spare hand in his.

"I never thought I could share you with another man, but when I look at our boy, it would seem that I was wrong," she says as he sits down beside her, looking at his son with doting eyes. "He is so tiny."

"Ha, at nearly nine pounds, he is hardly a tiny baby, my dear."

Andrew beams at her with an admiration that only a husband and father could have for a woman that has brought their first child into the world. "I do not know what to say, I don't have the words or the tongue to say what I feel. I'm just numb and in a world of my own."

Margaret looks at him. "You do not need to say anything, my dear, your expression and the pride I can see in your eyes tells me all I need to know. With so much going on, this was always going to be a massive challenge for the both of us. I can only do what I need to do because I know you will always be by our son's side."

Andrew laughs. "I'm not sure about that, I will always be here, but Anna is already broody. She has been baiting Wellesley again for his services. I fear that man has met his match in her. Besides, I think she will be watching our child like a cat with a mouse. Whatever the outcome, I feel we have the best of people around us."

Margaret chuckles. "That girl has changed him in so many ways, all of them for the better, I might add. He has lost and given up so much in his life in the service of the crown. It is good to see Wellesley have someone else in his life to give it some purpose and meaning. Don't get me wrong, I know she is a handful, but she brings so much good with her. Anna's heart is always in the right place, along with her ears and eyes and anything else she can use to watch over me."

They are interrupted by a knock at the door. Andrew looks at Margaret before getting up and opening the door, allowing Beth in with a tray of soup and bread.

"I thought you might like some food, Margaret." She turns to Andrew. "I have an extra bowl for you as well, sir, just in case you wanted some."

Andrew steps forward. "Beth," he says as he puts his hands out to take the tray from her, "thank you very much. I will take it from here, for today is the day my wife gave birth to our son. For the next eight hours I wish to be alone with my wife and child. Rest assured we will call if we need assistance with anything, but, if not, I will shoot the next person who knocks on that door. Please don't take it the wrong way, for I am very, very grateful to you all for everything you have done, but as the man of this house…" He turns to look at a sniggering Margaret, watching him from the comfort of her bed. "I have decided we need a little personal time to enjoy the moment."

Beth is taken back and unnerved by Andrew's forceful but polite words. She swiftly leaves the room, closing the door behind her without looking back.

"That was a little strong, Andrew. Strong, but right, I must admit that I am a little tired of being poked and prodded about, especially with how tender parts of me feel. As you have so finely put it, I have all I need now right here in this room, the rest can wait until we are ready to face them all again tomorrow."

Andrew moves back toward the bed and sits down by his wife, then lovingly at his son's face. Margaret reaches for his hand and clasps it in hers. "I still cannot believe we have a son, Marge, he is just so beautiful."

"You have not used that name with me in an age, my dear."

Andrew kisses her hand and looks at his beloved wife. "It was the name I first knew you by. Around the others Margaret always feels more appropriate, but to me Marge seems somehow softer for us away from prying eyes."

They both look round as they hear a chair being dragged down the corridor and placed beside the door to the room. Andrew gets up to investigate, but Margaret holds onto his hand.

"No, my dear," she says kindly, "They are outside and have kept their word. Besides, that can only be Anna, for Wellesley would not make a sound. Do you want to feel the wrath of that young girl? I feel she will give you back more than what you give her." Margaret raises an eyebrow at Andrew before continuing. "Remember what she does to Wellesley on a daily basis." She can see the fear dawn in Andrew's face.

"Yes, yes, my dear, you are quite right. We should not dismiss those that only wish us well." He then whispers quietly to Margaret, "She can stay outside in the hall, but if she knocks on the door I will give her a piece of my mind, you see if I don't."

Margaret's rolls her eyes at him before staring sternly. "Really, so why are you whispering? You men are all alike, you all fear a strong woman who fights back or an opinion that is not of your own making."

Andrew lets out a false laugh. "Ha, that is so not true, I am just speaking quietly because, well because…you are resting, my dear, and I wanted you to be calm and relaxed."

"Well, why don't you come the other side of me and lay on the bed next to me, that way I can relax and get some sleep before this little one needs feeding again."

Andrew smiles at her. "You are of course right. Perhaps she can be a little intimidating but look who she has for a mentor and teacher. You are no pushover Margaret, even the soldiers take instructions from you more than their officers when in battle, and that I have seen with my own eyes, so do not dare say it is not so."

Margaret smiles at her husband. "Those soldiers don't need my instructions, they are the queen's own grenadiers, the best this country has. They enjoy the banter with me, for I have known most of the men many years and spoken to a great number, if not all on different occasions in the past. You would have seen many of them yourself when you were visiting Stoneheart Manor before our wedding." Margaret chuckles to herself, and it makes Andrew curious.

"Why do you laugh, my dear?"

She looks at him with loving eyes. "I was thinking back to the time Anna went to the Manor for some training. Wellesley thought it might help her build up her skills in protecting the Queen and myself if she was taught some combat training."

Andrew looks at her with a shocked expression. "Anna! She trained at Stoneheart Manor?"

Margaret lets out a chuckle. "Oh yes, she made quite an impression in fact. For Staff Sergeant Hansen, the hand-to-hand combat instructor, it was a life-changing experience."

Andrew looks at her suspiciously. "Why, what did she do?"

Margaret tries to give the innocent butter-would-not-melt-in-her-mouth expression. "It is only a rumor mind, and Wellesley and Anna will not talk about it with me or each other, but the training for Anna was very physical and intense. You know what she is like, never able to give up and refusing to be beaten. Well in the combat arena she was thrown around and worked very hard, but no matter how hard they forced her to submit, she would not yield, and at one point she actually passed out under the pressure of a chokehold from the big sergeant. When she came around he was laughing at her, a bad thing to do to Anna at any time, but worse to do it in front of other cadets."

She hesitates a moment, thinking of the right words to say before continuing. "Well, the last morning before the passing-out ceremony for the cadets on the parade ground, the barracks awoke to the sight of a bed in the middle of the square by the flag. Tied to the bed quite firmly was the sergeant, not a stitch of uniform on, bare as our little man here was born, and clamped to his bits was his own sword held firm by a piece of wire. The blade was starting to cut in under its own weight and the pressure being applied by the wire. It took a skilled physician and two others to remove the weapon without further damage. Nobody knows how he got there or who did it to him and he refuses to speak about it to this very day. What I do know is that when that man entered a room later that day and saw Anna inside, fear shook him to his very boots and he left without speaking a word."

"She has always been a very resourceful girl, but to train her for combat, is that not a little extreme, my dear?" Andrew asks.

Margaret is quiet for a while, thinking about the past. "A long time ago, in the royal palace, a group of men got into the building under false pretenses. They attacked the king, queen and their daughter just after they had dined together in an act of utter betrayal. The fighting was said to be savage and unyielding. Wellesley defended the king's honor and body long after he had fallen, while his wife, Constance, gave her life in the defense of the queen and her daughter. She could not save the queen, but her last act was holding onto the young girl just long enough for help to arrive. No woman had ever fought so valiantly and with such courage as she did that day. Struck and wounded many times, she refused to give in until the fight was over and the aggressors laid strewn at her feet. Our young Anna is so much like Constance was, determined, cunning and resourceful beyond her years."

She turns to look at Andrew. "Wellesley felt that Anna needed training, I do not question his judgment, for he knows people and what they are capable of more than any person alive. I am only here today because of his ability to keep me safe in the early days. But I will ask you this, my dear, in these troubled times, who would you sooner look after our child while we do our duties and requirements to the crown, Anna or a group of soldiers on guard around the house?"

Andrew does not hesitate to respond. "Anna, without doubt Anna, but can she handle the pressure of serving the queen, you and watching over our child while you are away in the months ahead, my dear?"

Margaret thinks. "The queen cannot have us both, Andrew. If she requires me, Anna stays with you and Wellesley comes with me. I will not risk our son with anyone outside of the people who have seen him today, otherwise be dammed to her."

It is the first time Andrew has ever heard Margaret put someone before the queen. Not that he is complaining, for as he looks at their son again, he realizes that the boy is the most beautiful thing he has ever seen. Margaret turns her body, then gently lifts the baby and places him between the two of them.

"I would say I have an hour before he will wake up and want feeding. Let's take this moment while we can, my dear, and get a little sleep." She looks at her husband, who is staring at their son. The smile on his face makes her grin with pride as they settle down for a brief period of peace and quiet before the little one wakes.

CHAPTER 10

Organizing

From the moment young Henry is born, he becomes the center of attention for all the people around him. It is hard to keep his presence in the house a secret from all the visitors and people working in the war room as he bellows like a bull when he wants feeding or requires attention. But with only known and trusted people allowed on the grounds, Margaret and Andrew are comfortable that they have the best possible security, while still having a functioning house.

Over the next few weeks, the household gets into a well-regulated routine. To keep everything running on an even keel the entire inner group have duties to attend and complete before more people arrive. First thing in the morning, Wellesley walks the grounds and ensures he knows every guard and person who is in or around the estate. Beth and Anna check every room of the house, take charge of checking all deliveries and look after the baby for a couple of hours each morning to allow Margaret and Andrew time to get dressed, eat, and plan the day out.

Today starts just like any other day. Margaret has finished feeding young Henry and passes him to Andrew to burp while she tucks herself back in.

"My God, Andrew, if these get any bigger they will explode," she says as she struggles to tuck her breasts inside her dress. "As for all the milk, I seem to have enough to feed a dozen little ones, not just the one we have. Why does it have to keep leaking out when I squeeze them into my clothes? It just shoots out everywhere, like from a cow's udder."

Andrew chuckles as he watches his wife struggle with her ample proportions, and as she looks up at him he raises an eyebrow and gives her a seductive look. "You can wipe that smile off your face, my dear, you've got no chance there. One pair of lips sucking on me is more than enough, well for now, anyway," she says with a smile on her face and love in her heart. "I will just have to get Beth to adjust the fit for a few weeks and wear darker-colored clothes to hide the stains." She finishes dressing herself, walks over to her husband and kisses him gently on the lips before reclaiming her son from Andrew's grasp. Rocking him in her arms, she walks over to the window and looks out over the garden and river beyond. "Well, my young man, I think it is time we call in your nanny so Mummy and Daddy can get some food for ourselves."

She turns her son to look admiringly into his face, the grin on her face growing wider as the baby fidgets and creates little bubbles of saliva at the sides of his mouth. Andrew goes and stands close behind Margaret, puts his hands gently around her waist and kisses her neck and the bottom of her ear. Margaret leans back into the comfort of her man with a smile on her face, allowing Andrew to access more skin. "My dear, I do not think I have ever been happier than I feel at this moment in time. A beautiful son, loving husband, and good friends around me." She then sighs heavily. "I look forward to the day that this feeling I have is the normal every day for me and everyone in the land, but I fear the road to this will be difficult and paved with many obstacles to overcome before we get there."

Andrew gently gives his wife a little squeeze. "You have helped the queen get this far, I see no reason why you will not be able to see it through to the end, my dear. Besides, it needs to be over sooner rather than later as our son and I will need more of your time going forward as a family."

Margaret turns to face her husband. "As always, you never stop me doing what you know I must do; just encourage and support me. The things I need most to hear, you say without hesitation when most partners would fear to talk about it." She kisses him on the lips. "When this is over, I promise you, we will have a good life together free of tyranny and oppression."

Andrew smiles at her. "Whatever makes you think that that I am not enjoying our life as it is? There may be many changes and differences that are new to me, but one thing is for certain, I've done things, seen things, and had adventures that a few years ago would not have even been a possibility in my life." He chuckles as he kisses her on the forehead. "Come, in the words of somebody I know well, 'I'm hungry, let's eat.'"

With wide eyes and a big smile, Margaret pinches his side with her spare hand. "I know who you are talking about, and I resent that. I was eating for two and now I feel I am eating to feed several the way I'm producing milk."

"Don't say that near the cook or she will start milking you for ingredients for her baking!" Both Margaret and Andrew laugh as they head toward the hallway. Andrew opens the door for his wife and son, and, as Margaret steps through, Beth stands up from the chair in the hallway and comes to take Henry from her.

"He has just been fed and burped after he slept for a whole three hours this morning," Margaret comments as she passes Henry to Beth.

"Hello, little man, asleep for a full three hours, that must be a record for you," she says to young Henry.

"I will eat, review the day's needs and be back in an hour or so, Beth," Margaret says as she heads along the hallway to the stairs. Andrew kisses his son on the head and puts his hand on Beth's shoulder.

"She slept a little better last night, and this morning she was like her old self for the first time in a while."

Beth nods at him. "That's good to hear, I was beginning to worry that she was stretched too far and would break down."

"She knows that we all have her best interests at heart, it is just getting her to listen that is the problem. Still, we are winning at the moment, let's hope we can keep it this way," he replies.

Andrew leaves Henry in the capable hands of Beth and follows Margaret down the stairs and into the dining room, where they take their seats around the table and are served tea by the young maid, Maggie, who assists Bunty in the kitchen. Anna is already at the table tucking into her favorite, a plate full of sausages and crispy bacon.

Margaret looks at her and smiles as she shakes her head. "You eat like a horse yet remain as skinny as a rake, my dear Anna. Oh for the chance to be young again."

"It's all that running around the old man makes me do. Always got me doing something, he can be quite a meanie when he wants to be."

"Meanie, is that way you think of me, you young whippersnapper? I need to keep you working to stop you getting into trouble, young lady!" bellows Wellesley from the doorway before entering the room and taking the seat beside Anna.

Anna looks at Margaret. "Where is little Henry?"

"He is upstairs with Beth; he had just been fed and will be asleep for an hour or so before he wakes again."

"Aw, I was looking forward to seeing him." Anna turns to look at Wellesley. "He is so cute; I still want one of my own."

Wellesley sighs heavily as Anna flutters her eyes at him. "Not again, you say this to me every morning and I say the same thing back every time. The world cannot handle another Anna, one is enough in any country." As he finishes speaking, the maid places a plate in front of him containing a large piece of smoked haddock with a poached egg on the top. It takes but a few seconds for the smell to reach Anna's nostrils.

"Oh my God, that smells like wet sheep," she complains loudly.

"Wet sheep! I will have you know that this is finest smoked haddock and I always have it on Fridays."

Anna sneers at him. "It gives you old man's breath all day." Margaret and Andrew burst into laughter as Wellesley looks at her, shaking his head. "Your breath smells all day, and I don't like it, how am I supposed to work on having a baby with you when you smell like that? It makes me feel ill."

Wellesley smiles at her. "If it keeps you away from me, I will have smoked haddock every day." He pauses for a moment. "Every day for life, my girl."

Both Margaret and Andrew are still laughing when their

breakfasts arrive. As the maid places the plates before them, Anna can see they have grilled smoked kippers. The smell of them adds to the already strong odor of haddock and Anna puts her thumb and finger over her nose and squeezes to block the smell.

Wellesley looks at Anna with a mouth full of fish. "Are you sure you do not want some before we go upstairs and make a baby together?"

Anna looks at him in disgust, stands up and grabs her plate with her other hand and heads off into the kitchen, still holding her nose. Margaret and Andrew are roaring with laugher as Wellesley starts to chuckle, proud of getting one over on Anna.

"You know she is going to get you back at some stage today, Wellesley," Margaret says as she debones one of her fish.

He smiles at her. "Oh yes, I know she will be coming back with a vengeance, but for now I will enjoy the sweet taste of success and finish this piece of fish in peace and quiet."

Not five minutes has passed when Anna reappears from the kitchen. She has a thin strip of cloth wrapped around her head, covering her nose to prevent her smelling the fish. She sits back down at the table next to Wellesley and places her plate down in front of her and starts to eat. Wellesley turns to look at her and notices that she has added more bacon and sausages to her plate. "That is a lot of food for a petite lady to eat in one sitting, Anna."

She looks back at him, nodding her head. "Yeah, it is," she says, stabbing one of the sausages with a fork and raising it from the plate to look at it. "I need to build up my strength and energy for later as I'm going to need a lot of it."

Wellesley looks at her curiously. "And what are you doing later that will need all that energy?"

Anna looks away from her sausage to face Wellesley. "Why, to be with you, silly. As you said earlier, after we have finished breakfast we are going upstairs to make us a baby. I can see us grinding away for at least three or four hours, maybe more as I want to make sure of a good job, so get eating and build up your energy levels, old boy, you're going to need them."

Andrew and Margaret are barely able to contain themselves

as Anna speaks; both are desperately trying not to laugh and struggling to stay composed as she continues.

"I'm already feeling hot and excited about what is to come, but also worried you may not be able to stay the course or fade out during the performance, because if I am not fully satisfied…" She slowly shows her teeth and moves them over the end of the sausage, suddenly snapping her teeth down hard and severing the sausage in two. She swallows the piece in her mouth with a single gulp. "I can get a little feisty if I do not get what I need and feel anything less than content and fully satisfied with the performance."

The cutlery drops from Wellesley's hands as he turns to look at Margaret and Andrew in a desperate plea for help. Margaret bursts into laughter first, closely followed by Andrew. Anna starts to smile and chuckle herself, and, as for Wellesley, he slowly lowers his head into his hands and covers his eyes.

"Oh God, when will the suffering end?" he says as the others continue to laugh out loud. Anna turns and hugs the broken Wellesley with both arms, then she kisses him on his exposed cheek.

"It's only cos I luv ya that I tease you this way, my beloved big bear." She shakes his whole body before retaking her seat and continuing to eat her breakfast.

After a few minutes hiding, Wellesley slowly looks up from his hands. "Somewhere out there in the vast lands of this country is a man mad enough to love this woman and take her off my hands. Please, if you can hear me, hurry up. I will pay anything for you to get here quicker and whisk her away."

Anna looks at him with wide eyes. "Big bear, I will never leave you. If I should marry, we will still be living with you forever, for I cannot leave you to fend for yourself, not at your age," she replies to the poor, broken Wellesley.

"Three campaigns, six great battles and many skirmishes I have had over the years and survived them all. I have injured and broken most areas of my body at one time or another, once I crawled for days through a forest with a sword through my leg. None of this prepared me for the day I carried this girl from the coach to the palace and the torment I was to endure in the years to follow." He raises his hands and eyes to the sky above. "What have I done to deserve this, O Lord, I am but a peaceable man."

"Poppycock Wellesley," Margaret says. "I have been told many a tale of your escapades in the past by my father and a good few other people, some of which would make Anna's toes curl up. I remember one story about a barn in the Black Forest th—"

"That's quite enough, Ma'am. Anna does not need to know past deeds; they were difficult times and we had to adapt to difficult situations to survive."

Anna's face lights up. "I do, I do, I need to know of Wellesley's past, please tell me these stories, please, please, please!"

Margaret looks at Anna. "I think you have had your fun, young lady. It is time to get the war room ready, we have a couple of gentlemen scholars arriving soon and we need to be prepared for them."

Anna looks at Margaret with a sad face. "But what about Big Bear, can he come with me to the empty room upstairs? I don't know if it has been checked for strangers this morning and I might be in danger." Her sad face transforms into a wicked smirk as she turns to look at the stressed expression on Wellesley's face. "Just me and you alone in that room, Big Bear, we could, you know, get it going a little and work on my needs at the same time."

"No, he has other things to be getting on with. Besides, no matter what you think, I doubt you could handle him, for there is more to that man than you realize, my dear," says Margaret swiftly.

Anna looks at Wellesley again. "Are you hiding things from me, Wellesley? What secrets do you have that I ne—"

"Anna. Go," commands Margaret in a stern voice. Anna is up like a shot, grabbing her plate and giving Wellesley another peck on the cheek as she skips off toward the stairs and out of sight. Wellesley goes to speak, but Margaret stops him. "Don't say a word, I already know what you are going to ask and you will regret it later. You know she is the best thing to enter your life in many a year. Anna may be a little hard work sometimes, but she has been through a lot in her short life, she knows without you she would not be here today. That girl loves you like a father and needs you to keep herself going, just like another little girl all those years ago. As they get older, they go through troubled times, but they still need you, it's called growing up and finding your place in society. Do not give up on her now when she needs you most."

Wellesley sighs heavily and nods. "I know. I think I will go into the village and check for any strangers."

"Good idea, and while you are there you can give the garrison staying at the farm new instructions for the week."

Wellesley looks up at her with a surprised look on his face. "How on ear—"

"I have my sources and they are far better than you give me credit for. Now go before I decide to have words with you and Lord Ashby over the arrangements we had."

He dips his head at Margaret before getting up from the table and leaving the room.

Margaret turns to Andrew. "Would you take me for a walk around the garden, my dear? Today is going to be one of those days when I will have little time for us later, so let us make the best of it now while we have a moment to ourselves."

Andrew is up swiftly to pull the chair from behind Margaret as she stands up and together they head out to the garden. They walk slowly along the river's edge, arm in arm talking constantly, then make a couple of circuits of the garden. On the second circuit Andrew notices movement behind one of the large oak trees at the far end of the garden. He discreetly watches the area and spots a head peer round the trunk of the tree and then slip back out of sight. Andrew instantly does as Wellesley has trained him to do and puts himself between Margaret and the possible threat without her realizing. He edges her toward the house, still talking and laughing, and notices Wellesley about to mount his horse. Catching Wellesley's eye, Andrew gives him the signal for danger and follows with a discreet change of direction to maneuver Margaret towards the house.

Wellesley checks his horse's girth and walks round the far side as if to adjust the straps holding the saddle. As he looks round and forms a plan of action in his mind, he looks up to someone at the side of the house while keeping out of sight of the direction Andrew had highlighted. Not more than thirty seconds have passed when Anna comes round to the back of the building, steps into the kitchen doorway for a moment, then turns and walks towards Andrew and Margaret with a smile on her face as she speaks.

"Those men you have been waiting for have just arrived and would like to see you Margaret." As Margaret looks up at Anna to answer, Anna passes something to Andrew in a sleight of hand move, as she turns and walks with Margaret towards the house. At the same time, Wellesley leads his horse around the far side of the stable block.

Andrew slows his pace, dropping back from Margaret and Anna, as he cocks the hammer on the pistol Anna handed him before turning and walking toward the intruder. At the same time Wellesley appears from behind the outbuildings of the stable yard at a gallop, sword drawn, and in full cavalry charge. It is a magnificent sight as he is out of the saddle, leaning forward, his sword pointed forward ready to take on any threat.

Two men come running out from behind the trees, one with his rifle drawn and aiming as they move forward. Anna shields Margaret, pulling her to the ground behind Andrew. Andrew knows he must face the men full on and hope the man's movement reduces the accuracy of the shot. The intruder fires the rifle with a flash of powder smoke, and red flame, along with a loud bang. Andrew judders, but stands his ground as the rifleman starts to reload his weapon. The other assailant, with two pistols in his hands, continues his sprint toward Andrew, screaming loudly as he charges.

Margaret, now aware of what is happening, watches helplessly as Andrew stands between them and her and raises his pistol at the man as he closes in, he controls his breathing, and squeezes the trigger, firing at the first assailant. His shot strikes him in the chest, and the assassin continues to stagger forward a few paces before falling to the ground, blood instantly beginning to drain from his body.

Andrew looks up as he hears the click of the hammer being

pulled back and the pan being primed by the rifleman. He has no way of reloading his pistol, so he looks back at Margaret, smiles at her, then turns to face the gunman once more. As he begins to raise his rifle to aim at Andrew, the assassin is aware of the rider charging him but has misjudged how fast Wellesley is traveling. As the man's weapon lines up to his eye to aim Wellesley strikes down with the fatal blow, slicing through the man's shoulder and chest with a precise, clean cut. The rifleman holds his position for a moment as Wellesley turns his horse and races toward Margaret and Anna, knowing the damage has been done. As he dismounts, the assailant drops to the floor behind him, firing the weapon into the ground.

"Are you hurt, Ma'am?" he asks as she gets back to her feet.

"I am fine, but who are they and how did they find us? This was supposed to be a secure location," she comments angrily.

"I will deal with that later, Margaret," He turns to Anna. "You did well, Anna, really well, now get Margaret into the house, quickly." Wellesley turns to look at Andrew, who has not yet moved, notices something is wrong and turns back to Anna. "Go, go now, for there may be more still around."

Anna knows by his tone of voice that something is wrong but doesn't show it, she takes Margaret by the arm and escorts her towards the house as Wellesley walks his horse in the direction of the stationary Andrew. "You remembered the signals well. Not only that, but it was also a good shot, you stood your ground valiantly, my lad, saved Margaret's life, of that I am sure."

Andrew grimaces a smile as a tear begins to roll down his cheek then begins to wobble and leans into Wellesley's arms. "I did not think I would be able to shoot another man, but when I saw my wife in danger I just reacted. She cannot see us, can she, for I cannot stand any longer and I, I, I don…" He goes limp and slumps in Wellesley's arms.

Wellesley releases the reins to his horse so he has a free hand to undo Andrew's jacket. He looks and feels around to see where he has been hit and finds a lot of blood both front and back of his body, staining his shirt heavily.

"You've been hit between your bottom rib and your hip. It has gone through and out the other side, but it is in a thick part of your body and will need some work, my friend. I am going to gently lower you to the ground, so lean on me and I will take your weight." As Wellesley lays him down, he continues to speak to his friend. "Come on my boy, work with me, I do not wish to face Margaret alone for she is going to have the skin off my back for this one, of that I am sure."

While all this has been going on, the guards have arrived at pace from various areas of the grounds. One has taken hold of the loose horse and is leading it away while the others investigate the bodies of the assassins and the fallen soldier they had killed near the small boat used to get ashore.

Margaret has reached the door to the kitchen, but as she enters the doorway she turns to look back just as Wellesley lays Andrew on the ground. "Oh God, no! Andrew!" she yells, pushing Anna out of the way and rushing back to his side. She kneels next to him and looks at his wound. "Andrew, my love, why did you not say anything?" she yells, then glares up at Wellesley. "Anna, go get the physician," she barks out without looking up.

Anna has already anticipated what is required and left on her own initiative to get him and ask Bunty to get water on the stove and honey in a small pan on the heat as she moves through the kitchen.

Wellesley organizes the guards to help him move Andrew to the house, as they gently lift him up, Margaret snaps at them, "Let's hope they can do a better job of lifting him up than they did protecting us, or God help me, I will make them suffer."

Within minutes Andrew is in the house and being placed on the cleared table in the kitchen. The physician has arrived and wastes no time in looking at the wound with Margaret and Anna by his side, assisting where they can.

Outside, Wellesley is barking orders at the soldiers on duty, trying to work out how they managed to get so close to Margaret without them knowing. "Go to the farm and get all six cavalrymen back here now." He points at two of the men. "Find out where they got the boat and launched from. Check if it came from the far bank upstream somewhere, as it would be too difficult to row against the current. They usually work in threes or fours, so look for people with extra horses along the river's edge and bring them to me alive. If they are killed, don't come back, for I swear to God you will join the fate of these two men lying before you." The guards look at each other with shock in their eyes. It is the first time Wellesley has ever spoken to them like that. "Do you know how close they came to getting her? If it was not for Andrew, our lady would be dead. As it is, he has been wounded severely, now move like you have a purpose and get me some answers."

Wellesley leaves his soldiers and joins the others inside to see how Andrew is doing. He cannot find the words for his own shame and disappointment that these men got past him and nearly succeeded in their objective. As he approaches Andrew, the physician and Margaret are cutting away the clothing around the wound and cleaning away the blood with hot, wet strips of cloth.

"This will have to be cleaned out right through to both sides, and cauterized at both ends," the physician says to Margaret.

She thinks for a moment. "Let us get on with it while he is unconscious, with a bit of luck we can get it done before he comes around and without using laudanum. We can use that later to relieve the pain as I am sure it will be needed."

"This is no easy operation, Margaret," the physician warns. "It's risky and very dangerous, a lot could be damaged that we do not know about on the inside, even the shock of what we are about to do could finish him off."

Margaret looks at him. "Listen to me. That man has a baby son upstairs barely two weeks' old. I know the mettle of this man, he will fight and he will get through this. Now, let us get it done while the wound is fresh." She looks around the room at everybody present, pausing for a moment. "Everybody but Anna out of here. Wellesley, go do what you have to do, we will be fine here. I need you to find out who ordered this and only return when you have the answer."

The room clears in a matter of moments, leaving the physician to work on Andrew. Beth has gone upstairs to check on Henry, while Wellesley leaves and walks briskly down to the yard to mount his horse. As he does so, the six soldiers from the farm arrive at a gallop fully armed. As they pull up abruptly, he looks at the soldiers with steely eyes.

"Follow me, men, we have some assassins to find and not a lot of time to do it before they disappear into the hole they came from." Wellesley turns his horse and kicks it into a canter as they head along the road that follows the river upstream. It is not long before they are out of sight of the house and heading through the woods that takes them to the farms and outbuildings on the outskirts of the village.

An hour has passed since the attack, Margaret and the physician have completed the invasive work on Andrew. They have done all they can for now and Anna and the physician are just finishing off the bandages that wrap around his torso and preparing to move him to a bed upstairs. Margaret has tears in her eyes as she watches them cut off the loose threads on the bandages. With one last look she turns and washes her hands and arms before heading upstairs to see and feed Henry. The last thing Margaret wants to do is leave her husband's side, but the baby needs feeding.

A few minutes later, as Margaret is feeding young Henry, the physician knocks on the door.

"Come in," she says in a calm, quiet voice.

The old man enters the room and looks at Margaret. "I thought I had better give you my assessment of Andrew. I am not sure if the bullet has bruised or damaged the edge of his liver or kidney; the signs are good as the blood was not too dark and no other liquids were leaking into the wound, but only time will tell. If it has, we may have another problem to overcome and that may be a bigger threat to his life. In the next day or so we will have our answer either way."

Margaret nods at him. "Thank you, my old friend, I cannot

express how grateful I am that you decided to stay around for a few weeks to keep an eye on my son and me, for had you not been here I doubt my husband would have survived."

He smiles at her. "How could I not stay and see the girl I delivered become the woman you are today with a child of her own? As for that husband of yours, I hear he stood his ground to protect you. That takes some courage, I think you have chosen wisely with him, my lady."

"I did not think it would ever happen, not with all that I must endure, but I found a man I love dearly and he loves me. Despite all that I have put him through and the duties I must entertain, he has never once not been there for me, or prevented me from attending my duties to the crown and country. Now he lays terribly wounded having defended me with his life"

The physician frowns slightly. "You do know at some stage you will ha—"

"Yes," Margaret interrupts, "I know what you are about to say, I think it at least once a day, if not more, but the time is not right yet. There are far too many things in a state of flux to worry about myself at the moment, but thank you for your counsel, it is nice to know you are thinking of me." Henry finishes his feed and Margaret tries to hold him and tuck herself back in at the same time, a difficult task until the physician steps in to hold Henry.

As the physician holds Henry, she calls out for Beth. Within minutes the door opens and she enters the room, nodding at her old friend the doctor as she passes him.

"He has just been fed and I am going to be with Andrew for a while, look after him and put him down for a nap once he has finished belching, when he wakes, please bring him through to me in our room and I will feed him there." Beth nods in acknowledgement as Margaret moves toward the door. "Would you mind checking on Andrew with me before you go for a smoke, Herbert, it would help to ease my mind a little."

"Of course, Margaret, we would not want anything to happen to our hero now, would we?" he says as they leave the room.

*** * ***

Several miles away, Wellesley and his cavalrymen have just finished checking the last farm on the river's edge. They have found nothing out of the ordinary and frustration is beginning to build up amid the group.

"Nothing. Every building checked, every farmer, their families and workers all spoken to and not a thing. Where the hell have they come from? There must be a base camp somewhere in this area," barks Wellesley to his men, kicking out at a tree stump in frustration. He thinks for a moment, then speaks again. "Jenkins, take O'Sullivan and continue along to the next village and look around. Check the taverns and see if any strangers have been seen in the area. I will take the others, cross the bridge and ride along the riverbank on the far side all the way back to the house." Both men salute Wellesley before flicking the reins and turning their horses and, with a kick of their spurs, they head off toward the next village, a few miles away.

Wellesley leads the other four along the water's edge, sometimes along the bank and other times in the water to go around trees or other obstacles. It is in one of these areas, where the horsemen are walking in two feet of water and the men have a low silhouette behind the riverbank, that Wellesley hears the whinnying of a horse and faint voices traveling on the light breeze. He signals his men to stop behind the scrub willows they are just passing.

"Wait here," he commands before moving his horse forward enough so he can see through the thinning branches. As his eyes focus on the encampment he can see six horses tied up to a wooden rail between two trees. Two men are sitting around a fire warming their hands while a third is sitting on a rock at the water's edge with a rifle across his lap.

Inching his horse backward, Wellesley speaks to his men. "There are two men sitting by a fire, their weapons are leaning up against a tree some six or seven yards behind them. A third is sitting on a rock by the water, armed with a rifle. You four go back around twenty yards and come through the woods at them. Walk until you are as close as possible, then charge at the gallop once they have spotted you, the ground looks flat all the way to them from the edge of the tree line. I want them alive, so butt them with your horses if you can, try to push them toward the river; that way we will have them trapped. The one with the rifle is too much of a risk, so I will shoot him the moment he spots you charging in, we should get all the information we need from the other two."

As the four horsemen move back, Wellesley slides off his mount into the water. He ties his horse to one of the branches and takes his long rifle from its sleeve on the side of the saddle. Filling the barrel with a charge of powder from his flask, he takes one of his musket balls and wraps it in a small piece of silk, then rams it down tight on the powder in the barrel. He slowly moves along the bank to get to a position with a clear view of his target. He cocks back the hammer and pours some powder onto the pan ready to fire, aims down the sights of the rifle at the man on the rock, and waits.

It is not long before he can see the three men looking round and getting to their feet as his troops can be heard charging the last fifty or so meters. Wellesley waits for the man with the rifle to aim his weapon, as only then will he be motionless for a moment. As he does, with a thunderous crack, a puff of smoke and a small flame exiting the barrel, Wellesley fires his long rifle, hitting the man on the side of his head. He staggers for a second, then falls from the rock to the floor.

The other two men first move toward their guns, but stop and look around when they hear the shot ring out and watch as their comrade drops. Realizing that they would not make it to their weapons, they turn to run toward their horses just as the cavalrymen enter the camp. Both men are bounced off the chest and necks of the charging horses, spilling them across the floor with the impact. As they get back up, one man draws his pistol and aims at the lead rider, only to be struck down by the saber of one of the other men behind him, cutting across his shoulder and down his back. As he drops to the ground, the soldier dismounts and checks over the body of his victim. "Damn it!" he yells as he realizes the man is fatally wounded.

The last assassin realizes that there is no way he can get away and remains on his knees as the three other riders surround him and dismount their steeds. They tie his hands in front of him and wait a few minutes for Wellesley to arrive.

Wellesley enters the camp leading his horse with one hand while still holding his long rifle in the other. "I wanted them both alive, but not at the cost of one of you. That was a nice strike with the sword, young Percy, same technique as your father used when he was in the brigade."

Wellesley passes the reins of his horse to one of his men as he turns to look at the assassin. He walks up to him and removes his hat and looks him in the eyes. The man just stares back at him. "Yes, you're one of them, now let's see where they found you." He rips off the man's jacket and throws it on the floor, then takes a small knife and cuts his shirt open to reveal the skin on his left shoulder, giving him the answer he requires. "Three small black crescents that form a triangle, so you're from the Nomads Brotherhood, you're a long way from home, aren't you?" The man just stares at him and does not say a word. Wellesley looks around at his unit. "I fought some of these men when defending a merchant caravan in the deserts, died to a man if I remember right. You do not come cheap, so they must really want something badly to hire some of you to travel all this way."

Wellesley turns and walks over to the dead man on the ground, then bends down and searches him. Pulling his money pouch from his waist, he pours its contents into his hand. "Twenty-five gold coins," he comments. Returning to the man on his knees, he pulls off his money pouch and checks its contents as well. "Another twenty-five gold coins."

He continues walking round the camp, looking at all the signs. "Well-used fire pit, good stack of firewood, half a venison carcass hanging from a branch, you have been here for a while now. You must have been watching us for some time, planning your attack on our people." He moves over to the horses, checking out their equipment. "Six horses, six saddles." He freezes for a moment before looking back at the prisoner. Drawing his dagger, he walks straight back to the man and places the blade at his throat. "Always in threes, three here, two at the house. Where is the third one?" The man just stares at Wellesley, a small grin appearing on his face, then he starts to chuckle. "There is one still at the house," says Wellesley to himself while looking away as his mind races.

"If he is still alive, she will not be for long as it is our way," the prisoner says, smiling at him.

Wellesley looks back at the offender, the anger filling his body is turning into rage as the man continues to laugh at him. Wellesley grips the knife tightly and slices the assassin across the throat, watching him fall to the floor gurgling in his own blood as he fights for air. Without looking around, Wellesley issues his orders. "Bury them here, no markers, I'm going back to the house to check on Margaret." He does not look back, just mounts his horse and heads off at a gallop down the small track.

Back at the house, Margaret is sitting beside Andrew stroking some hair away from his ear. He has just opened his eyes and is looking directly at her, for a while he just stares before a small smile appears on his lips. "Thought I was dreaming, took me a while to realize you were not an angel come to take me on my way."

"How did you know I was not an angel?" she asks.

Andrew thinks for a moment before replying. "The smell of your perfume, the ring I gave you on our wedding day, and the fact that you are leaking a little milk. To my knowledge, angels do not have babies." Margaret looks down at the front of her dress and sighs. "Did I miss much while I was out? I feel like I have been kicked by a horse," he says, moving to a more sitting up position to get comfortable.

"No, not really, just had a man save my life. He took a musket round that was meant for me," Margaret replies as tears start to flow from her eyes. "Oh, Andrew, the things I put you through, the danger you are always in. I don't think I can take much more of this."

Andrew reaches out his arm and gently pulls his wife to his side on the bed. She willingly curls up beside him and kisses his cheek, putting her hand on his chest as she does. "Don't say that my dear, for we must go on as we have come so far. Besides, I do not want to have been shot for nothing." Andrew can see Margaret is greatly upset and tries his best to reassure her. "You believe so much in the queen and this country, don't give up now. Stay the course and finish what has been started, as once it is done we will have all the time left in our lives to enjoy each other."

The click, click sound of a pistol being cocked fully back breaks the conversation between the two of them, Margaret looks round and sees a pistol pointed at her from the far-side half opened bedroom window. Slowly the window slides the rest of the way upwards and a man's head wearing a crumpled black hat appears inside the room.

"Let's keep this quiet, shall we?" he says as he slowly slides himself through the window and into the room.

Margaret sits up on the bed. "Just what do you want here?" she asks as she stands up and faces him. "Have you lot not done enough damage already? I have an injured man here, a good man, one that does not sell himself to the highest bidder, regardless of it being right or wrong."

The man keeps his pistol aimed at Margaret as he looks first at Margaret and then at Andrew, who drops back down unconscious on the pillows. "Spare me, woman, I watched what happened from the rooftop by the chimneystack. He was a brave man indeed, standing there facing my friend with a rifle in his hands. But look where it got him! A gut wound and probably a slow death for protecting you. Better to be paid well and take your chances of a high life for a while, than be paid a pittance and suffer the same fate for far less of a lifestyle."

With a rap at the door, it opens and Beth walks in carrying Henry. "I think he is ready for his fee— Aaahhhh!" Beth yells as she notices the man with the pistol pointing at Margaret.

"Close the bloody door and move over there by the others," the man orders, while flicking the end of the barrel at her.

As Beth shuts the door and shuffles over to Margaret, still holding the baby tightly in her arms, the assassin is thinking and putting things together in his mind. A baby, his target with stains on her dress, the fact that they are not in the usual place for this time of year. "Well, this is a turn up for the books, I was not expecting such an opportunity when we came here this morning." He looks at Margaret. "You've been busy behind the scenes, haven't you, my lady?" As the assassin slowly moves round the room toward the door, Margaret tries to stand between him and Andrew. "I think I will have to take that little one with me," he says as he continues slowly moving round.

"Over my dead body," replies Margaret, with a scowling glare at the assailant.

"Oh, there is no doubt of that, but the baby will fetch a pretty penny to my employer, I would say enough to last out the rest of my days without ever having to work again."

Margaret stares at him, keeping his eyes focused on her by looking like she might try to react in some way. "Last out the rest of your days without ever having to work again, eh! I can willingly arrange that for you right here."

The man looks at her curiously. "How would you be able to do that?"

Margaret points in the direction of a large tortoiseshell box on the side table. "First, I would slowly move over there and open the secret panel at the back, then I would hand you some jewels that would blow your tiny mind," She slowly takes two steps toward the box while being closely watched by the man pointing the pistol at her.

"Easy, I would hate for this pistol to go off before you have had a chance to put your case across," he says, following her with the barrel of the gun.

Margaret stops. "On second thoughts, let's not waste any more time and end it now. Andrew!"

The man looks back at the bed where Andrew is sitting up with two pistols in his hands pointing straight at him. "Oh sh——"

He moves to aim his pistol at Andrew, but the first shot hits him in the shoulder, causing him to drop his pistol to the ground. Knocked back but not out, the man pulls a knife from his belt with his good arm and moves forward. The second shot hits him in the hip, spinning him around and dropping him to his knees.

Andrew drops back onto the pillows, the pistols falling from his hands. The jolts to his body have started his wound bleeding again and the pain of sitting up has caused him to pass out. While the intruder attempts to sit up, the knife still clasped in his hand, Margaret steps forward and kicks at his arm. He drops back to the ground and the knife spills from his hand and spins away across the room.

She bends down, picks up his pistol, and looks at it. "H Nock of London, a fine maker of firearms. I have two myself, as you now know, having just felt the sting from them both."

As she points the gun at the stricken man's head, the door crashes open and a sweating, out-of-breath Wellesley bursts in. He has two pistols in his hands and looks wildly around the room before turning and aiming his weapons at the assailant. Anna is behind him with her small knife drawn, she steps in and moves next to Beth and the baby as Wellesley stands over the man with Margaret.

"We found their camp and three more of them," he says while trying to catch his breath. "They are being buried, as we speak, in unmarked graves. Each one had twenty-five gold pieces on their persons. Seems the price is going up all the time."

Margaret's eyes have not moved with the commotion but stay focused on the man in front of her, as he looks straight back at her. "Check on Andrew Wellesley, I have this." Her arm is as steady as a rock, pointing the gun at the killer. "You come in here and threaten my family. Paid assassins with murder on your mind, and the thought that you would take my son for ransom. I despise you and your kind." The man coughs and splutters, still staring straight up at her. "One hundred and fifty gold pieces, blood money to kill a woman you have never met before. Now it will go to the family of the soldier you murdered, for Grenadier Haskins had a young wife and a daughter named Elizabeth. He was a good man, honorable, with a fine future ahead of him, a future that you robbed him of, shame on you." She sighs heavily as she thinks about the man she has lost. "To be fair, the bit that disappoints me most is that you were not even that good. Taking your eye off the prize for the thought of a better reward, you should have shot me from the window and made sure of your objective."

The man coughs. "I will remember that next time."

Margaret shakes her head. "No! you won't, your time is over," she says as she pulls the trigger and drops the man to the floor. Margaret tosses the gun on the ground beside the dead man as she turns to Wellesley. "You were right, I did not take our security seriously enough in the beginning. From now on you arrange what you see fit, for I fear Andrew has used all the luck he had in him this day and I cannot afford to lose him." She walks over and takes her crying son from the arms of Beth and sits down beside Andrew on the bed.

At the same time, Herbert enters the room still with his pipe in his hand. He looks around, makes his assessment of the situation, and moves over to Andrew to check the red staining seeping through his bandages. "I thought I said he needed to rest and not move, Margaret. This is not good, not good at all. I think I will need to stitch this side up to close it, I only hope he is not bleeding inside."

More guards arrive and the room begins to fill with people. Margaret, as always, takes control of the situation. "We cannot move my husband to another room, for that may do him more harm than good." She points to the man on the floor. "Roll him up in the rug he is on and take him away, bury him with the others in the woods far away from here. No markers, they do not deserve it."

Wellesley has caught his breath back. "They were paid well in gold; it would seem that someone is stepping up the fight to find and kill you, Margaret. We cannot afford for them to succeed, not when you have sacrificed so much. Perhaps it is time we went on the offensive and hit them back."

She thinks on his words before replying. "Well, they failed today but we did lose one of our own. Take our fallen soldier back to the manor and arrange for an honorable burial, I will say some words myself on the day. Give the gold from these murderers to the family he leaves behind, for they will not go short while I live. As for striking back, I would love to, but we cannot show our hand until we are ready, and we are far from that at the moment." She looks at Wellesley with her steely-eyed stare. "Worry not, my old friend, our time will come soon enough, and, when it does, we will rip them all from the very foundations of our lands and remove them forever."

As her men-at-arms take the body out of the room, Margaret assesses the situation. "Beth, take Henry into the room next door, I will feed him there. Anna, stay with the physician and help with Andrew. Wellesley, check out the grounds personally, I do not want any more surprises, and include the roof on your search this time, for that is where this one came from. The roof and then through the window over in the corner." She takes a long look at Andrew before following Beth out of the room, leaving the others to contemplate what has just happened.

Once the door has closed, Anna turns to Wellesley. "How can she be so composed? People have tried to kill her twice in one day, Andrew is badly wounded, and she just calmly walks away to feed Henry, I just don't understand it."

Wellesley turns to Anna, his eyes filled with shame and anger. He grabs her arms and shakes her firmly. "What do you expect her to do? People have tried to kill her many times over the years, this time it was different. *We* failed her, I failed to check the grounds and secure the area properly and you should never have left her side, not for a second, that is why you are here," he says angrily. "That woman is torn up on the inside, but she cannot show it because it will finish her and if she is finished, so are we and all we are trying to achieve." He turns and points at Andrew. "Look on the bed by Andrew's hands. Two spent pistols. He has opened his wounds firing at the assassin from the bed. Twice in a day a baker has done what we failed to do and we are trained to do this.

Now he lies gravely wounded. Stay here and help Herbert tend his injuries and pray he pulls through, because if he does not, I fear it will be the end of her and the end of her means the end of us and this country." Wellesley storms out of the room, slamming the door behind him and leaving Anna shellshocked and speechless.

Probably for the first time since her own attack, the reality of what Margaret is going through, and the severity of the events of the day are beginning to sink in. It suddenly dawns on her that this is not just a game, the stakes are far higher than she ever imagined. Andrew has put his life on the line twice for his wife, stood and faced a bullet with only his body to defend her without a second thought for himself, could she have done that? Face a bullet to protect Margaret. Would she have what it takes to face down a killer? The look of shame she saw in Wellesley's eyes now surges through her own body. She has been taking this all too lightly up until now, but the reality is finally dawning on her. She could have lost everybody who helped her when she was in need, all the people she loves in one day, gone! Could she live in a world without Margaret, Andrew, Wellesley, baby Henry and all the others? "This will never happen again, I swear it," she vows to herself as she turns and walks over to the physician with a more determined attitude. There is no way she wants to let Margaret or Wellesley down again.

"What can I do to help?" she asks.

"Oh, you are back with us now, are you?" he says while cutting away the bandage around Andrew's waist. "It's not hard for me to imagine what you are thinking, my dear. When you are my age you have seen it many times before; when and if the time comes, you will be ready. It will be like second nature to react, for you have the best teacher there is in Wellesley. I will need hot water and bandages to redress this wound and some brandy to clean the needles."

"Brandy, we do not have any of that here," Anna replies.

"My dear girl, go and see Wellesley, ask him for some of his private stock, he will have some." Anna is swiftly out of the room, leaving Herbert to continue removing the dressings and poking around the wound to see the extent of the damage Andrew did while defending Margaret and Henry again.

Nearly ten minutes have passed when Anna reappears with a pot of hot water hanging from her hand, bandages tucked under her arm and a bottle of brandy in the other hand. She crosses over to Herbert and places the water beside the bed on the floor and the brandy and bandages on the sideboard. Now the supplies have been collected, Anna prepares one of the bandages and begins to wipe away the blood around Andrew's wound. Herbert takes the brandy and pours it into a glass containing two needles and leaves them to soak while he strips out a length of thread from a spool he has taken from his bag.

Anna moves back to the far side of the room and watches as he dunks the thread he has taken off the spool into the brandy to give it a good soak and allow the brandy to help soften the material and make it more pliable. She stares in awe as he meticulously works away on Andrew's wound. Without a word spoken, the man cleans, stitches, dresses, and bandages Andrew's wound, then clears away all the rubbish with such efficiency.

All finished, Herbert packs everything away into his small bag just as the door opens and Margaret steps in. "That is all we can do for now. I will be off to finish my pipe and will be back later to see how our patient is doing. You must also get some rest, my dear, I know you have a lot going on, but you are no good to us ill or exhausted. You must also think of yourself and the baby."

As he picks up his bag and hat he notices the half bottle of brandy on the side. "I think I will take the rest of Wellesley's brandy as well, purely for medicinal purposes of course." He smiles and nods at Margaret before leaving the room, closing the door quietly behind him.

Margaret stares down at Andrew, lying asleep in the bed. "I had two gentlemen arriving this morning; with all that has gone on, I had completely forgotten about them."

"They came about an hour after the first incident in the garden," Anna tells her. "I showed them to the war room, they viewed and collected what was left out for them and left after around two hours later. With all that was going on, they did not want to disturb you, just told me to let you know they would work on the material, come up with suggestions and a plan and see you in around three weeks at a time that suited you."

Margaret nods in her direction. "Thank you, Anna, I appreciate what you have done today. I am sure the men will know what they must do."

Anna can see that Margaret is beginning to get emotional as she stands and just stares at Andrew lying in the bed. Tears are beginning to run down her cheeks as she sits on the bed beside him, stroking his face with the back of her hand. All day Margaret has been able to hold on and control her emotions but, in the empty silence of the room staring at her beloved, she can hold on to them no more. As she starts to cry, Anna stands up and heads toward the door, tears running down her face as well as she quietly leaves the room. She looks around and spots a chair further up the hallway and, making as little noise as possible, moves it in front of the door and sits down in it, just as she hears Margaret inside finally break down.

"Oh, Andrew, what have I done to you?" she says as she starts to sob. "Please don't leave me, for I do not know what I would do without you."

Outside the door Anna also has tears running down her face, it is all she can do to hold on and not break down as well, for only now does she truly realizes how much these people have put on the line for her and everyone else to better this country. Anna is finally experiencing firsthand how high the toll can be to do the right thing against the tyranny that this land has been put under by the Three Heads and their paid army of mercenaries.

Hearing somebody coming up the stairs, Anna wipes her face to hide the tears as best she can. Soon she can see Bunty carrying a tray with some food on it.

"I have some food for Margaret, I'll just take it in to her," Bunty says.

Anna shakes her head. "Just put it on the side there and I will take it in to her later," she replies.

Bunty continues past the side table. "Don't be silly, child. Get out of my way and I will take it in to her."

Anna stands up and steps forward, angry at the woman's disobedience to her request, raising her voice as she speaks again more firmly, "Step back and put the tray on the side table, I will deal with it when she is ready to be disturbed. Bunty is taken aback, but still thinks she has the right to push on. "One more step and it will go badly for you," warns Anna, as she reaches down the side of her trousers for one of her small blades.

The door opposite opens and Wellesley steps out into the hall. He looks at Anna, then turns to look at the cook.

"Wellesley, this child is preventing me from ta—"

"Let me stop you right there, woman. When this girl tells you to do something, you do it. Don't question it or argue it, just do it or you will be out of here before you have a chance to speak again. When it comes to Margaret, it is me who calls the shots, then Anna. Period. So put the tray on the side and leave before I make it a permanent arrangement."

Bunty turns and places the tray on the table, then looks back at them both with a shocked and disappointed expression before heading back down the stairs.

Wellesley turns back to Anna. "For the first time, you have finally grasped what it takes to be able to protect Margaret, but also give her the space she sometimes needs from her friends and enemies alike. Well done. Now, Margaret will no doubt have heard us out here, so let's give her fifteen minutes and then take the tray into the room, as you know what she is like when she be hungry."

As if by some divine intervention, they hear a voice from inside the room. "I heard that, Wellesley, and shall we say ten minutes as it just so happens that I am feeling a little bit peckish?"

Anna and Wellesley smile at each, "She misses nothing" whispers Anna as Wellesley shakes his head, turns, and goes back into his room and closes the door. Anna retakes her seat outside the room Margaret and Andrew are in, She sighs heavily, looks at the time on a wall clock, leans back in her chair to wait the ten minutes before she is to take the tray into Margaret.

CHAPTER 11

Preparing for the Day

After the assassin's attack, the house has taken some time to return to normal and come down from high alert. The stable block has been converted to allow six guards to be moved on site, along with four grenadiers patrolling the grounds and three more working in the war room. The farm in the village now has a count of twelve grenadiers in support, ready to rotate with men at the house and visit the surrounding villages to show force. They often visit the local taverns for a drink to see if any new faces have arrived in the area.

As for the locals, they have enjoyed the additional income from the purchases the soldiers make in the village, along with the security they have from the army being around. Crime has virtually stopped overnight, not just in the local area but the surrounding farms and estates as well, as the cavalrymen and women go round all of them at least once a day on a routine patrol. As for the military personnel, a chance to get out of the barracks, to be in close proximity to Wellesley and many other renowned people, is an opportunity all of them have requested. A rotation of two weeks per tour allows as many as possible to have the chance to support Margaret and the others and gives Wellesley the opportunity to put them all through their paces with the sword and cavalry skills.

With no more intrusions during the past four weeks, the conclusion that Margaret and Wellesley have come to is that the six assassins they eliminated had not reported that Margaret had been found or seen. They were probably one of several groups that had been sent round the country looking for Margaret with the intent of removing her at the earliest opportunity. All of them had the same gold payment on their bodies, so they were not expected to make contact again with their employers. Just tasked with finding Margaret, completing the contract, and then disappearing to eliminate any suspicion being laid at the feet of the Three Heads. They had a contract to fulfill and were left to get on with it, so the feeling is that they have killed everyone involved in this particular group, hence no return of others to take their place since. It could now be assumed on these facts that the Three Heads would not know whether Margaret is dead or alive until she shows up for the opening day in the debating chambers with the royal envoy of negotiators and diplomats.

Andrew has been recovering well and is spending more and more time with the troops, learning to ride, better handle a sword and pistol, as well as being a bit of a legend for his actions protecting Margaret on two occasions in one day. As always with Andrew, he plays down the role he had in foiling the assassins' attempts to murder Margaret as just being in the right place at the right time; nothing more and nothing less. "Any of the guards would have done the same if they were in my place," he says every time someone asks him about what happened. But to the guards he has become a man that has earnt their respect, stood his ground to protect Margaret and showed stiff resolve to the enemy, a fine example for all the new recruits to follow as a role model.

Anna has become far more disciplined when she chooses. Her skills to blend in around Margaret but still be in a protective position have greatly improved and her alertness to her surroundings and the people within it is now near perfect. As her role sometimes needs her to blend in with military personnel, she now has her own uniform made especially on commission by Wellesley, with some additional features to allow her knives along with various other items to be hidden discreetly on her person without being visible. To Anna this is the best uniform ever and she is always ready to put it on when the opportunity arises. Especially when she can take her position beside her mentor Wellesley, and they are both seen walking around together in uniform.

As for Wellesley, he has struggled to come to terms with the fact that contract killers had twice got so close to Margaret without him and his men spotting them. He is happier now the security is up to the level that he requested to start with. But the knock to his confidence has taken its toll, the only saving grace to his pride is that it was his training with Andrew on how to use and fire pistols and the pair he insisted were kept primed and ready at the base of the headboard of the bed that won out at the end of the day. It has made him realize that in this situation, defense and protection of key people is not the full solution; he must somehow start an offensive at the source and eliminate the people employing the assassins before they have a chance to fulfill their objectives. It is time he started to have some men of his own taking a closer interest in certain people and observe what they get up to on a daily basis. He needs to find a way of deterring any future contract killers from wanting to take the bounties put on offer by the Three Heads. The best way for this to happen is to ensure that any that are found, disappear and are never seen again.

A plan is starting to form in his mind. It is dangerous and will put at risk one he holds dear and close to his heart, so for now he will think on it a while before speaking to them in the hope an alternative solution can be found in the meantime. Whatever Wellesley comes up with, he will have to keep it hidden from Margaret as she will not approve any offensive actions until she is ready. As that is going to be some time away, however, he wants to start taking the fight to them as he has lost too many men over the years to keep waiting.

A more immediate challenge for him is the return of diplomats to the negotiating table. It is the end of the summer break and with the government back in less than a week's time, he will have to split his forces to cover several potential targets as state duties and diplomatic meetings will require Margaret and the growing number of other people working for the crown's interests to attend various events around the country. The only advantage he now has is that many of his troops have been working with him at the house in rotation and understand how to protect without being too intrusive. This is a big improvement on resources as he has more people he can depend on in his absence to cover the additional people that are working at the house.

Margaret has been dividing her time between her son, a bedside watch over her beloved Andrew as he recovers from his wounds, while reviewing and overseeing the plans in the war room. As Andrew's health improves, she devotes more time to the planning required by the monarchy to get the country back from the hands of the politicians. The only time Andrew and Margaret have been away from the house was for a picnic Andrew had organized two days ago, a mile up the river next to a small inlet in an area surrounded by pink flowers and bullrushes along the river's edge. Anna, as always was with them and in the trees, just out of sight, Wellesley and two guards were secretly watching to ensure no danger was present.

Even then, there was no rest for poor Wellesley as Margaret spotted just a glimpse of one of the soldiers in the woods, she fired off a pistol and screamed out loudly as if under attack. Moments later Wellesley and his men came charging through the undergrowth, sword in one hand and a pistol in the other ready to take on the world. He was met with the scowling stare and wrath of Margaret's tongue ripping into him about wanting to be alone for just a few hours, explaining they had Anna with them for protection and did not need people hiding in the woods as well. Wellesley was used to Margaret's scathing remarks, it was like water off a duck's back to him now, but after the incidents that had happened recently, there was no way that he would leave her without a proper escort. Anna was purely a last line of defense, he would never again leave her without support close by to back her up should anything happen.

As always with Margaret, later that evening after thinking on what she had done, she seeks out and apologizes not just to Wellesley but the two soldiers as well, sharing time with them and expressing her appreciation for watching over her and the family despite her sometimes-gruff mannerism.

Margaret has now started planning the trips and meetings she must attend around staying at the house or the palace's end wing, out of the way of most people so that she can be close to Henry. Whatever else happens, one thing is for certain; to pull the next few months off, Henry will become the most well-traveled, secret and protected baby in the history of Kelsey.

As another day draws to an end, Andrew and Wellesley enter the living room. Margaret and Anna are already there, sitting by the fire. Anna has her legs tucked under her body and baby Henry in her arms, rocking him gently back and forth.

"I never realized how comfortable these old chairs were until now," Margaret says to the men as they approach.

Andrew extends his hand and flicks it up in the air. "Come on, give up the chairs, you have a dozen new ones you chose around the room. We fought tooth and nail to keep you from throwing these two away. You dumped the rest, remember?"

Margaret grips the arms of the chair with her hands and spreads her body across the seat. "We have decided that these are more comfortable, like old worn cloths." She rolls her fingers along the arm of the chair. "I think we will stay right where we are and you can have the new chairs, my dear."

"Oh no, not a chance. You made your choice, you stick with the chairs you wanted," replies Andrew.

Wellesley is having no more success with Anna. With a typical Margaret-style stare, Anna speaks as he approaches. "Don't even try it, old man, this chair is taken and you aren't getting it."

The men look at each other. This is not good news as the new chairs are hard, upright and uncomfortable, more a stylish fashion statement than something comfortable to sit in at the end of the day. They had opposed the change and fought hard to keep one chair each for themselves, while all the others were removed.

With the baby in Anna's arms, there is no chance of Wellesley fighting for his chair, but Andrew is not giving up without a fight. Straddling the arm of the chair he sits down and leans on Margaret as he tries to slide into the seat with her, but Margaret is prepared to put up stiff resistance to hold onto her position. With arms and knees pushing back, she holds him off by wedging herself between the arms of the seat and pinching his thigh as he tries to wriggle in.

"Ouch!" Andrew yells, holding his wounded side and turning away from the chair.

Margaret is up like a shot. "Andrew are you all right, my dear?" she asks. As she goes to his aid, Andrew spins her around, slips past and takes the seat for himself. She puts her hands on her hips, frowning at the sneaky, underhanded move. "That was a cheap trick, but if that is how you want to play it, so be it." Margaret just sits on top of him, turning sideways to hang her leg over the arm of the chair and put her arm around Andrew's neck as she settles into position.

Wellesley drags one of the new chairs across the floor, puts it beside Anna, and takes a seat. He squirms around a bit before resigning himself to the fact that he is as comfortable as he can be in that particular chair.

As the group settle down to the evening in front of the fire, Bunty enters the room with a large tray covered in slices of cooked meats and pastries and places them on the side table. "I thought you might like some savory items with your tea," she says before leaving the room. The smell of the hot, succulent morsels soon fills the room with wonderful smells, causing them to start looking at each other, each one debating if the risk of losing a comfortable seat in front of the fire is worth the food on offer. Bunty returns with another tray with a teapot, cups and everything required to make a cup of tea and puts them next to the other tray.

Beth follows her into the room. She walks over to Anna to check on baby Henry, he is fast asleep in Anna's arms and she is giving all the signs of not wanting to give the little one up. Beth smiles and says, "All right, Anna, but in half hour, he must be woken up to feed or he will not sleep properly tonight." Anna nods with a huge smile on her face and settles back with little Henry.

As Beth steps back and looks round, she cannot help but notice something seems odd. She cannot put her finger on it, but as she goes and picks up a plate and starts to collect items of food, Andrew speaks,

"Could you do me a plate of food as well, please, Beth?"

"Don't you dare, he can get his own food!" snaps Margaret.

Beth looks at them both curiously, thinks for a moment, then smiles. "It's the chairs, isn't it?" she says. "I said them new ones were not very comfortable when they arrived, but somebody insisted they looked better than them old, tatty 'grandfather chairs,' if I remember the correct words they used to describe them."

"No, it's not that, I just cannot move because Margaret is on top of me," Andrew says.

"Then I will get up, my darling, it is no bother."

Andrew holds Margaret tightly. "No, no, you are fine where you are, my dear. Beth is more than able to assist me in such a menial task as to pass me a little food."

Beth laughs. "Yes, Andrew, I can see why you are happy with Margaret in that position, most men would be, but I think she is right. If you require any food, you will have to get it yourself."

Wellesley stands up, turns, and kicks the chair. "This is impossible, how can they make a chair so uncomfortable?"

Beth looks at Wellesley, chuckling at his frustrations. "You do know we didn't throw out all the old chairs? I believe some were put into the old stable block for the guards to use." Wellesley raises an eyebrow as he turns to look at Beth, freezes for a moment as he thinks, then storms off out of the room.

"You've put the cat amongst the pigeons now, Beth," says Margaret with a smile. "I have a feeling there is about to be a calling out of the guard any time now."

With the absolute refusal of anyone to give up their chair, for the next ten minutes there is an eerie silence as nobody moves. Then they hear voices and doors slamming, and Wellesley appears back in the room. He is followed by six soldiers, two to each of three armchairs. Two of the men are wearing only long johns and boots.

"Now, lads, we cannot have our finest sitting in these old armchairs."

"But, sir, they are absolutely fine," replies one of the soldiers.

"No, not for my men, place them down here and take three of these new ones back." Wellesley turns to the first two men. "Swap that one for the one in front of the fire, that's a good lad."

"But, sir, these are brand new and look expensive, they will get messed up with all our equipment over them," the soldier comments again.

"For my boys, nothing is too good. Now, take them with you and do not worry about any damage, you deserve to have nothing but the best, my lad."

The men do as instructed, within minutes they have switched the three chairs and are out of the room. Wellesley goes with them as they head out of the house, holding open the doors to allow them to get the chairs out more easily. When he returns to the room he can see that the five chairs have been put in an arc around the front of the fireplace, filling the entire space, though the one at the end has only partial access to the heat of the fire. Beth has joined the others and along with Margaret they have occupied the best four seats, each with a plate of food.

Wellesley stares at the four smiling faces looking back at him. "Really," he comments as he walks over and picks up a plate, only to then see that almost all the food has been taken and only the bits that nobody wanted are left. He slowly turns his head while muttering under his breath.

"Fear not, Wellesley, more food is on the way. Bunty is making up another tray as we speak," Margaret says as Wellesley takes his seat at the end of the fireplace. From the shaded area at the end of the row he looks at all the others with envy in his eyes, as they are all tucking into the food they had collected in his absence.

He does not have to wait more than a few minutes before Bunty appears with another large tray of sliced meats and pastries. Eager to get to the best bits before anyone else, she has scarcely put the tray down before he is up out of his chair and across the room with his plate. He selects all the things he wants with a grin on his face and turns to take his seat. He takes only two steps before he stops, and, with a huge sigh his shoulders drop. "You have got to be kidding me," he mutters as he realizes Bunty has taken his seat and is talking to Beth beside her.

Margaret is the first to notice. Barely able to contain her laughter, she taps Andrew's shoulder, and as he looks up she flicks her head in Bunty's direction. Andrew instantly notices what has happened and clenches his teeth to prevent him breaking out in laughter as well. Before Wellesley says anything, Margaret stands up and puts her plate on the side, then turns to Anna. "Time to feed my little man, I think," she says as her arms go out to collect young Henry from Anna's protective grasp. "Wellesley, you can take my seat for I doubt I will be back down tonight. It's been a long day, I need my bed and some rest," she says while looking at Andrew.

Andrew immediately gets up, stretching out his arms and yawning. "I think I will join you, my dear." Margaret collects Henry from Anna and the pair of them head toward the stairs, Andrew putting his arm around his wife's waist as they slowly move away, looking at their child and talking in low voices.

Beth has been so focused on her conversation with cook she has only just realized that the others have left with the baby. "Oops, duty calls Bunty, the baby is on the move, so it is time for me to go." She stands up and follows the others up the stairs to the baby room.

Anna is sitting back in her chair; with no baby to occupy her she is now bored and trying to think of something to do. She looks at Wellesley, who is eating. "I still need to adjust my uniform to fit that new blade in the side pocket, so I will see you in the morning, O great one," she says as she jumps to her feet and slips out of the room. Wellesley pays her very little attention while occupied with his meal, just gives a small nod and a raise of his finger as she passes and continues eating the food on his plate.

Within seconds of leaving, Anna quietly pokes her head back in the room and watches as Bunty makes her move. Although being quite a few years younger than Wellesley, her interest in him is no secret to Anna and the others, especially when he is dressed in his uniform and displaying all his medals. Anna watches as Bunty gets up and moves to the chair next to Wellesley and sits back down again.

"Looks like it is just me and you left on this cozy night, Wellesley." Suddenly a sense of fear grabs him, he struggles to swallow the mouthful of food, taking an extra-large gulp to get it down. Bunty leans toward him as she speaks again. "What you need is a good woman to look after you. You have been on your own far too long now, it's not good for a man in your position to always be single. You need the attentions of a real woman to keep you at your best, I mean, look at your uniform." She flicks at some of the lapels and stitching with her hand. "Some of the buttons are hanging on by a mere thread and your hat and trousers need the seams repairing before you fall out of them." She moves her attentions to stroking the top of his leg with the nails on her fingers. Wellesley flinches and sinks lower into his seat, fear seizing him as he looks for a way out of this sticky situation.

Anna hears a noise beside her and turns to see Beth is right next to her, desperately trying not to laugh, as she has also been watching everything unfold over Anna's shoulder.

"I also know how it feels to be alone, Wellesley. I have been without a man in my life for over a year now and I feel like I am wasting away with so much yet to offer." She moves closer to him and leans over the arm of his chair.

Outside the room the two girls are still desperately trying not to laugh as they can see Wellesley shrinking down lower and lower into his chair as Bunty moves in on him, her lips getting closer and closer to his. They hear a click from the direction of the stairs and turn to see where the noise came from. Halfway down the stairway is Margaret with a frown on her face. She points to the bottom of the steps and the girls follow her directions, first Beth and then Anna after she quietly closes the door, trapping Wellesley inside.

"I know what you two are doing. I leave you for less than a minute and you're both up to mischief! Now come up the stairs, the pair of you. As for you, Beth, I thought you would know better at your age." The three women have barely made the top of the stairs when the door downstairs slams open and Wellesley comes briskly out, closely followed by Bunty.

"I have to do one last patrol of the grounds before it is too dark to see," he says as he passes the bottom of the stairs.

"But you have not finished your food yet, would you like me to keep it warm for you? Wellesley, speak to me, darling. Slow down so we can talk, do you need somebody to keep an eye on you while you are outside?" bellows Bunty as she chases after the fleeing Wellesley.

The three ladies cannot help but burst into laughter. Louder and louder they laugh, as the three of them can still hear Bunty calling and giving chase to Wellesley as he swiftly moves through the kitchen and out into the grounds via the door at the back of the building.

Margaret is first to control her emotions and she looks at the other two with her hardened stare. "You two should be thoroughly ashamed of yourselves. You know Wellesley better than most, leaving him in a room alone with Bunty is not the best idea you have ever come up with.

Anna, you can work out a way to put this right by tomorrow, and I mean by tomorrow. Now, I'm going back to be with my son and husband, deal with this before he speaks to me about replacing the cook, as it will be the first thing he will ask before threatening to retire and leave us like he did before." They both lower their heads as Margaret walks away, but as she enters her room and closes the door behind her they start to giggle again.

"Oh, Wellesley, take me now, I ache for you," mimics Anna as she feigns passion by putting the back of her hand on her forehead and throwing her head back. "My dear Bunty, passion runs so dee—"

They look round and notice Margaret standing in the doorway with her arms folded. "Perhaps you two need to be replaced as well," she says as the girls look at her, then each other, before bolting down the stairs, giggling and laughing as they go. Margaret watches the stairs for a while to ensure they have gone before entering her room again and closing the door. She sighs and looks at Andrew, "Those girls will be the death of me, Andrew. They are always up to something and poor Wellesley seems to get the rough end of the stick and be on the receiving end of it all."

Andrew shakes his head and smiles at her, waiting a moment before answering. "I think if he did not like the attention he would deal with them rather swiftly, my dear. I have a feeling that, deep down, he likes the fact that they are thinking of him. It keeps him feeling wanted and part of the group and, besides, Anna would never let anything happen to him, not while she has breath in her body and blood in her veins. Now come to bed, we have little enough time to ourselves as it is, so an early night is something to enjoy. In less than a week you will be back on duty at the palace with the queen performing all the state and diplomatic duties and requirements they see fit to throw your way."

Margaret walks over to the wood and leather cot beside the bed and looks dotingly upon baby Henry fast asleep in his blanket. "So cute now, but in three hours he will scream the house down for his feed," she says, taking a seat on the bed beside Andrew and shuffling back to lean up against him.

"Do you regret having him so soon, Marge?" Andrew asks hesitantly.

Margaret swiftly turns to look at him. "Absolutely not, these might be difficult times and we may have some eventful challenges to overcome in the months ahead, but our Henry makes the fight all the more worthwhile, for it is his future we are fighting for, along with all the children in this land."

He smiles at her and kisses her on the forehead. "I was only asking, my dear, the answer was never in doubt, just the amount of pressure you put yourself under to get to the end goal worries me a little, that's all."

Margaret puts her arms around Andrew and holds him tight. "I am more worried about losing you. If not to an assassin, to you finding the path too much to take and falling out of love with me. Let's face it, you have been on the receiving end of some terrible situations so far, I fear deeply that I ask too much of you."

As Andrew looks into her eyes, he can see that she is sad and truly worried that she is slowly pushing him away from her. "This is not the time to get all sentimental, I would not be here if it was not my choice. I'm not the kind of man to run just because the going has got a little bit tough. Besides, as you so often tell me, 'If it is not worth fighting for, then you do not want it enough and it is not worth having in the first place, a statement that I agree whole heartedly with."

"But, Andrew, I nearly lost you twice in one day. The risk is a lot to ask of someone loved so deeply, for I fear I would struggle to live with myself if you were not in my life to share it with me."

He holds her tightly and kisses her passionately before speaking. "If I had not been there ready and trained by Wellesley, I would most certainly have lost you and Henry would be motherless. He taught me how to use a pistol, to stand my ground, observe my surroundings, and pick the right moment to go on the offensive. It was also Wellesley who advised me to keep two loaded pistols hidden at the base of the headboard, and, if I remember correctly, it was against your wishes, but he was right to insist that I did it anyway. It just goes to show that we are thinking of each other all the time and risking all that we have to watch one another's backs." He sighs and looks around at his son before continuing. "The only advantage we have is that we are as prepared as we can be and have friends and experience on our side. An old friend of mine once said, 'We cannot face the future unless we have a positive outlook'. Do not look back at what could have been, for there were so many choices made between then and this present moment. We are here now, and that time has gone, look only forward with the past as reference to lessons learnt on our way to this moment, for chance favors the prepared mind. So, with that in mind, I intend to be ready for all that those three men can throw at us, for one day it will be our turn to return the favor."

Andrew pauses to kiss his wife before continuing. "That day will come soon enough, and, when it does, I will take my vengeance for all the wrongs they have done you, me and all the others affected by their greed and lust for power and money. I will not fail like they have done on so many occasions to remove you from us. Or hesitate at the opportunity like that man did at the window. When our moment arrives, I will strike such a decisive blow for what is good and right that they will never return or influence this country again." He flicks her nose with his finger. "You may have married a baker, but he is fast learning to lay his cloth over many duties and professions. Who knows, one day I may even rule the kingdom, such is the ladder I seem to be on since I met you."

The sadness and worry in Margaret's eyes subsides as she looks proudly at her husband. "I saw something in you when we first met, but even I cannot believe the changes that have taken place and made you the man you have become today. In my eyes, you are already every bit a prince of this land, more so than any I have known. You might not have been born into the position, but I see more nobility in you than a thousand kings and queens that have long since passed, my love." Margaret turns her body, slides down the bed and reverses into Andrew, pulling his arm around her waist and moving a pillow under her head before holding his hand in hers.

As the pair of them settle down for the night, the house falls into silence, not a sound can be heard. That is, not for around three hours, then, as if on a timer, Henry bellows out a roar like a young lion. It takes only seconds for Margaret to respond, up and out of bed and lifting Henry out of his cot and into her arms. Moments later, as Henry starts to feed, he is silent again and the house is quiet once more.

Over the next few days, preparations and plans are made for Margaret to travel first to the palace, then to the city the following day to attend meetings with politicians and discuss the agenda for the next term in office. It is not an easy time for Andrew, as he worries for his wife's safety, but he makes the best of it, and, with the help of his close friends Anna, Wellesley, Lord Ashby, and Beth, they make all the preparations for Henry to travel discreetly. He will be in a safe escort with guards and officers that Andrew knows well, traveling on pre-checked roads and avoiding any towns and villages where possible.

The hardest part for Andrew will be the fact that he will have to take a step back and allow Beth and Anna to take the lead on the traveling arrangements with his son while he remains at the house alone. If he were to travel with them and be seen with Margaret or the others by spies or informers of the Three Heads, it may put everybody in jeopardy and make him a potential target for assassins in the future. However, most of the plans they have drawn up show that for a good part of the time Henry will be at the house safe with all of them around him. With this in mind, the estate is now a place where security is so tight that even deliveries are done by the same people or not at all, and guests are allowed entry by invitation only. Turning up uninvited and without a password has you escorted away from the area under the barrel of a gun, such is the efficiency of the guards on duty.

As the first day of Margaret's meetings arrives, all are on edge, but none more so than Andrew. He has checked, re-checked and triple-checked everything he can think of. As her bags are taken out to the carriage, Andrew escorts his wife to the open coach door. It is hard for him to let his beloved go when he knows she will be putting herself in harm's way, but this is the woman he married. He would not impose his will on her as it would not be taken kindly. All he can do is plan, prepare, and be there when she needs him, with the hope that she is kept safe by all those around her. To be fair, as Andrew has learnt in the past two years, she can handle herself in most situations and give back better than many would expect.

Andrew kisses Margaret one more time before she mounts the steps and enters the carriage. As she takes her seat she looks at her husband as he closes the door behind her. "Try not to worry, my dear. As you see, I have Lord Ashby leading my security detail today, and Wellesley driving the team upfront. Nobody wants a run-in with those two and their bodyguards, not if they want to live, anyway."

Andrew sighs heavily as he steps back and watches the reins flick onto the backs of the two horses up front. They move off following the six riders at the front, with another four at the back. The last to move off is Lord Ashby, who takes off his helmet and nods at Andrew.

"Fear not, my boy, your lady is in good hands with me and the boys. We will see she arrives at the palace safe and sound, mark my words." As he places his helmet back on his head he kicks his spurs into the sides of his horse, making it lunge forward into a canter after the rest of his troop.

Andrew stands and watches the convoy of friends leave and head off along the driveway and onto the track at the end. He continues to watch as they follow the road along and into the woods. Even then, when they are out of sight, stares in their direction and listens, until even the sound of them has long since faded from earshot. He turns and heads back to the house, where Anna is holding Henry on her hip in the doorway, rocking him slowly side to side while waiting for Andrew to return. As he approaches the door, she steps inside, and when Andrew enters the house the door closes behind him and a guard moves forward and takes his position in front of the door.

CHAPTER 12

The Shock Return

All the plans Margaret and her team have made are put into action, the rumors of Beth having a baby have gone round the palace and high society like wildfire. Speculation on who the father is and the fact she is a little older than most women for her first child make for a great deal of gossip and rumors. For Beth, Margaret and Anna, it has been fun to spread misinformation see how long it takes to get around the people working and serving in the Palace and diplomatic circle. As well as making it easier for Margaret to be seen around a baby without suspicion, though they remain vigilant and keep Henry well away from prying eyes and strangers just to be safe.

However, the biggest surprise by far that Margaret delivers is the following day as she is walking down the corridors of the parliament building flanked by Wellesley and Lord Ashby and followed by several diplomats and guards. As always, she is late for the meeting by exactly ten minutes, to play on the mind of those she is about to negotiate with. She likes them to be talking about her as she approaches and have to stop and look away as she acknowledges them. A technique her father taught her to do; he used to say it gave him an edge when he was about to go into negotiation with the opposition or heads of neighboring states.

As the party turn a corner and reach the entrance to the negotiating hall, they stumble across the Three Heads, Bonner, Mallory and Stone talking just outside the doorway. The three of them double-take as they look up and see Margaret and her team walking toward them. Margaret does not even look at them, just speaks as she passes, "Morning, gentlemen, shall we get on with this? I have a lot do today and do not wish to hang about unnecessarily as we have to meet envoys from the church this afternoon." The entourage passes the shocked and bewildered men and file into the room, taking their places around the large oval oak table. The table has gold inlay and is decorated with golden candle sticks, gilded bowls and ornate place mats with the Kelsey coat of arms engraved on them, along with other items of great value. They take their positions, pull up chairs and await the arrival of the Three Heads to arrive before preparing to run through the agenda for the meetings to come over the following weeks.

Outside the door, Wellesley and Lord Ashby stop and face the three men. Bonner and Mallory first look at each other, then at Stone as if waiting for instructions. After a few seconds they look back toward Wellesley, Lord Ashby moves off and stands inside the doorway while Wellesley continues to stare hard at Mallory.

"Yes, she is still alive despite your best efforts, but it seems the price is going up all the time. Are you running out of takers for this kind of sordid work, as they never seem to be seen again? Let alone the cost in gold you need to keep finding from the people's pockets to pay these would-be assassins." He looks down at Mallory's wrists. "I see you still wear your long sleeves to cover your wrists, always the cautious man if I am possibly going to be around. Still, it does not matter, I know it was you and it is only a matter of time before I act on it."

Stone steps forward. "If you know anything, why don't you do something about it right now, like prove it or just shut up and return to that woman, old man." He pauses as he thinks of the right words to take a dig at Wellesley and try and get him to retaliate. "I don't know why she would want you protecting her, you did not do a very good job of protecting the last king and queen!"

Wellesley does not turn from staring at Mallory as he answers. "Every assassin sent that day was killed and soon the people who instigated that terrible crime will pay the same price, but it has to be done within the law, unlike others who think they are above such matters." Wellesley moves away and enters the room, still keeping his eyes on Mallory until he disappears inside. He is closely watched by Lord Ashby, who had taken up a rear-guard position, as he also moves away from the doorway and vanishes from view, leaving just the three men standing outside in the corridor looking at each other.

Stone turns and snarls at his accomplices, "Hell's teeth, thirty teams out looking, seventy-five gold pieces per team and yet despite all your assurances that she would be dead, that bloody woman walks into this building bold as brass. Not only that, but her protectors also have the cheek to belittle you two in front of me! The shame and embarrassment of it all. This has now gone too far, can you two get nothing right? I would have been better off spending the money to be rid of you both for all the use you are to me at the moment. This should have been resolved years ago, not being dragged out in front of me time and time again." The two men look at each other, lost for words, all they can do is stare at each other with blank expressions.

Stone growls as he continues, "We will talk about this after the meeting, for I am sure that this is now going to be an eventful few hours to say the least. Still, it will give you two time to think up some imaginative excuses for your epic failures over the past couple of months."

He storms into the room, closely followed by the other two men as they take their places at the table. As they are seated, Lord Ashby closes the door and takes his seat with Wellesley on the back wall of the room. They have no voice in the debates that are about to take place, present only to bear witness to the meeting and to act as security to the queen's negotiators and envoys should they be needed.

Nearly four hours of intense negotiations pass, voices are raised and heated arguments ensue as Stone and his associates demand more taxes from the people for public services and the removal of the queen from her right to govern and rule over the laws of the land. "The queen should represent the country as a figurehead and representative only, not be able to set laws and involve herself in politics and the laws it is governed by. That should be left to the politicians who know how to run a country and make these difficult decisions," bellows Stone.

"The queen represents the people and the interests of the people, we all know where your loyalties stand and where they have taken this country over the years, Stone. It is the ruling monarchy's birthright to rule and a long time since the queen did so. I request this house return state powers back to the queen so she can take up the rightful duties she should have had returned years ago," replies one of the diplomats in favor of the queen.

"Gentlemen of the house, the queen does not understand the complexities of running a country being of such a soft disposition for her subjects. It must be left to those that know best to lay down the laws of the land in the interests of its people. Making those difficult and sometimes unpopular decisions in the best interests of the country and its residence," replies Stone.

As expected, the house fails to come to a clear two-thirds decision on any of the bills requested, to pass them into law. Them that are loyal to the queen remain loyal to her. Those loyal to The Three Heads will remain as long as they continue to be paid well for their support.

Stone is first to storm out of the room, closely followed by Mallory and Bonner. "That fucking woman has an answer for everything! How am I supposed to raise more money to pay off our supporters and creditors if she blocks every move to raise taxes or sell off land and produce to neighboring countries? You two should have finished her when you had the chance, but no! 'She is just a child, what harm can she do us?' Well, by the look of it, plenty! See what she has become now! You two wanted a seat at the high table, now earn it. Find a way to get rid of her fast, before I make it my personal objective to raise money by removing you two and claiming your assets as my own to fill the void I now find myself in."

He storms off, leaving Mallory and Bonner looking blankly at each other. After a brief moment, they also begin to move on, albeit at a slower pace and arguing with each other before going silent as they hear Margaret leaving the room.

Wellesley and Lord Ashby are out front and lead the group as usual at these events, and, as they reach the two men, Wellesley cannot help himself, he stops to speak to them both as the rest file pass. "That is the difference between a diplomat representing a nation and a dictator with no negotiating skills, just force, blackmail, and murder," he tells them. "They only get you so far, when it comes to running a country, you need the people behind you, and not just so you can take their money and then treat them like slaves and keep them oppressed. In time you will have nothing left to offer. Even now you turn on each other; how long before he makes good on his threats and you cease to be? I feel that day will soon come to fruition the way he speaks to you now". Wellesley looks at both of them in turn before he continues, "When that day comes and you are running for your very lives, where will you go? Your own country will not want you and no other land will want the burden of harboring people suspected of having a hand in the murder of a reigning king and queen! They would fear the repercussions or worse, their own deaths at the hands of the same murderers."

Margaret stops and turns to look at Wellesley. "Let them be, they are just puppets for their master Stone. Come Wellesley, we have more important things to be getting on with. If you would be so kind as to join us, we can move on to our next appointment with the Church representatives at St Bennett's Abbey."

Wellesley smiles and tilts his hat at the two men. "Hope to see you at the negotiating table next time, that is if you are still around. Or perhaps by then you will have a more suitable position in a hole in the ground somewhere. Well, I cannot hang around here chewing the fat with the condemned, I have places to be and people to meet. Stay safe, if not well hidden Mallory, for soon I will be coming for the vengeance my wife so desperately deserves, God rest her soul."

Wellesley turns and walks away with a smirk on his face, he has sown the seed in the minds of the two men just as he had planned. Now he will wait and see what they do next for he knows the mettle of these men and they will now be frantically trying to come up with solutions to ensure the safety of their own skins. As he rejoins Margaret and the others, Lord Ashby whispers into his ear. The words are not heard by anyone else, but he looks and smiles back at Lord Ashby as they move off as a unit away from the watching Mallory and Bonner.

"Do you think he will follow through with his threats? We are doing the best we can to be rid of that woman, she just has better men defending her than we have to put against her," Bonner says to Mallory as they watch Margaret and her dignitaries walk off down the hallway.

"I don't know," Mallory replies. "Rightly or wrongly, we have made our bed and now must live with the consequences and defend our position. He cannot possibly run all that he needs to in this country without our support and assistance. What scares me the most is that he believes he is above all others and has yet to be satisfied with all he has. His own ambitions will pull us all down if he continues the way he is going. Come, let's leave this place and see what we can come up with over a bowl of hot broth, for I think better while I am eating."

The two men head off in the opposite direction to Margaret and her companions. They continue talking and hatching plans as they leave the building through the library exit and head toward the high-end eating house 'All But The Sink'. As with any place they go, they are shown to the very best table in the house and have people doing all they can to impress and pamper the two men with fine wines, champagne, and servers falling over themselves to take orders. Within minutes of sitting down, the two men are approached by two beautiful young ladies who introduce themselves as Silvia and Angelina who, after a short conversation, take seats with them at the table.

As waiters add two more place settings to the table and pour glasses of champagne for the four of them, the girls smile and laugh with the men, who are trying to impress the ladies with jokes and conversation on a variety of subjects. The daft thing is that they do not have to be impressed since the girls are going to be paid for their services, all that is to be decided is how long the men will want them around for. The girls are thinking that if they play it right, they will have a nice bed for the night rather than the damp, dingy space they share at the back of a warehouse. With the day starting off so badly for Mallory and Bonner, the two girls laughing and giggling at all their jokes makes them feel better and they start to forget their problems and drink heavily. The more the men drink, the more they want to impress the women and enjoy being complimented by them in return. Minutes turn into hours and soon the men are quite drunk. When the two girls leave them to use the rest room, Mallory and Bonner start to talk.

"I'm too pissed to go home, start a row with them that have been waiting for me, for they will be feisty and not best pleased, that's for sure," comments Mallory as he throws back another brandy.

"Aye, besides that, us being drunk and the women at home being sober, it won't go down well and I still want to enjoy myself and have a bit of fun with these lasses. I know, why don't we stay at the Grand tonight and go back in the morning? Say that the meeting had gone on longer than expected," Bonner slurs in reply.

"That, that be a good idea. We can still have some fun tonight with er, er Silvia and Anger... wasser name and toss them out in the morning." The men stagger to their feet as the girls arrive back, arm-in-arm. Mallory throws down some notes on the table while Bonner puts his arms out toward the two ladies.

"Come, we are going on an adventure." The young ladies each take one of Bonner's arms while laughing and joking and turn and leave with the drunken man.

Mallory looks at the head waiter. "Be needing a carriage out the front to take us to the Grand Hotel right now, boy."

The head waiter is only too pleased to send a man out to get a coach as they have become very loud and offensive, upsetting many of his regular customers and causing some to leave. With a click of his fingers a young waiter rushes over to him and after a few brief words rushes outside to secure some transport for his noisy guests. "Would there be anything else you require, sir?" the head waiter asks as he leads Mallory to the exit.

"No, your service has been exemplary and the food as exquisite as always. I am sure now that the diplomatic negotiations are back on the table after the summer holidays we will be here a lot more often." He tucks a note into the waiter's top pocket and pats it with his hand. "For yourself, keep up the good work and thanks for the female company, keep it coming and I will make sure you're well looked after," he comments as he puts on his hat, spins his fingers around the rim, and makes his way to his friends and the waiting carriage.

Ravenger, the head waiter, manager and owner of the establishment, walks back toward his booking station shaking his head. He hates the thought of his restaurant having those men regularly attending, especially when Stone is with them, as they treat the place as if they own it. They lower its standards with the constant demands for loose women and loud, undesirable, villainous guests who insult and offend other regular and decent clientele with their behavior and manners. But, alas, as with everything in the city, they have the power to decimate anything they choose to, so he must appease, smile, and make the best of a bad situation, or lose what he worked all his life to build up and make into one of the finest eating houses in the country.

Not two miles further along the road, overshadowing Remembrance Park, stands the Grand Hotel. It towers over all the other buildings that surround it with its nine floors of decadent rooms and balconies. There is true opulence in the design and architecture of the building, combining old and new techniques and materials to show the very best that can be achieved by modern architects. Chief of whom is the legendary Bowen "Fence down" Derby, a legend in the development of all best buildings of all shapes and sizes.

Remembrance Park was built by the queen to honor her mother and father after they had been murdered, a place for all to remember them and take sanctuary when one's mind needs peace and quiet amongst the hustle and bustle of city life. Years of development and donations of statues and works of art from people across the known world fill the three-hundred-acre site. At the center of the park is a large monument, surrounded by four full-sized bronze Ambulette horses rearing and throwing their feet and manes as they reach for the sky. Between them is a small foal and on the wall behind them a shield with the coat of arms of the royal family. Each side of the shield there is a large plaque featuring a picture of the old king on one side and the queen on the other. Below, a wavy brass ribbon hangs with the words "A loss to a nation greatly missed but never forgotten" carved into it.

Around this area and the rest of the park are hundreds of well-used seats. All the benches and resting points throughout the grounds are made from the roots and stumps of great trees that have fallen. Each one is individually carved and shaped into a usable sculpture, as comfortable as they are beautiful. It is often said that since being built, over eighty percent of all couples in the city have proposed to each other at one place or another around this park, a tradition that has grown and now pulls people in from all over the country for such a special personal moment. These areas also hold another surprise for those who walk round this hallowed ground. For years it has been a tradition for lovers to tap in a small brass disk with their chosen words or names to the back or sides of the chair they proposed on. Thousands now adorn these seats across the whole park and glitter like confetti in the bright rays of sunlight or shimmer and seem to make the benches and chairs look as if they are moving when the wind picks up.

Many people regularly show their families or children their own special place in the park as they walk around the enchanting gardens, while others like to read the inscriptions left by fellow sweethearts. Such is the popularity of this modern tradition, there is now a small kiosk in the corner of the park that has been set up by a retired grenadier, 'Cherub' Charlie as he is now known. He will engrave a disk to order, or in some cases, while you wait, for a small donation to assist people injured during military services. Small brass hammers can also be borrowed from this hut as long as they are returned after use. All the brass disks are cut from a melted down statue of the former king and queen that Stone had removed from the main entrance of the town hall. It was found and rescued by Lord Ashby while he was at a smelter's placing an order for twelve eight-pound canons for a new ship. Now it seems that using a disk from this statue represents love to the very end and many people want to believe in that for themselves.

The grounds are maintained and patrolled from the queen's own private finances for all to enjoy and visit at no cost. The Park is considered one of the most romantic and safest areas of the city, as her own retired household cavalry and grenadiers watch over the grounds and the people who use the facilities, protecting all who enter with the same vigor and pride they showed as soldiers serving the old king and queen.

As with everything good the queen tries to do, there is always opposition by a select few, in this case it is the usual suspects Stone, Bonner, and Mallory. As well as it being a reminder that they would dearly like to remove from history, the park reminds the nation of a terrible murder and is a focal point for people to congregate without The Three Heads having influence over them, keeping the tragedy alive in the memory of the people.

Stone also wants the land for himself to build a new house on as well as selling part of the park to the Grand Hotel to enlarge their grounds and make a better area to hold garden parties and functions. Being a silent partner and the major shareholder in the hotel, he has a vested interest in building the hotel up to increase his profits. He tries at every opportunity to break the queen's control on the land using any angle he can to bring it up at the negotiating table and wrest it from her grasp. What really hits a nerve with him is that it was he who sold the land to the young queen in the first place, when it was derelict and used as a dumping ground by the whole city. Never thinking that after years of hard work and development, it would be near pristine and one of the main attractions of the city. A beacon of hope and a place that would come to mean so much to so many in the years to come.

As the carriage pulls up outside the Grand Hotel, the door is opened by a well-dressed footman in his red uniform with gold thread trimmings. He helps the two ladies out before stepping back as Mallory near falls out of the carriage, closely followed by Bonner. "Come this way, ladies, the view from the top is exceptional," shouts Mallory as he staggers into the hotel lobby. Passing the reception desk, he yells out again, "Champagne and frosted cakes to the top floor and be snappy about it." The others try to keep up as he continues on toward the wide, curved oak stairs that arc around the room. He mounts the first steps and staggers ever onward, half tripping and half falling forward as he does his best to charge up the stairs. The Three Heads hold the top floor year-round as a place to take important guests and politicians, or to use themselves when the opportunity presents itself.

Silvia and Angelina are a little out of their comfort zone and try to be more dignified as they walk up the stairs arm in arm. Although slightly tipsy, they do their best to look ladylike and fit in with others using the hotel. To the untrained eye they carry off their act reasonably well. But for the hotel staff, who are used to the Three Heads and what they get up to, they know exactly what the girls are and look at them with disappointment and disgust for entering their hotel. Still, they have a job to do and these two men carry a lot of influence and sway so they busy themselves satisfying the needs of Mallory and Bonner.

Two of the staff quickly run up the stairs past the four of them to open up the room and prepare the interior to receive guests, while others organize champagne and fresh cakes from the extensive kitchens. Silvia and Angelina help Mallory up the last few flights of stairs to the suite, as they enter the room they stop and stare at the elegance of the decor inside. The rooms are absolutely beautiful, with statues and works of art on every surface and plush burgundy velvet curtains hanging both sides of every window, held back with gold embroidered sashes. The two girls walk over to the double doors and open them onto a large balcony and look over the park grounds below. The symmetrical flower beds, shapes of the angle-cut borders, and positioning of shrubs and small trees around the crescent lakes now makes perfect sense.

The gardens may look good from the ground, but it does not hold a candle to the views from above. The colors, patterns, and designs all merge to make a mosaic that has to be seen from above for its display to be fully appreciated.

Inside the huge suite Bonner has just made it to the room and is throwing his coat and hat onto one of the many chairs while Mallory is in the bathroom relieving himself. One of the porters is standing by the hand pully elevator winding a rope on a wheel until a large ice bucket appears with five bottles of champagne, four glasses, and a three-tier cake stand covered in delicious pastries of all shapes and sizes. The other porter moves everything to a presentation table and then collects cutlery and plates from a side table along with cloth napkins and various serving implements. Looking over to Mallory for final approval, he opens one of the bottles of champagne and fills the four glasses. Once done he is approached by Mallory who tips him before the two porters tilt their heads at him and leave the room, closing the door behind them as they go.

Mallory picks up two of the glasses and takes them to the girls on the balcony, handing each one a glass, he looks them up and down, and, as the girls turn back to look at the view, Mallory moves up tight behind Silvia. He puts his hand around her front and cups her breast, squeezing it as he starts to kiss her neck and shoulder.

"Easy, tiger, we have the whole evening to go," she says while rubbing her spare hand up and down his thigh without turning around. This is the sign he has been waiting for, he brings up his second hand and cups both breasts, rubbing her nipples with his thumbs as he massages her breasts and continues to kiss her neck.

It is at this point that the strategy begins as the girls put their skills and abilities to the test. They are now in the hotel suite and what they get from the deal depends on how they plan their moves. The men just want one thing, and it would be easy to give them what they desire, be paid, and leave, but the girls have other ideas. This is an opportunity to spend the night safe in the best hotel in the country and enjoy themselves in the process. The cat and mouse games begin as Angelina walks over to Bonner and gently kisses him while stroking the back of his neck with her fingers.

"Let's have some cake and build up our energy, my dear, for once you get me going, I take a lot of satisfying and you're going to need all your stamina to keep up with me." She lowers her arm and brushes her hand over the front of his trousers, gently squeezing. "Well, we certainly have a little action beginning to firm up here," she comments as they move toward the champagne and cakes. Mallory and Angelina closely follow the two of them and as the girls select pastries to eat, Bonner pours out more champagne for them to drink.

Over the next hour or so the girls work their talents and abilities, switching their full glasses with the men's empty ones to keep them drinking. Lipstick or not on the glasses, the men are already so drunk that finesse is not required. Teasing them with a few kisses and allowing them to have a fumble here and there, they soon get the men to polish off four of the bottles of champagne. With the men looking worse for wear, Silvia and Angelina step it up a gear. Stripping off their dresses, they start to touch and feel each other intimately, watching the men as they do so. This excites Mallory greatly and he starts to take his clothes off and throw them across the room, but as he pulls off his trousers he falls over the legs of the passed-out Bonner and collapses to the floor. The girls laugh as they help him to his feet and virtually drag the dribbling and moaning man to one of the bedrooms, rolling him onto the bed and stripping the last of his clothes off. To their surprise he is wearing a money belt. After looking at each other and smiling with delight they swiftly remove the item and check inside the pockets.

"Blimey, one hundred and eighty ductares," says Angelina. They look at each other again. "Are you thinking what I'm thinking, Buns?" Angelina asks, using her pet name for Silvia.

Her face lights up as she smiles. "Shall we?" she replies as the girl's giggle and head back to where they left Bonner. As they enter the room all smiles disappear as Bonner is not where they last saw him. As they look at each other and begin to panic, then they hear the awful sound of a man throwing up in one of the bathrooms. Again and again they hear him retching, then silence.

After a few minutes of waiting, Silvia taps on the door. "Bonner, Bonner, are you there?" With no reply she opens the door and peers inside. "Oh my God, that is disgusting," she cries. Angelina rushes to the open door and looks inside. Seconds later she turns away trying not to retch herself, for inside the room Bonner is slumped up in the corner, surrounded by vomit and his own piss, a trail of champagne and part-digested cake all down his front.

"Is he dead?" Angelina asks as she tries to compose herself.

"No, he is still moving and breathing," Silvia answers. "But we can't leave him like this, we need to get him out of there and onto a bed." Angelina stares at Silvia with wide eyes.

"No! I can't go in there, I'll be sick."

Silvia grabs her hand and drags the shaking Angelina toward the room. "Hold your breath and we will go in, grab him, and put him on the bed by Mallory."

Against her better judgment, she follows Silvia into the room. Several swear words and ten minutes later they reappear dragging the intoxicated man between them. It takes the girls several minutes to get the man onto the bed with Mallory and roll him on his side, while Angelina goes back to close the door to the bathroom to keep the smell inside. Silvia starts to undo the clothes around Bonner's ample waist and finds another money belt. Opening it, she counts up her findings.

"Another one hundred or so ductares," she calls out as she walks back out of the room and throws the belt on the side with the other one.

She turns to look at Angelina, who is outside the main bathroom sliding her top over her head, her breasts bouncing enticingly as she wriggles down her underwear. She walks into the bathroom and begins to fill the large bath with water from the tap on the wall. While she smells bottles of perfume and adds scented oils to the filling bath, Silvia opens up the last bottle of champagne and collects two new glasses from the sideboard. She walks into the bathroom and places the bottle and glasses on the side of the bath before turning to Angelina. As Angelina lifts Silvia's dress over her head, she begins to caresses Angelina's breasts while kissing her passionately. Slowly they step into the bath together, still holding each other tightly in a lover's embrace.

An hour passes before the girls reappear from the bathroom wrapped in towels. Silvia checks on the state of the two men in the other room, then returns to Angelina who is in the master bedroom pulling back the silk sheets on the bed.

"They have not moved, Ange— What are you doing?" she asks with a curious voice.

Angelina looks at her with a seductive smirk on her face. "You didn't think I would go without trying out this bed, did you?" She moves forward and takes Silvia's hands in hers and walks slowly backward, taking Silvia with her, and when she reaches the bed she falls backward onto it. They land giggling together and Angelina wraps her legs around her partner, holding her in position. They begin to kiss passionately before Silvia starts to unwrap Angelina from her towel. "I think we should stay here for a couple of hours, then leave this place for ever. We have enough money to buy a little place in the country far away from here where nobody knows us and we can start afresh.

Nearly three hours later, down in the reception of the hotel, two well-dressed ladies step down the last flight of stairs from the rooms above. They are arm in arm, giggling and whispering to each other as they reach the bottom and look around the room. There is a pride and elegance to them as they walk across the entrance hall that they did not have when they arrived, an attractive look that gets more than a couple of approving looks from the men sitting around in the reception area reading newspapers or talking with friends. As they head toward the entrance to the building they are intercepted by two well-dressed gentlemen.

"Could we be of service to you two fine ladies? Perhaps a drink or two at the bar over there." The man points toward the counter at the far side of the room.

Angelina smiles at them, turns to look at Silvia then back at the two men. "I think not, I have all I need on my arm and she is more than a match for any man." The ladies smile politely as they pass the two men and continue on their way, then laugh and giggle as they go out of the main entrance to the hotel. As they approach the first taxi carriages waiting along the side of the hotel, the doorman opens the carriage door, they climb inside and take their seats as Silvia gives a destination to the doorman as he closes the door. He in turn passes the destination to the driver, who flicks the reins at his two horses to get them moving.

It is the last day the city will ever see these two women, as that afternoon they will start a journey that will eventually take them to the far side of the country, to the coastal village of Angel Sands about five miles from one of the large navy ports. Up on a hillside overlooking this community is a small homestead on the edge of a chestnut wood surrounded by open fields and small streams. The two ladies will start a small cattle and sheep smallholding that will quickly grow in size and produce some of the best cheeses in the land. In time, their produce will even find its way to the table of the royal family and get the coveted royal seal of approval as the queen's favorite soft cheese.

CHAPTER 13

Final Plans

Over the following five months life has been hectic for Margaret and Andrew as the country falls deeper into civil unrest. Stone's demands for more taxes and a tighter grip on the economy have the country divided more than ever. The resilience and determination of the queen and her administration to block all his proposals keeps them busy and most times they manage to rebuff the proposals, but not all the time.

With state-fixed prices on all grain and food not changing in more than fifteen years, and the right to buy all that is produced, they can buy cheap and sell to the people at a far higher price. Farmers and country landowners are now pushing back and smuggling grain and food stocks across the borders to get better prices for their produce, leaving the country and in particular the poor in towns and cities with barely enough food to survive. Stone has also started a diplomatic incident with the neighboring kingdom of Denmark over trade rights and a disputed area of land that he now feels should be under the rule of Kelsey.

The lord living on the land is from Kelsey, married to his Danish wife for many years with three children, but the land has title to Denmark and fair tribute is paid for the use of the land each year by him with no quarrel to the arrangement.

But, as always, Stone likes the area, with open fields, several lakes and a river running through the middle of the Estate, making it a prime location spot for the development of a grand estate.

Also on this land are three small villages situated along its length, the villagers that live there pay a small levy to the lord which goes towards the tribute given to kingdom of Denmark,.

With the lord's manor house in an ideal location facing the banks of the largest lake between two of the villages. Stone has his own plans for this estate and has started proceedings to acquire the land by any means available to him, even if that means starting a diplomatic incident. Leaving Margaret and her team to resolve these two discrepancies:

Restore faith with the royal family of Denmark.

Try to negotiate a better deal for the farmers to prevent them needing to sell their produce abroad to get a reasonable price and make a living.

It was a tough ask, but honor had been maintained with the Danish royal family after two in-depth meetings and a personal gift of a dozen ambulette horses from the queen. As for the farmers and their crops, all she can do is raise the issue with the representatives at parliament and try to negotiate a better deal with the politicians, a far harder and thankless task as Mallory, Bonner and Stone oppose everything the queen and her team will put forward.

Young Henry, as expected, has become a well-travelled baby, transported to various areas of the country for feeding and being with his true mother without raising suspicion. With locations like churches and cathedrals being useful meeting places for mother and son. He is now eating solid food on a regular basis along with less milk from his mother, allowing Margaret a little extra time to plan her days and workloads over a longer period of time. This has helped as she has been meeting and negotiating more and more with the diplomats and royal families of the countries and kingdoms that surround Kelsey in an attempt to ensure support for the up and coming events being planned.

Back at the manor house Andrew is having to take on a more active and changing role in steering daily events and overseeing the larger number of people working in the war room. It is becoming clear to him now that whatever the queen and Margaret are planning, it is not just a rouse to regain control of the country, but a total revamp of all the countries political affairs and how the country will be managed going forward. A task that has been many years in the making, not just in the time he has known Margaret. The scale of the preparation that is underway is enormous, using Young bright graduates, honest politicians, professors, and skilled professionals from all the universities across the country. All working hard, preparing and waiting to implement a total change to the complete running of Kelsey with all areas and aspects covered and planned to the smallest detail. So many people committed and dedicated to bringing the country back to its former days of prosperity and greatness.

Andrew's only fear now is that it would only take one mistake or a single person to betray the queen and this would all fall apart; his beloved Margaret and all she has committed to, along with so many good people lost. He now understands that this is a one-time, fully committed attempt to free the people from tyranny and oppression; failure would mean the loss of the country and, worse, probably the death or execution of all the people involved.

While the Three Heads have been bitterly blocking and preventing the queen from accessing her rights to rule, Stone has also been blocked and has not been able to pass any new meaningful laws or find any legal way to remove the queen from any right to rule the country permanently. All he has been able to do is delay and postpone her right to reign in an ongoing and constant battle using the diplomatic arena as his battleground.

Her role at the moment allows her to represent the nation as its figurehead, but the politicians have been in control of the country until she was to reach an age where she was no longer considered a child. Since she came of age to rule, they have used every trick in the book to keep her from taking back full power. However, from the age of twenty-one, the queen can veto any new rules and laws if she can prove they are not beneficial to her subjects in the assembly as long as she has a majority vote of all those present.

Stone, Mallory and Bonner may still be a controlling power within the government, but they have failed to get any additional taxation or billing laws through, with the monarchy's representatives and finance ministers combining to block all his attempts to take total control. This continuous stalemate holds the country in limbo, neither improving nor descending deeper into total chaos at the hands of the Three Heads.

This stagnant predicament has been frustrating Stone and the others to distraction, as the money that has been levied from the people is now less than they need to continue support from some of the more dishonest diplomats from the neighboring countries and rogue dignitaries to keep the pressure on removing the royal family from ever regaining state control again.

Margaret's team has also managed to block any reserves being transferred from the country's national banks or any finances being borrowed against the bank's reserves and used as bridging loans. This has been done with the help of the intellectuals and mathematicians she has been working with in anticipation of putting the squeeze back on Stone, Mallory and Bonner as she tries to bring the country back to being ruled by the queen.

At present The Three Heads just about have the finances to keep control of the country and the people needed to help retain their positions, but, like all rich and powerful people, they do not like using their own money to fight the queen or paying for support with their own reserves, as the transfers involved would leave a trail that could possibly be traced back to them.

Also, greedy men do not like using their own ill-gotten gains when they could be using somebody else's money, in this case the people's taxes and state funds. Stone is all too aware that if they continue to hemorrhage money without being able to replace the used finances, they will eventually run out of assets. And when the assets run out, paid mercenaries and support from those he relies on, like his fleet of pirate ships. Pillaging and plundering supplies and goods on trade ships running the shipping lines, soon dwindles in its willingness to take the risks needed to hold the country at bay,

It is now the beginning of winter, a time when the weather always takes a swift turn for the worst at some time, covering the land under a thick blanket of snow and ice. So far this year it seems to have been a little milder than many that have gone before. But sharp frosts and heavy snow could be only days away, depending on the direction the wind blows. Northerly winds coming off the sea usually bring the more severe weather conditions, while southerly winds tend to hold the milder weather for a little longer. Diplomatic meetings begin to slow as foreign officials do not like to travel at this time of year, as bad weather can add weeks to a journey at sea and even potentially strand them in a foreign country for a month or more.

With a two-week recess in the meeting schedule due to the trade diplomats from Saxony being delayed, and political disputes on borders between Hanover and Prussia preventing a state visit from the Hanoverians while they resolve their own differences.

Margaret is returning back to the house early, her arrival, as always is greeted by Andrew standing at the entrance to the building, waiting for the coach to stop so he can open the door for her himself. He has been fortunate that she has been able to return to the house quite regularly in the past month and as he opens the door to the coach, he is greeted with a smiling wife. She steps down to the ground and into the arms of her beloved Andrew, first kissing him passionately before moving back and speaking.

"It is good to be back, my dear," she says as she looks firstly at Andrew then behind him to Beth standing in the doorway of the house. She is holding baby Henry in her arms, rocking him gently from side to side as she acknowledges Margaret. Instantly she makes a bee line to them and takes her son from her grasp. "Hello, my little man, Mother's home for a little while". She shakes her head at him "Mother has missed you so much, yes she has." Looking back at Beth, she asks, "How has he been?"

Beth smiles. "He has been a little gentleman, eating well and sleeping in regular patterns, all has been well for the one day you have been away."

Margaret shakes her head. "So, it is only a day then, but I still missed him as if it was a month." The pair of them chuckle together as Margaret dotes on her little boy.

Behind them Anna has just stepped down from the coach. She smiles at Andrew as she walks straight past him to see Henry, patiently waiting for her chance to see and hold the little man. "Hu, Hu, Hu," she murmurs.

Margaret turns to look at Anna. "Really, Anna, I'm beginning to wonder who the mother of my child is! He seems to spend more time in your arms than the rest of us put together!"

They walk into the house and through to the large living room where the fire burns brightly and it is nice and warm, a far cry from the chilly weather outside. Margaret suddenly stops and looks around the room. Something is not quite right. She sniffs the air, then looks back at the others and then back at the room. It takes her a minute to realize what has changed.

"The chairs, they are slightly different, why have we changed them again? It nearly caused a riot last time."

Beth smiles and shakes her head. "Same chairs, we just had them re-covered with identical fabric and added a little extra padding in the ones where they were sagging a little. They needed a little touching up to make them presentable".

Andrew walks up to Beth and puts his hand on her shoulder. "Told you."

She sighs heavily, "Fine, you said she would notice and you were right" Beth turns to Margaret. "But how did you know? There is barely a difference to what they were previously and you have not even touched them to notice the padding."

Margaret raises her head a little higher and puts her shoulders back just a touch more in a show of superiority "The smell"

Beth looks at her curiously "The smell?"

Margaret nods "Wellesley always smokes the same pipe tobacco, I remember it since I was a child, as he and my father would smoke pipes together in secret away from my mother. Even now he would take a pipe in this room when I am not around as he knows I do not like it smoked when I am there, it makes my eyes water. Do not get me wrong, I like the smell it left in this room as it brings back fond memories, but now the scent has virtually gone. As it was embedded in the fabric of the old chairs, the chairs must have changed in some way". She walks over to one of the re-upholstered chairs and takes a seat while still holding Henry in her arms. She wriggles, sits back, stands up and then sits down again, twisting this way and that before settling into the chair. "They are

still extremely comfortable, if not just a little better than before"
She nods her head with approval "I like them a lot, good job with
getting them done Beth"

"Thank you" Beth says as Andrew and Anna sit down beside
her. "I will see about some tea, and I know Bunty has been making
cakes and biscuits all afternoon so I will bring some of those as
well". As she leaves the room, she closes the door quietly behind
her.

Anna is watching Margaret and Henry like a hawk, a sight
that has not gone unnoticed by Andrew, who starts chuckling and
shaking his head. Margaret looks at her through the corner of her
eye, then sits back in the chair and gets comfortable with her son.
Every now and then she takes a look over at Anna, and every time
she looks Anna is watching her like a cat ready to pounce.

"Have you told her yet, Andrew?" Margaret asks Andrew.

He shakes his head. "No, I presumed that it should be addressed
by you and you alone"

She nods her head in agreement. "I will wait for Wellesley to
arrive, for he will be a cantankerous old bugger if he does not hear
firsthand" she replies while playing with Henry's hand with her
index finger and pulling faces at him.

Anna is desperate to ask about what it is that they are not talking
about, but she also knows that if it is to involve Wellesley, then it
must be of great importance and well worth the wait. As she thinks
about it, the door to the room opens and Wellesley looks around,
nods at Margaret then enters. He takes no time heading for his
favorite chair, front and center of the fireplace. Grabbing the arm
in one hand he turns and takes his seat, letting out a huge sigh as
he does so. He leans back and sinks his shoulders into the fabric,
pauses for a moment, sits forward, and then pushes back again.

The others watch as he wriggles to try and get comfortable
then, standing up, he turns and starts pushing down on the seat
area with his hands. Andrew and Anna start to laugh as they watch
him trying to work out why the armchair is not as it should be. He
moves to the next seat and sits down in that one, bouncing on it
three or four times before getting up and sitting back in his favorite

chair.

"For God's sake, Wellesley, will you stop flapping about? It is only a chair, either sit in it of find another place to park your behind," barks Margaret as she watches him squirming and pushing back in the chair.

"It's this chair," he complains. "It doesn't fit like it should and I don't know why. It looks and feels right, but it's not the same as it was."

Beth walks into the room carrying a tray laden with a teapot, crockery, and other items for accompanying an afternoon tea. She places them in the side while watching Wellesley fidget about with his chair.

"Perhaps it's the shape of your behind that has changed. It does look a little bonier than it used to, and them trousers don't seem to fit as well, a little looser and hang down more than I remember" comments Anna, to a barrage of sniggers and chuckles from all the others in the room.

Wellesley is up out and out of his chair in an instant and looks at his bottom before turning to Anna. "I would have you know that I am in my prime, my trousers fit as they always have, filled to perfection with a fine figure of a man."

"Oh yes, I would agree with that, you are certainly a fine figure of a man, still able to turn any woman's head should you choose to with a firm rump like that," replies Bunty as she crosses the room with a tray full of cakes and fine pastries for the group. She places the tray down on the side while beaming a huge admiring grin at Wellesley.

As he looks around at her she winks at him and gives him a little wave. There is no description worthy of the shock and fear on his face as he swiftly sits back down and sheepishly tucks himself firmly back into his chair.

"A man beyond fear in battle, survivor of countless engagements with the enemy, struck down by a smile, wink, and wave from a woman. Seems that the chair fits you well now it has a purpose, Wellesley," says a smiling Margaret, who has been watching his reaction to Bunty.

Anna and Beth are giggling as they look at each other, they love it when Bunty speaks to Wellesley as she is the only person they know who puts the fear of God into the old war horse, shutting him up in an instant and keeping him quiet while ever she is around.

"Tea, Margaret?" Beth asks as she starts to pour out the cups. Margaret nods and is served first while Bunty offers her a choice of pastries she has just taken out from the ovens in the kitchen. Margaret does not hold back, collecting four, then five items on a small plate while balancing Henry on her side.

"Would you like me to hold Henry for you?" asks Anna, who is now standing right beside Margaret in anticipation of getting her hands on the young Henry.

Margaret chuckles and shakes her head. "You be a canny lass, my dear. Yes, you may take my little man, just while I eat, though, it is not for the rest of the night." Anna lifts the young Henry from Margaret's side and holds him gently in her arms as she sits back down in her chair and begins to play with the baby's hands.

Wellesley is desperate to get amongst the food on offer, but with Bunty still by the side of the tray waiting like a predator watching a fresh kill, he has to wait and pretend he is not interested in food. Fortunately for him, Andrew is a gentleman, and, knowing what is going on, he collects a plate, places a few items on it, and passes it to the hungry Wellesley.

"That should start to fill those loose trousers they are all talking about," Andrew says as he passes him the plate. Wellesley willingly accepts the plate Andrew has offered while on the far side of the room. Bunty realizes her chance has gone. With a disappointed expression at failing to get near Wellesley, she lowers her head and leaves to attend her duties in the kitchen.

"Would you please close the door as you leave, Bunty, as I do not wish young Henry to get a chill from the draught?"

The door soon closes and with that and a few more mouthfuls of cake, Margaret speaks again. "Well, as we are all together, it seems fitting that I should say a few words. The past few months have kept us busy and on edge, especially with my son needing to be moved around so much, for that I thank you all from the bottom of my and Andrew's hearts. All has been quiet with no incidents or risks to any of us for some time now and, again, I thank you for all you have done to keep Henry safe and away from danger. However, it will not last forever, the more we resist and push back, cutting them off from finances and stores looted by his pirates plundering the coastline. The more they will try to infiltrate and take us down to save their own way of life. We must keep Stone and his associates on the back foot, be alert to anything different for they will surely try to break us up and take us down"

She turns and looks directly at Wellesley. "Well, that is for most of us. Wellesley seems to be handling his greatest foe with less decorum than usual, but then again he has not come across a woman with such steely-eyed determination before and Bunty seems to be quite determined in her own ways to make good her ambitions with our great protector here."

As the others chuckle, Wellesley curses and mutters several words under his breath. "Sorry, Wellesley, is there something you would like to say?"

He shakes his head and gives Margaret a sinister stare while he snaps off another piece of pastry, listening as Margaret continues to talk. "Well, this is where I drop another big one on you all, for it would seem that we are going to have to go through it all again, for I may be with child again."

The room goes absolutely silent. Anna's jaw drops as her eyes widen before a huge grin covers her face, Beth takes in a deep sigh, while Wellesley just stares at the plate he is holding as it lowers and some of the items fall into his lap. He speaks without realizing he has done so.

"Bit keen, aren't we? First one has barely hit the ground and is not even walking."

Margaret shrugs her shoulders and gives an innocent expression. "To be fair, we were not intending on having another one so quickly, it just seems to have been fate."

Before she can say any more, Anna speaks up. "This is so wonderful! Can I pretend this one is mine and keep it with me when it's born, for Wellesley here is not up to much and I am still waiting for him to get going?" She covers her mouth with her spare hand as she says, "I think he is a bit o-l-d and past it now."

Wellesley looks at Anna, flabbergasted at what she has just said. He tuts and shakes his head at her. "You little, little thing! I am not past anything, nor am I skinny or afraid of Bunty! I am in my prime." He stands up and brushes himself down from the food he has dropped on his lap. Walking over to Margaret, he kisses her on the cheek and hugs her. "This is great news, but I am not sure how we can pull it off again. We used every trick we knew to get away with it the first time." Then he turns to Andrew. "Congratulations, my boy, you are a far braver man than me, you show good grit." He shakes Andrew's hand and pats him on the shoulder.

Beth is next to hug Margaret, whispering in her ear, "Are you strong enough to follow all this through? You have put so much of yourself on the line."

Margaret hugs her back, and replies at the same time, "It must be done while we still have supporters in court and my body is young enough to endure. Besides, Andrew is far more capable than I ever dreamed, I love him dearly and know he will stand by me in my time of need. That being said, when this is all over I will be by his side until the end, for he has given up everything for me, I would be a lesser person if I did not do the same for him."

While the others are talking, Anna places a cushion on her stomach with her free hand and starts to rub it. "I will say it's Wellesley's if anyone asks, call it Wellina if it's a girl and Wellesley the 2ed if it is a boy. To make it known to all that he still has it in him at his age and make Bunty jealous at the same time." The others cannot help but burst into laughter at this cheeky girl as Wellesley looks up to the heavens.

"Oh God, what did I ever do that you would punish me so badly? Just tell me what I must do to make amends and I will do it."

Anna looks at him and smiles. "Of course, I would expect you to do the right thing and marry me now I am to have your child. White carriage, big cake, and a party that goes on all night."

"Baby, marriage, Wellesley!" yells Bunty, just entering the room with another tray of pastries. She places the tray down on the nearest empty space and runs out of the room in floods of tears. Margaret is shaking her head and desperately trying not to laugh, finding it hard to control herself and stay straight faced, but with the others laughing out so loud she is fighting a losing battle.

"No, no, Bunty, it is not what you think" calls out Wellesley. He goes to catch up with her then realizes what he is doing and stops, puts both hands on his head and sighs heavily, then, looking at Anna, he reaches out with his hands before curling them into fists and turning away. "If you were a man I would st—"

"You would harm the woman carrying your child, your own wife to be?!" Anna says with a shocked look on her face. "Did you hear that, Henry, he would do us harm?"

Wellesley stops and tries to gain some composure before speaking. "You are not my wife, you are not with my child, you are definitely not with my child" He pauses to collect his thoughts. "I think I will patrol the grounds one last time."

As he moves toward the door, Andrew speaks.

"I will come with you; I could do with the fresh air." The two men head out of the room leaving the ladies with Henry to talk amongst themselves.

"Anna, funny as it was, go see Bunty and clear the air. You can let her know my condition, too, she is trustworthy and would know soon enough anyway".

As Anna gets up and heads toward the kitchen, Margaret speaks again. "Are you forgetting something, Anna?" Anna stops, lets out a sigh and turns towards Margaret, handing over Henry with great reluctance. Margaret smiles and shakes her head.

"Thank you. Now go, and when you next see Wellesley on your travels, let him know what he means to you, for he is an honorable man and you tend to push him a little past his comfort levels."

Anna nods her head. "You're right, as always, Margaret. I think I will see him first, for he means more to me than most." As she glides across the floor to the exit, Margaret turns to Beth.

"As funny as they are with each other, I fear what would happen to the other should something befall one of them, they have a true father–daughter relationship. As for me and Andrew, the time is fast approaching when the truth will need to be talked about.'

Beth sits down as Margaret continues, "The day that we are working toward has been decided, It will be the queen's official thirty-fourth birthday celebrations at the palace. Everyone of note will be invited to the occasion so it will allow greater freedom for people away from the palace. We will plan and act on all areas at the same time. God willing, good will prevail and we will see an end to this tyranny, but if it does not, I will count on you to protect the children until they come of age Beth."

She looks at Margaret in shock. "What do you mean, my lady, look after your children?"

"Dear Beth, you have always known from the start that this could only have one of two outcomes, either we are successful, or they continue to rule the day. If they rule the day, many of us would have perished. So, I ask you now, look after this here little Henry and, if I am so lucky, the one I carry at present, for I fear the price of failure will leave them wanting both parents and many of our great friends would have perished as well."

Beth's lip starts to tremble as she realizes what Margaret is asking of her and she becomes upset at the thought of it. She reaches out with both hands to hold Margaret's free hand. "Oh Margaret, you must promise me you will not fail! The thought of losing you would break my heart, especially after all you have been through."

Margaret looks at her, a slight smile appearing on her face. "Now come on, I'm not gone yet and I intend to be around for a long time. So, let's get to planning an outcome that betters us more than the enemy."

Outside in the semi darkness, Andrew and Wellesley are walking around the edge of the riverbank on the far side of the garden, talking as they go. As they pass one of the more mature trees, Wellesley stops to relieve himself while Andrew steps away and waits.

Looking back toward the house he can see Anna quietly walking toward them with a finger over her lips, Andrew smiles when he sees her and starts to walk firstly towards her, then continues straight past and heads back toward the house while Anna makes her way to the tree and waits the other side of its thick trunk.

Moments later, Wellesley appears still looking over the river to the far bank. "As I was saying, it will be difficult to hide two children from the eyes of th—"

He cuts himself off and looks down at Anna as she tucks her hand between his arm and ribs and hooks his upper arm with hers. "You were saying about the children? And don't touch me with that hand, I know where it has just been!"

He bends his elbow to allow Anna a better hold. "You, my dear, are a right royal pain, not since my late wife Constance have I had a woman drive me to distraction like you do."

She slows her pace a little. "Challenging me to distract you more, are you?"

He chuckles loudly. "Oh God no, you are on the limits of my endurance as you be now."

"Tell me more about Constance, like how did you first meet?"

"Ha, did Margaret put you up to that one?" he asks as Anna starts to chuckle.

"She may have hinted a while back that it was a good question for me to ask."

"Well, it was a long time ago, she was just about the age you are now." He lowers his head and looks at the floor as he reminisces on the day he first met his beloved Constance. "It was a freezing cold day in January, the ground was frozen solid and a good ten inches of snow had fallen in the past day. I was a young corporal in charge of a group of eight men on a so-called training exercise. We had been blindfolded, driven around in a cart for hours, and dumped in the forest in the middle of Black Heath moors on the peat beds. We were to stay there for two days, then make our way back to the outpost using the skills of survival, compos and map reading they had been teaching us. We could approach nobody, be seen by nobody, and were not to purchase any resources on the way. On top of that we had people searching for us from another division, if they were to find and capture us, they had up to twenty-four hours to make our lives as uncomfortable as possible before our return to our own unit.

"Take into consideration we were already at an outpost far away from civilization to start with and quite isolated, so we were as far from any inhabited village or community as possible in our country. It was just our luck that, within hours of us being dropped off, the snow began to fall heavily. While we built a small shelter and got a fire going, I decided to let two men follow the cart tracks that delivered us to our drop off point to get a head start on the direction to travel as we could not get any direction from the sun and visibility from any hilltop was minimal due to the weather.

"It soon became clear that the sergeant who dropped us off was as crafty as me, as he had traveled in a five hundred meter square a few times to lay down heavy ruts in the ground and then had covered his tracks as he moved off the square to avoid detection. With the snow falling and covering everything in a white blanket, it was about fifteen or twenty minutes later that the two men I had sent approached our position from the other direction, still following the indented tracks on the ground."

Anna chuckles. "So what did you do?" she asks curiously.

"I did as anybody would do in the army, followed my instructions to the letter. We waited two days in the freezing cold, fed on the odd squirrel and rabbit we trapped in snares and anything else we could scavenge from the land, and then headed off in a southerly direction. The snow was the worst we had seen in years for that time of year and having traveled for two days hard and fast, we were exhausted. So, we stopped to rest and warm by a fire at a shepherd's shack, well, more like a few stone walls cobbled together, but it was welcome shelter for the group of us. I had thought we would have reached the outpost by then or at least found some road or features to help guide us back, but the weather made everything white, and we could see nothing. With virtually no food and precious little in the way of resources to keep us going, the next day I made a decision that we would take any opportunity to get food on our way, steal from a house if we must, but we needed something in us to keep going.

"To our good fortune, just before dusk we came upon a highland farm, lots of outbuildings and sheds along with twenty or thirty pens in the neighboring fields. It was obvious that it was used in the summer for rearing animals on the high fields and meadows but closed down in the winter months. We checked all the outbuildings and found nothing to eat, so decided to break into the house, being that we were so cold, wet, starving, and numb to any feeling in our hands and feet. We could not undo or discreetly pick a lock or pry open a window as our fingers were near frozen, so we just barged the door open with a shoulder charge. To our surprise, the house was warm and the fireplace had not long been used as the embers still had heat in them.

"I knew then we had made a mistake but being so cold we piled wood on the fire to get it going again and explored the house, calling out to anybody who may have been around not to be alarmed, we were there for warmth and food, not to steal or harm anyone. We had had no reply from anybody and saw no one in the house or connected extensions and no livestock in any of the outbuildings. All I could deduce was that they had left some time that day while there was light to see the road under the snow and where they were going. As for us, we huddled back around the fire to get warm. It was then that young Perking's noticed something hanging inside the fire flume, which turned out to be nearly a full leg of ham being cured by the smoke coming off the fire and up into the chimney stack. Poor thing never stood a chance, we had stripped and consumed the lot within twenty minutes, leaving Perking's gnawing on the bones for any scraps left on it." Wellesley chuckles. "By God, even now I remember the taste; to us at that moment in time it was the best-cured pork in the world. In reality it probably wasn't all that good, it was just that we were starving hungry and near to eating the soles on our boots.

"It was about that time that I noticed the square shape cut on the floor. Closer inspection showed it to be a trap door into a cellar, and, as I opened it and pulled back the hatch, a pistol shot rung out with the ball just missing all of us and hitting the ceiling above, followed by a warning to stay away. I tried for an hour to convince whoever was down there that we meant no harm and would pay for everything that we had used or eaten. When it went quiet for around ten minutes I convinced myself that the person or persons below would tolerate me going down and checking out the area and speaking to them face to face.

"Despite all my men's warnings and reservations, I got on the ladder and started to descend, certain those below would not do anything until I had reached the ground. Oh, what a mistake." He chuckles as he thinks back on the moment.

Anna stops walking and looks at him. "What happened next?"

He shakes his head, still chucking. "I got down about three or four steps before someone had at me, and there was a searing pain as they stuck me with a sword through my right buttock. I let out one hell of a yell and shot back up the steps. I bled like a stuck pig for nearly an hour, could not sit down, nor stand up. My men could not stop chuckling and laughing as they patched me up and seared the wound closed with a hot knife. That was the first of many wounds in my career, but, without doubt, the one that taught me the most. Never show your behind to the enemy, always face them head on".

Anna cannot help but laugh at Wellesley's misadventure, it is hard for her to imagine Wellesley being a young soldier green as the grass on the ground below them as they walked on. She has only known him as a skilled, high-ranking officer of great honor and esteem .

"Being dark and now near midnight, we stayed in the house that night, most slept in chairs and various areas of the room around the fire and I stretched out flat out on my belly with my behind up in the air. I was the first to wake in the morning, not that I got much sleep in my condition, and as my eyes opened and focused I was faced with two pistols not three feet from my nose. Over the barrels I saw the face of a young lady peering over the open wooden hatch to the cellar, she had fear in her eyes, but the pistols were rock solid in her hands. As the rest of my unit woke and came around she did not flinch, as they picked up their weapons she did not even turn to look, just kept her focus and aim on me. To start with it was a stand-off, but, as we started to converse and I told her of our plight and where we were from she finally lowered her weapons to the ground, a moment that could not come too soon for my pounding heart.

"We found out her name was Constance and she had been locking down the farm for winter while her family were moving the last of the stock to the lowlands. She got caught out by the bad weather and was going to ride out the winter snowstorm in the house and catch them up in a day or two.

She informed us that we had walked near thirty miles past our outpost and already knew about us, as the day before she had been visited by a cavalry patrol searching the area for a unit of grenadiers and asked to keep an eye out for them. It would seem that if we had knocked on the door instead of sneaking around the farm, Constance would not have hidden in fear and I would not have had a hole in my behind.

"I knew from the moment I saw Constance that she was the woman for me, and, after weeks of walking round like a penguin with smiles, laughter and comments from every man in the troop, she had ensured I would never forget our first meeting. That lady had the face of an angel, a heart as big as a lion, and compassion and kindness second to none. On the flip side she had the fire of the Devil in her when it came to a fight. She had been trained well by her father and brothers in the use of a sword and pistol, was expert with a rifle, and able to show up most men from the saddle with a sword."

Wellesley chuckles as he remembers Constance. "Half the barracks fell for that woman and she chose me over them all, not that she let me know at first, she made me work and played me for months before allowing me to call on her. From that first visit, I knew there was no other person in the world for me. So opposite in our upbringings, yet so complete when we were together, we became inseparable from that moment on. Little did we know then that fate would move us to both serve the royal family, though it was different circumstances for each of us that would make it happen.

It was her mother's closeness to the queen that gave Constance the duty of queen's companion and close protector of her child after she defended her at a royal ball from some foreign diplomats drunk on their own self-importance. By the time she had finished with them, one had a broken arm, another would never have children by his own abilities, and a third lost his eye. As for me, I was the young officer known for being a scrapper in the ranks, fast with a blade, but not so good as a gentleman.

Lord Ashby took an interest in me, saw something others did not. He took me under his wing and developed my diplomatic skills to match my abilities with fists and weapons. Soon I was with him at all the royal engagements and regularly in the presence of the king and queen, not to mention my beloved Constance.

But it was when I saw the king practicing his swordplay with one of his instructors that our friendship began to grow. He saw me smiling and shaking my head as he and his instructors danced around, wiggling their blades at each other. He ordered me to explain what I found amusing, so I told him: "The enemy would not prance around all puffed up and civilized but would go in for the kill with no decorum or etiquette." He instructed me to show what I meant and offered me forward with his three of his instructors. Me being me and given the nod by Lord Ashby, I took up the challenge and stepped forward to demonstrate.

"After two or three steps, one of them lunged forward with the point. I flicked away his sword with mine, stepped inside and head butted him. I watched as he fell to the floor, out like a candle hit with a snuffer. The second pranced and danced around, flicking his sword backward and forward at me with little effect, making strange grunting noises every time he stepped forward to thrust. On one such occasion I moved to one side, flicked away his blade and punched him in the head with the hilt of my sword. As I turned to the third he prodded me in the shoulder with the point, "touché" or something he muttered, smiling at me. I grabbed his sword in my hand, holding it as he struggled to pull or push his weapon free from my grip and shoulder. Kicked him in his jewels, and then, as his head came down, I raised my knee and struck his nose. As he fell backwards, I pulled out the sword from my shoulder and threw it beside him.

The king looked at me with shock. 'That was not gentlemanlike, not at all, young ruffian,' he said as I plugged the hole in my shoulder with a small piece of cloth from my pocket. I remember Lord Ashby replying. 'One of my men has taken out three of your finest instructors in less than two minutes sire, were he an assassin you would now be dead and the country without its king. The pomp and fluff of a peacock has no place in teaching or defending a king, you finish them off fast and by any means necessary to get the job done, for you know not what is coming up at you next."

"A week later, by order of his majesty, I had been re-assigned to the king as his personal bodyguard and master-at-arms. We practiced weaponry near every day. I took a lot of cuts from our king, and to my shame, gave one or two back, but I was under orders from him not to hold back but to push him harder and harder as his skills developed. Over the years we became remarkably close. Constance and I spent most of our lives around the royal family, her protecting the queen and daughter and me and me serving his majesty in the same way. We had many a scrape and conflict with people sent to do their worst against our king and queen, all of which were dealt with in the same manner, fast and swift and without hesitation. That is until the day our own countrymen betrayed them.

"Politicians out for their own greed and ambitions, they were punching way above their stations in society and had paid a lot of people to look the other way or support them. I was not prepared for people on the inside to assist and plan such a despicable act of treason, it had not even crossed our minds that the worst danger was within our own walls. The price I paid in my failure was far too much to take, the loss of the monarchy, Constance as well as my pride took me down to a new level of self-loathing.

But, as always, Lord Ashby was there to keep me from harm's

way, pulling me back from the brink of despair and rebuilding a broken man into a useful tool, giving me purpose again. This time we will be ready on levels not yet even considered, and nothing will be left to chance. By the time the queen is prepared to make her move, all will be ready to strike at once, quick and decisive."

The two of them arrive back at the entrance to the house, and Wellesley follows Anna inside. in the hallway he speaks to her one last time. "When the time comes and we are in the thick of it, think not of me or yourself. Protect the queen at all costs and strike first and without hesitation. Do not ponder in the years that follow what you could have done differently, for that time would have gone and the outcome cannot be changed. Make sure you do all you can in the here and now while it matters, for we will have only one shot at this and Margaret and Andrew will need us at our very best. As they are the ones putting everything on the line this time and will need all the support we can possibly give them." He kisses her softly on the forehead before turning and walking away, disappearing up the stairs.

Anna returns to the lounge, where she looks around at everybody then heads toward the empty seat beside Margaret and Henry, nodding at her as she sits down. All the while she is thinking on what Wellesley said about her actions in the here and now. Sadness fills her eyes as she realizes how much her beloved Wellesley has lost over the years and yet he is always there for her and all the others when they need him. She wonders if there is a man anywhere that is more deserving of admiration and praise for what they have done than her mentor Wellesley.

Margaret is watching Anna and can see that the young lady has many things on her mind. As she reaches over and touches the back of her hand, Anna looks up at her and Margaret can see the sadness in her eyes. "I think now you realize now how much pride and love he has in you Anna, for I know he tells you more than he would any of us."

Anna nods as the tears start to flow. She tries to wipe them away with her fingers but more follow, faster and faster. "He has been through so much and still gives without any thought to himself, never asking for anything, yet he has lost so much in his life."

Margaret sighs while Andrew gets up from his seat, walks over and passes her a white handkerchief to wipe away the tears. Then he turns and leaves the room, taking Beth with him and leaving Anna and Margaret alone with young Henry.

"Now that is not true, he has me, his godson Henry here, and you! Do you know that when he watched over you he prayed to God for the first time since Constance was taken from him all them years ago?" She nods at Anna as she looks up from wiping his eyes. "Oh yes, it's true, on more than one occasion I heard him offer himself in your stead to Him in the hope He would spare your life. When you were at your gravest and he thought he was going to lose you, he took it upon himself to take revenge for what had happened that night. It took a dozen men including Lord Ashby and his bodyguard Olson, to hold him down while they took the men that harmed you from the holding cells to the ship to serve their sentences. Many sustained injuries protecting those prisoners even though they all wanted the same revenge for what they had done to you. But death would have been too easy a way out, Lord Ashby knew hard labor on a ship of the line for years would break them far worse than Wellesley's blade. He knew at some stage during your recovery that Wellesley would want to take revenge for what they had inflicted on you and had his best men waiting to prevent Wellesley disgracing his honor by killing those worthless wretches."

"But why me?" Anna asks. "Why do I mean so much to him? I had never met him before I woke in that bed!"

Margaret smiles. "Because you are who you are, a fighter, a young lady with spirit. You gave yourself up for young Billy knowing the consequences of your actions would cause you harm. You fought for your life and hung on when most would have lost the will after what had happened. These are all the qualities he admires and respects in people, but if you feel it is too much, I—"

"No, God no! He is all I have, I love him more than anyone I have ever known, he has been a better father to me than own ever was. Nobody means more to me than Wellesley, it is just that it always seems to me that I let him down and disappoint him at every turn."

Margaret laughs. "My dear, you and I have so much in common, we both love our men to distraction, me with Andrew and you with Wellesley, a man who is like a father and mother rolled up into one for not just you, but the both of us. We both would not be here if it were not for them and their dedication and love for us, yet we hide secrets from them and pray our white lies never get found out or put them in harm's way.

"I came close to losing my husband twice in one day, yet if he had to do it again tomorrow, he would do it three times over without a second thought. Do I deserve such devotion from a man who does not even know all about me? We both could not live without these men in our lives, yet feel we never give our fair share of love back to them. Well fear not young lady, we do, and we will make sure they are aware of it in the months to come. You and I are the daughters Wellesley always wanted but never had the chance to have, yet he still loves us as though we are. He keeps us safe and out of harm's way, a shadow that watches over us no matter what we do. Always there, always present ready to protect us should mortal peril be close by. He is as proud of us as we are of him, so worry yourself not, my angel in wolf's clothing, for that man would stand by you no matter what you did. I also know for a fact that you make him proud, for he tells me as much every day and we both see it in his eyes and that raw growl of a smile he sometimes lets out, even when you act up a little and test his patience to the limit."

Margaret stands up. "I think it is time me and this little man said our goodnights. You also need to get some sleep as well, as I require you to go to the city tomorrow and deliver some documents and plans to Professor Simmerson Hibbot at the university. You remember him, one of the two men you entertained the day Andrew was shot by the assassins.

"The man who smelt of mint and carried a small leather briefcase with him, he was very charming."

"That is how I always know he is near me Anna, that strong

smell of mint. He is pivotal to our plans as he can pass information to other intellects that I cannot get to without raising suspicion. These papers are far too important to be lost or found by others, I trust nobody else with them as they must not be seen being delivered or be read by anyone other than the professor."

Anna nods as she listens to her instructions and thinks on the task at hand. "It would probably be best if I was in military uniform then, so that I would be hard to tell apart from any of the other officer cadets that attend some of the lectures. I must go early though, so as to arrive at the same time as they do". The two ladies and Henry leave the lounge together and head up the stairs. They say their goodnights on the landing before separating and going to their respective rooms, with a brief look back and a wave at each other they close the doors, putting another day behind them.

CHAPTER 14

Anna's First Mission

It is just coming up to six in the morning and daylight has yet to break out and invade the night sky. Margaret and Anna are already downstairs having breakfast while young Henry is in the nursery being watched over by Beth. Outside, Wellesley is in the stable yard giving instructions to the new house officer 'lieutenant Doolan', a young man fresh from the barracks. He is a stocky, brown-haired and brown-eyed soldier of good standing in the regiment. He is on his first tour at the house and eager to prove his worth to all, especially Wellesley as he is a legend with all young officers and cadets. Doolan has been tasked with being Anna's driver today, as well as watching over her and keeping her safe, a challenge far harder than he is aware of due to the mischievous nature of this young lady.

This is his first mission out of uniform and Wellesley is laying down the dos and don'ts in great detail to ensure he fully understands his role. "Do not stop for anything on the way to or back from the university. Once there, watch over her from a distance and wait for her return. She is a capable lass, so be patient and watch, she will signal you if you are required for any purpose so be alert to any signs she may make."

The young man clicks his heels and salutes. "Yes, sir, I will watch over her like a hawk."

Wellesley sighs heavily before speaking. "Boy, you are a coach driver, no saluting, no stiff back and upright pose, just hat pulled down at the front and act slovenly, as if you hate being alive. You are to be inconspicuous in the crowd, not the best-drilled soldier in the barracks."

It is the first time Anna will be away on a mission on her own, without Wellesley around as backup. Like everyone else in the house, he is concerned for the safety of his beloved little girl but would trust nobody more with this mission as he has trained her well.

"Now, Doolan, one last thing. Anna may look like a cute, innocent young lady in her pretty dresses and frills, but be warned she is anything but. She can hold her own in a scrap, and ca— What the hell?" Wellesley exclaims, as he catches a glimpse of Anna walking toward him in her full modified military uniform.

She marches straight up to him. "Morning, Wellesley, you look well today, if not a little shabby." She flicks his lapels with her fingers and rubs her fingertips together. "Could do with a clean you know, don't want to disgrace the colors, do we?" Wellesley grits his teeth and clenches his fists as he tries to refrain from saying anything that would turn the air blue or throttling this cheeky young lady that always seems to have an edge over him.

Anna looks at the man with Wellesley. "Are we ready for me to depart driver? I have places to be and duties to fulfill and still be back here by dark to tuck this old boy in bed." Wellesley and Doolan just stare speechlessly at her as she climbs into the carriage and closes the door herself. Moments later she leans out of the window and speaks again. "Well let's get on with it, I must arrive at the same time the other cadets get there or wearing a uniform would have been a waste of time".

Wellesley shakes his head. "Boy, I fear for you, with what she has hidden in that uniform she could start a small war." Doolan has no idea what Wellesley is talking about, but he turns and climbs into the driver's seat on the front of the coach and prepares to leave. With a final nod from Wellesley, he flicks the reins at the two horses and they head off down the driveway. Anna is still hanging out of the coach window waving to Wellesley and remains in this position until he is out of sight, at which point she takes her seat and quietly thinks out in her mind what she must do when she arrives at the university.

Wellesley returns to the house, moves through to the kitchen and takes a seat beside Margaret. She can see that he has a lot on his mind and knows exactly who he is thinking about most. "She will be fine, my old friend, you have trained her well and you know there is no better person for the task at hand."

Wellesley gives a slight nod. "I know, it is just that she has become a little important to me." He pauses for a moment before speaking again "It is not the risk she is taking, but the knowing what I would do should she be caught and harmed, for all the planning and good you propose to do would be in vain as I would wipe them out in a heartbeat, destroying your dreams and my honor in the process."

Margaret smiles and places her hand on his. "There is no way you would disappoint me, for you are one of the cornerstones of this country and a friend beyond repute. We are beginning the final chapter in a plan that has taken most of my life and a great deal of yours. If we can stay the course, all the ills that have been thrown our way in these dark times will be avenged. Not only that, we will have a chance to bring our people into a new era, just hold on my friend, hold on."

The moment is broken by the arrival of Bunty, placing a hot plate in front of Wellesley and a large silver tray in the middle of the table covered in bacon, sausages, and an assortment of kidneys, mushrooms, and liver. She has her usual smile and doting eyes as she stares at Wellesley. "Eat up and gain your strength, my good man, you may be needing it later if you play your cards right." As she turns and walks away, Margaret starts to smile and shake her head as Wellesley breaks into a chuckle.

"She will never give up on you, Wellesley, no matter what you do or where you go, she will be close by waiting to pounce like a cat on a mouse."

"I know she means well," Wellesley says as he starts to fill his plate, "And I am flattered she thinks on me so, but alas, the woman needs to find another for my heart belongs to one and one alone. I cannot share it with anyone else even though she has long since gone from my arms."

Margaret pats the back of his hand a couple of times. "Believe me, I know, I have the same feelings for the man I am forever leading into the pit of hell and back. God knows why he has stuck with me for so long, but I am so glad he has. Now, if you will excuse me, I need to see Andrew and reassure that man I am not just using him to make babies before bumping him off, as he seems to think that of me at this moment in time," Margaret says chuckling as she stands up to leave.

He laughs out loud. "I must admit he seems to have a point; you do push him to the limits of what a mortal man can take. But then again, until he came along I never thought I would meet anyone who could satisfy the exacting standards you had set. For you are stubborn beyond belief, hard-headed and determined. Fair play to him for being the man you have always deserved my dear, you have definitely found a keeper there if he can just stay alive long enough to finish what you have started."

Margaret stops in her tracks and looks at Wellesley "My God, Wellesley, am I hearing you right?! After what you originally said, you finally, actually approve of Andrew?"

He sits back upright in his chair and looks at Margaret. "When you first started to look in the city and amongst the people for 'The One', I thought you were mad and had lost your sanity, but you have proven me wrong. It was better to pick fresh from the tree rather than the old wind falls on the floor, just like you said. Lord knows what he will say when he finds out the truth from you, but in my opinion, I think you have underestimated his resolve, he is no fool and knows there is more to you than you let on. The man loves you for what he sees and feels, not what you are."

Margaret stares at Wellesley for what seems an age before speaking again. "It is the thing I fear most. I love him to distraction, but cannot show it as I should, such is my commitment to the monarchy and its people. I often wonder, would he be strong enough to handle more or have I pushed his limits to the edge?"

Wellesley is quick to answer. "Andrew has a way about him, he is far tougher on the inside than he shows on the outside. I gave up trying to underestimate him a long time ago, that lad is resilient without even realizing and continues to surpass my expectations.

Perhaps as you said yourself not so long ago, you have come too far to turn back now, so roll the dice and take the chance, finish the game you started and then see where we stand when it's all done."

Margaret does not speak again, but she thinks on his words before leaving the kitchen and heading up the stairs to her room and Andrew.

* * *

It's a little before nine in the morning as the carriage arrives outside the university entrance. Cambria Percival Institute of Life Sciences, or CP's as it is known to all those that attend its educational offerings. At first it was only open to the rich and wealthy, for they were the only ones who could afford to pay to learn about the sciences of life. But with heavy poverty hitting the country, Lord Ashby had secured a great many places for the military and people with abilities in all fields including finances, business, diplomacy, and engineering to attend and learn from skilled masters and add to their repertoire of knowledge. As he founded the building and pays the wages of all the lectures in the establishment himself, he has ensured that even females could attend if they chose to do so, something unheard of in more prosperous times. But with him holding the purse strings it became a case of teach them or find employment elsewhere. For many lecturers with no other place of employment, they reluctantly do as requested, not that they give the females much consideration. For the women of the time with a strong disposition, they could be educated to a far higher standard than ever before, but it took a strong will to carry it off, and a huge amount strength to take the criticisms some lecturers would put on these women, still some did endure and have become well educated in their fields.

As the carriage pulls up, Anna looks out of the window at the many people walking by, waiting for a group of military cadets to move past. When one such group appears, she lets herself out, swings her green cape over her shoulders, and follows them into the building. Once inside she takes a small notebook from her pocket and follows the directions written down by Margaret that morning. Within ten minutes of following the notes, she comes across the door marked 'Professor Simmerson Hibbot,' and taps on the glass panel before waiting for a reply.

"Enter and wipe your feet on the mat, please", says a voice from inside the room. As Anna enters and cleans her boots, she can see the man she is here to deliver the package to on the far side of the room with several other people sitting in armchairs very similar to the ones she is used to at the house. Anna walks over to them and is greeted by a smile as he stands up to receive her, reaching out to shake her hand. Professor Simmerson Hibbot is often a guest of Margaret's at the house, along with his friend Dr Percival Jacobs, the man sitting to his right.

"My God, it's a woman in your common room!" bellows an unsavory character in a tweed outfit and smoking a long, thin white clay pipe. He stands up, walks over and starts poking Anna with a thick willow cane with an ivory handle and brass tip, pushing her backward into a side room. "Out, out, out!" he commands as he drives her backward, following the retreating Anna into the other room.

Behind him, Simmerson and Percival try to stop the man from being so aggressive toward Anna, but he just ignores them and continues to push her. With one more forceful poke from the man, Anna has had enough and finally responds. She grabs his waistcoat with one hand, spinning him around and up against the wall behind the door, while her other hand presses a long, thin blade to his throat.

"Prod me again, I dare you," she says while staring into his eyes. The man is taken by surprise at the swift and aggressive response from this young woman, then releases a clip on his cane handle. Anna is quick to see the shine of metal from the hilt of the swordstick blade ready to be pulled from the walking stick and pushes her blade harder against the man's neck.

"That's enough, Smyth," says the professor. "Your behavior is totally unacceptable, leave this room immediately before I have you removed from this building. As for you, young lady, release him. This is not the kind of response I expect from one of Lord Ashby's cadets, provoked or not." Anna slowly steps back two small paces, then and only then she removes her blade from his neck and moves away to allow the man to get to the door.

The man closes his cane sword with a click, straightens himself back up and rolls his head on his neck before turning to Simmerson and speaking. "Having women in this establishment has not only lowered the standards set here, especially with these military types, but also allows common rabble to assault gentlemen without fear of retribution. Mallory will hear of this insult, mark my words," he says before taking one last look at Anna.

"I am sure we will meet again soon, my dear, then we will see who is the better man." With that, he turns and storms out of the room. "Out of my way, you clumsy clot!" he yells at some poor student just outside in the hallway he has pushed into and knocked to the floor.

He was followed to the entrance by Percival, who stands and holds the door open while signaling to the other three people present to leave the room. "Please, gentlemen, would you excuse us? I believe the professor will require words with this young lady on her conduct and attitude to a member of staff." The three men look at each other before getting up and exiting the room, each one tilting their heads at the professor as they pass him on their way out. As the last one leaves, Percival locks the door while Simmerson leads Anna to one of the now-vacant chairs.

"Please take a seat, my dear, Percival was just protecting you with what he said to the other people."

Anna takes off her cape, lays it over the arm of the chair, then takes a seat. "That man is not a very pleasant person, and his eyes were as shifty as any I have seen before" she says as Percival and Simmerson take seats opposite her.

"He is a particularly distasteful man, but it is better to have him close at hand to watch than be looking over your shoulder as to where he may or may not be. He and a dozen others watch all that work and learn here, they are the eyes and ears of Mallory and the other two, Stone and Bonner. Since Lord Ashby started sending people to be educated and trained in the many fields we have on offer, they have been paying close interest to the entire goings on of the university. They are not stupid, young lady, they know that it will take educated people to run a country and this being the best educational building in the land means that it is always under close scrutiny. They want to know who is attending the lectures, who visits the establishment and why they are visiting. To ascertain whether they are a risk to the Three Heads and their puppet government. So many things they worry about, it makes me chuckle to know we put so much fear into the daily lives of these terrible men."

"Why do you not just remove them from the building if they pose such a risk? It is what I would do," she asks.

Simmerson nods slowly at her as he smiles. "Yes, it would be the logical thing to do, but that would tip our hat and they would then know something is going on. Far better to use them for training the students. We have them all under constant surveillance, no better way to learn than to actually use what you have been shown to good effect. Drop false information, mislead those that are looking for something, leave trails of breadcrumbs that lead to nowhere, we run them a merry dance without them even realizing how much they are helping the cause. Now, my dear, you have something for me, I believe?" Simmerson asks as he sits forward in his chair and awaits Anna reaction.

Anna looks at him for a moment. "I know who you both are, as I have seen you at the house and the palace on several occasions, but I cannot give you what you ask for without the answer."

Simmerson smiles. "Excellent, my dear, just excellent, it is always right to be cautious, but before I can give you an answer, you have to ask me the question." She stands up at the same time the professor does and leans over to whisper into his ear. After a short pause to think, he then whispers back his answer to her. Satisfied with his answer she nods and turns to her chair. She undoes her utility belt and places it over one of the arms, then starts to undo the eighteen gold colored buttons down the side of her tunic. Opening up the front of her clothing, she takes out a stack of papers wrapped in a thin sheet of leather binding and hands them to him.

Unwrapping them, he starts to sort the papers into different piles on his desk while Anna redresses herself, puts on her belt and waits for him to finish sorting. Percival collects two of the piles of paper and moves to another room, moments later he returns without the documents in hand and is passed another pile by the professor and moves off in the direction of another room and does the same thing. This happens several times before all the paperwork is gone from the table, with Percival leaving the room into the main hallway with the last sheets.

"I have been forgetting my manners, dear Anna," Simmerson says as the door closes behind Percival. "Would you like some refreshments or a tour of our building before you leave us? I have so many wonderful things I would like to show you. For example, this building we are in is incredibly old and has many secret passages and hidden rooms you may find interesting, including one Margaret was very fond of hiding in during her two years under my guidance."

Anna smiles at him. "That is the kind of thing I would really like to see, but another time perhaps. For now, I must return to Margaret as I have other duties that need my attention before the day is out and as you well know, she does not like to be kept waiting when it comes to her instructions."

He sighs and shrugs his shoulders. "It's a pity, but I understand, you are very similar to her in many ways, but do please come back and visit some time and I will show you around then."

Anna steps forward and kisses him on the cheek. "Goodbye, professor, I am sure we will meet again soon." She turns and lets herself out, closing the door behind her and following the route she took to get there backward to leave the university grounds.

It is as she crosses one of the small, square gardens, where a few students and cadets are walking, that she gets a feeling she is being followed. Slowing a little, she looks down at the ground and hesitates while listening to hear if any footsteps slow as well. Sure enough, she hears the slowing of steps behind her, confirming her suspicions. Anna moves off again at a swift walking pace; with so many people around, she is not worried about being attacked but is concerned they will follow her back to the coach and then back to the house. Leaving the main entrance to the building Anna stops and looks around while thinking on her options. With a plan in place, she crosses the road to a small teahouse away from the waiting carriage, taking a seat at a table set outside that is facing back in the direction she has arrived.

Doolan has seen her pass in front of his horses and watches as she sits down at the table. The fact that she does not enter the coach has his attention and he carefully looks around while keeping his hat well tilted down. A young female server approaches Anna and she places an order for tea and a cake from the card on the center of the table. As the girl leaves to collect Anna's order, she keeps a discreet look out for whoever was following her. A smile of satisfaction appears on her face as she notices the man Smyth on the grounds of the university talking to two senior students. There is a brief moment when the three of them take a casual glance in her direction before one of the students moves off along the path and around the corner of the university.

It is enough for Anna to know she was correct in her assumption that she was being followed and that Smyth was the man following her out of the building. Moments later, he and his younger associate cross the road and walk toward Anna, they pass and enter the building without looking in her direction, taking a free table just inside the door behind the window opposite. They constantly look in Anna's direction to check what she is doing while pretending to look at the menu cards they are holding.

Anna takes no notice of them; to her they are rather amateurish and she was on to them from the start, but she is curious to know what they intend to do, so for now she waits to see what happens next. In her mind this is an opportunity to find out who else is working with them or who they are working for, as she assumes the other person must have gone for some kind of instructions or backup.

As Anna's order arrives and is placed out in front of her

while another server is taking down the order from Smyth and his companion on the other side of the window. Anna adds two lumps of sugar and milk to her tea, then stirs it several times before tapping the cup with the spoon and placing it on the saucer. As she takes a sip of tea, she looks toward Doolan. He has been watching her closely and when she gives him the hand signal to stay back, wait and be ready, he is on full alert. Not knowing what situation Anna is in he waits and watches, giving her a slow nod to say that he understands before preparing two small pistols by his side.

Ten minutes pass and Anna is pouring a second cup of tea from her small silver pot when a coach pulls up outside the teahouse, just a few yards ahead of where she is seated. Anna looks up as the footman jumps off the back of the carriage opens the door and pulls out the step to allow the people inside to exit the vehicle, but it is a while before the two men finally step out of the carriage to the side of the road. They are still deep in conversation with each other while having their backs to Anna. With cloaks and top hats on she cannot recognize them, but their voices seem vaguely familiar and the identical canes in their hands are similar to some she has seen before, but just cannot remember where.

"Driver, return in an hour and don't be late" one of the men calls out to the nodding man on the front of the coach. As the carriage pulls away and the men turn and head toward her and the entrance to the establishment, now she recognizes them. Mallory and Bonner, two of the men she has grown to hate the most in the world.

She watches as they move past her table without recognizing who she is, which puts a little smile on her face for a moment as the uniform idea has done its job. But she knows they will soon be back for a closer inspection and when they do, she will be instantly recognized by them.

Anna thinks through her options. If she gets up and leaves, she may get to the carriage, but it is facing this way and they would stop and apprehend her as she passes, finding any excuse even if they have to make one up to do so. If she walks off, who knows how many are now watching her ready to follow? Away from the main street, where it is quieter, they may try to abduct her, or worse, and nobody would be around to witness the attack. She decides her best option is to play it here in public view with Doolan watching over her, and see how her charm, wit, and adaptable skills perform under pressure against these evil men.

She takes another sip of her tea and sits back in her chair and waits. She can already feel the chill of many eyes watching her but does not react or respond. Then ignoring a tapping on the glass, knowing it is one of the men's canes being used just to get her to turn around and look at them and be recognized. Instead, Anna sits forward and takes another sip of tea and a bite of cake while she waits for them to come out and look at her for themselves.

Anna does not have to wait long. First Mallory, then Bonner come out of the doorway and stand at the other side of her table and look directly at her. "My dear Anna, I did not recognize you in your new attire, it is not as fetching or as elegant as we are used to seeing you wear. What brings you to the city alone and without your masters?" asks Bonner in a polite but curious manner.

Anna smiles at him, "I recognized you two as soon as you stepped out of your carriage with your fine cloaks, top hats, and matching canes, but as I have had people follow me from the university, then staring at me through a window for the past half hour. I chose not to say hello as they were sure to tell you I was here".

Mallory looks to Smyth and the other man, angry that they were so easily spotted and that he has now been put in the situation of having his men known by Anna as well as the fact that the university is under observation. Something that would soon be known by Margaret if Anna was to leave the teahouse. "Go, before you never have the chance to go again you imbeciles. I have pet dogs at home with better manners and abilities than you two."

He turns back to Anna as the two men scurry away, crossing the road and heading back to the university. "Forgive me Anna, my dear, good staff and especially good, skilled, and talented staff are hard to find these days, and the best like you seem to be attached to the queen". He leans forward and takes Anna's hand in his short white glove and kisses the back of it, pausing as he does to look into her eyes.

Anna's skin crawls as she looks back and smiles at him. Suddenly she notices something that piques her interest, as Mallory has reached his arm forward, his sleeve has risen up slightly and between that and his short white glove his wrist is exposed, showing the long white line of a scar across it, about an inch and a half in length. "My dear Mallory, that is a nasty scar on your wrist, it must have hurt terribly when you got it," she says in a polite, dainty voice.

Mallory shudders slightly as she talks, his facial expressions getting serious for a split second, then he smiles as he thinks for a moment before speaking. "Yes, it did rather, a dueling scar from my days as a hot-headed youth, it taught me a big lesson in life, one that I have never forgotten."

Anna looks at him curiously as she takes her hand away from his. "Oh, and pray tell me, what might that be?" she asks politely.

"Always finish what you start, don't leave anything unfinished for you never know when it will come back to bite you."

Anna smiles at him, "Then I would presume from those wise words that the person who did that to you is now not of this world?"

He smiles at her. "My dear, he was well broken that day, never the same again I would say." He straightens up and speaks again in a serious tone of voice. "Now comes the duller side of our conversation. I would ask of you two things, my dear, firstly what business did you have at the university with Professor Simmerson? Now be warned, I am very serious on this matter, do not test me with a silly response as I do not wish to become unpleasant, was it on instructions from the queen."

Anna smiles at him while she thinks of a plausible answer that would not be far from the truth. "Well for once we are in agreement, while in town I am to purchase some clothing for Beth's child, Henry, as a present from the queen. Lord Ashby also had asked me to see if the professor could fit in another class of twelve officer cadets for a term of strategy teachings on great battles of the past or something like that, it was in a letter I gave to him, but, me being me, I read it before I gave it to him."

Bonner pulls a sheet of paper from his pocket, opens it and passes it to Mallory. "Our friends gave this to me just now inside the building, it was taken from that man Percival, a friend of the professor's, just after he put it on the requests pile for the attention of the university governor."

Mallory reads the letter closely before continuing his conversation with Anna. "It would seem that your explanation has merit, my dear. Great navy battles and their commanders of the sea, if I was to believe this was not planted to throw suspicion away from another alternative."

He leans forward and places his hands on the table. "My second question would be to ask how much you would want to work for me and supply us with information on the queen's activities, along with those of her friends Lord Ashby, Wellesley, and the others? But being an orphan, knowing how and where your parents died, and having no known relatives still alive to use as extortion against you, I could never trust one so cunning to be honest with me. You, my dear, are a very dangerous opponent, far better to be removed from the game we play than be trusted or employed."

Anna slowly stands up, leans forward, and puts her hands on the table besides his. Face to face and looking directly into his eyes, she speaks her piece in a quiet voice. "You could not afford me, as it is not money or position in society that drives me, and I would never work for a murderer like you. I know what happened to my parents well enough, and only instructions from my queen prevent me plunging my knife into your heart and finishing you off here over this table. That and the fact *he* is watching you over the barrel of a long rifle at this very moment, waiting for any excuse to let fly with a shot, because, you see, in this case he has more right to you than I do."

Mallory does not move, but his eyes give away his fear as he looks around, scanning the horizon for any sign of Wellesley. "You did not think I was here alone, did you? I was but the bait and your associates were the game drawn in. Once we had them on the hook, you would surely follow, and that you did."

"She's bluffing, there is nobody out there, we would have seen them by now," says Bonner.

Mallory grits his teeth and shakes his head "Shut up, you fool, and let me think," he replies. As the fear of the situation begins to sink in, beads of sweat begin to form on his forehead.

"Now, I am going to leave," Anna says calmly. "Once I have left, I will pick up a certain gentleman on my route round, only then will you be safe, so I suggest you both take a seat and wait a while. You should try the tea, it is quite good here."

As Mallory slowly takes a seat, Bonner looks around. "This is stupid, he is not out there anywhere I can see, and with one shot what can he really do? He will probably miss. Let's just take the girl and be done with it, besides, she may be good entertainment given some encouragement." Anna stares at Bonner sternly as she gets to her feet.

"For God's sake, Bonner, just take a s—"

"I did not say he was alone," Anna interrupts Mallory. "Perhaps Lord Ashby and Olson are around as well, I believe both have unfinished business over some farms and stud horses with you. Three shots and two targets does allow for at least one to miss, so I would say the odds are in their favor, wouldn't you agree."

Anna has played her cards well, as the fear that gripped Mallory now has the same effect on Bonner as he realizes he could be a target as well; his body language changes as he looks around with a concern he has not had up until now. Anna slowly moves along side of the table until within striking distance, discreetly takes a long blade from the thick pleat down the side of her trousers and thrusts it toward his groin area, stopping only as she feels cloth on the tip of her knife. Bonner lets out a whimper as he looks down to see the blade in a precarious position.

"You think I am some sort of entertainment, do you? A cheap piece of meat to be used as you see fit?"

"Now, now, don't be hasty," he says as he starts to tremble.

"I ought to do us all a favor and slice them off, but I think I will leave that to *your* master Stone, for he was right, you are weak and lacking intelligence, or should I say 'a jester in the house of kings' as he says of you." Anna is quick to put the seed of doubt in Bonner's mind, as she knows he has been feeling the pressure of being unwanted by Stone for a while now. Looking up, she signals Doolan with a flick of her other hand to bring the coach over to her. Moments later, he approaches, pulling the carriage up beside her before calling a halt to the horses. She takes the knife away from its target, points it to one of the spare chairs, and allows Bonner to take a seat. "I will be leaving you now. If I were you, I would sit and watch for a while as I will be picking up people on my way round the square, the more I pick up, the safer you will be, saving your favorite friend until last, Mallory."

He looks at her with steely eyes and a hatred that screams revenge. "You have the advantage this time, Anna, but the next time we meet, it will be on my terms and I will not be so lenient, I swear it."

Anna chuckles before speaking. "You could have sat at the table with me and had tea with no malice at all, I would have taken you for who you are and you the same with me, but you have to push and dominate everyone. I pity men like you, never to have true friends or real love, just those who take payment for their services or because you threaten to destroy them if they do not show obedience to you."

She ponders for a moment, then asks Mallory a question that has been on her mind for a long time. "I have often wondered, was it all worth it? Betraying your country, assisting in the murder of the king and queen, stripping the people of their families, homes, and wealth. Bringing this beautiful country to its knees and near bankruptcy just to keep you and the other two in clover? If you had the chance, would you do it all again or would you have chosen another way after seeing all the damage and destruction it has caused?".

Mallory sits back in his chair and takes a deep breath. "I do not know what you think I have done, young lady, but to answer your question, I have made my cloth, my dear, I must now wear it and live with what I have done, for even I cannot turn back time even if I wanted to".

Anna walks up to the side of the coach and the door held open by Doolan, pausing a moment to speak quietly to him. "Drive around the square, stop when I hit the roof twice, wait ten seconds then move off. When I hit the roof three times head home. But take the back roads out of the city with haste, our lives may well depend on it." As she takes her seat he slowly nods in understanding of the request before closing the door and climbing back up into the driving seat, releasing the brake and flicking the reins. Anna watches the two men from the small window in the coach door behind the netted curtain. Mallory and Bonner are like coiled springs, watching the coach intently and waiting to shoot out of their chairs in an instant. At the right moment she bangs the coach roof with her fist twice and Doolan pulls up instantly.

At the teahouse, Mallory and Bonner can see the horses but the coach body is obscured by a vending cart selling fruits and vegetables. The men move their heads to get a better view but are unable to see if anybody got into the vehicle or not. Doolan moves off and on command stops again another fifty yards along the road, this time with the coach hidden behind a stonewall about five feet high with just the heads of the horses and the top part of the carriage in view. This time Bonner and Mallory sit back in their chairs, believing Anna was telling the truth and realizing that without transport or sufficient men at arms, they have been out outgunned and have given up on any chance they might have had to get at her.

The coach moves on another four hundred yards and turns side on behind a small piece of grassland and stops again, this time in full view of the men but so far away they are only just visible. The coach waits for about a minute to ensure both Bonner and Mallory are watching closely before Anna sticks her head out of the window and waves to the two men, then the carriage pulls away again and disappears into the back streets of the city. The last thing Anna saw of them was Mallory clapping his hands as he has just worked out Anna has out-bluffed him. While Bonner was standing up and throwing his chair into the road in a fit of rage.

It is only now as Anna sits back in her seat that she realizes what a dangerous game has just been played out. Her expression becomes very solemn as she realizes that if she had made any mistakes, or shown any weakness or fear in any way, she would have been at the mercy of two men who would have stopped at nothing to get information from her. And the way Bonner was talking she may have been violated as well, a thought that sends shivers down her spine.

A small grin then appears on her face as she thinks of the fear on Mallory's and Bonner's faces when she used her friends names in her defense. What a move that was, she thinks to herself, if only Margaret and Wellesley had been there to see how she played it, they would have been so proud of her.

The journey back is uneventful if not a little bumpy and uncomfortable due to their speed, but it is of no matter to Anna, for she cannot wait to tell Margaret and Wellesley what went on and what she has found out. Only five hours have passed since she left and the coach is already moving down the driveway back towards the stable yard, the horses near exhausted, blowing hard with a white froth forming around where the leather straps rub on their sweating bodies as they pull up at the front of the house.

Wellesley is the first to greet them with two of the patrolling guards by his side, with hot steam rising profusely from the horses he realizes they have been worked to their limits and need immediate attention. He turns and calls to the stable hands for assistance and moments later two come running up from the yard towards him.

"Right, lads, the horses have been pushed hard and have a sweat on, get them unhitched and walk them round the yard for a while to cool down. Give them water to drink and a few buckets over their backs to wash them down, hold off any feed for an hour or so then bed them down well." He walks past the horses to Doolan. "Report then, why were you in such a rush, are we expecting anyone to have followed?" Wellesley asks as the man steps down from the driver's position, then turns and salutes his commander.

"Nobody followed us, I am sure of that. As for the speed, I was under instructions from Miss Anna to push on at pace. We arrived at the university as planned, Miss Anna went inside, half an hour or so later she came out and went to a teahouse across the road about a hundred yards in front of me. She signaled me to wait and observe as she had tea and a cake at a table outside. Some people went into the building, she seemed to know them but did not make conversation. Then a coach pulled up and two men got out, they also went into the building, then came out and struck up a conversation with said lady. After about thirty minutes she got in the coach and we left, I made some stop-start maneuvers around the square under her instructions, then, I headed back as fast as possible."

Wellesley nods his head. "Thank you, Doolan, that will be all. Get some food from the cook and well done on your first mission."

As Wellesley goes to move off, Doolan speaks again. "Sir, if I might add, I think the lady Anna was in a lot of danger. She handled herself with the utmost skill, but I believe more went on at the teahouse than I was aware of sir."

Wellesley takes in what Doolan says as he approaches the carriage and opens the door, looking inside and to see Anna fast asleep in the corner. As he reaches in to touch her, her eyes open and she smiles.

"I knew it would be you who would look for me first." She sits up and takes Wellesley's hand and steps down out of the coach, then locks her arm in his as they walk toward the house. "A whole lot went on today, I will explain everything once I get changed into some more appropriate cloths to meet Margaret in."

Wellesley shakes his head. "Women, why do you have to look good just to speak to someone? I don't get it, and, besides, Margaret has been pacing up and down the front of the fireplace ever since you left, I think she has been more nervous than me over how you were doing at the university."

As they step through the door into the hallway, Margaret is standing in front of them with Henry in her arms. She has been watching the coach since it returned and had let out a sigh of relief on seeing Anna step down from the vehicle. "More nervous than you, Wellesley, really! I was not the one on the roof with a spy glass looking at the horizon for the last hour."

Wellesley puffs himself up. "I was checking the far bank of the river, I thought I had seen something, something suspicious moving around and needed to check it out."

Margaret raises an eyebrow. "Oh, I see, so if the river is behind us, you were checking the far bank by looking in the opposite direction across the fields and toward the city?"

"I was using due diligence and on occasion I viewed all the surrounding countryside, but it was the far bank of the river I spent most time viewing." The ladies both start to chuckle as Wellesley tightens his lips in an attempt to make sure he says nothing more.

"No need to worry about getting changed, Anna, come through and warm yourself by the fire and tell us how it went today." They move into the lounge, where, to Anna's surprise, Lord Ashby and Olsen are sitting by the fire drinking wine and dining on a bowl of cook's meat stew, with Andrew for company. As Anna approaches, they all get up to greet her with smile and a kiss on the cheek.

"It has been a while, Anna, since I saw you last and you seem get more beautiful each time," Lord Ashby compliments Anna as she takes a seat between him and Margaret. "So, tell us of your adventure and what you found out, for I know if Margaret sent her very best close protector, something was bound to happen."

Anna tells them everything, from the professor being watched, Smyth and his group of senior students that watch over everything that goes on at the university. To being followed by Smyth to the teahouse, right through to the arrival of Mallory and Bonner. She also explains the little ruse she used to make them think they were being watched by people with long rifles and how it gave them an edge to get away, a part that Lord Ashby and Olson in particular found highly amusing, giving Anna a round of applause for her ingenuity.

While the group discuss all the new information Anna has given them, she takes the opportunity to walk out of the room with Wellesley, stopping him in the hallway. "There is one thing I did not talk about in the room, for I believe you need to hear it first.

Mallory went to kiss my hand, and as he did, his sleeve moved up his arm and exposed his wrist below a short white glove. I noticed a thin white scar at the top of his hand where it meets the wrist, about an inch and a half long that was running down the side. He was taken aback that I noticed it and explained that it was a dueling scar from years ago and that the person who gave it to him had suffered ever since."

Wellesley is frozen to the spot with a hundred thoughts running through his head. "I knew as much, Anna. Thank you for bringing it to my attention, now you get changed as you wanted to while I return to the others." Anna starts to climb the stairs, still looking back at Wellesley as he slowly moves back into the lounge, deep in thought.

Inside, conversation stops as he walks steadily toward the fireplace. All can tell something serious is on his mind.

"What is it, Wellesley?" Margaret asks with a concerned look on her face.

Wellesley looks at her for a moment, then speaks. "Anna just confirmed what we already thought. It was Mallory that night in the palace. She saw the scar on his wrist when they met at the teahouse when he introduced himself. She said he reacted badly to her noticing it and when she asked him about how he received such a wound, Mallory explained it was an old dueling scar from years ago."

The room goes quiet as everybody has their own thoughts on the news they have just heard. After several minutes, Lord Ashby finally speaks up and breaks the silence. "They will not take kindly to what Anna has done to them. She has humiliated them in public and they will want satisfaction, especially if she has seen evidence that would incriminate Mallory for what happened that night in the palace. We will need to watch over our young lady a little more carefully until this is over, a job I fear will be very challenging, knowing her and the way she gets involved in everything."

Wellesley is still staring at the floor, looks up and says "I want it known now, when the day comes, leave Mallory to me, I have a fate in mind for him that he will never forget. The rest you can do with as you see fit, but that man is mine and I will have words with anyone who stands in my way."

Margaret nods her head. "It was always my intention for you to deal with the situation for the both of us, Wellesley, I see no reason why that would ever change." She thinks for a moment then speaks again. "This is enough conversation on the day's events, we have guests tomorrow so let's finish the evening with friends and enjoy our time together, for these moments have become few and far between of late."

"Hear, hear," comments Lord Ashby. "And to start this off, I have a little gift for young Henry here." He walks over to his bag and takes out a small cloth-covered package and passes it to Andrew. "Now don't dally, my lad, open it and look what is inside." Andrew unfolds the cloth to reveal a painted picture of a small colt with its mother. "His name is Oscar and he be near six months old. On Henry's first birthday he will become his first horse, a pure Ambulette pony with a bloodline that traces back to my grandfather's stock."

Andrew is speechless, he has only ever seen pictures of these smaller versions of the great Ambulette horses, never before thought that his son would ever have one of his own. "I do not know what to say, I thought only royalty and people of high standing were allowed this kind of beautiful animal."

Lord Ashby turns and looks at Margaret before looking back at Andrew. "Every father's son is a prince, my boy, and yours to you is no exception. You have earned this prize for him with all you have done. Besides, I always have one or two surplus to requirements." Andrew shakes his hand then walks over to Margaret and Henry to show them the picture.

Just then, Anna returns to the room in a pale-blue dress. She makes a beeline for Margaret and stands beside her looking at the picture of the horses and then at Henry with sad eyes, before finally looking back at Margaret.

"Fine, Anna, you win, you can hold Henry for a while, but that is only because it gives me a chance to play a game of cards with the others. Having you out of the game means I only have one card shark to watch." She stares at Wellesley, who tries to give an innocent look back.

"It's a deal" Anna says immediately as her arms shoot out to take Henry from her.

"Still up to his old tricks, is he, Marge?" Lord Ashby asks as he frowns at Wellesley.

"Between him and Anna, it is impossible to get an honest game around here, and as you know Lord Ashby, I do like a game of cards now and then, she replies as Andrew and Olson start to pull out the gaming table and open it up with the additional extension as there are more people than usual. Wellesley covers the table with a green cloth and then opens the drawer to take out the cards and starts to shuffle them.

"You can put them back, Wellesley" calls Lord Ashby as he moves back over to his bag and takes out a dozen new packs of cards and gives them to Margaret. "As you requested, my dear, one dozen new sets of cards with a green and gold diamond pattern on the back. They are like no other cards that can be purchased."

Wellesley looks at Margaret's smiling face. "Really, that is just mean, do you think I would cheat my friends?" he asks as he watches Margaret walk over to an ornamental tea chest sitting on a side table. She opens it up and places ten of the packs of cards inside, then closes the lid and locks it with the small key on the front, which she places in a locket around her neck. "Do you not think you are over doing this a little, Margaret?" Wellesley asks.

Margaret looks at back at him sternly. "I'm not finished yet. Bunty!" she calls out loudly, and moments later Bunty arrives in the room.

"You called, ma'am?"

"Yes, would you take this tea chest and put it somewhere Wellesley will not dare touch it, please?"

Bunty collects the chest from Margaret and as she turns, looks directly at Wellesley. "I will keep it somewhere safe, certainly, it will be in my room." Wellesley cannot help but be taken aback by her answer.

"I think under my bed," she continues, leaving a look of shock and horror on Wellesley's face. Everyone in the room is laughing as Bunty marches out with a smile on her face. "I will be waiting for you should you want to knock on my door, darling," she calls over her shoulder, blowing him a kiss before closing the door.

Wellesley's face is a picture, full of shock and fear as the rest of the room laugh at his misfortune. As the laughter subsides, Margaret is first to take a seat around the newly positioned gaming table. She places one pack of cards on the deck and the other she tucks inside the bodice of her dress.

"Now they have finally gone down a little there is enough room fit them in there, and if I feel your hand on me Wellesley, Andrew will shoot you, friend or not."

Poor Andrew shrugs his shoulders and raises his hands toward Wellesley, he has managed to stay neutral so far, but Margaret has now pulled the husband card into play so he must respond. "As my wife has so graciously pointed out, I will have to watch for any close physical contact between you and Margaret for the rest of the evening, any such conduct will result in me requiring satisfaction and a duel at dawn on the lawn outside."

As the others rekindle their laughter, Margaret has one more thing to say. "You are to sit opposite me Wellesley, with Olson on one side and Lord Ashby on the other. Andrew, my dear, I would like you on my right side and, Beth, please be on my left, to keep him at arm's length."

As everyone takes their seats around the table, Beth passes out stacks of gaming disks to everyone in the game. Anna is sitting by the fire, holding and playing with young Henry, periodically looking up to see who is doing what in the game.

Wellesley looks up, leans forward and speaks "Do you not think this is taking it a little over the top, Margaret?"

Margaret raises an eyebrow while she is opening the pack of cards and checking what the face values look like. "I can always ask Bunty to come back into the room and take a seat beside you if you wish me to."

"No! I am fine with the arrangements as they are, I was just expressing my opinion, that is all. I just feel that you have an ill-conceived picture of me and the art of playing cards, I only cheat when I am struggling to win, and I would not practice my sleight of hand on my friends. Only those that would do the same thing to me," he replies while looking at Anna sitting by the fire.

Olson is laughing so hard it is beginning to hurt his sides. "You be a funny man, Wellesley. In times of war, I would want no other but you and Lord Ashby by my side, but when it comes to cards, I would sooner play against Anna."

Wellesley looks at him with a shocked expression, "But she cheats worse than me and is bad at doing it."

"Yes, but she is prettier than you and we know she is cheating, so if the lady wins a couple of extra coins, we do not mind as she has a nice smile." At this moment everyone is laughing, including Anna.

As the laughter dies down, Anna asks from the other side of the room "So, Olson, you think I am bad at cheating at cards, do you?"

"My dear Anna, do not take it the wrong way. Olson is only being honest, it is easy to tell when you are being underhanded as you always flutter your eyes and bite your bottom lip, as well as push out your chest to try and hide the move with a distraction. We watched you do it to many of the young male cadets at the barracks when you were training, to great effect I might add. You fleeced many of them of the coins they had, but they were only amateurs and easily distracted. When you play us, you are playing against masters? We only pretend not to notice and bide our time, waiting for the right moment to take the bigger pots or fold and give you precious little in reward for your efforts," replies Lord Ashby.

Anna sighs heavily. "I admit, it is true, I have been taken down the path of wrongdoing by a terrible and corrupted man. I have tried so hard to resist his teachings, but Wellesley is a determined mentor, ever pushing me into the darker arts of subterfuge, not to mention the pay being so poor that if I did not supplement my income, I would be walking around in rags not dresses."

Wellesley looks round at Anna. "Ha, you needed no teaching

on anything, you were born slippery and have remained so. All I am guilty of is trying to make a silk purse out of a sow's ear, a task that many would have found just too difficult to attempt."

Anna puts her hands over Henry's ears. "Don't listen to him, Henry, he is a bad man, he is using me as a distraction while he cheats on the others at the table," she says, chuckling to herself.

"How can I be cheating? The cards have yet to be dealt," he replies.

"Cards, yes, but the disks are on the table, I would be watching them if I was playing at the table," she responds swiftly.

Instantly, everybody looks at their own stack, then at their opponents stacks, counting to ensure they all have the same amount to start with. Already Anna has set the seed of doubt in all their minds and put a smile on Margaret's face before the game has even started.

The group continue to play cards for the rest of the evening and well into the early hours of the morning, only ending the session when it becomes apparent to Margaret that she and Lord Ashby are the only ones left who are not falling asleep at the table. As they wrap up the session, Margaret counts the cards before packing them away in their little box and putting them into her pocket, much to the annoyance of Wellesley, who watches her every move to see if he can lift one of the cards for a while to get a set of similar ones made.

CHAPTER 15

The Price of Revenge

Time is moving swiftly for Margaret and her close team of friends and family, with a date set at the palace to action the queen's plan to regain control of the country. The house is a hive of activity as everybody is pulling together to have the people trained and in position ready to complete each detail of the plan.

Margaret and Wellesley are on their way to join the rest of a diplomatic party for a meeting with envoys from the neighboring empires of Saxony and Hanover now they have now resolved their own issues and are ready to negotiate on long-term trade and treaty agreement going forward.

It is a key time for diplomacy as the royal envoy will also be strengthening the queen's position in Kelsey and ensuring the support of neighboring kingdoms on the day she fights to retake control of her country. As with everything they do, discretion is of utmost importance as they must keep these negotiations away from the eyes and ears of The Three Heads and the rest of their corrupt diplomats and informants. It will be a dangerous time for all involved, but they must ensure that they have a strong bond with the rulers of these two nations to secure a stable future.

✳ ✳ ✳

Around the same time in the capital city, a less-than-cordial meeting is taking place at Mallory's city mansion between Stone, Bonner and Mallory.

"Yet again that little tramp has made you look foolish and stupid for all to see. I want her fucking head on a plate, do you hear me? On a plate!" bellows Stone.

"Your men could not even do the simplest of tasks like discreetly watch a university without being discovered and now they know we are on to them and aware they are hatching some kind of plan. I fail to understand what I pay these men for as they seem to create more problems than they are fucking worth."

Bonner tries to bleat out an excuse. "It is not our fault, we do not have anything to bribe or blackmail her with, we don't even know anything about the woman that would help get her on our side or break the little bitch, her past seems to be a bit of a mystery since she lost her family."

Stone swallows down a large glass of brandy, then throws the glass into a fireplace in frustration, making the others jump as it smashes on the metal grate.

"Well, I might have the information you need to resolve this issue, you see a certain politician friend of ours has recognized Anna at one of our recent diplomatic meetings with the queen. I am sure you are aware of Hubert Forcedyke and the incident with his son over some sort of assault charge." The two men nod at him as he continues.

"He is bitter over the incident, and it would seem that Anna was the woman that cried wolf on his boy and caused his incarceration. She is the reason his son and three others are now coscripted to a ship of the line for the foreseeable future, patrolling the coastline and assisting to bring our pirate friends to heal and costing me yet more money in smuggled goods and trade. If what he says is correct, she was once living on the streets along with several other children in an old building that has subsequently been rebuilt to house some of the unfortunates of this country. Perhaps some of her friends now reside in that building, someone there may even be a close friend of hers and be of use as leverage. In particular a young boy named Billy, they were said to be close, he might be the key to getting to her to comply with our needs. Get the boy and the girl may well be fall in our pocket."

Mallory speaks up, "I had a meeting with the leaders of all our street associates just yesterday, all have been hit quite hard recently and have struggled to maintain the level of chaos they were achieving earlier this year. The Penny Rips have been wiped out to a man, and the queen's own forces are now actively hunting out all the gangs at every opportunity they get.

I think some of them would appreciate the opportunity to take the fight back to the monarchy and collect a bit of pay back for the losses they have endured. If you give me the name of the street, I will have them look into this place and the boy 'Billy', see if this new information is good and can be used to our advantage."

"You do that, here is the street and number." Stone passes Mallory a sheet of paper. "Make it sooner rather than later as it would be nice to have an insider in her camp for once and find out more about what that bloody woman is up to."

There is a knock on the door before a servant enters the room, "Your food is ready to be served in the dining room, sir."

"Excellent timing, Denver, we will be through shortly." Mallory turns to the other two. "Gentlemen, shall we continue this at the dining table?" With a nod from the pair of them, Mallory leads the three men through the open door and into the dining room.

A few days later, a little after one in the afternoon, Ned is making his way back from his routine check on the bakery. He has a loaf tucked under his good arm for Dick and himself and is approaching the house with the orphaned children. As always, his intention is to visit Penny and see how she is doing, ask if they require anything done around the building and spend a little time with the younger children. They always have lots of questions to ask him about his life in the army, more so young Billy who loves the idea of being a hero and protecting everyone like Anna does.

As he approaches the building, he can see three men on the other side of the road, they catch his attention as they seem to be tucked slightly back down the side of a house and garden wall so not to be prominent and stand out in the street. He decides to cross over and walk past them to get a better look at who they are. As he approaches, he begins to slow and listen to what they are saying, as well as discretely getting a good look at them.

"Seems to be just an old woman downstairs in the window, should be an easy in and out tonigh—" The man stops speaking and looks at Ned as he slowly moves past, fainting a limp and sluggish movement.

"Be on your way, old man, there is nothing for you to see here but the back of my hand," one of them comments as he passes them by.

It only takes Ned a moment to realize they are a gang-related group as all three are wearing tall hats and red scarfs. He tilts his cap at them and shuffles along past them, heading straight back to the cottage to speak to Dick about what he has just observed.

One of the men is curious and steps forward to watch Ned and possibly catch up to him, when another speaks out, "Ah, forget it, it's just a one-armed cripple. Nothing to worry about, let's get back to the others, we're wasting time here."

Ned makes his way back home, deliberately not looking back at them as he moves on, so not to draw any more attention to himself. On arrival he enters the house, drops the bread down on the kitchen side and moves out into the garden. He takes a seat by Dick, explaining what he has just seen.

"Do you think it was just coincidence that they were there?"

"I don't know, they were definitely looking at the orphans' house as if for a purpose, but it doesn't make sense; it's just full of children, no money or value in the place. It does not hold anything that would be of interest to a gang or syndicate."

"Well log it in the ledger so we have a record of it and we will do a couple of checks tonight and ensure that all is safe for Penny and the children." The men talk about the incident for a little longer before getting on with making a meal for themselves then clean and prepare their pistols in case they are needed later.

The afternoon passes swiftly and as the two men light the fire in the house and settle down for the evening, suddenly Ned stands up. "No, it does not sit easy with me, my friend. I have that feeling something is not right, and you know if I have that feeling, then usually something is going to happen."

Dicky looks at him. "What do you intend to do about it then?"

Ned has made up his mind. He reaches for his jacket and large brown shoulder bag. "I think I will go and see Penny, may well stay the night with her at the house, just in case."

"Well, if you are taking that bag, then you must really have that feeling that something is going to happen, do you want me to come along with you?"

"No, it is probably nothing, but I must still check it out. You keep warm by the fire, and I will see you later, if not, in the morning."

As Ned puts his heavy boots on, Dick thinks on his actions. "I will make a few walking visits in the night and early morning, just to ensure that nothing is going on outside, I will see you tomorrow when you have got this feeling out of your system."

Ned puts his jacket on and heads for the door. "See you later, my old friend, and don't drink too much as I am not here to help you up the stairs," he comments while chucking to himself. "It took you nearly an hour the other day and I could not stop laughing until I was near fit to burst."

The sound of Ned's hobnail boots can be heard by Dick for some time, tapping away on the cobble stones as he makes his way up the road towards Penny and the children.

It takes him around ten minutes to reach the house and another fifteen minutes to walk around the building and the surrounding lanes to ensure nothing is out of place before he knocks on the door. Within a few seconds the door is opened, and he is confronted with several smiling children. "Hello, Ned, what brings you here so late?" Abbey asks with a smile on her face.

"He has come to tuck me in," shouts out little Katie, as Ned laughs and enters the house.

"That will only be if you have been behaving yourself, my young ladies." Katie grabs his hand and leads him through to Penny in the kitchen before running off to play with her friends.

Penny is just putting the finishing touches to a bandage on one of the boy's legs. "Hello, Ned, it's a bit late for you to be visiting. Still, it is nice to see you and the children always enjoy the stories and adventures you tell. Though I must confess, some seem to be more of the imagination than what I consider factual."

She lowers the boy to the floor. "Now this time keep the bandage on you for more than a few hours, young James, as it will help it to heal and get better."

"Yes Miss Penny, I will try," he replies while running off to join the others as they play, leaving just Penny and Ned in the kitchen.

"I would have you know that young Richard and myself are still actively in the Fusiliers and drawing full pay, it is just that our bodyguard duties have changed a little, that's all."

Ned puts his bag on the side and takes a seat at the table as Penny offers him a welcome glass of cider while laughing at his comments and shaking her head.

"You always look after me and know what I like, Penny, thank you."

"Well, you would not come visiting this late in the day unless something was up, so out with it my boy, are you still on duty as it were, or just passing by?"

Ned looks around to ensure no children are around before speaking. "That I am, I saw a group of men watching the house today, tall top hats and red scarfs. I think they were gang members."

"Tall hats and red scarfs you say. Yes, they are gang members, but they are a long way from home. For they are Tom Ruddies from the city. What would they want with a children's home this far away from their patch I wonder!"

"That I cannot tell you, but if it is alright with you I was going to stay the night just to be on the safe side. I would like to be around just in case they decide to visit during the night."

Penny thinks for a moment. "We can set you up a makeshift bed using the large chairs by the fire if that is good with you, as all the beds upstairs are taken by the children. I have used it myself several times before and it is quite comfortable if set right."

"Just a chair will suffice, Penny, I do not wish to be a burden to you. I just have a feeling and want to make sure all is well, that's all."

"Core blimey, it's Ned!" hollows a boy as he enters the kitchen.

Ned turns to see who it is.

"Billy, that is no way to address a man who has come to visit us," Penny comments while flicking him on the top of his head. "Improve your language when you speak to somebody."

"I'm sorry, Miss Penny, I was just excited, that's all. He is a real honest-to-God hero, served our queen for many years and has been wounded in battle several times. His charge at the enemy to protect her is famous you know."

"That may be so, but it is time for your bed along with the other younger ones, so go before I give you a spoon full of my special medicine to help quieten you down."

Billy's face drops to a disgusting expression. "That stuff is nasty, more like poison than medicine, it should not be allowed."

Penny reaches for a spoon from the sideboard, opens up the top cupboard and reaches inside for a dark-brown glass bottle. As she turns to face Billy, he makes off out the door as swiftly as he had entered the room.

She chuckles and places the bottle back where it came from. "Never seems to fail having the fear factor of medicine over that one, one spoonful of this castor oil and he is off faster than blowing out a candle." Ned chuckles as Penny takes a seat beside him and begins to write down her expenses for the day in a small ledger book.

"Must keep the daily accounts up to date, Ned, every coin counts with so many to feed and clothe in this house."

She writes a few lines down before speaking again. "What would the gangs want with an orphanage? There is no wealth here, just a group of homeless children and one old woman."

"I do not know Penny, but I be seeing them earlier and heard enough to conclude that they may be up to no good. You have a lot of vulnerable people here. Perhaps it is nothing, but for now just humor me as I am tasked with watching over you all."

Penny smiles. "You and Dick are always welcome here, Ned. Besides, I like the feeling of having men watch over the children; makes me feel safe and it ensures that nothing will happen again like it did with young Anna and some of the other girls in the past." Penny closes the book and gets up.

"Now I have to get the younger children to bed. Make yourself at home while I am gone, I will sort your bed out on my return." She gets up, taking one of the lanterns from the side with her as she leaves the room and makes her way up the stairs.

No sooner has she gone from view, Ned pulls his bag up from the floor and lays it out on the table. With a quick look around to ensure no children are present, he begins to load and prime one of three pistols, lining each one up once done, ready for use should they be needed. Then he goes to the window and looks outside. It is getting dark as night closes in, he can see very little apart from around the two streetlamps that are lit at the entrance to the path leading down to the building. He still has a feeling that all is not as it seems and is apprehensive at what the night might have in store for them.

Penny arrives back near an hour later. "Well, Ned, it was not easy to get the younger children to bed, they all wanted to see you. In the end I have promised them that you will spend a little time with them in the morning before you go."

Ned chuckles. "It will be my pleasure Penny, it is always nice to still feel wanted and useful at my age, It is like having children of my own, but I can at least walk away when I have had enough of them, unlike yourself."

Penny laughs, "Come let's sit by the fire and talk with the older ones, for they have been waiting patiently for you to see them, But I warn you, no blood and guts talk, I want them to sleep later, not have nightmares."

The pair of them move to the fireplace and begin to make conversation with some of the children that are still awake. They are eager to ask Ned about his days in the army and things he used to get up to with Dick and his fellow soldiers. This makes for an interesting couple of hours before all decide to call it a night and get some sleep.

Ned is woken early the following day by the sound of people moving around in the house; it is still dark but there is a glow of light coming from down the hallway and into the room he is sleeping in. He gets up and makes his way towards the sounds and the light. As he peers into the kitchen through the doorway he can see Penny along with three of the oldest boys and Rose, a girl he knows well as she now runs the bakery under Penny's guidance.

"Hello Ned, we tried to be quiet so not to wake you," says Rose.

"We were just off to get the bakery up and running, get the ovens lit and up to temperature ready to start the day's baking."

Ned lets out a sigh of relief; he is standing in his long johns and white cotton shirt full of holes. He looks at the smiling Rose, Penny and now chuckling young men, then he realizes what he must look like. "What you all be laughing for? It's my lucky shirt, so enough of the mockery, I have had it a long time."

"We can see that, Ned, perhaps you could leave it with me and I will see if it is possible to sew it up before it falls apart completely," Penny says while trying not to laugh out too loud.

"Thank you, but no! This shirt is a part of me, and it fits and feels simply fine as it is. Now, with your permission, I think it is time I go and put the rest of my clothes on." As he leaves, he can hear the others chucking and laughing over his attire.

"Ned, you have always been a stubborn old coot, but if you do not leave that shirt behind when you go, I will have the boys take it from you forcibly. You cannot continue to wear that rag of a shirt, it is disgusting!" yells out Penny.

Ned pretends he does not hear her as he leaves. A few minutes later he returns to the kitchen fully dressed and takes a seat at the table with the others.

Rose pours him out a mug of tea, adds milk and a couple of pieces of sugar to the mix and stirs it before placing it in front of him.

"This should warm you up," she says with a smile on her face.

She then turns to the boys. "Well, them ovens will not light themselves, we had better get going as there will be a lot to do before we are ready to serve our customers."

As they leave, all give Penny a kiss on the cheek as she is considered mother by all of them. As the last of them steps out the house into dawn's light, she quietly closes the door and the building becomes silent once more.

Penny sighs and then speaks, "They have become so good at what they do, Ned. Once orphans of this town, chased, beaten and ridiculed for years, now they are feeding hundreds of families every day. And yet they are still the same people they were, just a little older. I could not be any prouder of them if they were my own flesh and blood."

"I could not agree more; it would seem that people are slowly beginning to pull together more and more, it was only a year or so back that nobody would have given those children the time of day. Now, the same people are depended upon them for their very survival."

Bang, bang, bang. There is a loud knock at the door, Penny looks at Ned and then towards the doorway. "They must have forgot something", she comments as she moves towards the door and opens it, "And what did you forg—" Penny is taken back as she is confronted by a group of men in tall hats.

"Sorry to bother you at this hour, but we are looking for somebody, a young woman called Anna."

Penny knows exactly who they are and composes herself. "No, there is nobody here by that name." She tries to close the door, but the man has put his boot across the step, stopping her from closing it.

"Well perhaps some of the others here know of her, do you mind if we ask them a few questions and find out."

"This is an orphanage for children; we do not allow strangers in here at all, let alone to visit so early in the morning. Come back later if you must." She tries with all her strength to close the door, but to no avail as the man's boot holds fast.

The door is forced back open by one of the other men, pushing Penny backwards a few feet. "I insist," the man snarls as he pushes his way into the house followed by some of his companions.

Penny keeps stepping backwards and moves into the kitchen area, still being followed by the advancing men. As she makes her way around the table, the men notice Ned sitting down with one arm inside a brown leather strap bag. They are taken back a little, not expecting any other adults to be present, but, with numbers on their side, they advance forward into the kitchen.

"Seems to me the woman has asked you to leave."

"Yeah, well, what she wants and what we do are two different things, old cripple." He looks back at the others. "Take a look around, we will deal with these ones here."

Some of the men split off and head along the corridors of the house, while the ones in the entrance to the kitchen watch Penny and Ned. Moments later they hear the yelling and screaming from the children upstairs, along with the crashing of furniture and the shouts of the men asking about Anna.

"Well, are you going to do something, Ned, that is what you are here for, isn't it?" Penny asks in a stern voice.

"Yes, just give me a minute, it is not easy to fill the pans with one hand when you cannot see what you are doing." The men all look at Ned as they realize to late that he is preparing to act against them.

Click, bang! The pistol in the bag fires and hits the first man in the chest, knocking him backwards and to the floor. The second man panics and reaches into his jacket as Ned lets loose a second shot, hitting him in the torso while the third man runs out of the kitchen and back outside the building and into the arms of some of his associates.

"They were ready for us; shoot to kill and burn this place to the fucking ground when our men come back out!" he hollers.

Inside, Ned has got up from the table and moved to the doorway, speaking as he goes, "Load the two pistols for me Penny, that's a good lass."

He pops his head out into the hallway and back in, taking only a second to look around. It is followed by two shots ringing out and missing their mark, hitting the door frame and the wall in front of him. He then leans out again for a better look and spots where the two men shot from. He checks back to ensure that Penny has already started to reload the first pistol.

The men outside are entering the house through the front door. Ned makes his choice and as they creep in, he leans out and shoots one of them in the head, killing him instantly. The others run back outside to take cover and reassess the situation.

All goes quiet for a while as the gang members do not know how many people are armed in the house and are reluctant to move around at any great pace. They are thieves and murderers, not trained soldiers; bravery and discipline are not built into them like it is Ned. As Penny hands him a loaded pistol, she works on loading the next one for him.

Outside, the men at the doorway are distracted by what they see heading towards them,

"Get a load of that!" one comments as the others look up. Far in the distance, Dick is hurtling towards them wearing nothing more than his long johns and a long black trench coat. He is pendulum swinging on a pair of crutches as fast as he is able to cover the ground between him and the orphanage.

"What do you make of it?" one asks.

"Be fucked if I know." Another replies.

They watch as Dick continues to swing towards them. As he gets closer, the men raise their pistols ready to fire. At about twenty yards from them, Dick begins to slow and at fifteen yards he stops. Leaning on his crutches he coughs and splutters while attempting to catch his breath. He puts one of his hands out as if to ask the men to wait while he continues to cough and dribble profusely. The men start to laugh and chuckle at the state of the old man in front of them, lowering their pistols as they do so.

Dick slowly looks up at them, still panting as he wipes the sweat from his brow with a handkerchief. "You have no idea how hard that was to get here so fast on one leg, nearly took it all out of me."

"Old man, I would say it has, you are not even dressed and your timing to be here is not good either, for we are in the middle of something."

Dick puts the handkerchief in his huge coat pocket. "No, laddie, my timing was perfect."

He tilts the pistol in his pocket and fires at the lead man, hitting him near the heart. Leaning over onto the opposite crutch more, his other hand raises another pistol in the other pocket and fires at the second man, striking him in the stomach. With a blood-curdling roar, he flings one of his crutches at the last man as he moves forward while trying to free his sword from his belt.

The crutch hits the man across the head, staggering him backwards as he fires his pistol into the side of Dick, who falls onto one of the men he has shot. Unable to get up, he somehow manages to free his sword and swing it wildly in the direction of the third man, missing him by some distance.

He looks down at the floundering one-legged man, still struggling to get up or reach him with his sword.

"You were good, but not that good as to beat me, old man," he says while he slowly begins to reload his pistol. As he finally places the small ramrod in the barrel to push down the shot, he looks down at his target. Shock and fear fill his eyes as he finds himself looking down the barrel of a pistol pointing directly at his face.

"Still better than you will ever be, boy," Dick comments as he fires the pistol and drops the last of the men outside the building. Dick turns to look at the man he is laying on. "Thanks for the loan of your pistol," he says as it falls from his hand. He then looks at the wound in his side, grimaces with pain before dropping back down onto the floor, the last of his reserves now spent.

Inside the house, Ned has heard the firing of pistols outside and he knows it would have been his friend getting involved in the fight. Now, with Penny by his side with two more loaded pistols in her hands, he makes his move; first a quick lean out and in, followed swiftly by the firing of two more pistol shots by his opposition. Ned then leans out and shoots at the wall by the door, knowing it to be a thin wooden parting wall. The bullet finds its mark as he hears the man fall to the floor. He switches pistols with another from Penny and let's fly another shot at the man on the ground, ensuring he is out of the way and no longer a threat. Then swapping to the last pistol Penny has reloaded, he waits for his next moment to strike at them.

Upstairs, the yelling and shouting from the children has stopped. As he takes another quick peek down the hallway he can see two men, one holding a child by the arm while the other is behind them.

"Seems we have found what we are looking for, be grateful we only want the one," the man says as he looks for a way to get out of the building with the child.

"Well, that's one too many in my book."

"What are you talking about? There are many of us here and only you and an old woman to stop us."

"No, I think you will find that you two are the only ones left alive my boy, my friends have taken out the rest of your group outside."

"A likely story, Sid, Drake, Fitch. You out there!" the man yells and waits for a response. With no response he calls out to them again, "Answer me, damned your eyes, where are you?" "As I said, you two are all alone now, so why don't you give it up and come peaceable like, it may well save your lives."

"What should we do!" one of the men says to the other.

"Quiet, let me think for a moment." He pushes young Billy out in front of himself while keeping a tight grip. "Follow tight behind me, Burt, and watch our backs."

"Right, we are coming past and going to take our leave of you. Get in our way and the boy gets it, do you understand?" He squeezes the boys arm tightly to make him scream out with pain. Penny instantly goes to move forward, but she is stopped by Ned.

"No, Penny, if they leave with the boy, you will never see him again. His best chance is with us right now," he reassures Penny before responding to the two men.

"No chance, hurt the child and I will finish you off. He is the only reason you're still alive as it is, just give it up, it is not worth your lives, not for one small child."

The two men begin to slowly move down the corridor in tight formation, pushing Billy along in front, using him as a human shield against Ned. Young Billy, however, has other ideas in his mind; he has been in this position before and saw what they did to his best friend Anna last time men used him as a bargaining tool. He fumbles in his pocket for his small penknife, opens the blade and grips it tightly in his hand, then, as they push him further along he strikes down hard with his clenched hand and jabs the small knife into the man's thigh.

"Aaaahhhh, you little bleeder!" the man yells. Billy then pulls the knife out and strikes it back down again. This time, as the man yells out, he lets go of him at the same time.

Billy makes a run for it, making ten or twelve yards before the man instinctively raises his pistol and fires at the boy, hitting him square in the back. Billy staggers a few more paces before he falls to the ground with barely a sound made. At the same time Ned leans out round the doorway and fires a shot of his own, hitting Burt in the throat; he swiftly drops to the floor holding his neck in his hands as he gurgles and splutters, the shot having ripped open his windpipe, leaving him choking on his own blood.

Penny rushes out to aid the stricken Billy; she still has the last pistol in her hand and the man notices it and lunges forward. Anticipating she is about to shoot him, he pistol whips her across the face, knocking her unconscious as he rushes for the door and an escape route from the house.

Ned grabs at the man with his one arm as he passes, "Come here, you bastard!" he yells as he tries to hold onto the man's shoulder, but with only one hand his assailant eventually breaks free and runs out of the house. Ned picks up the last loaded pistol from the floor and looks at Penny and Billy lying motionless on the ground. Gritting his teeth and growling with anger, he rushes out after the man.

To his surprise, the villain is only a few yards outside the door. As he raises his pistol and looks around, he can see that the man has stopped as he is surrounded by sixty to seventy people from the neighborhood; all armed with whatever they had to hand, ranging from pistols, rifles and knives to gardening implements.

With the man resigned to the fact that there is no escape from his situation and surrendering, Ned looks around to finds his friend. He spots him leaning up against the house by the side of the doorway, blood oozing from his wound.

"Oh no! Dicky my friend, what have they done to you?" Tears well up in his eyes as he moves to the side of his best friend and kneels down.

Struggling to get his breath and speaking in a near whisper he speaks, "I, I came as soon as I heard the first shots, but I'm not as f-fast as I once was, my friend. See, look at me, I'm not even dressed in my uniform or wearing my boots." Tears are flowing down Ned's face as he holds Dick in his arm with his head supported on his chest, blood leaking from his mouth as he struggles to breathe from the wound on the side of his ribs that has punctured his lung and is slowly filling with blood.

"You did just fine, Richard. You came to my aid when I needed you most as you always do. Saved my life yet again and helped protect so many children; nobody could have asked more of you."

"S-serving with you by my side has been the greatest honor I could have wished for. I will tell our comrades that you are doing w-w-well my ffr-fr…"

Dicky's head slowly drops as the life drains from his body, while Ned holds onto him and looks to the sky, tears flowing down his face as his lifelong friend finally succumbs to his wounds and leaves him for the first time since they were children.

Inside the house, Penny is being helped to her feet by some of the townspeople; she has a nasty open wound across the side of her temple, but her first concern is for Billy and what she can do for him. More and more friends and neighbors enter the house and offer their services to help in any way they can.

Penny, as always, has them working within minutes; this time to get the bodies out of the house so the younger children do not see them, while others help move Billy Infront of the fire while they wait for a physician to arrive.

Rose has arrived back from the bakery; she is quick to help with the rest of the younger children, keeping them upstairs until the others have cleaned up all the blood and cleared the house of all the gang members and their weapons.

* * *

It is near eleven when an unannounced rider appears at the

manor house to deliver news of the attack on the orphanage. He is instantly descended on by three guards and dismounted from his horse as they begin questioning him. After some time, one of the guards finds Anna and lets her know that a man is desperate to speak to her or Andrew.

Anna is cautious to start with, but, as she approaches the man, she instantly recognizes him as one of the men who helped build the house for the children. With the guards satisfied that he is no threat, they return to their duties while she listens to what he has to say.

Horrified by what she has just heard, she rushes into the house calling out to Andrew as she takes to the stairs and heads to the war room where she last seen him.

Andrew responds to the sound of her voice and they meet in the hallway outside the room. As she approaches him, he can see something is terribly wrong by the look on her face.

"They have attacked the orphanage, Andrew. Penny and Billy have been hurt, and several more have been killed in the assault on the building."

It takes a moment to sink in as Andrew thinks about what Anna has just said: "We must leave immediately. I will get the horses ready as it will be the fastest way to get there."

As she turns to go, Andrew speaks. "No, wait a moment, let me think."

"There is nothing to think about, it's Billy and Penny, I'm going now."

"Anna, stop."

She looks at Andrew with watering eyes. "I must go to him now, he needs me." She starts to cry as Andrew steps forward to hold and comfort her. "This is revenge by Mallory and Bonner for what I did the other day. I know it is, they have attacked it to get back at me, this is all my fault." She sobs as she holds Andrew tight.

Beth has stepped out from the nursery as she has heard the commotion. She stands nearby and waits for Andrew's next move.

"Anna, listen to me, we do not know anything yet. We will go to them, but it is the bigger picture we must consider; we cannot afford any rash actions. It could be a decoy move and we must prepare for all possible outcomes."

Andrew looks at Beth. "I want this place locked down, all non-essential people are to leave the premises immediately. You know who is needed here and who is not, please see to it at once."

Beth moves off with a purpose, walking straight into the war room. "You, you and you, time to leave. This place is now being sealed up until further notice and watch yourselves as you depart, stay safe and ensure that you are not being followed. If in doubt, head to the garrison at Stoneheart Manor, they will protect you."

Andrew speaks "Anna, send one of the guards to the village, I want all the reserves called in, any on patrol to be recalled. I want all our people back at the house on full alert. Also, the rider that came in with the message, ask him to return to the village and let them know we will be there as soon as we can."

Within twenty minutes, three coaches and several riders are leaving the house down the gravel driveway and splitting off in different directions. Over a dozen cavalry men have arrived and taken up their allotted positions around the house and grounds, while Andrew stands by the front door looking around in all directions to ensure all are in position.

By now Anna has changed into her military uniform with all her attachments in place, including her new pair of small lightweight pistols. 'A gift from Lord Ashby', much against Wellesley's wishes as he felt Anna was dangerous enough anyway.

Since owning them, Anna has become quite a markswoman, having practiced on several occasions with Lord Ashby himself and other times with Olsen and Captain Hawkswell.

She joins Andrew at the front of the house. As always, it brings a smirk to his face to see Anna armed and ready to go. Anna has also become quite a favorite with the guards as well; being pretty, curvy, attractive. She is the secret mascot of the troops; they respond to her commands and requests as if from Wellesley himself.

For many, she is one of the men, able to drink, gamble and fight as well as the rest of them, but none would dare approach her or ask her on a date for fear of her response and that of the people who watch over her.

Andrew leaves Beth in charge of the house; it is the first time that all but her will be away from his son, but he must go to the orphanage and see what has happened for himself.

Instructions are also left that Margaret and Wellesley are not to be informed of the incident until they return from diplomatic duties. Andrew feels it might compromise their negotiations and Anna and himself are more than capable of dealing with this situation. Besides, there is nothing they will be able to do being so far away at this moment in time.

As horses arrive at the house from the yard, He mounts up and is soon joined by Anna. They are taking only two guards with them to ensure the house is heavily protected while they are away. This is not Andrew's usual way to travel, but time is of the essence in his mind and needs must.

They arrive at the orphanage in a little under two hours and there is still quite a crowd of people present outside the building. A wagon is parked outside and the bodies of the gang members are being loaded on to be taken away for disposal.

Andrew and Anna dismount, leaving the horses with their guards and head straight for the house. Inside they find Penny in the kitchen being attended to by a physician; she is relieved to see Andrew and reaches out a hand to him while the doctor sees to a cut across her eyebrow. It has already been stitched and he is wrapping a bandage around her head to cover the wound. Rose is sitting beside her while Ned sits close by, staring at the middle of the table in a trance-like state.

Andrew comforts her as she is still heavily shaken from the incident. "They came in the early hours of the morning Andrew, looking for young Anna. Ned was staying over as he had seen some of them watching the place yesterday and was suspicious of what they might be up to. I should have listened to him and taken it more seriously, but this is just a home for lost children. I did not think they would attack us."

Anna looks at her and wonders why they would be looking for her in this place while Penny continues to speak, "I said there was no Anna here, so they went after the children, looking for some that knew her. That is when Ned stepped in; he fought them all on his own, protected us all and held them off until Dick arrived."

Penny starts to cry, "Poor Dick, he was so valiant, he gave his life protecting the children." She looks up at Andrew. "If these two men had not been here, who knows what would have happened to the children." Penny breaks down as Andrew steps forward to hold her in his arms.

Ned looks up at Anna, he is filled with remorse and sadness, his eyes are glazed over as he speaks to her in a quiet voice. "I tried to save them all lass, I really did. But I failed, and they got one of them, your friend young Billy. I'm so sorry, but it is not looking good for him."

Anna's world falls apart as she hears Ned speak; her lips quiver as the shock of what she has just heard sinks in. She trembles and is near to tears as she speaks. "No, not Billy, where is he?"

"You will find him in the room down the hall, I have done all I can for the boy, but we cannot move him as his wound is too severe," says the physician. "The young man is in God's hands now; it is just a matter of time."

Anna immediately turns and leaves the kitchen. Dread is in her heart as she wonders what she will find when entering the room, she can see Billy lying on the makeshift bed with two of the older children beside him on the far side of the fireplace.

As they see her, one of them speaks, "Are you Anna?"

She nods.

"He has been asking for you for some time now, he is so weak."

The two children move away as Anna kneels by his side. The tears run down her cheeks as she begins to stroke the side of his face, moving his fringe away from his eyes.

The little boy's eyes begin to slowly open and blink. "Is that you, Anna?" he asks in a quiet and frail voice.

"Of course it is me, I am right beside you. Can't you see me?"

"I cannot see anything, but I can hear you and feel you touching my face."

"I can see you, and as usual, look at the trouble you get yourself in when I am not around to watch over you."

Billy smirks, then shudders with pain. "They came back Anna, came back looking for you again. This time though, I was not afraid, not like before." He pauses to try and swallow a few times before continuing.

"I fought back this time Anna, stabbed him in the leg I did with that penknife you gave me for my birthday. You would have been so proud of me, me and Ned! He is a real hero you know, Lost an a-arm in battle. We beat them t-together A-A-nnaaaaa."

Billy's head slowly drops to one side as his last breath ebbs from his body. Anna watches him for a moment before she lifts him up gently into her arms. She sobs as she slowly rocks him backwards and forwards. "This is all my fault," she says as she holds him. "I swear to you Billy, I will get the people responsible for this and make them suffer."

Behind her, Andrew and Ned have just entered the room and are watching.

Finally, after several minutes has passed, Anna lowers Billy's body back down, straightens his hair and closes his eyes before slowly raising the sheet over his head. With a few more deep breaths to calm herself, she wipes the tears away, then stands. She turns, looks up at Andrew and Ned and walks towards them.

Ned takes his cap off and lowers his head. "I'm sorry, lass, we did all that we could, I just could not get them all quickly enough."

Anna smiles at him, steps forward and kisses him on the cheek. "I know Ned, and I am sorry for the loss of Richard, you two had been together a long time. Margaret is forever telling me stories of your escapades, along with all the others that have long since gone. Even retired and missing an arm and a leg, you two were more than a match for so many of these nasty villains."

Anna looks across at Andrew, then back at Ned. Tears start to flow again as she speaks. "Billy's last words were that he fought back at them with Ned. A real hero, he called you. He was so proud of you, Ned. Thank you for spending time with him, he never did have much to be proud of after he lost his family."

"That young Billy, he was the real hero, not me, my lady. A

soldier knows who he is fighting; they stand before you under another banner and come at you with all they have. If we die in battle, it is what we are paid to do; no regrets nor sorrow, just our time to die. But back here these youngsters live hand to mouth looking over their shoulders all the time. Not knowing who, when or where somebody is going to get at them." He lowers his head and stares at the floor.

"This house was supposed to be a safe place for them to grow up in, give them back a chance to become young adults and make something of themselves, like those that now work in the bakery."

Anna looks at Ned. "They were attacked here because of me Ned. They wanted to get back at us and take revenge because I refused to spy for them against the queen. Using the gangs was a cheap option to them and now Billy and Richard are dead and Penny is injured."

Anna sobs as Andrew steps forward and takes her in his arms to comfort her. "No Anna, these gangs have been terrorizing people for many years now, but they all work for the same people and we know who that is."

Andrew may not show it, but inside there is an anger and a rage that is building, the more he thinks on what has happened here, the more he feels hatred towards those responsible for the attack. He stays calm and collected for those around him like Anna and Penny who need him to support them. But, inside, he wants so badly to destroy all those that had a hand in this atrocious act.

He puts his arm around Anna's shoulder as they turn and walk out of the room. While Ned looks down at the lifeless body for some time.

"You had spirit, lad. You were braver than most I have known, now rest your bones for they can hurt you no more." He puts his hand around the back of his head, undoes a silver chain from his neck and places it on Billy's chest. He adjusts the cross until he is happy with its position, then places his hand on the boy's heart. Lowering his head, he quietly says a small prayer before placing his cap back on his head, turning and leaving the room.

Outside, Andrew is organizing for the body of the fallen soldier

Richard to be taken to Stoneheart Manor for burial. It is the place where many fallen comrades with no families have been laid to rest in the past, and a fitting place for a hero like him to be put to ground as it has been his only home most of his life.

Ned arrives as a transport wagon is being arranged with a man to arrive shortly and collect Richard's body. "I would be grateful if I could ride with him, sir, the man being my best friend and all. It will give me a chance to say my goodbyes with the rest of the troop one last time."

"Of course, Ned, that goes without saying. Margaret and Wellesley are not due back from their state visits for another two days, that will give us the time for the preparations required for Richard to have a proper sendoff with all the honors he deserves."

Ned tilts his cap at Andrew, Anna and the other people present. "I will collect his best dress uniform and boots for the occasion." Then he turns and leaves for the cottage to obtain all he needs for him and his best friend.

"What about Billy?" Anna asks.

"We have several quiet areas of the church grounds that would be fitting for the young man," the undertaker answers in a calm, quiet voice.

"No, Billy never wanted to be alone. He was afraid to be on his own; bad things always happened to him when others were not around to protect him. I need a place for him nearest the church with people already around him to keep him company."

The man looks at her. "Those kinds of places are usually reserved for people of influence and cost a lot of money to secure, my good lady. Not really affordable to one such as the young boy."

"Maybe so, but Billy has powerful friends in high places and cost will not be an issue. Please make the arrangements for tomorrow afternoon at three," Andrew says in a stern authoritarian voice.

"A day to make all the arrangements! That will take some effort to make all the necessary requirements happen."

"Then go and make a start on it. Anna has given you the information on what is needed. Have the boy collected from here within the hour and readied for the occasion. In the meantime, we have other things that need to be looked into while we are here."

The man scurries off as Andrew turns to Anna. "Would you check on Penny and the children, Anna, I have some other business to attend to and will return as soon as possible."

"No, I think I will come with you. For I know where you are going, and I want to see the man who killed little Billy as much as you do."

Andrew looks at the steely-eyed and determined Anna. He could order her not to come with him, but, knowing Anna, far worse would happen behind his back and if anything was to happen to Anna the repercussions for so many who love her would threaten years of Margaret's careful planning.

"Well let's be on our way then."

The two of them return to their horses and the guards that have been holding them while they were in the house. Tightening the girths back up on the saddles, they mount up and head to the local magistrate's office and holding cells where the last gang member is being held, pending being charged for his actions.

On arrival, they are surprised by the size of the crowd of people protesting outside the building; hostile and yelling at the officers defending the entrance over the attack on the orphanage. Dismounting their rides, they make their way through the angry mob to the entrance of the magistrate's office and men standing vigilant at its doors. While residents of the area who are disgruntled with what went down, vent their anger at the guards while demanding to see the magistrate. Andrew recognizes several of the crowd present as he has known and fed them for many years. Some even helped and supported the building of the orphanage while others provided donations for the children who now reside inside it.

The four pistol armed constables standing guard at the entrance to the building are struggling to keep order; as Andrew and Anna approach, the people quieten and stop pushing, as they watch Andrew speak to the men holding firm at the entrance.

"I have come to see the prisoner."

"Sorry, nobody gets in today."

Anna thrusts a letter towards the guards. "You let us in or suffer the consequences of the queen," she barks at the men with anger and hatred in her voice. As the men crack the seal, open the letter and begin to read it's contents, she speaks again. "I do not like to be kept waiting, so take it to the magistrate and get the letter verified."

The man looks up at her. "I do not need him to verify this, I can read it myself. I apologize for the delay, but, as you can see, this is a difficult time. Please pass by."

Entering the building and walking down the corridor, Andrew looks at Anna, "How did you come by such a letter so quickly?"

"I always carry several with me, you never know when they might be needed," she answers without even looking back at him.

"Are they official or are they something y—"

Anna stops and looks at Andrew, "They get the job done. Any more than that, you need to speak to Margaret for I can say no more."

She moves off again and into a large room at the end of the hall, as the pair of them look around, they see the magistrate sitting at his large wooden desk on the right hand side. Two guards are to his left and on a bench on the far side of the room two more men in uniform are sitting and waiting. Andrew instantly recognizes the uniforms they wear as national guards, the personal bodyguards to Mallory, Bonner and Stone.

"I see it did not take long for you to arrive here; someone was swift to relay the failure of this little enterprise. Afraid the man might talk before you get him out of here?" Andrew comments sternly.

The men squirm but say nothing as the magistrate continues to read a letter on his desk. "Well, it all seems official; you have the right to take him into your custody under the authority of the government."

He looks up at the guard beside him. "Would you please collect the prisoner for me and hand him over to these two gentlemen." The guard nods and makes his way out of the room.

"Who has the power to authorize this?" yells Anna.

The magistrate looks at her and sighs. "This document is signed by our government; it authorizes the release of a prisoner to these two men so that he can be moved to the capital for questioning. I have no option but to hand the man over, even though I know, like you, this is not how justice should be served."

"They attacked an orphanage and killed a young boy and a queens grenadier. What kind of justice is this? He will be back on the streets within a day," she bellows. "All we ask is for a few minutes to question him and find out which one of them organized the attack!"

"I am sorry, but I must follow my orders and they say to release the man into their custody."

Within minutes the guard returns with the prisoner. Entering the room he pushes the cuffed man towards his waiting escort, he is no happier about his orders than the rest of the people there. The prisoner looks around at all in the room, then smiles at Anna in her uniform. "Hello, my pretty, I have not seen a guard like you before, are you here to personally escort me away from here?"

Anna is incensed. She goes to step forward towards the prisoner but is restrained by Andrew. "Anna, let it go for now, we will follow this up later."

"Anna! So, you are the wench all this has been over, you have cost me the lives of a lot of my friends today."

She stares at the gang member. "You killed a child named Billy. Why?"

"Dead is he! A shame that, seems that my employer had a use for him if he had lived. Still, that is the price for knowing you I guess," he says with a smile on his face.

Anna pushes against Andrew to get at the man, tears beginning to run down her cheeks as she struggles to break free of his grasp. "Anna, best you wait outside!" She tries again to get past him, but this time he turns her to face the doorway.

"Anna, wait outside, you are in no frame of mind to be here."

As she looks at Andrew, the tears flow ever faster.

"Please, my dear, wait outside and I will be there shortly."

She takes one last look past Andrew at the smiling prisoner

behind him, before storming out of the room, slamming the door behind as she leaves.

"Bit emotional be that woman, highly strung I would say, needs to let off a bit of steam. Perhaps I will be able to help in that department later," says the prisoner as he begins to cackle.

Andrew looks at the magistrate, then at the prisoner and his new escort, then turning back to the magistrate, he speaks, "I know you are only following orders, but this is wrong. You are here to serve the people, not assist in corruption and murder. Times of change are coming, and you will need to decide what side you are on."

He then turns to face the smirking prisoner, "There is not a place in this country you can hide from me. I will find you and bring you to justice for what you have done this day. As for that girl Anna that you mock so badly, I would fear her more than the Devil himself, for he would have more mercy than what she will show should she cross your path before me."

The smirk has gone from the prisoner's face as he is marched out of the room. "You can't touch or threaten me, I am a protected man, you hear, a protected man!" he yells as he is pushed down the corridor and out of the building.

Outside, the crowd is closing in to try and get at the prisoner and it takes the four guards from the entrance of the building as well as his two escorts to funnel him towards a waiting carriage. The closer they get, the tighter the space they have to move in, until just before they get to the door of the transport where the people have got them in a compressed space. Suddenly the prisoner lets out a gasping "huuuah", then again another, quieter moan as he is shunted into the carriage by his escort.

Inside he hangs onto the small window in the door with his hands and looks into the crowed as he struggles for breath. Staring straight back at the man is Anna, her face like stone, eyes burning a hole deep into his soul. As he falls back onto his seat, he continues to look at her while attempting to speak as the carriage drives away. But it is all to no avail, for Anna has done her work well; two puncture marks, one to the bottom of his lung and the other piercing the side of the heart. It will take around five or six minutes for him to bleed out while he gasps to get a breath of air into his lungs. Just far enough away from the magistrate's building to keep everybody guessing as to how it could have happened and who is responsible for the attack.

Anna makes her way back to her horse while discreetly wiping down the needle-like blade and placing it back into the stitching of her uniform. The only person to have noticed her act is Andrew, who has been watching her walking back through the crowd of people. As they mount up, he says nothing, they just stare at each other for a moment before Andrew nods and they move off together under the escort of two cavalrymen.

Billy's funeral service is a somber affair; all the children from the orphanage attend with Penny, along with many local people paying their last respects. As people leave, Anna places a small penknife on his coffin, along with a large, thin blade of her own. "I am so sorry I was not there for you, Billy, but rest assured that he did not get away with it." She slowly turns to walk away, comforted by Andrew as the waiting gravediggers move in and begin to lower the body before filling in the grave.

It is the first of two funerals for the pair of them as, days later, they are standing over the grave of Richard beside Margaret with Wellesley, Ned and near four hundred of the regiment paying tribute to a loyal servant of the queen.

Full honors are given to the man who has served his country all his life, yet, at the same time, there is a feeling of anger in the air and amongst the troops that such a loyal man should have lost his life to the likes of petty gang members attacking an orphanage. There is a growing feeling amongst those present that the fight should be taken to those that flaunt the law and harm the innocent. Not less Margaret and Wellesley, whose anger at what has recently happened in their absence is burning like a fuse inside them.

CHAPTER 16

The Ambush

What happened at the orphanage has given a greater sense of urgency to the preparations. Two large wooden outbuildings have been constructed on the grounds of the estate and are filled with all manner of equipment, uniforms, and boxes full of documents. Each building has its own group of people filing in and out during the day and even part of the night as they prepare and train people for the roles they must take up in an instant. Security has tripled as escort duties are needed during the transport of people and supplies around the country and Bunty now has three people working with her in the kitchen to feed all the people that attend the house daily.

Margaret and Andrew have another addition to their family in the form of a young daughter they have named Katherine. She is now five months old and is already a favorite with Lord Ashby, who is now a regular at the house due to all the preparations he is carrying out. Young Henry is pushing two years old and is keeping everyone around him on their toes as he is every bit a terror as he is cute and cuddly, preferring to be with Aunty Anna or sitting up front on Wellesley's saddle as he rides around the grounds, overseeing all that is going on.

With less than three weeks to go before the day Margaret has been working and planning for with her team, she is beginning to feel the pressure and stress that comes with such a huge undertaking along with two young children. As always Andrew is by her side ready to steady her when she needs him and be her rock when times are truly testing. But even he can sense that this is going to be a life-changing event and has noticed she is becoming more apprehensive and cautious for the first time since he has known her.

Margaret spends most of her days split between the war room, feeding her daughter, and planning for the day and all that it will require to see it through. On the odd occasion Andrew can get her to sleep, it is deep and usually in his arms as they sit in front of the fire wedged in one of the armchairs or on rare occasions, in a bed after a particularly long stint of planning lasting a couple of days or more.

All who know her are worried that the strain is becoming too much for just one person to contain and bear the load it carries, but Andrew understands Margaret and knows now that she must stay her course and finish what has started if she is to resume any kind of normal life after the event is over.

Andrew's role has dragged him into many areas of the project that he never intended to get involved with, from reading the charts on the walls to working with the different groups of people who are now dedicated to specific parts of the plan. He has come to his own conclusion that the events that will unfold on the day will be carried out in many areas of the country on several different fields of expertise, and that all must be executed at the same time to have the desired impact and effect the changes needed.

But at what cost? The more he looks at all that is going on, the more he fears for his beloved wife as he wonders what risk she will be taking to stand up against the Three Heads and what the Queen is doing to protect his wife throughout this, considering Margaret seems to be doing all this for her.

Andrew searches around the grounds of the house looking for Wellesley. If anyone will be able to explain what safety precautions will be in place on the day for his wife, it will be this man, who he trusts above all others. He finally catches up with him in the stable yard with Henry, talking about his young pony, Oscar.

"Yes, we will soon be putting a saddle on him for the first time, young Henry, and a few months after that you will be learning to ride as one with him." The boy looks at Wellesley with a gleam in his eye while stroking the head of his pony. There is no hiding the excitement in the child's expression; it is infectious and makes all that witness it smile with pride. "But for now, we can only watch him grow, as he is not strong enough to carry a person yet. Just feed him a treat and visit him every day just like you are doing, so he knows who his master is."

Andrew arrives just as Beth is calling out for Henry to join her for something to eat, but Henry spots his dad and staggers up to him with his arms out for a hug. Andrew willingly obliges as he picks him up and spins him around. "You seem to have grown bigger since I saw you this morning," Andrew says as he holds him in gently. "Now run along to Beth, for she has something nice for you to eat in the house, my boy." As Andrew places him back on the floor, Henry turns to Wellesley and waves a hand before shuffling his way to Beth under the watchful eyes of both Wellesley and Andrew. The men continue to watch until both Henry and Beth have entered the house and closed the door behind them.

"That boy has the makings of a fine man one day, Andrew, a man I'm sure will make you and Margaret proud in the years to come."

Andrew smiles. "How could he not be? Look at the people he has around him to guide and influence his growing mind, I could not wish for better people." The two men walk together toward the river at a slow pace. "I need to talk to you about Margaret," Andrew comments.

Wellesley stops in his tracks and looks at him, his face changing from a smiling, contented expression to one of a more serious nature. "I know you have a lot of questions and deserve many an answer you have never received. But now is not the time, in a couple of weeks all will be different and you will ha—"

"No, not this time, a truer friend in this world I do not have than you Wellesley, but if you do not speak with me now, I swear I will use all the training you have given me on you, for there is much for me to lose here."

Wellesley tries to walk away, but Andrew grabs his arm and twists him around to face him. "I am not joking my friend. I have too much to lose and I do not see the queen or anyone from the palace taking the risks my wife does, so talk or I will draw on you here and now and be done with it."

Wellesley stares back at him. He should be standing his ground and put Andrew in his place as he has the skills and ability to do so, but he also knows Andrew will stand to his last as he has done on several occasions before. If he takes on Andrew now, he will lose a great friend and ally, he sighs heavily as he reluctantly nods his head as he speaks. "We never had this conversation, and I will only answer what I can. But be aware, you may not like the answers you get and with a nation dependent on the outcome I would sooner lose a friend than my country, so ask and ask wisely my friend."

Andrew thinks for a moment before asking his first question. "How much danger will my wife be in come the day?"

There is a moment's silence before Wellesley answers "More danger than she has ever been in before and there are only two outcomes: total victory or death. Our opponents will be up against the wall and they will not give up what they have easily."

Again, there is a small period of silence before Andrew asks another question. "Who will be there to protect Marge should things go sour?"

"Everybody. Every single person you have ever seen within our group, as well as friends, soldiers, sailors, politicians, gentlemen, and ladies from society who will also be putting themselves in harm's way at the same time. It has taken near twenty years to set up for this one day and we have already lost so many people to get this far. Friends, family, civilians that have had all they own stripped from them or worse, even your own parents fought for what is to come in their own way, and that is to mention but a few."

"What of the queen? I have yet to see her putting her life on the line like the rest of us," Andrew snaps out.

Wellesley answers immediately, "And you will not, she faces danger every day of her life, and if she were ever to be tied to this place or its people they would kill her in a heartbeat, and we would lose our monarchy forever. Her only salvation comes from this being separate and discrete, but I tell you this, not a moment goes by that she is not thinking of all the people who are risking all they have to support her."

Wellesley is almost shaking with passion and holding on to his self-control by a thread. "The sacrifices that woman has made makes what you are going through seem like nothing and if, and I mean *if*, we get through that day and you have the chance to see our queen at the end of it, you will understand why she is so important to us all, including you."

The heated conversation is broken up by a voice coming from behind them. "Is everything all right here?" The pair of them turn at the same time and see Margaret standing but a few meters away, baby Katherine in her arms and Anna standing by her side.

Wellesley is first to respond, sighing heavily with his hands clenched in front of him. "These are difficult times made harder by the circumstances and rules I have to play by. There is nothing going on here that needs discussion with yourselves, just me needing some air." Wellesley storms off toward the stable block while flinging his arm out in front of him. "I think I will take a patrol out to the woods to the east, as it has been a day or so since we last checked them out." They watch as his pace picks up and he marches away from the group, mumbling and muttering to himself.

"Anna, go with him, help him to calm down while I speak to my husband."

As always with Anna, it is like she has read Margaret's mind and is already turning to follow Wellesley to the stable yard. "Wait up, old timer, I could do with letting off a little steam myself, as well as showing you how to ride a horse at a canter, if your bones will allow you to travel that fast." She skips off after him while holding up the hem of her dress.

Wellesley turns to look back at her and bellows, "You're not dressed to ride and I'm not waiting!"

Anna stops, plays with her waistline for a second, and then drops a ring of skirts to the floor and steps over its frills, exposing loose trousers underneath made from the same material as the dress. "Wanna bet, old man? I'm always ready for a challenge."

Wellesley turns again and cannot believe what he sees before him, this girl is just so full of surprises. She runs after him and hooks onto his arm as only Anna can do, for any other person would surely have been dispatched in a second by the old war horse. But Anna has a way with him, and Margaret knows that and uses it to her advantage when she needs to, as it is important to keep her family together in these demanding and difficult times.

As the two of them move out of sight and into the stable block, Margaret turns to Andrew. "That is the first time I have ever seen you and Wellesley raise your voices with each other, my dear, what was it all about?" she asks in a calm and kindly manner.

Andrew looks at her and then his daughter. "It was nothing, just a debate on something we both care about deeply."

Margaret looks into his eyes. "Oh! I see, so it was about me then?" Andrew is taken aback by how Margaret has worked it out so quickly when she has only just arrived.

She smiles at him. "I have been negotiating all my life, my dear. Before you were around sometimes I was but a kind word or a quick bit of thinking away from being with my parents in another place." She passes Katherine to Andrew to hold as she links her arm through his. "Walk with me my darling, like we used to?"

The pair of them slowly move toward the riverbank. "I have dragged you through all manner of my problems, been close to losing you on more than one occasion, yet I am afraid to say that the worst is still to come. I would hazard a guess you approached Wellesley about my safety during the coming weeks, as I have seen you brewing and brooding over it for the past few days, if not weeks."

Andrew looks at her but does not say a word. "Wellesley and Lord Ashby have been on and on at me over the very same thing at least five times a day for a month or more now. Please understand it is difficult for me to ask for help or favors from other people as it almost always carries an element of danger and the chance of losing another person I care about. I have lost so many close friends over the years, each time, a piece of me dies as it tears my heart apart and I crumble inside."

She pauses as she thinks on what she is about to say. "In three of week's time, at the queen's official birthday ceremony in the palace's great hall, a declaration will be held in front of thousands of people. Dignitaries and royal families from neighboring countries, as well as all the prominent people from this country along with more than a few from the masses. They will be attending so that all can hear and enjoy the news and celebrations that I hope will happen from that day forward."

The three of them turn and follow the riverbank along the edge of the grounds while Margaret continues to speak. "You see, it is at this state event that the queen intends to put an end to the tyranny of the Three Heads, Mallory, Bonner and Stone. She will fight back for control of the country she should be running by now and end years of suffering for the people of this land. But it is difficult, as so many corrupt officials and politicians will have to be replaced at the same time to make it work permanently. We will all have to be there, including the children to show support and to allow everyone to know of their existence. It is vital to the queen's objectives and strategy that this all be done at the same time to ensure success."

Andrew stops walking. "That could put them in danger," he says.

"Yes, but you and I along with everybody else we know will be there with them to ensure their safety as best we can". She can sense that Andrew is struggling with this request and thinks fast to reassure him. "We will be right beside them, that I can promise you, side by side with them the whole time." Margaret takes a deep breath. "If you say no, I will understand and try to find an alternative solution to not having them present, but it would suit our purpose better to have them there, for in that one day we could undo years of wrongdoing and end a terrible oppression".

Andrew thinks for a while on the request his wife has made, it is difficult for him to even consider his children being exposed to any kind of danger, least of all from the ruthless people that have taken over control of Kelsey. There follows near five minutes of silent walking as Andrew thinks on all that has been discussed before coming to a decision. "If we are going to be there in harm's way, with everybody we know around us, it would be right to assume we would be the ones more at risk, not the children. It would be unlikely that the opposition would carry favor with the entire country if they were to attack children in full view of diplomats and envoys from other countries." Margaret nods at his assumptions.

"If we were to fall, our children would be looked after by Beth, Wellesley and Anna?"

Margaret pauses for a moment before answering. "Beth, yes, but if we fail, I fear all of us will be no more. Not just you and me, but all that you see around you here and at the barracks. This is our one chance to right the wrongs so many have suffered. There will be no going back if this goes wrong."

Andrew takes a deep breath and exhales. "Then it would seem that we must not fail, for I want to live a long life with my wife, children and friends."

Margaret turns to look at Andrew, nearly in tears as she holds her husband and daughter in her arms and kisses them both. "I know that I put you through such terrible things, my dear. Thank you for trusting me one more time, it means so much to me that you are by my side."

They slowly head back to the house, it has been a difficult and challenging day for the pair of them and they, like so many others, are glad to see the back of it, for each day that passes brings them closer to the end goal that they hope will bring change to the land.

The next couple of days begin to see the evacuation of the house as all the preparation that has been carried out there now moves off to different areas of the country. Coaches arrive and depart daily with documentation, soldiers, and people who have been working on specific tasks. By the end of the second week only Margaret, Andrew, their children, Anna and the immediate staff are left at the house and security is back to four people as they prepare the last two carriages to take them all to the palace.

More nervous than any of them is Andrew; he has never stayed at the palace before and is apprehensive about seeing the queen and what he might say should they get into a conversation about his wife Margaret. All the work and risks she seems to be doing and taking on her behalf has caused more than enough friction between the pair of them. Yet the queen is never around to help or support her, this plays heavily on Andrew's mind as he worries for his family.

As they finish loading up their bags and cases for a trip that will last several days, Andrew is surprised by a guard calling out, "Riders approaching." He looks out across the fields and spots the arrival of a cavalry unit in the distance. He watches as they turn off the road and down the driveway toward them. It is only as they pull to a halt in front of him that he recognizes the officer leading the troop. A smile appears on his face as the man takes off his helmet and nods at him respectfully, while Andrew steps forward and shakes the officer's hand.

"It has been a while Andrew and I hear you have two children now!"

Andrew smiles and nods his head with pride. "That we do Captain Hawkswell, the addition of a baby girl called Katherine. As beautiful as she is, I fear she is already getting as stubborn and hard-headed as her mother and has that stare that could have only come from Margaret." Both chuckle as the captain knows exactly what Andrew talks about firsthand.

"Well, we have been sent from the barracks with instructions to escort a special cargo to the palace". Looking toward the house, captain Hawkswell spots Margaret exit the front door and start walking toward the carriage with baby Katherine in her arms and behind her, Beth is walking with Henry and carrying a small bag. "I see by what is moving toward us that the special package Lord Ashby was talking about is about to be loaded into the carriages."

Margaret looks up at the captain and smiles. "If it was Lord Ashby who sent you, it was to watch over his goddaughter Katherine. The rest of us are now considered less important for some strange reason. It is good to see you again captain, how is your wife and the two boys? The rumors I hear suggest that they are becoming rather good in the saddle and have both made lieutenant in the grenadiers."

The officer beams from ear to ear. "That they have ma'am. I hope in the days to come they will see you for themselves, as the boys have not seen you since they were teenagers at the palace ball some years ago. They are so immensely proud to wear the uniform of the queen's grenadiers and my wife and I could not be happier with the careers they have chosen to follow."

"I will make a point of it, for I also could not be more honored that Robert and Ethan Hawkswell have followed in their father's footsteps to serve the monarchy. How lucky we are to have such good people in our ranks, I look forward with great anticipation to see if they become as finer officers as their father." The captain somehow seems to sit higher in the saddle as he hears her words, brimming with pride at the fact that Margaret mentions both his sons by name It makes him feel all the more prouder as a father.

As the party load up into the coaches, captain Hawkswell splits his unit into two groups, one to lead the carriages from the front and the other follow up the rear. As he looks to the drivers to ensure they are ready, Margaret pokes her head out of the window. "Captain Hawkswell, if I remember rightly, the last time you were in charge of my security we had a running battle for several miles."

He nods politely at Margaret. "That is correct, ma'am. I think that is why Lord Ashby specifically requested me and the lads of the 1st to escort you again. I believe his exact words were, excusing the language, 'You have fought with that stubborn, hard-headed woman before, no man or assassin would want to take on the pair of you again after the thrashing you dealt out last time."

Margaret looks at him with her steely-eyed look. "Quite right too. The charge your men carried out that day is still considered one of the bravest acts witnessed by men alive today. But with children in the coaches on this occasion, let us hope we do not have to take such drastic action."

The captain salutes Margaret before turning his horse and heading off to the front of his troop and leading the way for the others to follow. With one look back to check that both drivers are ready, he raises his hand and signals everybody forward.

The convoy of mounted troops and carriages moves off along the driveway and out onto the track as one solid unit. It is the start of a journey that will last around three hours, depending on any events that may occur on the way. As with everything captain Hawkswell does, he has ridden the route twice in as many days and has areas along the route that he wanted additional security present. As they enter the first of many wooded areas, two mounted riders are waiting for him to arrive. As per his pre-planned arrangement, they will all call out a password as he approaches the sixty-yard mark, in this case, one of the mounted cavalrymen yells out, "Ranger!" In the event of danger or something wrong, they will call out "For honor", allowing the men in the convoy to prepare for an attack and adapt accordingly. Finally, as the captain approaches the men they take off their helmets for him to see their faces. With only seventy active men in the unit in total, he knows all in his troop by sight, even if he cannot always remember their names.

As he passes the men, they replace their helmets and fall in at the back of the convoy. This will be repeated a dozen or so times during the journey and as each pair of cavalrymen moves to the back of the group, the front pair of the rear guard will move to the front of the convoy and slot in behind the lead riders to ensure an even split of soldiers during the journey.

Over two hours into the journey and the group have made good time, they are now only around eight miles from the palace and the relative safety of its walls. In the distance the captain can see the next pair of riders waiting on the side of the road. As they near the sixty-yard mark, one of the men calls out the password, "For Honor."

Captain Hawkswell and the others continue on at the same pace, as he reaches the two men they take off their helmets as is the procedure. The captain turns his horse and moves off the road between the two riders. When he reaches them, he draws his sword and slices across the throat of the man on the right before plunging his sword through the shoulder of the other rider, knocking him to the floor with the sword still through his body.

As the man falls screaming in agony, the other rider slips from his mount, choking on his own blood before dying on the spot where he fell. The rest of his troop responds to the incident in a well-practiced manner. Two men dismount and take hold of the injured man, gagging him with a cloth to prevent him making any more noise. Another dozen men split up and start searching the surrounding wooded area, while half the cavalrymen from the back of the group move forward, taking up positions along the sides of the halted carriages.

"Sir, over here, we've found them," calls one of the men searching the scrub area to the right, captain Hawkswell rides over to see what he has found. It is a somber sight that meets him. Two of his men, blood-drenched and stripped of their uniforms. The man who found the bodies is kneeling beside them. He looks up and speaks. "One is dead and the other near death. They had their hands tied behind their backs and were beaten and tortured." As he is reporting his findings, the other man drops limp from the soldier's arms. "He be gone as well, sir."

Margaret has got out of the coach and has just seen the last moment as the grenadier's life slipped from his body. It is a sight she has seen too often and every time it breaks her heart to see men die protecting her.

Captain Hawkswell lowers his head. "Post two guards, we will send a wagon for them once we have deli—"

"You will do no such thing captain. We all knew these men." She turns and looks at one of the dismounted grenadiers. "You, soldier, get some blankets from the luggage on the back of my carriage, wrap them up carefully and put them inside, we will take them with us." Margaret turns and shouts out, "Beth, move the children to the second carriage, quickly!"

As she moves back past the captain, he stops her. "Thank you, I did not want to presume I could use your transport, not with the children here."

Margaret puts her hand on his shoulder. "They are our men captain, good men who did not deserve this butchery and they deserve our respect and compassion now they are not with us.

Now that man you stuck, find out what he knows and do not spare the lash, for he does not deserve it."

The officer looks at Margaret, his eyes becoming more focused as he replies. "Yes, ma'am." He turns and cuts a path through the undergrowth to the wounded man on the floor, leaving his horse to another to collect. He looks down at the man with contempt and disgust for the murder of two of his men, men he has trained and rode with for many years. He can see just from his posture and weathered face that this man is a hardened murderer, used to this kind of work, with cold, expressionless eyes that are presently focused straight at the captain. A foreign mercenary paid to kill his friends and fellow countrymen by his own government. The captain has seen his like many times over the years, now captured, he will be expecting to be taken prisoner and escorted away for questioning once his wounds have been patched up. As usual, he will say nothing of any use, bide his time in the cells until being freed by his employer somewhere down the line in some quiet, backhanded trade-off.

But not today, for today this man's past and wrong doings have caught up with him, this was one attack he should have stayed away from. The captain removes the prisoner's gag. "I will ask you only once, where is the ambush to take place? People like you always work in packs."

"I ain't got nowt to say, so clap me in irons and be done with it, for I will say nothing to the likes of you."

Captain Hawkswell looks around and realizes how close they are to the coaches and the passengers, then looks at the men guarding the prisoner. "Take him into the woods away from the children. Sergeant, get the white pouch from my saddlebag and bring it to us, it would seem that this man requires a little encouragement."

The man starts to yell and scream as he is dragged through the scrub by a soldier holding his arms, causing the sword that is still through his shoulder to catch on the vegetation as they push on deep into the woods. In a small clearing they release him, allowing the man to drop to his knees before slumping back to the ground in a heap. The captain wastes no time in grabbing the sword handle and twisting it to inflict maximum pain, making the man scream.

"I have no time to fuck about!" captain Hawkswell yells at his prisoner. "You murdered two good family men who were just doing their duty for a few coins in your pocket. So, forget any sympathy or leniency from me. If you want to live, tell me where the ambush is to take place, if not, you will die where you are."

The man just looks up at him and shakes his head. "It were more than a few coins, more than you will see in your lifetime," he mutters as he spits in his direction.

The sergeant arrives with the small white bag and passes it to his commanding officer. Captain Hawkswell asks about the ambush again, but the man just spits at him. Grabbing the sword, he twists it and pours some of the contents of the bag into the gap the rotated sword has left in the man's body. The response to the salt in the wound is immediate as the man screams out in pain.

"Go to hell! You'll all be dead soon, you wait and see, I'll be dancing on your grave in the hours to come!" the man yells defiantly, pointing at the soldiers. The captain pulls out his sword, swings it around his head, and strikes down on the man's wrist, severing the hand from his arm. The cut is so clean and swift that it takes a few seconds before the prisoner to realizes his hand has been removed. As he looks at the stump on his arm, pain and disbelief in equal amounts set in. "My hand, you took my fucking hand!" he yells. One of the grenadiers covers the wound in a rag and binds it with a leather cord.

"Still do not want to talk." The captain looks at his men. "Put out his other arm and let's see how he survives with no hands."

As the men start to pull his other arm from his body he cries out "No, no, for pity's sake, no!" Captain Hawkswell raises his sword for a second time. "Fine, stop! It's down by the lake, they are in the woods on the left, they will trap you against the water!"

The captain thinks for a minute. "How many are there and what was your role in all this?"

The prisoner is whimpering and crying and starting to go into shock. Hawkswell raises his sword back up. "Wait!" he yells. "About thirty with long irons. We were to strike down the men at the back of the convoy to create confusion just as you enter the wood by the water's edge."

The soldiers release the man's arm and he drops in a heap on the floor, sobbing and holding his arm, while the captain first wipes, then sheaths his sword and turns to head back to the carriages, deep in thought of what to do next. He looks up and sees Margaret and Andrew standing in front of him, having heard everything that has gone on with the prisoner. The captain takes a moment to compose himself. "We know where the ambush is to take place, so if we turn west, we can avoid them and reach our destination safely ma'am."

"Hmmm," Margaret murmurs as she thinks. "You are right of course, captain, but it would have been useful to rid us of so many of the paid assassins so close to the palace, it could have put a large dent in Stone's manpower come the day." A silence comes over the group as Margaret and Andrew think about their options and what they should do next.

"I have an idea that just might work," Andrew says slowly. "I have seen the terrain with Wellesley, but it is risky, and we would need some volunteers to take a chance and be in harm's way for a moment." About twenty of the soldiers around them instantly step forward.

Captain Hawkswell looks at Andrew. "You have your answer, for the men that were slain back there were our comrades, all would volunteer if it involved payback." The three of them talk for a while, as Andrew explains his idea to Margaret and the captain, more and more of the grenadiers move closer and listen in to the conversation.

Nearly an hour later, over the crest of a small hill, two carriages begin to come into view. First it is just their roofs, but as they reach the top of the climb the whole convoy can be seen. Two mounted grenadiers lead the group, with four bringing up the rear. They move along the track toward the lake and heavily wooded embankment, on which a group of men lay crouched, waiting to spring an attack on the convoy. Up on the open ground the coaches move ever closer, and the men in the ambush prepare to attack.

Suddenly the two cavalrymen at the back of the convoy draw swords and attack the men in front of them, slashing away until they both fall from their saddles. The two mounted men at the front of the convoy turn and give chase to the attackers, pursuing them back over the hill and down the other side.

"No, it's too soon!" shouts one of the ambushers. "You were to wait until you were beside us!" He stands up and makes his way forward, soon the rest of his group are up and running toward the carriages. The two drivers see the group of thirty or so men moving toward them and try to turn the horses to go back up the hill, but they struggle to get moving on the soft ground away from the track and soon the armed men are taking pot shots at them. One is hit in the arm and falls to his side before rolling off the vehicle, while the other driver decides it is faster to jump off and run away on foot than try and get the coach moving on the soft ground.

With both coaches now at a standstill, the ambushers approach them slowly, for they now have their prize and just have to finish it off for an end to a good operation. At around a hundred yards from their objective, they can make out two women in large hats inside the windows of one of the coaches. At fifty yards, one of the men calls out to them. "Out you get if you want to live, if not we will blast you to kingdom come!"

For a moment there is silence, then a few muffled sounds followed by a woman shouting out in a panic-stricken voice "No, no, you will kill us all! Help us, somebody, please!"

It is all the ambushers need to hear to build up their confidence and they quicken their pace, moving toward the carriages with vigor. The first man arriving looks in through the window and freezes on the spot. Several more approach both stationary carriages before a thunderous volley of pistol bullets, smoke, and flames is let loose from the windows. The front six or seven men fall while the others behind begin to raise their weapons. A second volley of pistols lets loose its shot and more ambushers fall to the ground before a few shots are fired back into the smoke-filled windows.

At the same time on the ridge of the hill above, overlooking the attack, a line of twenty-two mounted cavalrymen watch on with swords drawn. They begin walking forward in a line as Captain Hawkswell shouts his orders. "Have at them men, charge!" The troop hit a canter from the off, then a gallop with their sword points forward as they lean over their saddles, keeping low to their horses.

The villainous band of murderers and cutthroats have been completely taken by surprise. Some are trying to reload their weapons while looking at the grenadiers in full charge, others are picking up wounded comrades, the rest are already trying to fire their weapons while running for cover. Sheer terror fills them all as the Grenadiers descend on them from all sides. The carriage doors burst open and soldiers rush out to join the attack, swiftly followed by Andrew, Margaret, and Anna. The driver and the other two men on the floor get up and add to the attack, all of them letting rip with pistol fire and chasing down any that are fleeing. In a last-gasp attempt, the leader of the group, a huge man dressed in black robes and a head bandana, charges at Captain Hawkswell, grabs his body, and pulls it from his horse, throwing him to the ground and knocking the wind right out of his lungs. The man stands over the captain screaming and shouting some kind of war chant as he raises his curved hanger sword above his head. He is about to strike down when Andrew steps in and thrusts a sword deep into the man's chest, at the same time raising a pistol and letting loose a shot that hits the man in the throat and knocks him backward to the ground. It is the last act of the skirmish as air falls silent. Slowly the breeze pushes the smoke from the gunfire away, bodies can be seen strewn everywhere as Andrew helps his friend back to his feet.

In less than five minutes, thirty-eight assassins have been dispatched with only a shot to the arm of one of the drivers in return. There is a roar of cheers and sword waving by the gallant men of the queen's own as Captain Hawkswell returns to Margaret with Andrew beside him and salutes her with his sword.

"That helps even the score a little for Butler and Collins. They were good and loyal men to the end," he says.

Margaret nods in agreement and thinks for a moment. "Captain Hawkswell, I will take the men from the carriages back to fetch their horses and pick up the children, Beth, and our fallen. We will then make our way to the palace with the grenadiers we have. Would you please organize the burial of these mercenaries in the woods up by the lake. No markers, they do not deserve them, also check each one for gold coins, I am sure they would have been well paid and we have two families that will be in need of such finances in the years to come. Be sure to have a search party find their camp as well, they will have mounts somewhere around here and the cavalry can always use good horses."

The captain wipes the blood from his sword and returns it to his side. "It will be done as you command." He then turns to Andrew. "That was a fine plan, sir, worthy of any commander's merit."

Andrew smiles. "Well executed by you and your men, I might add."

Margaret turns to head back to the coach, stops, and looks back to the captain. "I almost forgot; I will send their friend back with the grenadiers. Please ensure he joins them in the woods, because, as you said yourself, they were both good men, so a sentence of death is the decree." She then turns and leads her team back to the coaches and climbs inside, closely followed by Andrew, Anna, and some of the soldiers.

After a few minutes' wait for the drivers to get the horses turned back onto the road and make their way back to the others at a brisk trot. Captain Hawkswell watches them until they disappear over the hill and out of sight before turning to his men and calling out. "I could not be prouder of you men, a fine and gallant charge worthy of any I have seen before. To a man you all carried your duties to the highest standard, well done to you all."

All the men stop and look at their captain and cheer. "Hurrah! Hurrah! Hurrah!"

Hawkswell beams with pride at his troop. "Now you know what you are fighting for, the highest in the land stood by you and fought shoulder-to-shoulder with us, put themselves in danger to help avenge our fallen comrades, isn't that something worthy of telling your families and friends about?" bellows the captain as he raises his sword. The men cheer and rally to his words, all of them proud of what they have achieved.

It is a mighty victory for the 1st, but as with all battles, victory or not, clearing the battlefield and burying the dead is a more somber time. Be it your own men or the enemy, you cannot help but feel a little sadness for the people who will not return to their families or friends, for their lives have ended and in this case nobody will ever know what happened to them or where they are laid to rest. As the men dispose of the bodies in shallow, unmarked graves, their mood becomes that of quietness and humility, for once the ground has grown over the graves in the coming months, they will cease to exist and will never be seen again.

CHAPTER 17

Day of Days

Margaret and her party have arrived at the east wing of the palace via a side road so as not to make too much of an entry and the grenadiers have already moved on to the stable yard and palace guardhouse. The carriages stop outside the ornate marble staircase that leads to a small patio and entrance to the wing and the party dismount, Anna and Beth swiftly take the children up the stairs, into the building and away to one of the prepared bedrooms, while the drivers of both vehicles start unloading the luggage from the carriages. The house servants start moving the items into the building as quickly as they are unloaded, rushing up and down the stairs in an attempt to clear everything as fast as possible to reduce the chances of people spotting them.

Upon dismounting, Margaret and Andrew walk over to the second carriage and look at the two blanket-wrapped men inside. "I knew both these men, Andrew, met their families on more than one occasion." She reaches out for the comfort of his hand and holds it tightly. "Another two men killed protecting me, why? It is all starting to get too much." Her eyes well up and her lips start to tremble.

Andrew puts his arm around his wife to comfort her. "If they were given the choice, they would do it again whether you want them to or not my dear, for you have become a symbol for not just them, but their families, children, and many others in this time of great need. You stand and fight with them when most in your position would not. So many people look at you for inspiration these days, you have to hold on just that little bit more. If not for yourself, for all the others that will willingly lay down their lives to give you this chance to change things."

Andrew looks up at the coachmen who are now mounted back up in their driving positions and waves them on with his eyes and a twist of his head while still holding on to his wife. As the coaches start to move off he slowly turns Margaret toward the building and gently guides her inside.

"Let's hope they are the last men I cause the deaths of, for I fear I cannot take much more loss in my life," she says while dabbing at her eyes with a small piece of cloth handed to her by Andrew.

"My dearest Margaret, it has been yet another difficult day, let's be grateful that it was only two people, for it was a bold move to take on so many paid assassins. The grenadiers did well today, perhaps a mention from you to the queen would be appropriate on the way Captain Hawkswell handled the situation, maybe even a mention for the 1st as they all played their part."

Margaret stops and looks at her husband. "I think you are forgetting something Andrew. It was your plan that saved many a death of a grenadier in that ambush today; the men look to you just as much as they do me these days. The humble baker who seems to have no limits; able to plan, strategize, always brave in defense of his wife. God knows where I would find another husband like you my love, so do not leave my side, for it would truly be my undoing. As for the captain and his men, you are right, I will have words in the morning and have something put in place to show mention of their valor. For now though, I feel it is my husband who needs my attention, and that he is going to have it for the rest of the evening. She kisses Andrew passionately before they move into the building and along to their chambers, closing the door behind them.

The next two days are marked more by the absence of people than their presence. Both mornings after breakfast, Margaret and Anna are off dealing with the preparations for the following day, ranging from dress fittings to flowers, linen to matching decorations and the position and seating for all those that will be attending the ceremony. Even the children have been whisked away two or three times during the day to be fitted out for various outfits. Wellesley and Lord Ashby have yet to appear and Andrew has spent most of his time with the children and Beth or occasionally wandering around the huge east wing on his own.

In one of the largest ornate rooms that Andrew has ever seen, he views all the items that are displayed, from suits of highly decorated armor to the stained-glass windows, exquisite furniture and many ornamental objects. The walls and some parts of the ceiling have various frescos and hand-painted scenes depicting honor and chivalry. Along the hallways are pictures of kings and queens of the past along with prominent figures from the church.

Young Henry has already broken a small blue vase while running around and bumping into a small pillar, sending the object crashing to the ground, From the look of horror on Beth's face when it happened, it must have been very expensive or rare, but she says nothing, just clears it up and disposes of the broken pieces.

Andrew is about to lose his mind with boredom and lack of anything to do when he hears a friendly voice call out to him "It's about time you did something useful young Andrew." As he turns to see who has spoken, Lord Ashby and Wellesley walk up to him in full military uniforms and dress swords, bringing a smile to his face as they shake his hand and smile back. "You seem glad to see us, lad, is anything wrong?" asks Lord Ashby.

Andrew shakes his head. "God no, it is just good to have friends around again, it has been a little difficult to sit idly by with everybody else busy doing things, and I am left roaming the walls of this huge building on my own."

"Well worry yourself not," Wellesley says, "For all our duties have now been carried out, our tasks finished. All we have left to do is be by your side until tomorrow is over."

Andrew looks at them strangely "By my side? Why do you need to be by my side? It is not me all the attention will be on but the Queen and Margaret along with all the others at the state gathering. People like yourselves, men of great importance and influence who have served the royal household for many years. I do not think that anyone is going to worry about me, I am of no importance to tomorrow's proceedings."

Lord Ashby laughs out loud. "Too many years in my case young Andrew. But you must learn to understand, it is both you and Margaret that need to carry on defending the people of this land along with all around you, for we are not getting any younger. Our duty is to protect you all while we have blood left in our veins and the strength to continue."

Wellesley and Lord Ashby head off toward the doorway out of the ornate room. "Come, Andrew, let's see the great hall where all the action is going to happen tomorrow. We can explain where people will be standing, sitting and all the pomp and fluff that goes on with this type of ceremony."

The three men head off down the corridors with Andrew commenting on how fine their uniforms are and how they look like dressed game birds with the feathers in their helmets. "If you think these are flash, you wait until tomorrow when we are in full dress uniforms with all the insignias and medals," says Wellesley. "Besides, you will be wearing a uniform of your own and it will be us having the last laugh."

Andrew looks at them seriously. "What do you mean, I will be wearing a uniform?"

Lord Ashby lets out a bellowing laugh. "You my boy, are part of the queen's own, married in their colors and you will be dressed accordingly as this state ceremony requires. Besides, you will need your wits about you and will be fully armed as a last line of defense for Margaret should anything happen during the ceremony."

"But I have no uniform to wear, and what little we brought with us is not up to me wearing tomorrow."

Wellesley swiftly replies "You, my friend, will find a perfectly fitting uniform waiting for you when you return to your room tonight, made by the very best tailors this land has to offer."

Andrew sighs heavily. "Oh, that's great, it means that if anybody is going to be shot, it will be me again." The others cannot help but laugh, as he does always end up in the thick of it every time.

"Do not worry yourself, Andrew, we will be beside you from now until tomorrow when it is all over, we will not be leaving your side for a moment," Wellesley reassures him with a smile and a slap on the back as he passes.

Andrew looks at them both. "Friends we are, but gentlemen, I will not be sharing my chambers with you two, that place is reserved for my wife and children. Besides, I doubt if even you two are brave enough to take on Margaret and tell her you will be in the bed with us." A roar of laughter from Wellesley and Lord Ashby echoes as they continue on down corridors that Andrew has never seen before. Each one filled with suits of armor, life-size statues, paintings, and all manner of decorative art pieces.

"Again, you are correct, Andrew, we are soldiers in Her Majesty's army, and even with all that training and countless battles under our belts we would not have been brave enough to take on the wrath of Margaret. You are the first and only man that has ever stood up to the challenge," replies Wellesley after he has stopped laughing.

"That be true enough, Wellesley. In the last five years this man has been shot, wounded to near death, hunted, had countless incursions including getting married. Been a hero, a father of two and saved many a life, what's more, he is still alive to this day. Our Andrew here is becoming a bit of a legend, but, alas, you will also not be with Margaret tonight, my boy. As she and the children are now in another wing of the building preparing for tomorrow with several handmaidens and all sorts of other people assisting them." Lord Ashby comments.

Andrew stops in his tracks; the smile has dropped from his face as he looks at them with a concerned expression. "What?" he says.

Lord Ashby put his hand on Andrew's shoulder. "For her and the children's safety, this night you must spend apart. There are far too many people around who could inadvertently put them at risk or say the wrong thing, plus tomorrow it will take most of the morning for them to dress her for the event. Now come, we have a lot for you to understand and be ready for as you have a huge role to play in the outcome of the coming event," Lord Ashby says as he gets Andrew moving toward the great hall again.

After another fifty yards, they reach the large arched double doors at the entrance to the great hall. Highly decorated with painted artwork depicting knights standing guard over a king and queen. The green and guilt-edged doors are pushed open by two men at arms, revealing a huge, cathedral-like room. The ceilings are covered with paintings of angels, kings, queens, cherubs and characters from the Bible flying and reaching down from clouds and blue skies above with open arms and outstretched hands. Huge stained-glass windows showing historical events and famous people bring in additional light as well as adding color to the already breathtaking design of the hall. The walls are decorated with curved covings and mounted turrets and an assortment of banners that add to the decorative effect of the room. While dozens of people busy themselves in almost every corner of the hall, putting up huge displays of flowers and pure white and peach sheets, all finished with bows and sashes of dark-green silk. Andrew stands in awe at what is presented before him, motionless as he looks around trying to take in all what is presented before him.

"It be the same for every person the first time they enter this room Andrew, all just stop and stare," says Wellesley as he walks past Andrew and turns to face him. "If this room could tell of the events that have unfolded here, we would be entertained for years." He sighs with a smile on his face as he remembers some of the good times he once had here.

"Now, pay attention, Andrew. Tomorrow this will be the main entrance for all the dignitaries and official people that will attend. To the left and right, front and back, there are four more minor entrances. The far end of the hall will be filled with people invited from all the various cities and countryside estates across the land. As we start to move further forward we will have more prominent people closer to the walkway, which will be lined with guards the whole way to the front. Behind them, more people and well-wishers from the capital."

Wellesley leads Andrew and Lord Ashby along the central, marbled pathway. "Now we have the area designated for the dignitaries and people of providence, lords, ladies, gentlemen and professionals in their fields of expertise." The men continue forward until they come to the head of the room and the raised marble steps to the throne area.

"Here is where the queen will sit once the throne along with other items have been brought up from the vaults below. They will be safely stored there until tomorrow, along with the crown jewels and staff of office."

Wellesley walks up the steps and turns to look out across the room. "On the right will be members of other royal families and heads of state from the countries that surround our nation, all with their own security personnel along with their families and honored guests. To the left, the high-ranking politicians and dignitaries of our own country including The Three Heads, along with the more lords and ladies of merit. By that I mean people who have served this country and been honored with state titles for their services to queen and country."

Wellesley pauses for a moment's thought before continuing. "The Three Heads, Mallory, Bonner and Stone will be closest to the front, no doubt with some of their henchmen close by. We will have a mixture of men around the area; queen's own grenadiers mixed in with some national guards from the state, or, should I say, Stone's private army."

Andrew thinks for a moment. "Where will you and Lord Ashby be during the ceremony?" he asks.

"Why, behind the queen with the rest of her senior officers, in a fan around the steps. Anna will be beside the queen, while you will be sitting beside Margaret as is the custom for these state affairs."

"What about my children?"

"To your right with Captain Hawkswell, Olson and my elite men watching over them," Lord Ashby swiftly assures him. "They will be protected closer than the queen, as she must address the nation with a speech and will be open to attack from those that might object to her rulings."

Andrew thinks a little and then looks at his friends, something in their expressions triggers a thought in his mind, he thinks a little more while looking away from them, then turning back to face them, he speaks. "She is setting herself up, isn't she? The queen is going to allow the opportunity for them to make a move against her and you're going to allow it to happen."

Wellesley and Lord Ashby look at each other before looking back at Andrew. "She has given us instructions to allow the opportunity to be available, should they choose to take it," Lord Ashby admits. "Yes, it is her wish to end this if she can tomorrow."

Andrew is uneasy. "But what if something——"

"It will not," snaps Wellesley in a crisp, sharp tone. "I will not lose another member of the royal family, not while I live and breathe. But I have been ordered to present the opportunity Andrew. Ordered by my queen to allow this to happen, so you just make sure all my training has not gone to waste on you and protect her should I fall or fail in my duties".

There is a silence between the three of them as they look at one another. "Now, let us leave this place and think on better things for a while, for I have thought on the outcome too many times this last week," says Wellesley as he leads the others out of the room.

On the far side of the city, Stone is entertaining Bonner and several women in his dining room when the door bursts open and Mallory swiftly makes his way toward them.

"It's the queen, she's at the palace! Not only that, the rest of her party have also arrived unscathed" he gasps.

Stone is up out of his seat in a flash and throws his napkin down on the table. "Leave us please, ladies, I will call on you again later." The women begin to tut and moan quietly as they get up, showing their disappointment at having to go. "Fuck off now! Before you never get the chance to leave again!" Stone yells, throwing his glass down into the center of the table, smashing it and another glass with the impact. The ladies shriek and grab their belongings before running for the door and exiting.

Stone turns his attention back to Mallory. "How is this possible? We had our best men waiting for them in ambush, it was a perfect set-up, so tell me what went wrong!"

Mallory shakes his head. "I don't know, but she has been seen in the palace today by our contact. Rumor has it she arrived two days ago and has been preparing for the ceremony tomorrow since her arrival. Along with that woman Anna, Wellesley and Lord Ashby"

Stone sighs heavily, then looks up into the air above. "How does she do it?" He shakes his head. "Two days ago you say, that means we have now lost our very best men, near as dammit forty well-paid assassins and mercenaries; the pick of what we had left. I thought it was odd that we had not heard from them these past few days. Now I know why."

He walks around the table, flicking things on it as he passes them. "No doubt they are dead and buried in some wood somewhere and we have that bloody Lord Ashby and Wellesley to thank for it." Stopping to look at Mallory, he speaks again. "You should have killed him when you had the chance Mallory, for he has some kind of knack for smelling out a trap."

Stone sits back down at the table and puts his head in his hands. "Who do we have left for tomorrow? I know she is up to something; I can smell it even if I cannot see what it is. Far too many dignitaries and representatives from Hanover, Prussia, Saxony, Denmark have arrived here in the past few days, even royalty from Sweden arrived this morning and we have not been on terms with them for years. This cannot be just a normal birthday gathering, something must be going on that we are unaware of."

"We have lots of scammers and knife men on the streets, but for use in a palace, where culture and education are required? Only our personal bodyguards, officers in the national guard and the few household security personnel come to mind as having the skills to blend in," Mallory replies.

Stone puts his hands together and thinks. "OK, replace some of our diplomat friends with national guards, double the men around us, and ensure all our bodyguards are present and I mean all of our bodyguards with no exceptions. And have them all armed for the event, including yourselves. Pistols will be the order of the day and we will see what the bitch has planned. Now I have women in the other room waiting to entertain us, join me or leave, the choice is yours, just be ready for tomorrow."

As Stone leaves the dining room for the gentlemen's library, he is followed by the smiling Bonner, while Mallory passes on the offer and decides to leave. Tomorrow is playing heavily on his mind and he decides to recheck and ensure all is organized ready for the showdown to come.

Back at the palace, it is now late in the evening. Andrew has retired to his bed, he can hear Wellesley and Lord Ashby still planning and scheming in the other room but does not pay it any mind. He has only Margaret and his children on his, wondering what dangers they will be in come the morrow.

With so many thoughts in his head it takes him a long time to finally fall asleep, and even when he does, he drifts in and out of his slumber. It is possibly the worst night's sleep he has ever had, only coming to an end with the banging on his door from Wellesley calling for him to get up. It takes a moment for his eyes to acclimatize to the light, as it is quite bright as he sits up. He looks around, it strikes him that the curtains are already open, and the sun has lit up the room from three separate windows. He tries to remember if they were drawn last night or whether someone has been in his room already this morning. A question soon answered as he sits up and notices a full-dress uniform spread out across a side unit. Surrounding it and on top are boots, belt, sword, short pistol and a decorative and ornate officers hat complete with feathers.

For now, he leaves them all and just wraps a robe around himself before exiting the room. In the adjoining hall, Lord Ashby is sitting in a chair also just in a robe, but still with his cavalry boots on and a small clay pipe in his mouth. Wellesley is helping himself to some sausages and bacon from a silver buffet trolley to one side.

"Ah, so you have finally decided to join us young man, well get some food down you as you will need your strength on this day of days," says Lord Ashby as he taps out his pipe on the heel of his boot, capturing most of the ash in a small dish which he then shakes out onto the unlit fireplace.

Andrew nods at him as he collects a plate and places a few sausages and thick-cut pieces of bacon on it, then moves to the table to join Wellesley. Moments later, Lord Ashby also sits down with them, plate piled high. "Where the hell do you put it all, Ash?" asks Wellesley. "You're barely bigger than Anna yet you put away more than Olsen and the rest of your elites in one go."

Andrew starts to chuckle as Lord Ashby ignores Wellesley and attacks his food like a rabid dog. After three or four minutes he stops chewing and replies, "I eat when I can, as much as I can, when food is available, for there has been many a time when I have gone without food for a week or more in the field."

Wellesley slams down his cutlery, "You stubborn old goat, Ash, the last time you were out in the field we used bows and pikes and the queen's father was king!"

Lord Ashby downs another two sausages before speaking again, "As an officer I must always be ready." He thinks for a moment before continuing, "Besides, I do not want to be classed as having a bony arse and being a little thin in the trouser department like you were the other month."

Wellesley sits upright in his chair, rolls his eyes and stares at Lord Ashby. "How dare you, I know just what you're talking about. My bottom is as firm and muscular as it has always been, it was those armchairs, they had been tampered with."

Andrew is near in stitches as the pair of them dig away at each other for the next half hour, only stopping when Lord Ashby dives into his food for a few more mouthfuls before continuing about Wellesley's physique.

Andrew carries on laughing for a while before adding to the fire of the conversation. "If I remember rightly, Bunty was more than happy with his behind, in fact she paid it quite a compliment and if there is something she does know a lot about, it is the physique of a man."

Wellesley jumps straight on what Andrew has just said. "That's right, she did, was quite impressed with what she was presented with."

"Bunty, you're talking about the cook Bunty? Now there's a good woman, kept me warm on many a cold night in the past," replies Lord Ashby as he winks at Andrew.

Wellesley's jaw drops. "No, no, it can't be, you're old enough to be her grandfather."

Lord Ashby smiles at him. "I can still get cold on a winter's night you know, old or young, the cold can still cut deep and a man likes to be kept warm, especially if a woman is involved." He winks at Andrew again, but this time Wellesley sees him doing it out of the corner of his eye.

"I saw that, you, YOU despicable old war horse." The three of them chuckle and laugh together as they finish off their breakfast and get washed and dressed up ready for the day's events.

Andrew is just putting on his belt and attachments when there is a rap at his door. "Yes, come in," he calls out.

Wellesley enters the room with Lord Ashby in close pursuit. They are both a sight to see in full military dress; row upon row of medals and bars of commendations across their chests and looking every bit the great men that they are. Walking straight up to Andrew, the men start to straighten up his uniform. Lord Ashby opens a box he is carrying and starts to pin four medals on left side of Andrew's chest, perfectly in a line with one of his buttons. Andrew looks at them as they are placed in position. Two are similar but one has the addition of a clasp and a short, dark green and gold piece of ribbon, while the other two are fancier, one an ornate cross and the other a circle with a star inside. Both have words written on them in Latin, a language that Andrew has seen in his time, but is unable to read.

"Are these so I do not feel naked next to you two?" Andrew asks.

Lord Ashby looks at him with a serious expression. "These, my boy, are what you have earned over the past few years. I will explain their meanings later, but understand, they are not for pomp and show in any way; these represent courage and honor for things that you have done, deeds that you and you alone have achieved."

Wellesley then places a three-inch-wide green sash with gold trim to its edge over his head and down to his side, showing the badges of the queen's own grenadiers, Royal Navy and queen's coat of arms on a silver badge crested by two rearing Ambulette stallions, that he does not recognize. Around his neck and under his collar Lord Ashby places a large colored ribbon with a jewel-encrusted cross hanging from a short gold chain. He centers it at the front of Andrew's uniform, then pins it in position with a small clasp.

"Your sword is a full-dress cavalry commander's sword, but the blade has a fully sharpened edge on it Andrew, use it if you must for the protection of Margaret. This pistol at your side has a paste-like powder dried on to the pan, something from my own designs, cock it and fire at any angle and it will discharge but with just a little more smoke than usual, again use it in the defense of your wife if you need to." Wellesley tells him as he tidies up every little detail on Andrew's uniform and equipment, taking particular care with the positioning of the large, ornate hat with a white feather plume on the side; the same as Wellesley and Lord Ashby are wearing.

"Now, there is less than an hour to go before we get to the staging point," Wellesley says, finally satisfied with Andrew's appearance. "Your role is to walk alongside Margaret and sit beside her, sit when she sits, stand when she stands; there will be changes to many things and you will not understand them all, just go with the flow. Margaret thought it would be better to just try and hit the ground running rather than explain everything in minute detail. There will be a lot of people around you that are watching every move you make, but just think on Margaret, she is all you need to focus on, for she will be the one in most danger. We will be right behind you and your friends are all around us, so do not worry yourself, just stay focused."

Andrew is deep in his own thoughts as Lord Ashby taps his arm and offers him a nip from his flask. He would usually say no, but this time he accepts the offer and takes a few swift gulps from the silver vessel.

"Thank you," he says, passing it back to Lord Ashby.

"Just think, Andrew, three hours from now it will all be over, Margaret and you will have a totally different agenda going forward. Until then, sit by the fire and warm yourself, for no amount of worrying now will change the outcome later. Just remember to act first, worry about the consequences later."

Andrew gives a short, sharp nod before taking a seat, moving his sword to one side while sitting back into the folds of the chair and watching the flames in the fire dance and flicker.

For the first twenty minutes, the time drags on slowly, but as Andrew dreads the moment they must leave, the time seems to pick up pace and within what seems minutes to him, an hour has passed.

"Well, this is it Andrew. Time we make our way to the assembly hall and get ready for all the action my lad," says Lord Ashby as he takes one more sip from his flask before passing it to Andrew, who also takes one more sip before passing it back.

"Keep it on you for now, it may bring you some luck lad," he says as he walks over to the door and opens it. Andrew stands up and straightens his jacket, sliding the flask into his breast pocket. His heart is pounding and his throat dry, but he keeps thinking on Margaret and his children and the fact that he would sooner be with them than not. As he walks to the door he asks, "So, how many people do you think will be present, Wellesley?"

Wellesley raises his hands. "Ah, just a few thousand."

"Four thousand, eight hundred and forty-seven guests and three hundred and fifty-six servicemen and women," Lord Ashby says swiftly.

The life seems to drain from Andrew. "I do not think I have ever seen that amount of people in one place, let alone walked past so many, what if I faint?"

"Well, you should have been on the battlefields with the Prussians years ago, my boy, twenty thousand of us there were, facing down thirty thousand on the other side. The ground shook with the thunder of our cavalry charge, and the rows of men marching forward on one another. You had to see it to believe it, what man would do to one another over a disputed border line still troubles me to this day."

Wellesley looks at Lord Ashby. "I don't think this is helping matters Ash, perhaps we should leave your old war stories for another day and concentrate on today's performance."

Lord Ashby huffs a little as the three men make their way down the corridors toward the main entrance to the great hall. As they move ever closer, the roar from all the people inside the great hall grows louder and louder.

Apprehensively, Andrew turns the corner into the start of the procession corridor, at the end of it he can see the unmistakable small, curvy figure of Anna in her royal green uniform. She is standing at the side of what must be the queen in her full state ceremonial attire. A large, bell-shaped dress, dripping with encrusted jewels and thread that seems to sparkle in the light. A huge sash across her body, studded with badges and emblems of status on the front and back, and the royal crown on her head. In her hand she holds the famous staff of office, a three-foot decorated metal rod with six huge, perfectly cut sapphires of piercing blue, evenly spaced around the gold band of the neck. They in turn are surrounded with a pattern of white and pink diamonds, creating a continuous figure of eight pattern that brings the design together. On the top of this is the symbol of Kelsey, a flawless rich-red ruby the size of a baby's fist, hence its nickname little angel's heart, for it has always been known to represent the beating heart if the country. If it should it ever leave the shores of Kelsey, the country would fall into a deep hole and become a lake that would be so deep and dark that nothing could live in its water, or so the legend says.

Andrew can only see the back of the queen and part of one side, but it is enough for his hands to start to sweat as his nerves begin to get the better of him. It is all he can do to keep walking toward his country's ruling queen. His legs are like jelly and seem to have a mind of their own as they feel like they could buckle at any moment. With Wellesley and Lord Ashby supporting him on either side, he approaches and stands to the left of his queen, looking straight ahead, far too scared to look around as he wonders what he should do next. The hairs on his neck stand on end and his heart pounds as if it were trying to force a way out of his body.

"You look rather good in that uniform, it suits you well, Andrew."

She knows my name, he thinks to himself. *What should I say or do now?*

She turns and looks at the side of Andrew's face. "You are going to create quite a stir in society after this Andrew. All will want to know who you are and where are you from," she says as Andrew slowly starts to turn his head and look directly at the face of the queen.

He stares blankly for what seems an age as his brain tries to reason out who he is looking at, then it registers. "Margaret! What are you doing here, where is the queen and what are you doing wearing her clothes?" Behind him, Wellesley and Lord Ashby are chuckling to themselves. Andrew turns to look at the two men before looking back at Margaret, then back at his friends, and then once again at Margaret.

"Andrew, it is me, Margaret, your wife and also the Queen of Kelsey. It has been the hardest and most difficult secret I have ever had to hold from someone. But for your own safety as well as my own, I had to keep it from you until the very last moment. But now it is time for all to know and for us to get our county back from those that want to destroy it."

Andrew's mind is still trying to piece it all together. He looks back at the smiling Wellesley and Lord Ashby. "There be words we will be having after this, for I feel that you two have played me and I am not sure how I feel about it yet."

"My dear, you are my husband, prince of these lands, commander-in-chief of all my armies on land and at sea, hence the sash of status over your shoulder and the cross around your neck. Those two men behind you report to you, do with them as you see fit." Andrew looks at the now-sheepish and quiet men who are looking anywhere but at Andrew's face as Margaret speaks again. "But for now, my beloved, escort me into the hall, take your rightful seat beside me as we try to take back our lands from them that would oppose me, for this might be the quickest reign of a prince in this country's history if we cannot pull this off."

She has a slight smirk on her face as she and Andrew look at each other for a moment. Then, Anna's head appears from the other side of the Queen as she leans forward and smiles at Andrew.

"Do I have any power over this young lady? I feel five years in the barracks kitchens would be a good start."

Anna's grin drops to a look of shock and disappears back behind the Queen. "No, this lady is ward to the queen, and answers to me and me alone, not that I don't feel that a little more discipline would not go amiss sometimes."

Anna puts on a sad face as Margaret smiles at her and then Andrew, then sighs heavily before speaking again. "I know you have lots of questions, Andrew. Let us see if we get through this first, for if we do not, the questions you have will be in vain and will no longer matter."

Margaret looks back at Wellesley and Lord Ashby. "Now, shall we begin before even I lose my nerve and turn away?"

Margaret steps forward and leads the group around the corner and the twenty yards ahead before turning to face into the great hall, where she pauses for the rest of the party to line up behind her and the plethora of the waiting officers and security to position themselves around them. As she steps into the room, a fanfare of trumpets and ı.   from the gallery above signals the arrival of the queen along with cheers and applause. All in the great hall are standing and cheering as the queen and her husband begin the long, slow walk down the central corridor to the head of the room.

As the group move further along the room, the people are more learned about protocol and start to realize there is something different with the procession and that this is not just a birthday celebration. Beneath the cheering, there is a growing swell of whispers and words of excitement as they begin to realize that the queen is not alone.

"Who is the man beside her?"

"Why all the decorations with green ribbons and bows

everywhere?"

The group reach the steps at the head of the room. The dignitaries and invited royal guests are abuzz with conversation and excitement, that is all but Stone, Mallory Bonner and the dignitaries and politicians around them. With expressions like granite, they watch in silence as Margaret takes the five steps up to the throne, turns, and takes her seat. Beside her Andrew takes a second, very slightly smaller, seat and they wait for the rest of the group to take their places around them.

Stone immediately starts talking with Mallory, Bonner, and several of the other corrupt politicians present, letting rip with angry comments and flailing his arms. At the same time, a large and a small chair are placed down between Captain Hawkswell and Olson, not far from the Queen's side. Moments later, Beth comes out from the side entrance carrying a child in her arms and young Henry walking beside her; they take the seats on offer and position themselves to face the public for the first time.

It takes a good five minutes for the crowd to stop cheering and talking to one another about what is happening in front of them. Margaret just smiles and acknowledges the people, nodding and rolling her wrist with small waves.

Andrew, on the other hand, is as comfortable as a long-tailed cat in a room full of rocking chairs. He is concentrating hard on his wife, family, and friends and trying his best to blank out the enormous crowd while coming to terms with who Margaret really is. It is one thing to have suspicions that all is not as it seems, but a completely different ball game when you are actually married to the queen!

For now their children are princes and princesses, and he suddenly wonders *What am I? A prince? A king? Is all this really happening? How can a common man be married to the Queen of Kelsey?*

Before Andrew has a chance to think on it anymore, Stone steps forward to face the queen, brushing off the hands of a few men who try to hold him back. "I am confused and a bit perplexed, my queen. Who is this man beside you and what is he doing there? What are these children doing beside you with their mother, your handmaiden Bethany Saddler?"

The entire hall goes quiet in seconds, so much so a pin drop could be heard as all wait in anticipation of her answer.

Margaret looks down on the man and, in a loud enough voice for most to hear, says, "Why this is my husband, Prince Andrew, and these are my children Prince Henry and Princess Katherine. They have been with their nanny Beth under the guise of being her children to protect them from harm's way." The crowd gasps and mutters between themselves, but swiftly quiet down as the conversation between Stone and Margaret continues.

"Your husband, your children? I don't understand, why do we not know about these things. Is this some kind of joke you be playing to make us look fools?" Stone replies.

Margaret looks at him with steely eyes but maintains a pleasant voice as she speaks. "Staying alive has been difficult since the murder of my mother and father near twenty years ago. I have survived many an attempt on my life, due in great part to my protectors Lord Ashby and Wellesley, along with Beth. They have kept me from harm's way and the ambitions of a few evil men to take over the country. So, when it came to marriage and children, I needed to give them the best protection that I could, invisibility to those that may do them harm."

"Yes, yes, it was sad about your parents, a tragic loss to the country. That is why we run the country's affairs on your behalf, to take the worries and burden away from your delicate disposition and leave it in the hands of people who know how a country should be run, your politicians and government. I understand that you are a woman and the hard compromises and tough decisions that must be made to run a country are not for you, that is why we continue to rule on your behalf. But what is known of this man? Who is he, what state or country does he come from, what is his family tree and royal connections, is the marriage legitimate and are these children really yours?" Stone asks with a sly look on his face.

"Spare me your weasel tendencies Stone. My husband, Prince Andrew is from Kelsey and we were married not far from here in a small chapel with witnesses and recorded in the royal affairs book. Our children were born from these very loins and assisted by the royal physician and several members of the royal staff, all of whom are here today. The events were also recorded and witnessed in the same royal affairs book.

As for running this country, *you* have run it into the ground for your own greed and benefit while others suffer and lose what they have, or worse, their lives to feed your ambitions. You have used blackmail, paid assassins and murder to keep a stranglehold on this country and its people, but no more. I could not be more ashamed of what I have allowed to happen at the hands of you and your parasites, content to suck the goodness and decency out of this once-great country and leave its people on their very knees, while you live like kings on their hard work. I know, as I have lost many a friend and relatives to your murderous ways. I myself have survived countless attempts on my life from your paid mercenaries, paid with money taken in taxes from the very people of this land. My husband himself has been wounded and near death on more than one occasion defending my life and the life of his son, but no more. The day has finally come when you and your kind will no longer be tolerated, the greed and corruption you have spread throughout the land is now your downfall. As of one hour ago, your government has been disbanded and ceased to exist, along with that of your friends and co-conspirators, Mallory and Bonner, for I know they also have crimes to answer to, along with those vultures that surround you."

The room may be filled with well over four thousand people, but not a word is spoken as all listen to their Queens words echoing through the great hall as she makes a stand on their behalf. Many of those present know what has been going on for years, but only now, with their queen making a stand, do they feel brave enough to make a stand themselves and support her.

"What are you talking about? I am in charge of this country, by appointment of the government, to enforce my will on the laws of the land until such time as the rightful heir to the throne came of age and was capable to govern for themselves. That is exactly what I am doing and have done for these twenty years!" he bellows back at the queen.

Margaret looks at him with her usual expressionless face. "That is exactly what you have done. When I reached eighteen you moved the age to twenty-one, then twenty-four, thirty, thirty-five. You have been so busy making up new laws to benefit the three of you and your lackeys, you forgot to look back at the laws of the land that pre-existed. No man can rule on behalf of a member of the royal family for over eighteen years, as this from birth is the maximum age a person could be before they would come of age. Secondly, when you act on behalf of a member of the royal family, it is a treasonable offence to invest or store items, artifacts and wealth belonging to the crown in another country without it being documented and recorded. You have been storing paintings, sculptures, other artwork along with wealth belonging to my family and this country's museums in houses in Hanover, Saxony, Denmark, and Prussia, not to mention my mother's personal jewelry in Sweden."

Bonner and Mallory look at each other and then at Stone, who, at that same moment, stares back at them. "You thieving bastard, you said that it was sold to make up the tax loss this country had made, not to go in your own private stash!" Mallory comments as he stares at Stone.

"Gentleman, I can assure you that this is absolutely ridiculous and total nonsense, I have done no such thing. Believe me, she is making this up just like everything else she has just said," Stone protests.

The feelings of anger and betrayal amongst the people of the great hall are beginning to grow. Whispers, murmurs, and rumblings are becoming louder as discontent and rage begin to fill the room. Margaret stands up and passes her staff of office to Andrew, then turns to the crowd and puts her hands out to get the crowd to quiet down. Before she sits back down and continues, "People, calm yourselves. You will note that we have representatives and royal guests from all the countries that I have mentioned. They have been here a few days now and returned all that had been removed from us as a goodwill gesture and a wish to help repair our relationships that have been tested these many years by these foul creatures."

People start to stand, cheering and clapping in a united show of appreciation as those that returned the stolen property stand up in acknowledgment of their kind gestures.

That is all but Stone, who turns and looks at Margaret with hatred in his eyes. "This is an outrage! I demand the return of my property at once," he spits out as he tries to control his temper.

Margaret looks directly at Stone, with Mallory and Bonner behind him. "You do not think you have got away with it so lightly, do you, Stone? Your properties abroad have been gifted back to the relevant governments as a thank you for their kindness and generosity with the aim of building better relations between our countries."

Stone grits his teeth and clenches his fists as Margaret delivers the news.

"But that is not all. Over the past two years, the final pieces have been prepared for this very moment. All twenty-four of your government offices around the country have had their officials arrested and have been replaced by people voted in by the lords, ladies and learned professors of this country. They are in session now, beginning to set standards that will put right the wrongs and atrocities you have committed against the people. The corrupt and cruel enforcement agencies you set up have by now had their people rounded up and removed. They will await trial for their crimes and have been replaced by newly trained personnel under the leadership of Lord Ashby and Professor Simmerson Hibbot of the university."

The government officials and diplomats behind the Three Heads look at each other and start to rant and rave in protest of what they are hearing.

"Don't listen to this mad woman, she is unfit to be queen and we will do well to be rid of her!" shouts Stone to the men behind him.

Margaret looks at him with her granite stare. "I have not

finished yet. Your homes and offices are now forfeit and now the property of the crown, to be returned to their former uses as museums, town hall and national library along with many other key establishments. In fact, they are already being converted, for the benefit of the people. As for your vault of deeds to all the farms, houses and other places you have stolen over the years, Stone, Bonner and Mallory. They are already being given back to the rightful owners or their families. Most of the people you have falsely imprisoned have been released and pardoned in full, it may take some time to find them all, but it will be done as soon as possible. But by now, I would say about a fifth of the people whose homes and farms you took away from them have begun to move back while we have been talking, and the rest will follow in the time to come."

Margaret smiles at Stone. "Now you know what it feels like to lose everything you have and be powerless to prevent it. What will you do now, traitor to your own country? Where will you go from here? No country on our borders will want you, not just because you are a criminal and a murderer, but also because they fear you will do to them what you did to my mother and father and have them killed to take their places."

Stone looks around at all his guards and protectors. Sheer rage and anger have taken over his mind. "Are you going to listen to the wailings of a weak and feeble woman? Take her away and be done with her madness; she is not fit to run a country, just like her parents, they lack the spine to make the difficult choices."

Stone looks around. "Did you not hear me? Arrest her and take them away!"

None of his own troops are even moving, let alone doing what he instructed them to do. Perplexed, he looks closer at the men on guard around him. They are still not moving, but otherwise nothing immediately stands out to him. It takes him a while, but finally he notices that many of the men have a thin dark-green ribbon around their arms, difficult to see on a green uniform. As he looks around the room, many of the security men are wearing them, including some of his own National Guards, and all of these men with ribbons have one hand on their pistols or short swords. He turns to face away from the queen and look at his own security henchmen. "A thousand gold pieces and a free pardon for anyone who can kill that bitch, ten thousand if you kill them all!" he yells while snarling with barely controlled rage.

There is a moment of silence as the mercenaries, henchmen and several of the national guards under Stone's command look around, but, as always, greed and stupidity go hand in hand with men of no honor. Some of the national guards try to move, but a blade or pistol swiftly in their ribs encourages them to stop. The mercenaries, bodyguards and a few of the diplomats with nothing to lose, however, lunge forward. Some do not even make it a meter before being swiftly cut down by the soldiers protecting the queen. Those with a little skill make it a bit further before Wellesley and Lord Ashby shoot them down on the steps.

Captain Hawkswell and Olson step forward at the same time and cut down two of the national guardsmen attempting to get at the children. While they are dealing with the threat, Beth and another soldier immediately take Henry and Katherine further back as more soldiers step forward to protect them.

The rest of the people in the hall can only watch as guards and soldiers take out their swords and pistols and stand alert around all the aisles, protecting the people and honored guests from any danger that may come their way. But expected by Margaret, the main action was always going to be around the queen and her family as the Three Heads try to take control of the hall and finally finish her and her family off. If they succeed, they will win the prize as there will be nobody left to contest them.

In front of the queen, two of Stone's bodyguards break through and advance on her. Andrew is up like a shot, pistol drawn and cocked. He lets loose a shot that hits the first man in the chest and, as he falls, Andrew draws his sword and takes on the second man. The swordplay is swift and decisive as the man is no match for Andrew's skill with a blade. With a flick of his wrist, the weapon slices through the side of the man's thigh, then across his shoulder, and finally Andrew lunges and drives the point into his ribs. With a gasp and last stagger, the man falls to the ground while Andrew looks for any more assailants.

At the same time, Bonner makes his move, charging toward the unarmed Anna. "I will have at you now, you bitch!" he yells as he slashes wildly at her with his cane sword. She ducks down under the slovenly swipe and steps toward him, her hand rising from her side and plunging a knife into his groin. He screams and looks down at his wound just as Anna strikes up with her left hand, pushing a second knife under his chin and into his brain.

"That's for all the women who could not defend themselves, you pig," she says as the man falls to the ground, violently juddering and twitching before lying motionless and dead.

Mallory also moves forward, a sword in one hand and a dagger in the other. Wellesley is immediately there to take him on and they exchange a few strikes before he speaks. "I killed your friend the king last time, this time it will be you." Wellesley defends from a couple of slashes and a thrust from the dagger before pulling out a long, thin, rounded blade that tapers down to a point with his other hand. "I have been saving this for you for a very long time," he comments.

"What! A toothpick? I will ram that where the sun don't shine!" Mallory yells as he cuts and slashes at Wellesley with both his weapons. Wellesley easily blocks all the strikes with his sword, weaving and dodging as he waits for the right moment. Several more strikes come from Mallory before he lunges forward with his sword tip, attempting to finish Wellesley off with a decisive move. But Wellesley is ready for it, for it is the move he has been waiting for. As he twists his body and allows the blade to pass across his chest it nicks his shoulder, taking a small button with it. At the same time Wellesley strikes forward with the fine blade, direct and straight into the center of his heart, pushing it right down to the hilt. Mallory's eyes widen as he gasps with pain, frozen to the spot for a moment before dropping to his knees.

Wellesley flicks his sword into the air and catches the blade in his hand, then places the handle over the point of the fine blade at Mallory's back he twists it, bending the soft blade tight to Mallory's back and preventing it being pulled. "My wife was far better and more accurate with a blade than I will ever be. I swear I once saw her take the wings off a fly in flight with two strikes of a sword, or so it looked to me. If she were to have placed that blade in your heart it would have been just a little lower, making it last that little bit longer." He sighs heavily. "I miss her and the king every day I breathe and die a little more every day I live, but what is worse is that I know you were the cause of her death with your betrayal that night in the palace all those years ago.

"Now that blade in your heart will allow it to beat for a while longer. Each beat it will leak just a little blood with the pressure. Touch it and the pain will be immense, far more than a man like you can stand. Pull it out and you would be dead in minutes, but I don't want that, hence the twist at your back. I want you to remember my wife and the cost of your betrayal to our king and queen for as long as possible before you die. It may be hours or even days, but I want you to know what it feels like to be slowly dying with not a thing you can do about it. I have often wondered what thought will be last in your mind as you slip from this world, but now I have avenged those you betrayed, I realize that to be honest, I don't really care as long as you suffer."

Wellesley steps away from Mallory and looks around. The room is silent, any resilience in Stone's men has long since been quashed, the men around him gone, leaving just a twenty-yard gap between Stone, standing with his arms folded, and the queen standing up in front of him.

"It would seem that I have underestimated what you would be capable of, for I did not foresee most of what has gone on today." Stone sighs and shakes his head.

"But then again, you did not see this coming, either." He unfolds his arms, pulling a pistol out in his right hand and raising it to point at Margaret.

Andrew is first to spot the danger and with no weapon to hand, dives in front of Margaret as the pistol is fired. The shot hits Andrew and he falls to the ground motionless. Stone's eyes have followed Andrew to the ground, as he looks back up at the queen she is staring directly at him down the barrel of a pistol.

"No, I did not see that, but my husband did and he was more of a man than you ever will be." There is a puff of smoke as Margaret lets loose the charge, sending the pistol ball toward Stone. It hits him right between the eyes and as a small trickle of blood begins to weep from the wound, he falls first to his knees and then to the floor, his reign of terror on this land finally over.

Lord Ashby is first to his knees beside Andrew, closely followed by Wellesley who rolls him to one side to look at the wound. "No, God no!" he yells as he pulls back a wet hand from Andrew's body.

Margaret slowly lowers her pistol, looks up a little as the tears begin to roll down her face, as she knows he could not have survived the impact from such close range. "What will I do without him?" she asks herself as her eyes lower to the ground and the pistol drops from her grasp.

"I'm, I'm not dead just yet," a voice says quietly from the floor, "But it hurts like hell".

Lord Ashby stands up holding a flask that has been crumpled in from one corner. "Look at the state of my flask! It is ruined beyond repair; you owe me a new one, Andrew."

Margaret moves next to Andrew and sinks to her knees behind his head as Wellesley gently sits him up. She can see where the shot hit his jacket, the flask taking the full impact on the corner, then deflecting the ball into his shoulder.

Andrew looks up at his wife. "Please tell me why is it always me that gets shot? Can't one of the others that are paid to protect you get hit once in a while."

Margaret is laughing and crying at the same time as she holds him in her arms. "Oh, Andrew, you have to stop doing this to me! It is not good for a mother-to-be to go through this kind of ordeal every time."

Andrew pauses for a moment as her words register, then looks back up at her. "What! Again? Surely not. I am beginning to think I am definitely being used and you are trying to be rid of me, my queen."

The group of friends that have formed around them begin to

smile and chuckle as Margaret's personal physician pushes his way through the crowd with his little black bag in his hand to attend the wounded. As he looks down and sees that it is Andrew on the floor, he speaks, "You again! Why can you not just stay out of trouble?"

The laughter is even louder this time as the physician gets to work on Andrew's wound and the guests begin to cheer an applaud the queen and her people for what they have just witnessed.

CHAPTER 18

A Man Never Forgotten

It has been some time since the queen's stand against The Three Heads in the great hall of the royal palace. Law and order swiftly returned once the corrupt politicians had been removed, leaving no place for the gangs and underworld to find salvation should they be caught. For the people of this great land, the standards of living have improved across the entire kingdom, borders are re-opened and trade with all adjoining nations is thriving. People who once risked all to escape the country are returning to rebuild what they once had. Farmers are harvesting the first crops under their own rule and producing enough food to supply a grateful nation with surplus to spare.

Musicians and performers fill the great halls and buildings, bringing back the crowds to again enjoy what they once had. For many of the children and younger generation, this is the first time they have seen a performance and they are captivated. A pride long since forgotten has been restored and the poverty that was so prevalent under Stone's rule is reducing by the day as the people are able to work their way towards better standard of living. The country is well on the way to restoring its position as a flourishing nation, but, as with many great and growing nations, sometimes it takes a tragic loss to truly pull the people together.

Prince Andrew has fully recovered from his near-fatal wounds again and stands alongside his beloved wife, Queen Margaret. Beside them, their three children, accompanied as always by Anna and Beth, stand and watch as their mother addresses the hundreds of thousands of people from a balcony, who are lining the streets on this solemn day.

"Lord Ashby was an inspiration to us all. Good or bad, he saw the potential in all of us, from all walks of life, rich or poor, the old and the young, he had time for each and every one. He dedicated his life to this country and never gave up hope. Even in its darkest hours, with the loss of my mother and father, he stood like a beacon of light and a ray of hope to all those he came in contact with."

Margaret's eyes begin to water and her lips to tremble as she remembers the man who stood by her until his very last breath. For his last words to her, as she kept vigil by his bedside, were: "I am so very honored to have served you my dear, your father and mother would have been so proud. I cannot wait to meet them again and tell them what you have become and achieved."

Andrew is instantly aware she is struggling. Stepping forward to stand by her side, he puts his hand on her back, giving her enough comfort for her to find the strength to control her emotions and continue her speech.

"He had few direct family members, but, without doubt, he had the largest indirect family I have ever known, as our nation now shows with its support of him in his passing. There is no honor, medal, award or mention that this man has not won, earned, or been given at least once in his life. It will come as no surprise that he has left most of his estate and holdings to the nation, from the great library, royal theatre, Ashby docks, Ambulette stud farms, hospitals, royal academies, and many, many more establishments."

Margaret is struggling to hold it together but, as always, she manages and keeps going with the speech that she has memorized word for word. "No monument or building will ever represent what this man has given for us, as it would only be in one place and he was everywhere, touching all who met him. For that reason, I have drawn up plans for a postal service, a place in every city, town, and village where collections of letters and packages can be sent and delivered across our great nation. The Ashby Post, as it will be called, should be in place by the end of the year. It will be a minimal charge to break even in costs and employ the many people needed, but when in full service all should be able to reach

each other within a week no matter where you live in this great country, just like he reached all of us."

The crowd start to cheer and applaud the idea, the noise swelling as more and more people join in and raise their voices. Margaret waits for the people's appreciation to quiet down enough before she continues. "Lord Ashby will be leaving the gates below the palace shortly, with the full military honors and escort he deserves. Please raise your respects as he passes on his way to be buried in Dewinter Cathedral, for I feel no man better deserves to be laid to rest in our most revered place of worship than Lord Ashby."

As the tears start to run down Margaret's face, she turns to seek comfort in the willing arms of her most-treasured Andrew. "Oh God, he will be so sorely missed," she says as the tears flow down her cheeks. Andrew, as always, stands firm and holds her until she is ready to leave the balcony and make her way to the cathedral for the next part of the ceremony.

Below them, the large iron gates slowly swing open and the cavalry escort starts the procession through the streets of the city. There are over 100 of the finest gray ambulette horses that lead out first, many of which were bred on Lord Ashby's stud farms and each one ridden by an officer of the guard. Some are still in full service while others are long since retired, but all of them are in full military uniform and what a sight they make, wearing all the honors and medals from serving the crown over their years of service.

They are closely followed by various units of both the army and navy. Each group of men and women is faultless in their dress code and shiny equipment, following the cavalry along the road to their final destination. After them, a gun carriage drawn by six horses exits the gates. On the back of the black and brass carriage lies the coffin containing the body of Lord William Harvey Ashby, Grand Master of the Barr. Behind, a plain black open carriage with Queen Margaret and Prince Andrew leads other carriages containing the children, Anna and Wellesley. Following them other dignitaries and important people a grateful nation, as well as royalty from other countries. The last out of the gates is a small detachment of cavalry from Lord Ashby's own unit that makes up the rear of the column. These elites, watched over the man in life and now escort him to his final resting place.

As the carriage containing Lord Ashby passes the people in the crowd, all hats are removed and heads bowed or lowered in respect. Not a sound is made, just the horses' hooves clicking on the stone road and the quiet rumble of the muffled wheels of the coaches as the column passes by. It is a thirty-minute walk from the palace to the cathedral and there is not a space along the roadside for a person to squeeze in; so many wanting to pay their respects to such an honorable man.

Aboard the coach, Margaret is thinking about her old friend. So much has passed in the time she has known him, so many things have happened. The bravery he showed in protecting her children, the advice he always had for her when it was most needed. Even if she did not act on it at first, it always proved to be the right guidance in the end. His ability to always give the worst in society a chance and always be right in his judgment, protector of the innocent and oppressed. *Oh God, how I will miss his counsel in the years to come, for there will never be another like him*, she thinks to herself.

The time seems to fly by so fast; before she realizes it, they have reached the cathedral. As the military escort and procession passes the entrance, Lord Ashby's gun carriage pulls up at the entrance and the queen's carriage takes a right into the grounds by the side to allow her to take her position inside with her family to greet the arrival of her fallen friend.

Outside the building, in front of an ever-swelling crowd of tens of thousands of people, eight pole-bearers arrive to take the coffin inside. Dressed to perfection in their uniforms, with shining attachments and gleaming medals, the eight men round the back of the gun carriage slide two long poles along the runners under the coffin, then ceremoniously lift and position it onto their shoulders before locking arms with the person opposite them. Two more men remove the poles from under the coffin and the bearers turn to face the entrance to the cathedral.

Below Lord Ashby's right shoulder the newly promoted

General Olson holds position; on his left is his good friend First Lieutenant Patrick Murphy. Tears run down the eyes of this man as they do several of the other men in the group, for at this moment he recalls his first meeting with Lord Ashby several years past, down an alleyway where he received wounds to both legs from the man now on his shoulders. What history never explains is that the same man tended the wounds himself for several weeks after the incident, dragged two men kicking and screaming into the ranks of the army, and mentored them both through years of rehabilitation and education. Lord Ashby taught Murphy to read and write his own name for the first time in his life and gave him the tools to become a better man in society, to earn the trust and appreciation of others.

At the end of the coffin, Sergeant Brendan is holding up his corner, the second of the two men from that fateful day many years past. With tears in his eyes, he holds the man's coffin with great pride and a huge sense of loss. To his friends and when off duty he is still known as Rabbit, on duty he is known as the queen's own color sergeant, in charge of all regimental banners and honors, and hell befall you if you are a private or snotty, a name given to a person not even at a level to be ranked, and you forget to call him that or disrespect the colors. He may not have had as big an impact as Murphy did in his rise through the ranks, but he had the same devotion to Lord Ashby and received just as much praise and time back from the great man himself.

Olson barks out his commands loudly and the pole-bearers' immediately focus on the task in hand as they follow his instructions with absolute precision. The slow march to the steps, the perfect ascent in unison, the slow walk through the cathedral doors and along the main corridor past many of the prominent guests, until they stop in front of the large marble stone at the altar. Slowly, and with absolute accuracy, they lower the coffin from their shoulders onto the marble stone, using perfectly choreographed moves, then step five paces back and turn to face away from the coffin and stand guard.

Until this very moment, only royalty have been laid to rest on this altar stone. Margaret, not for the first time, has broken with tradition to do the right thing for her country and the needs of its people. For in her time, she left the palace for the streets of her city, married a commoner and discreetly produced a family. Took down a dictatorship, borne arms and shed blood by her own hand in defense of her husband and country. The toll it has taken on her body and mind can only be imagined by a few people and realized by just five of her closest friends, one of whom now rests in front of her. At eighty-one, he may have died of old age after a great life with many of his friends around him, but in her eyes it was far too soon. He will be sorely missed by Margaret more than anyone else. For his counsel was second to none and his brain was as sharp at the moment of his death as it had always been, it was just his body that had given way to the punishment a true soldier endures in a life of service to the crown and its people.

Margaret does not hear most of the speeches given by the head of the church and guest speakers, her thoughts are with Lord Ashby as she stares at the casket of this special man and the many funeral wreaths of all shapes and colors that continue to be placed around the room. She does not need to be reminded of his deeds, for she was there with him for so many of them and knows a lot more besides of the realities of what he had been through.

She recollects the memory of that fateful day that her parents were murdered and how Lord Ashby was there to help and protect her within the hour. Remembers looking into his eyes as he picked her up and slowly walked through the bodies of the men who murdered her mother and father, along with Wellesley's wife, Constance. It was Lord Ashby and Wellesley that took a carriage and discreetly departed for Wellesley's home, where she would be protected and safe from any further attacks. It was there she stayed for many years, with Beth and the others looking after her until she was able to hold her own against the people who wanted her gone.

Stone, Mallory and Bonner may had succeeded that day in their aim to take power and control of the country, but failed to kill the princess along with her parents. Having moved her from the palace grounds to a military garrison, that would now not be an option as the security was absolute and her protectors were utterly dedicated to her. They had years to prepare and protect the young princess before she would be of age to take control of the kingdom. In those years Stone, Mallory and Bonner tried several times to remove her quietly and discreetly using assassins and infiltrators while bringing no more attention to themselves than was absolutely necessary. Each time they failed or were undone, but the cost was high and many loyal to the princess were killed protecting the young girl. While many more noble families loyal to the royal child were removed or murdered in a bid to sever the young princess from society and keep her in isolation.

Oh, how they would come to regret the failure to remove that little girl. Lord Ashby, Wellesley and Margaret were never going to let things remain unpunished, as she grew and matured, Lord Ashby and his good friend Wellesley planned and schemed retribution on those that had had a hand in the murder of their king and queen. Slowly, their idea grew into a mission and a long-term goal. Never could it be proven that they were investigating and removing those involved, but over the years, Lord Ashby and Wellesley carved their way through the lower ranks of those that had been part of the plot, leaving just the three ringleaders to the end, calling them the 'Three Heads' as a codeword, for that is what they wanted from them. Just their heads.

Inside the cathedral songs are sung, small speeches and anecdotes about his life are spoken by friends, and prayers are read out by the bishop and others from the church. Margaret hears them all, but her mind is thinking on him and him alone. But it is when they move his coffin to its final resting place in the far corner of the cathedral, below a stained-glass window depicting the pilgrimage of saints traveling to pass the word of God to the world, that the tears begin to flow down her face again.

Andrew offers her a handkerchief to wipe her eyes, but she gently lowers his hand. "Let the tears flow where they may, my dear, for he is worth every one of them and a million more. We will not see his like again in our lifetimes." Margaret looks back at Lord Ashby as they lower him inside his tomb and slide over the cap in the shape of a knight with his sword and shield on his chest. Carved on the shield are the words she requested: "Courage is not given, it is found when most needed. Here lies a man whose courage was beyond measure, his love for his country beyond reproach, passion for its people beyond words."

As the people who close and seal the tomb move away, Margaret walks up to his resting place with Andrew, their children, Wellesley and Anna. She places her hand on the shield and traces the words with her finger. "Goodbye, my old friend. You will be good company for all you meet in the hereafter, but sorely missed by all of us." She turns and walks away, allowing others to approach and say their last words to the great man.

Barely a word is spoken in the carriage as Andrew and Margaret make their way back to the palace, where they are soon reunited with Anna, Wellesley and their children. As they enter the area of the palace kept private for the queen and her family, formality is relaxed. Princess Annette is tired, still just under two years old and is now being carried on Anna's hip. Prince Henry is on Andrew's shoulders requesting his father walk faster as he pretends to be riding his Ambulette pony, Oscar. A gift from Lord Ashby, as he gave all the children a pony on their first birthday.

He used to say: "A yearling for a year old, by five the horse and rider know each other, by ten they can ride together and have bonded, by fifteen they are a team and fearless, by eighteen they are unstoppable." Ambulette horses are at their best from fifteen to twenty years old in service, fearless and brave by nature. At twenty-five their frontline service is over, but they are still used to break in new officers and cadets, for these horses want to work and do not like to be put out to pasture. Henry's pony may only be a smaller version of these great horses, but they are equal in character. Already Henry tears around the grounds at lightning speed, jumping anything he can get his pony's legs over, including Margaret's prize rose beds, much to her annoyance as he should not even be in the gardens let alone amongst her flowers.

Princess Katherine is just like her mother, headstrong and stubborn. Even at four years old she knows what she wants, and at this moment it is her mother's hand. She walks side by side with the queen, head up and facing forward. Andrew smiles as he watches the pair of them walk together. *God help the man she falls in love with, for he won't know what he's letting himself in for,* he thinks to himself.

As with every funeral, there is a wake afterward. Lord Ashby's is at the palace in a few hours, leaving the royal family a little time to relax, eat, and change ready for the formal event. The children are not required for this gathering and after they have a light lunch together, Anna escorts them to the royal nannies to rest and be entertained while their parents continue with their duties. With nobody around, Margaret and Andrew move to one of the smaller rooms to rest. As Andrew takes a seat in one of the suites, Margaret sits by Andrew, flicks her shoes off and leans up against him, putting her head on his chest, legs up on the furniture and toes under one of the matching pillows. The loss of Lord Ashby has Margaret thinking about her own life and what she has been through with her beloved Andrew.

"I have been nothing but a burden to you since we first met, my dear," she says while rubbing his arm. "When I think about it, you have lived in danger almost from the day I first saw you. Since then, you have been shot at more than once, wounded twice, near death for nearly a month, you even married me without even knowing who I really was, even started a family." She pauses to take stock of her words. "I never really told you the truth about anything in the first few years of knowing you. I have graveyards in every closet, not skeletons, and I took out all my frustrations on you, my unbreakable rock when things were at their worst. Why have you stood by me all this time?"

Andrew puts his hand over her shoulder and squeezes her arm gently. "I have wondered about that many times myself. You never actually lied to me, more never told the complete truth. The adventures, for want of a better word, certainly got the heart pumping on more than one occasion. As for the children, who's to say I did not impregnate you to keep you around? I mean the sex was not that bad in the end. Ouch!" he yells, as Margaret pinches his leg.

"Do not forget who you are talking to." She stares at him solemnly for a moment before breaking into a smile. "We certainly have been active when it comes to that, my dear." She comments as she settles down back into his chest as he rubs her arm again.

Andrew continues. "I think it was your reaction to Anna when you saw what they had done to her, your anger, compassion and determination to help that girl no matter what it cost. I think I knew then you were more than you pretended to be, for no normal common person would have the ability to call to arms all the people you did that day. But, at the same time, it was that moment when I fell in love with you. From then on, I cut my cloth to fit around you, for I knew you were the one for me."

She reaches up and kisses him on the chin. "I knew you were mine before then, my dear. But the children and your bakery serving the poor did strengthen your case greatly, as I do like a good cake". She smiles at him as he chuckles.

There is a rap on the door, but when Margaret and Andrew ignore it there is another, and moments later with still no answer, the door opens and Wellesley enters the room. He is met with the standard death stare from Margaret and a small smile from Andrew, as he knows it must be important for Wellesley to brave the stare. "I'm sorry to barge in on you, but he is here again. It is the fourth time this week and the sixteenth time this month. He is refusing to leave without at least an appointment". Wellesley pauses for a moment and then bravely speaks again. "I do think it may be time my queen. He has served you well and with honor these past several years".

Margaret stands up, anger in her eyes. "You do, do you? I will be the judge of that as your queen". Wellesley desperately looks to Andrew for help, for they all know whom he is talking about, and his opinion may help sway Margaret's decision.

Andrew thinks for a moment. "My dear, it has been near seven years now and Lord Ashby himself had requested this audience on several occasions".

Margaret turns to look at Andrew; she is wild-eyed and very

protective on this subject but takes a few minutes to calm herself down and think on the situation at hand. Leaving her shoes behind, she walks over to one of the facias on a chest of draws and pushes it to expose a secret gun drawer. She pulls out a pistol and starts to charge the weapon. Andrew and Wellesley watch with apprehension. "You want me to see him, then I will, but if I do not like what I hear, I will shoot him on the spot and that will be on your head Wellesley." After finishing the first pistol, she continues to load a second from the drawer.

Wellesley bravely asks, "Why do you need two pistols to meet him?"

"I do not know yet, maybe it is to ensure that if he is not dead with the first shot, he will be with the second, or perhaps I will turn it on you for bringing him here". She finishes loading the second pistol, packs up all the spare pieces and closes the drawer. "I will meet him in the cutting room by the rose garden entrance; it would be safer for all if nobody else was around".

Wellesley bows and is off like a scalded cat, closing the door swiftly behind him, while Margaret turns to her husband. The anger in her eyes has calmed a little as she holds both pistols in her hands and has the barrels resting on the desk. "I know it is what Lord Ashby has wanted for some time now, but if he harms or upsets her in any way I know I will kill him dead, for she is like sister and daughter to me."

Andrew looks at her and nods, then walks over to his wife and while standing behind her, puts his hands on her shoulders to reassure her. "If it came to that, my dear, I would kill him myself. Now why don't you put your shoes on and we deal with this together? For we both love her very much."

Margaret nods and walks over to her shoes, slipping them on while still holding onto her pistols, refusing the offer from Andrew to hold them. "Not this time, my dear. I may well be needing them both, and this is one instance you will not be able to convince me otherwise."

Andrew nods his head to acknowledge her wishes, then follows her to the door. As she reaches the doorway she waits patiently for him to open it and let her through, for there is no way she is letting go of the pistols she is holding. He opens the door and follows her out of the room and through the building, down two corridors and across several halls and rooms until finally she reaches the cutting room. Margaret walks straight in as there are no doors here, round the cutting table to take a seat facing down the middle of her private rose garden, pistols at the ready. She takes a deep breath through her nose to enjoy the scent of her wonderful roses and to calm her beating heart, while Andrew stands beside her wondering how this meeting is going to end. Margaret cocks the pistols with her thumbs and rests the barrels on the table, ready to fire if needed.

Within minutes the rhythmic tapping of footsteps can be heard heading toward them, the sound gets louder and louder until Wellesley arrives, leading a man in a blue naval officer's uniform, hat already tucked under his arm. Wellesley goes to speak, but, before the words come out of his mouth, she flicks him away with one of her pistols. With that he removes himself swiftly from her sight to stand by the side of a statue, just out of view of her position.

Margaret stares at the man bent over in front of her in a low bow. She says nothing to allow him to stand up straight, just looks at him for a while in a cold and uncomfortable silence. After a near two-minute wait, the queen finally speaks. "Well, you have the audience you have waited so long for, what do you want with me on such a sad day?"

The young man looks up at her for the first time, he is in his mid-twenties, with short, dark brown hair curling at the ends. Wearing the uniform of a first officer with the insignia of the gun ship *Vigilant*, a ship the queen knows well as it has defeated many a pirate vessel plundering off the shores of her coast over the past few years. Several honors are pinned to his jacket, including her gold family crest with two rearing Ambulette horses holding the sides of the mount and a green and blue ribbon above and below. The medal itself is cast from pure gold taken from a scepter thought to be carried by a Roman emperor in years gone by. It is known as the Kelsey Star and represents honor and valor above and beyond any other award presented to naval personnel; it is the highest award the navy can bestow.

He clears his throat with a nervous half cough. "I knew you would be here today and Lord Ashby himself told me never to give up until I had an audience. I believe his exact words were, 'She can only kill you the once my boy, go at her."

Margaret turns to Andrew. "That sounds like something that old goat would have said". She pauses for a moment before speaking again. "I recognize that medal, it can only be presented by a reigning monarchy, and I have given out only two of them in near twenty years. One to Lord Ashby and one to a man that was thought to be near-dead from his injuries, sustained saving the *Vigilant* by turning away a fire ship and steering it back into the pirate fleet. A fleet we now know was being funded and supported by the Three Heads. If I remember right, two ships were run aground and were captured, one was burnt and sunk by the fire ship, and another was chased down and boarded by men of the *Vigilant* in a violent and bloody battle that cost the lives of nearly half its crew."

The young man nods his head. "It was a bad day for the Navy with so many lost from that ship, but it was a great achievement, destroying the enemy fleet utterly. I was the fortunate one to be chosen to board and turn the fire ship. The injuries and burns to my hands, arms and chest were thought to have left me beyond surviving and I spent several months in Ashby infirmary. Lord Ashby himself collected this award on my behalf as I was not expected to see the week out. He was a good man and determined to see me buried with the honor rather than it be wasted, as I have no family to talk of and nobody to receive it in my stead."

The queen's expression softens slightly as she looks at him. "This country owes you a debt of gratitude, First Officer Daniel Turner. I presume that is your name, for I have it on a letter from Lord Ashby and it is the name of the person I recorded in the books as receiving that medal on your chest."

Daniel nods in acknowledgement of his name. "It was a

relief for us all that those pirate ships were dealt with in such a resounding engagement, for which I am thankful. Your bravery does you and the Admiralty much credit in the eyes of many who reside in this great country. For that reason and that reason alone, I have granted you this audience. But I would be careful what you ask of me, for I saw what you did to one of my subjects with my own eyes all those years ago, and I have an opinion of my own when it comes to you."

As Daniel first looks at her and then lowers his head; she can see the shame and self-loathing in his demeanor. "Several years ago, I was with a group of men drunk on homemade grog. There were five of us that night, and I followed like a sheep as we looked to entertain ourselves with some girls living rough on the streets. I did not partake in the entertainment, for it is not my way to put on others against their will, but what I did in my eyes was far worse. To my shame, I watched and did nothing to prevent the terrible situation from occurring. For when Finley could not find one particular girl, they set about finding her by way of others. They beat and tortured a small boy, making him scream and yell until she came forward. I still see her now, standing up and walking towards them. That young girl knew what was going to happen to her and yet she just continued to walk on. I watched as they pulled and tore at her clothes like a pack of wild animals, with no thought for her feelings. She just looked past them and stared at me as they had their way with her. That girl was far braver then, than I could ever be, more so than that day in battle on the fire ship for I was just doing my duty, she was sacrificing herself for a little boy."

Tears of shame start to roll down the man's face as he recalls everything that happened that night so long ago, he starts to shake his head and tremble with guilt as he continues. "What was worse, I could not stop them going back a day later to find her again. I tried to convince them that it was wrong and that we should leave them alone, but they did not care. To them the homeless were fair game that could be exploited when needed. They did not even consider those children as real people, just slaves to be taunted and used as they saw fit". He pauses to collect his thoughts. "Never was

I so grateful or relieved to find that someone cared enough to set a trap and catch the people who had done this terrible thing. My being there was just cause enough to be punished with the rest, I deserved no less for the crime that was committed that day."

Margaret turns to look at Andrew. The man's recollections of that night are bringing back all the anger and rage she had for the men as she remembers finding Anna and the condition she was in, wedged tight in the corner of that tumbledown building. This man's confession to all that had happened so long ago and his regrets and shame for his part in the debacle is not what Margaret or Andrew were expecting to hear.

"What has happened to the other four men that went to sea with you all those years ago?" Margaret asks him, even though she already knows their fate as she had demanded that she be informed of what happened to Anna's abusers.

Daniel sighs deeply. "The politician's son could not take the shame after his father disowned him and he leapt from the ship barely a week after we left port with a length of cannon chain wrapped around his waist. Finley, as always, found a way to make grog and, while drunk, picked a fight with a better man and lost. One deserted while in port getting provisions and was executed once he was apprehended. The final man Chester, died by musket fire during the boarding of a smugglers' ship a year into his service."

The queen nods at Daniel as he answers the fate of each person in turn. "Well, that leaves only you then, doesn't it? Why is it that you of all people climbed through the ranks? From the reports I have read from the ships logs, you volunteered for every mission that came along."

Daniel looks at his queen. "To start with, it was because I was so ashamed of what I had done and wanted to end my life. I am no coward, and it goes against God's will to take my own life, so I took every mission I could in hopes that someone else would end it for me. After one such close encounter I was wounded, which led to a chance meeting with Lord Ashby and Officer Horacio, who recognized me from that night. They could see something in me that I could not yet see myself. They spoke to me as a person, changed my way of thinking, and helped me to focus my shame into an objective. I could not change what happened, but I became determined to repay the girl for what I had allowed to happen that terrible night".

The queen is taken aback by his honesty, this man is not what she had been expecting. "So, what do you want here with me? For I was the one that found Anna that terrible day, and at present, I am still undecided as to using these two pistols to end your life right there where you stand."

Daniel nods in agreement. "Even if Lord Ashby and Horacio had not told me, I would know now that it was you that found Anna by the look on your face and the passion in your eyes. You are the one who set up the trap to bring us to justice and rightly so, we deserved no better".

The queen does not move a muscle, just continues to stare at the man before her.

Daniel nods his head. "So, if it is true about you finding her, then the other stories that Lord Ashby told me were not just stories from an old man, they were true events too. You did travel amongst your people during the reign of the Three Heads." He turns to Prince Andrew. "That would make you the baker that built a home for those children and married our queen".

Andrew also does not move or show any emotions, just watches Daniel as he tries to make sense of all the young man has said.

Daniel nods his head to himself as he thinks on things for a moment. "It says a lot for the quality of our queen that she is prepared to go to such lengths to take in an orphaned child from the streets, and I would fully understand your use of those fine pistols on myself should you desire. I would not take any offence to the action. In fact, in the early days, there was many a time I would have welcomed the opportunity to end this torment, but now, before you do, could I please ask one thing before you pull the trigger?"

The queen considers his request and after a brief pause she nods at him. Daniel steps forward and pats his pocket with his hand while looking at the Queen. "With your permission?" The queen nods again and Daniel removes a small square box from his pocket and places it on the table before her. As he does so, she can see the terrible burns and scars on the back of his hands and wrists. "From the moment I joined the Navy, every penny I earned, minus food and essentials, has been deposited. From my share of the prize from five ships and cargos captured, to all my pay until last month. I have but the clothes I stand in and a footlocker on the ship to my name. Everything I own is invested in this box. I have not partaken in anything other than my duties since the moment I boarded my ship seven years ago."

Margaret looks down at the box. "I recognize the gold and black box as being from Crystal Rose, the jewelers who made many of the items my mother wore and I still wear some on state visits."

Daniel nods. "Yes, Your Majesty. I have been depositing money at their shop for near seven years for the chance to own this item. The deal being that they would hold this for me, but if I died at sea they would keep all payments made and keep the contents of the box".

Daniel turns the box to face the queen and opens the lid. Inside is a huge ruby brooch, surrounded by a ring of sapphires, then dark green emeralds and finally a ring of diamonds. "This represents everything I own. I would like very much to apologize to Anna in person and give her this as a gift for all the suffering I caused her. I will ask nothing more and will do as you see fit, but I would very much like to say I was sorry in person."

The queen looks at Daniel, back at the brooch, then back at Daniel. "I know this brooch, for I had my eye on it a few years back before it disappeared from the display. If I remember right, it was master jeweler John Darcy senior's last piece of work. The Penrose Cluster. What a beautiful piece." The queen closes her eyes and lets out a large sigh as she reaches into her pocket and pulls out a letter, throwing it on the table between them.

"Lord Ashby gave me this letter on his death bed. It contains witness statements from Horacio and George, as well as one from the great man himself, people I know very well indeed. It would seem that you have fallen into good company, for these men are amongst my most trusted friends and I know them to be good judges of character. All of them report on your conduct that night; your honesty, bravery, and the speed with which you rose through the ranks serving our country. Your remorse for what happened to Anna that night is clear. On his deathbed, Lord Ashby himself humbly requested that you be able to speak to Anna and present her with a gift".

She turns to Andrew. "Before meeting this man I could think of a thousand reasons to say no and only one to say yes; the request of a man who was like a father to me. I was sure I would raise both these barrels and take satisfaction in using them on him, but on speaking to Daniel in person I am not so sure. Lord Ashby may well have been right. He would always have a way of knowing the right way of approaching me. Even now, when he has passed on and it is about my beloved Anna, he still finds a way to approach the situation in a just and fair manner."

She turns back to Daniel. "If I was to grant you an audience with Anna, are you prepared to handle the consequences of your actions? If she takes it badly, I will shoot you myself with no mercy or pity whatsoever."

Daniel nods without hesitation. "I willingly accept the proposition, and should you still see fit to end my life, I will blame only myself for the poor judgment I made all those years ago."

The queen looks to her right. "Wellesley, I know you are hiding round the corner, make yourself clear and present." Within seconds the man turns the corner with a pistol in his hand and presents himself to her.

"Ask Anna to join me here in the garden, please." Wellesley looks at her, turns to look at Daniel, then back at the queen.

"Go and find Anna for me now," she asks again. Wellesley acknowledges her request and leaves, placing his pistol back on his belt clip as he moves away. The queen closes the box on the table and slides it back to Daniel. "Be assured, should anything go wrong with Anna, I will kill you on the spot."

Daniel again nods in understanding of his position. It has taken him many years of service to get to this moment and he fully understands the importance of the next few minutes. He has only the one chance to make it right and apologize to Anna.

Daniel takes the small box and places it back in his waistcoat pocket. They wait for several minutes before the sound of footsteps can be heard in the distance; the dainty tapping of heals getting slowly louder as Anna comes closer. With each step the tension in the air grows and Daniel begins to sweat. It has been a long time coming and now he is finally going to meet her.

When Anna arrives, the first thing she notices is the officer in his blue uniform. She gives him a small smile before turning to the queen. "Yes, Your Majesty, you called for me?" She sneaks a second look at the officer. "I recognize that crest," she says, looking at the medal on his chest. "I have only seen it's like on Lord Ashby's dress jacket on formal occasions, with all his other medals." Then, looking back at the queen, she now notices the two pistols in her hands and her expression becomes more serious.

"Anna, this man would like a word with you, would you take him into the garden? But keep within fifty paces of me." Anna thinks for a moment before she curtsies and turns to the officer. They slowly walk down the steps and into the garden, where Daniel starts to speak.

Margaret is already regretting her decision to allow them to talk and is slowly turning the pistols in her hands to face the officer. The conversation between them starts off with a smile on Anna's face, but as the conversation continues the smile slowly disappears and a more serious expression takes its place. After a few more minutes speaking, Anna slowly looks round to Margaret. Even at this distance the queen can see the tears rolling down her face. Turning back to Daniel, she strikes him across the face with her fist and follows through with her elbow, just as Wellesley had taught her. The blow knocks Daniel to his knees, the box in his pocket falling to the ground in front of him. He hadn't expected the blow or the amount of force and venom behind it and he is stunned for a moment. Anna watches as he collects his senses and reaches out to pick up the box, as he does so, sees the burns and scars that cover the back of the man's hands and wrists. Her mind flashes back to Lord Ashby's meeting with the Queen, asking for a special medal to be presented to a man before he died of his wounds. She had heard the story of this man, who had risked all to save his ship and comrades. Lord Ashby had made a point of talking about the man's many deeds of heroism and his wish to right a wrong from many years ago. She starts to put the pieces of the puzzle together and realizes that the man has been trying to right the wrong he did to her all those years ago.

Anna looks back at the queen; she has stood up and is raising a pistol to fire at Daniel. Anna then turns to look at the man on his knees before looking back at the Queen. On pure gut instinct and nothing more, Anna steps between the queen and Daniel, preventing the shot from being fired. She cannot help but think there is more to this conversation and she must hear it all before making a judgment. She looks back at the queen, while slightly shaking her head, Anna then looks at Andrew in the hope he will understand she needs his help. She need not have worried, for Andrew has been watching and is already responding. He reaches out his left hand over the barrel, pushing it gently down, while his right hand gently goes around Margaret's waist as he whispers into her ear.

"My darling, you have made our beloved Anna as wise and astute as only a great mother could, trust her now to make the right decisions as she comes to terms with the reality of her own life. These next few moments may well close the past and open new doors for our girl, for she has never spoken of that night, nor of any man in her life since that terrible attack. Perhaps Lord Ashby's last wish may well be his finest moment in Anna's life, for this man does not deny his past, has not tricked or deceived us with his intentions. He has come to you with only a request to do what is the right thing in his own mind. The cost of getting this far has been an epic struggle for him, yet here he stands, just like you did when your country needed you. It is time to sit back and watch all that you have developed and worked for over the years come and grow into our future. These people, this kingdom, our family and friends no longer need rescuing, you have already done that for us all. What we need now is to heal and become a great nation again. Your people want to make you proud for all your sacrifices and everything you have endeavored to do for them. They need a queen to represent the best in all of them and by God I can think of no finer person to fit that role. You have made this country whole again, let your subjects enjoy the fruits of the seeds you have sown for them."

Margaret turns to look back at Anna and Daniel. He has by now stood back up and is brushing his uniform down, then places the box back in his pocket. Anna reaches out and takes one of his hands in hers. She is looks closely at the state of the scars and wounds present while speaking to him. Turning back, she looks at her beloved queen and mother figure with the pride of a loving daughter, asking for permission without speaking. Margaret gives her the gentle nod she was waiting for and Anna turns around and begins walking slowly through the rosary with Daniel by her side.

"It would seem they still have a lot to talk about," says the queen as she looks down at the two pistols in her hands, she uncocks the hammers and carefully places them onto the table. Then, turning to her husband, steps forward and holds him tightly in her arms, kissing him gently on the lips before whispering into his ear. "My dear, you are becoming quite wise in your choice of words to me. Perhaps we should leave them for a while, I know Wellesley is somewhere nearby watching over them, so let us take our leave and talk about our own future".

Andrew Smiles as Margaret attaches herself to his arm and they turn to walk away from the rose garden, as the walk down the corridor Andrew speaks, "And what is it you would like to talk about my dear".

"Well, I was wondering my husband, do you think four children is enough? I have included Anna in that number as I class her as one of my own. But I have heard that for a good royal family, five or six is a wise number to aim for."

Andrew rolls his eyes and takes a big, deep breath. "Well, I do not want to let my queen down, but I think we should take it one at a time, with a lot of practice to get it right." Margaret and Andrew smile at each other as they continue on their way, holding each other tightly as they move on. Both couples are being watched over by the ever-present Wellesley on the far side of the garden, tucking his pistol back into his jacket as he smiles and shakes his head at the escapades of his Queen and Prince Andrew. Then he turns to look at Anna as she walks around the roses. For now, it is her that he feels the need to watch over, well, just for a little while until he is happy that she is safe in Daniel's company.

As the two of them walk around the rosary for the second time, Daniel stops and takes the box from his pocket and passes it to Anna. She is hesitant at first, but, after a few more words from Daniel, takes the gift and opens it up to reveal the multi-colored brooch. It is an absolutely stunning piece of jewelry and Anna's eyes light up as soon as she casts her eyes upon the beautiful stones and their setting in yellow gold. After viewing them for a minute or so, she looks at him as she closes the lid and tries to pass it back. Daniel refuses point blank and pushes the box toward her, finally, after pushing it backward and forward several times, she concedes and lowers it to her side as they turn and continue to walk slowly along the rows of ornate blooms, still talking.

On the far side of the room, tucked in by one of the large stone sculptures, Wellesley has been watching everything that has been going on. 'Lord Ashby, you never cease to amaze me, even from the grave you always seem to get it right,' he comments to himself as he turns to a small white bench and takes a seat, leaving the couple to talk alone. After looking around for a while at all in view, he pulls a small hipflask from his pocket and flicking the lid up raises it in the air. "To the queen, God bless her," he says.

The flask is swiftly snatched from his hand. "I will drink to that," snaps Anna as she takes a sip from the flask and passes it back to Wellesley.

"What the— You're supposed to be talking to Daniel!"

"Been there, done that, got a nice piece of jewelry. Now let's go back and join the queen and Andrew, who knows what they will get up to without us around?"

Wellesley is speechless. He puts the cap back on his flask and places it back in his pocket, then stands up and starts to walk with Anna. "Is that it then, the conversation over that fast?" he asks as they continue walking.

Anna turns to him. "That is it for today." Then she smiles at him and turns back to continue walking into the palace. Wellesley is still trying to make sense of it all when she speaks again. "Oh, I nearly forgot, we are going riding tomorrow at six in the morning, it will be no side saddle for me, so if you can get those old bones up that early and keep up, you will be able to watch over me and Daniel like I know you will want to, old man!"

He looks at her with steely eyes and speaks through clenched teeth. "Why, you little..." Anna sprints off laughing, closely followed by the raging Wellesley in hot pursuit as they move through the palace in the direction the queen and Andrew had moved in just a little earlier.

Some way ahead, Margaret and Andrew have reached their private quarters and are taking a seat by the fire, as Andrew sits, Margaret takes her place beside him and rests her head on his shoulder and chest as she usually does. Andrew arm moves around his beloved wife to comfort her as she speaks. "I often wonder my dear, you have been through so much at my side, taking away all the danger and peril you have been through. For years I held a secret over you that everybody around knew other than yourself. Do you ever feel angry or annoyed that I did not tell you I was the queen and that I started a family with you to continue the monarchy and family line should we fail in our attempts to regain control of the kingdom?"

Andrew is quiet for some time before he answers her. "What makes you think I did not already know who you were and impregnated you to keep my position in the royal family. Was I as surprised as you thought I would be, stood by your side in the entrance to the great hall that day?"

Margaret thinks hard on his words for a moment, she lifts her head from his chest and looks him in the eyes while frowning slightly. "Did you know who I was" she asks curiously. Andrew chuckles, "That my dear is a question I will hold secret until my dying days, for surely I am entitled to have at least one secret in my closet". She smiles and lowers her head back onto his chest and resumes her position. "Well, whatever the truth, the cards have been delt and we have played our last hand, let us see where it takes us my dear".

END

Wendy Rundle
Frances Hawkswell
Nigel Nuilst.

Printed in Great Britain
by Amazon